Prairie Fire

Prairie Fire

LJ Maas

Yellow Rose Books
a Division of
Renaissance Alliance Publishing, Inc.
Nederland, Texas

Copyright © 2002 by LJ Maas

All rights reserved. No part of this publication may be reproduced, transmitted in any form or by any means, electronic or mechanical, including photocopy, recording, or any information storage and retrieval system, without permission in writing from the publisher. The characters herein are fictional and any resemblance to a real person, living or dead, is purely coincidental.

ISBN 1-930928-36-X

First Printing 2002

9 8 7 6 5 4 3 2 1

Cover design by LJ Maas

Published by:

Renaissance Alliance Publishing, Inc.
PMB 238, 8691 9th Avenue
Port Arthur, TX 77642

Find us on the World Wide Web at
http://www.rapbooks.biz

Printed in the United States of America

Dedication

There are so many people to thank for a novel such as this and so few functioning brain cells to remember them all.

To the folks at RAP, especially Stacia and Barb.

To my mates, the Misfits. Lor, whether I write out grocery lists or greeting cards, you and the gals always make me feel like a best-selling author.

Of course, to my own *Tashka* (warrior). For her love, support, and care - I give my undying love & loyalty.

Special Thanks goes to

Grant Gerondale, Communications Coordinator of The Nature Conservancy of Oklahoma. His fabulous photographs of prairie fires that he allowed me to adapt for the cover, were quite wonderful.

Lea (Chriss) King, my super lady-rancher whose knowledge about cows, bulls, and just about anything that walks on four legs made this author sound like she knew what she was talking about.

Ann & Clark at TK Wolf and Assoc., Inc. I would never have had the feel for this one without their Native American Cultural & Spirituality classes.

Prologue

Once again, the Spirits visited Taano. *It does not feel well, having this same vision for so long.* The old Shaman pushed aside the softened deer hide that served as a blanket. Taano couldn't remember a harvest season growing cold this quickly. He rose and added a small buffalo chip, a *chopi,* to the little fire that was banked in the center of the *chuka*. He warmed his hands and rubbed them together. After lowering his body to sit cross-legged in front of the fire, he reached for a wooden bowl. Inside the smooth, carved dish lay his *ikhish bahtushi*. The small pouch held herbs, roots, and anything else nature provided to prepare his Medicines.

Taking a pinch of sage from the bag, Taano tossed it into the fire after rubbing it between his thumb and forefinger. Then the old man cupped the rising smoke with his hands. He rubbed it into his joints, which seemed to ache more every day. He added cedar and then sweetgrass in much the same way. The Shaman's eagle feathers fanned the fire to produce the necessary smoke. Finally, he added a small bit of tobacco to his pipe and sent the smoke up to the Great Spirits above. He began the ritual this same way every night since the disturbing vision had visited him. His prayers were in a language long forgotten by his people, with the exception of Medicine Men and Women from kin Clans who still knew the Way.

He was *Ankahito*— his family had always been *Ankahito*—but the original Clans had separated and traveled far and away, so that now there were many sprinkled throughout the land. It would be a long journey for an old Shaman, and Taano wondered why the Spirits would call on one so weak for such an arduous task.

He spent the rest of the night speaking with the Spirits, sometimes friendly, sometimes arguing. The young people of the Clan held their tongues as they passed by the Shaman's *chuka*. He knew the language of the Old Ones, and it was never a good thing to question the ways of a Medicine Man. When the sun rose high up in the sky, the old man's talks were over. He went to the Elders and told them of his visions and of the task for which he found himself anointed. Although this would leave the *Ankahito* Clan with no Shaman, they all agreed that the old man must go where the Spirits directed him in order to deliver the warning.

The old man packed his *bahtushi*, taking any items he thought he would need to converse with the Spirits along the way. He looked into the sky and then consulted the small painting he had created on a piece of smooth leather. The distance was great, at least for his old bones. It would take him until the moon when buffalo dropped their calves, if the weather stayed with him.

The Shaman never thought to question the images the Spirits gave him. The message he had to deliver was clear; whom he would deliver it to seemed more uncertain. There were only two who were strong enough to deliver the proposal to the necessary people. The old man didn't tell the Elders that the two saviors to the land would be women. *Men and their pride.* He shook his head. He had seen many things and known many powerful women in his youth. He was too old to begin to question the ways of the Spirits now. The Spirits told him to search for the two in the area above the flatlands. One woman was a mighty warrior, the other a powerful Medicine Woman. *It has been many years since I have met with a Medicine Woman*, Taano mused. He remembered the Mother of his childhood Clan, who was part Healer, part Medicine Man.

The only other information made known to him was the nature of the women. The Spirits whispered the same thought repeatedly in his dreams at night.

You will know them by their contrast; as the sun cannot exist without the moon, so these two are. They are summer and winter, light and dark, hard and soft. Their contrast is an enigma to man, for one is neither completely hard, nor the other entirely soft. Where one is at first light and the other dark, they have the power to become the opposite. First glance will see the hawk, which swoops down to snatch the small fish from the safety of the water for its own meal, but you must look beyond the sight of men. You must see in them the small fish, who willingly gives its entire being to nurture the grateful hawk.

Look for them with the eyes of the Spirits, and you will find the Redhawk and the Salmon.

Chapter 1

A cold blast of fall wind swirled around the two women standing on the ridge. Sarah leaned into Devlin's tall body for warmth. The weather never seemed to affect the rider. Devlin quickly pulled off her newly cleaned duster and wrapped it around Sarah's small figure.

"Do you want to stay a bit longer?" Devlin asked.

Sarah shook her head, turning tear-filled eyes upward. "No, we're probably worrying Mattie. I just wanted to spend some time alone with Uncle Art. It seems like the house has been non-stop visitors since the funeral."

Art Winston had been killed just a fortnight ago. An unscrupulous cattleman had thought to acquire the old man's land as well as Sarah's ranch. Devlin and Sarah had worked together to foil the man's plan.

"I surely did respect that old man," Devlin added.

Sarah smiled up at the dark-haired woman, realizing the statement was as close as Devlin would ever come to openly expressing her emotions for the older man. The small blonde remembered how long it had taken the rider to express her feelings for her. Her smile grew.

"What?" Devlin asked self-consciously.

Sarah shook her head in answer, her eyes now filling with tears of a different kind. "I love you, Dev," she finally said.

The rider's stern expression evaporated with the wind. A

perfect smile graced her tanned face and she leaned down to place a chaste kiss upon her lover's cheek.

"I'll never get tired of hearing that," she whispered into the smaller woman's ear.

"Good," Sarah beamed back. "Because I don't think I'll ever get tired of saying it."

The small blonde took the lapels of the rider's jacket in a firm grasp and tugged gently, drawing Devlin's head down to meet her own. She pressed her lips against the warm smoothness of Devlin's mouth and felt surprised tension in the taller woman's body.

Devlin was immediately swept away by the gentle kiss and her body reacted quickly. She wrapped long arms around Sarah's shoulders, pressing their bodies together. Two weeks ago she couldn't bring herself to kiss the woman; now she was finding it damn near impossible to stop.

Devlin groaned, somehow finding the strength to gently pull away from the smaller woman.

The sound was one of sheer frustration, and Sarah wondered once more at her tall companion. She could scarcely believe that she alone could please and distress the rider with a mere kiss. She wondered if Devlin felt the same thing she did right about now. If that was the case, then Sarah well understood the dark-haired woman's need to groan.

Almost two weeks had passed since Devlin kissed Sarah in the middle of town and proclaimed her love. They made a number of assumptions about their future together, but in actuality, they hadn't spent one moment talking about what would happen or even what they wanted to happen. They only knew that their futures would be as one and that everything else would work out in time.

The problem with that theory, as Sarah saw it, was that her body was quickly saying that time was up. Of course, it also didn't help that since the day when Devlin first kissed Sarah, their lives and their home had been in a constant state of turmoil. Mattie and her children lengthened their stay in order to help out after Art's death, but there were now two ranches to care for, and Sarah and Devlin were spreading themselves as thin as possible. At night, it was all they could do to sit on the couch and hold one another, attempting to stay awake until the sun set.

The kiss ended, but the two women still stood there holding on to one another.

"We'd better get a move on, we're wasting daylight," Devlin said huskily, quickly clearing her throat to remove the sounds of passion and want. *Now isn't the time, especially not in the middle of the prairie.*

Sarah simply nodded, not trusting her own voice. They walked hand in hand to where their horses waited. The animals pawed impatiently at the soft turf and occasionally tossed their heads. Sarah turned before Devlin could assist her into the saddle.

"We will find time, won't we, Dev? I mean, time alone...just for us?" Sarah turned away in embarrassment on the pretense of mounting her horse, but Devlin laid a gentle hand on her arm and the smaller woman paused. She turned to look up into smiling blue eyes and felt almost ashamed for doubting the rider's attraction to her.

"Yes, *sachu-kash.*" The backs of Devlin's fingers grazed the small woman's pink cheek. "There will be time for us. Soon, I promise, and it will be wonderful." The rider whispered this last into Sarah's ear, watching the young woman's face turn rosy.

Tears misted in Sarah's eyes, as they did whenever Devlin called her that. In the language of the Clan it meant "my heart." Sarah rewarded the tall woman with an embarrassed smile. "You enjoy teasing me, don't you?"

"Yes, *sachu-kash,*" Devlin chuckled. "But it's because I do so enjoy that shade of pink on your cheeks."

Sarah turned to face the tall rider. Devlin knew she was in trouble by the look of determination that crept into Sarah's eyes. The small blonde slipped her arms around Devlin's waist, pulling their bodies tightly together.

"You like my blush, do you?" Sarah asked with a sly smile and a gleam in her eye.

Sarah's body slid against the taller woman's. The younger woman's hips pressed into the rider in a very suggestive manner. It wasn't out of character for Sarah to be so bold. When challenged, she would take any dare thrown her way, even if she was in miles over her head.

Devlin's breath sped up and a bolt of pleasure sliced through her. She could feel Sarah's breasts pressed just underneath her own.

Sarah knew she'd won when she saw the cocky grin disappear from her lover's face, and Devlin swallowed hard.

"Hmm, I kind of like the way you blush. It starts right here at your neck," Sarah traced a fingertip along the rider's collar line, "and it ends right here." She brushed the dark hair behind one of Devlin's ears and watched as the ear slowly turned scarlet.

Devlin quickly grabbed the teasing finger and placed a rough kiss on her lover's lips. "You," she said as she pulled away and turned Sarah toward her horse with a gentle shove, "are a wicked young woman."

The two laughed and mounted their horses, then rode back toward their new home at Art's ranch. Devlin enjoyed the playful banter. It was something new in her life. Sarah wasn't a woman to let anyone get the best of her and Devlin liked that. The rider remembered the way Sarah's body felt pressed up against her own and seriously wondered how long she could continue to control herself.

Like you just told her— soon.

Devlin and Sarah stepped into the ranch house just in time to see William Hennessy shaking hands with Madeline, Sarah's older sister.

"Well, here they are now," said the older woman.

"I'm sorry we're so late, Mattie. Mr. Hennessy, I didn't realize you would be coming by today."

Sarah was cool, but respectful to the businessmen of the town. While the remaining members of the Cattleman's Association went out of their way to offer condolences for the loss of her uncle, Sarah couldn't forget that they'd done nothing to actually stop the terrible events from happening. Hennessy was an old friend of her uncle's, she knew that much. She never had the time to get to know the Irishman, who owned the livery stable in town and did double duty as the only lawyer between their small town and Kansas City.

"Mrs. Tolliver." William Hennessy removed his hat and shook the hand that Sarah offered. "There are certain matters regarding your uncle's will that do need your attention. I thought it would be more— well, easier for you and Madeline in your own home."

"How thoughtful," Sarah replied.

Devlin laid a gentle hand on Sarah's shoulder. The smaller woman instantly felt the connection and the tender admonition from her lover.

"I apologize, Mr. Hennessy. It really was thoughtful of you to come all the way out here. Why don't we all go into the den?"

Once they were in the other room, Sarah motioned to Hennessy, indicating that the lawyer should make use of her uncle's large oak desk. She and Mattie sat beside one another in a pair of overstuffed leather chairs. Devlin closed the double doors to the room and stood a few feet behind Sarah.

"The information in Arthur's will is, of course, for the family only," Hennessy commented, gazing up at Devlin.

"Devlin is a part of this family," Mattie returned, beating her younger sister to the punch.

Devlin wasn't sure what to do, but once Sarah offered her hand, she grinned slightly and took it in her own.

"Miss Brown is my family, Mr. Hennessy. Actually, bringing this up now saves me a trip to your office. I'll need you to draw up the necessary legal papers for my own will. My assets and my children are to be left in Devlin's care should anything happen to me."

The hand around Sarah's tightened for a moment, then relaxed as the blonde looked up at the standing woman. "I know we haven't talked about this yet, Dev, but it's something I feel strongly about."

Devlin felt a brief moment of panic at the overwhelming amount of trust and responsibility Sarah offered her. The rider knew this relationship would be forever, but they hadn't yet talked of things so practical. This was a harsh land, and anything could happen in a season's time. Was she ready to accept the job of raising two young children should something unforeseen happen to Sarah? Devlin was an outlaw, or at least a reformed one. Staring down into the green eyes that always looked back at her with complete trust and love, Devlin felt the answer in her heart before it passed her lips.

"Are you sure?" Devlin asked.

"Absolutely. If you agree, that is."

The rider squeezed the hand in her grasp. That action and an unspoken communication that passed between the two women was Devlin's reply.

Sarah smiled and turned back to the lawyer. "I trust that you can handle the paperwork?" Her query was more of an expectation and left little doubt as to who was really in charge of this meeting.

"Um, well, yes, of course, Mrs. Tolliver." Hennessy stammered, pausing to glance between the two women in question. Finally settling his eyes on their entwined fingers, he saw it with certainty. "Well, let's get started, shall we?" he asked as a formality.

"You ladies, Sarah Tolliver and Madeline Caufield, being the next of kin to Arthur Winston, are the sole heirs to his estate and all its monies and properties. Mrs. Caufield, your uncle knew that you had a life elsewhere, so he left the majority of his properties to Mrs. Tolliver. However, he did leave you a sizable cash inheritance. To you he left the sum of two hundred thousand dollars and the deed to the estate in Kentucky."

"Good Lord, I didn't even know Uncle Art liked me that well." Mattie looked from the lawyer to her sister. "Where in the world did he get that kind of money?"

Mattie was more than surprised. She wrote to her uncle on occasion and came out every five years for a visit, but she had never been close to the man. Sarah, on the other hand, was like a daughter to him. It was apparent that as soon as Sarah came out west, she would be the heir to the family cattle business. Mattie never thought twice about that fact.

"Art was as shrewd a businessman as they come. Punching cows wasn't the only thing he concentrated on," Hennessy replied.

"Sarah, this is ridiculous for me to receive so much money. Surely you'll need something, now that you have to run both ranches?" Mattie asked her sister. "Richard's income has always been more than enough to keep us comfortable."

Sarah opened her mouth to refuse, but was interrupted by the lawyer.

"Actually, Mrs. Tolliver was left the bulk of Art's estate. Cash holdings from banks in New York, Chicago, and Kansas City, totaling nearly eight hundred thousand dollars. That's not counting all his land holdings." Hennessy paused and looked up into Sarah's shocked expression.

"I had no idea Uncle Art was putting away money like that. Every cent will come in handy to run this place, though. I have four hundred acres and Uncle Art has nearly a thousand– "

"Oh, there's much more than that, Mrs. Tolliver. As I said, Art was a heck of a businessman. He began buying land the minute he settled out here, when you were just a young girl. He owns nearly every acre of land surrounding the Arkansas River. Every cattleman for a hundred miles in any direction pays Art for water rights," Hennessy finished.

"People pay him for water that nature provides?" Sarah

asked in amazement.

Devlin had been quiet all this time, but now she smiled at the small blonde. It was the Clan way to share all of Mother Earth's gifts. Paying someone for water that flowed freely in the river seemed as ridiculous and unfair as having to pay to breathe air. The rider appreciated that the young woman's nature was as close to the Clan way as if they had raised her.

"Well, Art does own the land," the lawyer said. "Correction, Mrs. Tolliver, now you own that land. It adds up to hundreds of thousands of acres. Here in the Territory, Arkansas, Missouri, up toward Kansas and even Fort Laramie. To put it quite bluntly, you, Mrs. Tolliver, are now the wealthiest woman west of Chicago."

"Well, I just don't know what to say," Sarah said slowly. "I had no idea Uncle Art— I mean, I just thought he raised cattle." She looked from one face to another.

Finally, Devlin's low, rumbling laughter filled the room. "It's okay, Sarah. You don't have to apologize for it."

The blonde smiled hesitantly. "I'm sorry, Mr. Hennessy. I'm a little shocked by this news."

"It's understandable, Mrs. Tolliver." The lawyer closed the leather binder on the desk in front of him. "I know that many of the men of this town have been less than honorable in their dealings with you, but that doesn't hold for all of us. I apologize for myself and on the behalf of many of the respectable gentlemen in town. I know," he chuckled and held up a hand, "you're probably thinking that I'm trying to cozy up now that you're a wealthy woman."

"The thought did cross my mind," Sarah admitted.

"Well, I wouldn't blame you there, young lady, but you should know that I was once a riding partner of Art's. When I was a much younger man, of course," he added with a grin. "Art and I, along with some old hands that have long since gone to their maker, practically built this town. I guess with a town comes progress, and that brings men like that Montgomery. He was the exception, Mrs. Tolliver, not the rule. We may be getting on in years and not always able to put up as much of a fight as we did in our younger days, but there are still a few of us gents who loved and respected your uncle. All you ever have to do is call on us, and you'll have a few friends out there. There may be a little dust on us," he ran a hand through his wavy gray hair, "but don't let that fool you about the fight left inside."

The older man grinned amiably and Sarah found herself grinning back. She was glad to hear about this side of the men from town. She was beginning to fear that all the men in the Association were mirror images of John Montgomery, the man who had her uncle killed. If that proved to be the case, it would be difficult for her to live and raise her children here in spite of her newfound wealth.

"Mr. Hennessy, I can't thank you enough for everything you've done. I know Uncle Art trusted you and I hope you'll forgive me if I'm still a bit skittish, what with everything we've been through recently. I do accept your apology, however, and I'll remember your offer, should we ever need it."

Sarah signed paper after paper until Hennessy declared the matter of Arthur Winston's will concluded. He shook hands all around and then made his way to the surrey rig hitched in front of the house. He waved quickly as he gave the reins a light snap and the horse pulled away.

"Dev!" A grizzled looking rider walked up to the front porch, nodded to Sarah, and then hastily removed his hat.

"The nights are gettin' pretty cold out there. What do you wanna do with all them late calves in the herd up on the northern ridge?"

Devlin leaned against the porch railing and shrugged her shoulders. "Don't ask me. She's the one you work for." She jerked a thumb in Sarah's direction.

The rider seemed nonplussed and uncertain what to do next. He didn't know if Devlin was making a fool of him or not, but he didn't want to be the one to question the dark-haired woman.

"Um, Mrs. Tolliver...uh–"

"Start bringing them in ten or twenty at a time, Mr.– ?"

"Porter, ma'am. Grubby Porter."

Sarah paused and grinned at the man, who shifted his feet nervously and scratched a week's worth of beard.

"I don't want to know how you got that nickname, do I, Mr. Porter?"

"Reckon not, ma'am," he answered.

"Well, Mr. Porter, it certainly feels like winter will be coming sooner than usual in the hills. Get them into the valleys where they can winter, but be sure the men shift them between the two eastern lowlands. I don't want them feeding on green grass too long," Sarah said confidently.

"Yes, ma'am," the rider answered. He tipped his hat before

donning it and walking away. He shook his head slightly as he left, wondering in amazement at the first cattlewoman he'd ever met.

"I hope you enjoyed yourself." Sarah smiled at the tall woman still leaning against the railing.

"Yep, as a matter of fact I did," Devlin replied.

The rider had not intended to humiliate her lover, but she wanted the men on the ranch to know that Sarah knew as much about cattle and tending a ranch as any man on the place. The sooner they came to know her hard work ethic and learned to respect her as a cattlewoman of intelligence, the better for all of them.

Devlin washed the worst of the mud from her hair and clothes in the water trough outside. It had taken her and four other riders to finally maneuver the cow and its calf from the spring bog. Now, quickly drying mud covered her from head to toe. She stripped off her cotton shirt, but the mud had seeped through to her undershirt. After pulling off her boots, she entered the house through the kitchen and made her way up the back steps to the second floor. Her clean clothes were in Sarah's room, but she hadn't seen the young woman all afternoon, so Devlin was on her own to find a clean outfit.

Just as Devlin reached the second floor landing, Mattie walked out of Sarah's bedroom, pulling the door shut behind her. The older woman had an article of clothing draped over one arm and chuckled when she saw Devlin approaching.

"You look a fright."

"Yeah, some mutton-head let go of the rope and I ended up in the same spot as the cow," Devlin replied. "Sorry about the mess I'm making."

"Dev, this is your house, remember? You don't have to apologize to anyone. One of the girls in the kitchen saw you ride in. There's one steaming hot bath ready for you in the other room." Mattie indicated Sarah's bedroom. "Just drop those muddy things in a heap on the floor. You can wear this if you're overly modest." She handed what turned out to be a robe to the rider. "I'll see that you have a little privacy, for a while at least."

Devlin was speechless. She was just getting used to accepting kindness from others, but she didn't know what to make of this woman with the easy manner and cheerful personality. The rider wondered if Mattie's husband knew what he had in her.

"Thanks, guess all of this takes some getting used to." Devlin offered up an embarrassed grin.

"You're doing fine," Mattie replied with a smile as she walked past the taller woman.

Devlin went into the bathing room off the large bedroom that belonged to Sarah. It was hard to think of it as their room since Devlin and Sarah had yet to spend the night together there. *Doing anything beyond sleeping, that is.* She could feel Sarah's thoughts when she kissed her good night and held her. Some nights it took everything in the dark-haired rider not to let her libido take control of her actions. Devlin wanted the physical aspect of their relationship to be just as perfect as she thought the spiritual was. She didn't want to make love with Sarah for the first time in a room where those around them could hear every sound they made. The rider continued on to the bathing room, promising herself it would be soon.

The large ranch house didn't have complete indoor plumbing like the hotel Devlin had once visited in Chicago, but the separate bathing room was large and it had a wood-burning stove of its own. She remembered the fancy hotel rooms, a suite they called it. It had a water system that not only brought fresh water in, but also swept the dirty water away. Art's house was rather fancy compared to Sarah's two-room cabin where they had to bring water in one bucket at a time. Here, they had a pump that carried water from a well directly into the bathing room.

The rider eased her body into the hot water, reclining in the long tub that easily accommodated her tall frame. Eventually, looking for some soap, she picked up a delicate round bar, tinted a pale lilac color and smelling of lavender. She sniffed at it and smiled. She wondered what Sarah would think when she smelled this sweet scent on her instead of the harsh lye soap Devlin usually used.

The rider finished her bath and dressed in the clean clothes that Mattie had graciously set out for her. She walked through the kitchen and her mouth watered at the delicious aromas coming from the stove and fireplace. She just now realized that she hadn't eaten anything yet. After a quick cup of coffee, she and Sarah had ridden out to survey the land and had ended up at the spot where they had buried Sarah's uncle Art.

Looking around the house and then outside, Devlin became concerned when she was unable to find Sarah. The dark-haired woman spied Mattie on the front porch shaking dust from a small rug.

"Have you seen Sarah?"

Mattie noticed the concerned expression on Devlin's face, and the older woman had to remind herself that the rider and her sister had come rather close to losing one another just recently. "As a matter of fact, I haven't seen her for some time now."

She tried to remember where she saw her younger sister last, and a sly smile pulled at the corners of her lips. The last time she spoke with Sarah, the young woman had just received the shock of her life. Mattie shook her head. "I can't believe how dumb I am sometimes. I may have an idea where she's at, Dev, and why."

"What do you mean why? Is Sarah hiding from me?"

"Not from you, Dev, from life. I have a feeling that suddenly being the wealthiest woman in the Territory is having a slight effect on Sarah."

"I didn't think— damn, I should have noticed," the rider admonished herself.

"Don't worry, my friend. She hasn't gone far. I suspect that you and my sister are more alike than either of you will admit." Mattie raised her head just in time to see Devlin look away guiltily. "I think you should try the hayloft," she added as the other woman blushed. "When Sarah was a young girl, the slightest trauma would cause her to run and hide from everything and everyone. We usually found her sound asleep in the barn." Mattie chuckled.

"Thanks," Devlin said quickly and offered up an easy smile. She jumped from the top step of the front porch and made her way to the large barn behind the horse corral.

Sarah lay in the bundles of clean hay littering the large, airy loft of the main barn. She folded her hands under her head as though she were preparing to take a nap. She had snuck into the loft hours ago, once she was certain the children were off playing and Devlin had gone out on the range. A smile came across her face as she pictured the tall rider in her mind. Her stomach did a little flip and she pushed any other images from her head that involved Devlin.

It had been a long time since Sarah had the luxury of just hiding out from her problems. *Although this certainly isn't what* most people would call a problem, is it? More money and power than I could ever dream of. Those two little luxuries would guarantee her standing in the Territory for the rest of her life— no more scraping or begging. Now that Sarah had these things, she wasn't certain whether she wanted them. Suddenly her nice, easy life had grown complicated beyond reason. *Is this the kind of life I truly want? Does Dev even want this? Good Lord, we haven't even talked about just the four of us together, let alone what we'll do with all of this!*

The sound of booted steps in the dirt and the uneasy movement of the horses in the stalls below alerted Sarah that she wasn't alone. She rose to her knees and peered over the edge of the loft and into the barn below. She saw no one, but an attack of vertigo forced her to pull away from the edge. Sarah hated that weakness within herself. Ever since she was a child, she had suffered from attacks of nausea and lightheadedness when faced with the view from any sort of height. She heard the wood creak slightly by the ladder that led up to the loft. She waited, but no one appeared. Her heart was pounding in her ears. She remembered that it hadn't been that long since Dale Karsten had abducted her daughter. John Montgomery had hired the man, but thanks to Devlin, the outlaw had met an untimely end.

Sarah slowly and quietly crawled to the edge of the loft. Once she was within a few feet, she leaned over as far as she could, but still saw no one. Her position didn't afford her a view of the bottom of the ladder, only the middle of the barn floor. She carefully scooted closer, suddenly hoping it wasn't one of the large rats or opossums that occasionally nested in the barns. She was afraid that if she leaned forward any more, she would be completely off balance should anything or anyone try to attack her. Curiosity won out and Sarah cautiously poked her head over the ladder, fighting against the dizziness that threatened to overpower her.

Devlin popped her head over the edge of the loft, a large grin on her face. "Hi."

Sarah yelped and jumped backward into the hay, falling on her backside. "Son of a bitch!"

Devlin looked shocked, then leaned back and burst into a fit of raucous laughter. She almost lost her grip on the ladder, she was laughing so hard.

"What are you laughing at?" Sarah hissed.

"You. I've never heard you curse like that before." Devlin

continued to chuckle as she pulled herself into the loft.

"Oh, Dev," Sarah slapped the rider's arm half-heartedly, "you scared the holy hell out of me!"

"I'm sorry, but you should have seen the look on your face." Devlin couldn't keep the smile from her own face.

"I thought you were a rat."

"Well, I've been called far worse, that's for sure."

Sarah's anger dissipated, leaving an adorable face with a cute pout.

"I'm sorry, *sachu-kash*, I shouldn't have laughed at you," Devlin said. She leaned against a bale of hay and gently pulled Sarah into her lap. "Tell me, what can I do to make it up to you?" she added in a low whisper, inches away from Sarah's face.

Sarah smiled coyly, a look she never used before the rider. "Well, a kiss might help."

"Oh, it might, eh?" Dev responded. Sarah nodded and the rider began to close the gap between them, but pulled back at the last moment. "Wait a second. You're not going to pinch me or slap me when I close my eyes to kiss you, are ya?" The rider arched an eyebrow suspiciously at the woman in her arms.

"You're just going to have to take your chances, aren't you?" Sarah grinned.

"I think I'll risk it," Devlin said as she leaned in for a tender kiss.

One kiss turned into a few easy caresses and lingering looks before Sarah laid her head on the rider's chest.

Devlin rested her chin atop the blonde head.

"How did you know where to look for me?"

"Once I started to get a little worried, Mattie gave me a hint. She said that you used to hide in the hayloft when you were a little girl and life started to close in on you a bit."

"I'm sorry, Dev. I should have let you know where I was. I didn't mean to worry you."

Devlin touched the young woman's cheek, accepting the apology. "What troubles you, *sachu-kash*?"

Sarah took hold of the brim of the rider's Stetson and gently pulled it from the dark-haired woman's head. She placed the hat on a bale of hay, then leaned in and touched her forehead to Devlin's. "Are you okay with all of this? You're getting a lot more than you bargained for with me, Dev."

Devlin smiled at the younger woman. The rider had never before felt so comfortable with any one human being. She had always preferred her own company to all others. Things were different now and she could feel it in her heart. Things that she worried about previously seemed inconsequential now. There was only Sarah, Devlin, and their new family. *Family.*

It certainly was a daunting word, but Devlin had met one challenge after another in her life. She refused to back down from any of them. Would she rise up to meet this one with as much vigor? Devlin knew in her heart that she would. There would be rough times ahead, for all of them, but she realized the one thing that would make all the difference: the love they shared would give them a different kind of strength, one that would equip them to handle the joy as well as the adversity that life could show them.

"I think I'm very okay with this, Sarah." She chuckled. "That in itself should scare the thunder right out of you. I won't say I'm not terrified, or that I'm gonna be good at any of it, but I'll say one thing for certain. You've got me, Sarah Tolliver. You've got me for a good long spell, and for the first time in my life, I don't see the next range rising up to tease me. I don't hear the wind whispering my name and telling me that something better lies just over the next hill. What I see and what I want is lying right here in my arms."

Sarah looked up into the face of the woman she loved with all her heart. She had a feeling that their life would be one revelation after another. Devlin could be a hard woman, able to take a man's life in the blink of an eye; she could also be tender and forgiving. Sarah just stared into the blue eyes that held her own.

"You have a gentle side to you, Devlin Brown, and I'll wager you don't show it to many. Thank you for letting it be me."

A rush of intense emotion passed through the dark-haired woman, and she reached out and pulled Sarah against her. She cupped the small blonde's cheek and leaned closer. The rider said the next words to herself, too afraid to show the commitment of her heart. *I'll love you forever, Sarah. In this life and the next, I'll always walk beside you.*

The rider closed the remaining distance for a kiss through which she tried to impart the depth of her love. Sarah's hands entwined around Devlin's neck and the two women leaned back into a mound of dry hay. The smaller body lying atop her own felt like heaven to the tall rider. Her hands circled a slim waist and pulled their bodies closer together. Their kisses became deeper, rougher, and their breathing increased along with their heartbeats.

"What you do to me," Devlin moaned into Sarah's ear.

The small blonde pressed her body harder against the lean figure below her, eliciting a small whimper from the dark-haired woman. Sarah loved the way that sound made her body feel. She boldly released the two topmost buttons on the rider's shirt. Sarah kissed the dark skin and the tip of her tongue tasted the exposed flesh. She shivered at the way the salty taste lingered on her tongue and wondered what every part of the tall woman's body would taste like.

Damn it all, Dev, why don't you just take me?

Sarah was waiting for her partner to make the first move. The younger woman wasn't used to playing the aggressor and she wasn't quite sure if there were rules about that sort of thing when women were together. She'd given just about every subtle hint to her partner that she could think of, but it seemed as if the rider wasn't noticing her signals. She thought about telling Devlin that she was ready to consummate their relationship, but when it came right down to it, Sarah was plain embarrassed to talk about the physical aspect of their love. She thought long and hard about showing Devlin what she wanted, but she wasn't even sure what that was herself.

Sarah had a good idea of the ways in which women could please one another. She didn't consider herself a total fool. She knew it would involve touching and caressing. Simply thinking about the few times she'd ever pleasured herself made her stop and reevaluate the situation. Could she bring herself to touch Devlin the way she desperately wanted the rider to touch her? Whenever she let her own hand take care of her more personal needs, she ended up wracked with guilt. An image of the old Bible-thumper of a preacher that she grew up listening to would fill her mind. He would pound on the pulpit and say that if it felt good, it was probably wrong. Sarah was a long way from that Kentucky preacher now, but some lessons were hard to unlearn.

Hellfire, woman! If you keep kissing me like that, I'm going to lose what little control I have left, Devlin thought. *Does she honestly have no idea what she's doing to me? I want our first time to be perfect, Sarah, but you are getting dangerously close to something I don't want to stop.*

Sarah nipped at the skin on the rider's neck and it was enough for Devlin to cross the line of emotion that she had been carefully treading. The rider rolled, carrying the other woman with her, until her body covered the small blonde. The dark-haired woman paused long enough to look into the emerald green eyes that stared back at her, desire apparent in the gaze. It seemed an unspoken agreement passed between the two just before Devlin took Sarah's lips in a kiss that caused the young woman to moan in satisfaction.

Devlin almost unconsciously slid her hand along Sarah's body, coming to rest against a full breast. The rider stroked a hardened nipple through the cotton fabric as whimpers of pleasure escaped Sarah's throat. The dark-haired woman kneaded the flesh under her hand, her own hips pressing into the body beneath her.

"Oh God, Dev." Sarah groaned.

"Mother?"

Both women froze at the sound in the barn below.

"Hellfire," Devlin panted heavily in the small blonde's ear.

The tall woman rolled to one side, and Sarah rose into a sitting position, trying to get her breathing under control.

"Yes?" Sarah's voice cracked in the middle of the word and Devlin quietly laughed as the young woman tried again. "Yes?"

"Is Dev with you?" Matt's voice filtered up from the barn below.

"Um, yes. Why?" Sarah asked. She slapped the rider in the stomach as the dark-haired woman continued to laugh.

"Aunt Mattie says it's time for dinner. She says to tell you if Dev's up there too, you two can do that after dinner."

Sarah's face turned a bright shade of pink. "We're coming," she replied. Her face turned an even brighter shade of red when she realized her choice of words.

"Not anymore we're not," the dark-haired woman said, as she buttoned her shirt and winked at Sarah.

The small blonde hit the rider in the stomach once more and the two climbed down from the hayloft. Before they walked from the barn, Devlin pulled the smaller woman back inside for another kiss, then released her.

"Well, at least that answers my big question." Sarah nervously smiled up into sky blue eyes.

"Which question is that?"

"I thought...well, I thought maybe you didn't– didn't exactly want me that way." Sarah looked down at her shoes, unable to meet the rider's gaze.

"You thought– " Devlin stopped abruptly, wondering if she had heard right. She reached out and caressed Sarah's cheek until the green eyes rose to meet her own. "That couldn't be further from the truth. Woman, you and I have got to find a place to be alone very soon, so I can show you just how much I do want you in that way."

Sarah swallowed, unable to speak, very nearly unable to breathe. An undisguised expression of lust now smoldered behind the rider's blue eyes and Sarah wondered if she would be able to control her own needs for much longer.

Chapter 2

Sarah indicated the chair at the head of the dinner table, but Devlin didn't feel altogether comfortable sitting in that spot yet. The rider held the chair out for Sarah instead. The small blonde instantly recognized the rider's discomfort and graciously sat down. Devlin breathed a sigh of relief and took the seat to Sarah's right as the blonde woman situated Hannah on her left. Mattie sat down at the other end of the table just as the children came running in, breathless from riding.

Matt quickly took the seat next to Devlin. Sarah took notice of the hat on her son's head and opened her mouth to speak. Before she had a chance to say anything, Devlin leaned over to speak softly into Matt's ear.

"Boy, don't you know better than to wear a hat and spurs to your mother's table?"

Matt looked up with a guilty expression, first at Devlin and then into his mother's disapproving stare. "Sorry, ma'am," he apologized to his mother.

The youngster quickly removed the offending items, and Devlin acted as though she hadn't said a word. Sarah smiled at her son's efforts at civility. She had worried about Matt. She wondered if he would learn all that he should, especially with his father gone and no male influence in his life. She realized now that her worries were needless; as hard an edge as Devlin possessed, there was a tenderness and a graciousness about her. Sarah felt confident that Matt would learn all that he needed from this quiet rider.

When the children grew quiet, Sarah led them in thanks for their meal. Not a praying woman, Devlin felt a little uncomfortable the first time this happened. As time passed, however, she realized that Sarah didn't sound anything like the fire-and-brimstone circuit preachers Devlin had run into. The small blonde gave thanks for the family, their well-being, and the food. She always said the prayer in that order.

Sarah never thanked any god in particular. She never used a name at all. At first, the rider thought this was in deference to her own Clan beliefs, but she soon learned otherwise. Sarah was one of the only people Devlin had ever met who truly believed someone had created the whole world. Sarah trusted that someone held it all together, even though it seemed a tenuous grasp at times. The small woman once told Devlin that every culture had its own god and that there were a precious few who believed in nothing at all. She went on to explain that her father had taught her at a very young age that it was an arrogant man who thought that his way was the only way.

Once the meal began, the dining room filled with talking and laughter. Sarah had a dry wit and a quick one at that. Her sister was much the same. They easily traded barbs with one another and entertained the children with stories of when they were children in Kentucky.

Mattie was the talker and Sarah the introspective one, that much Devlin could see right off. It was amusing to the rider to see how much in life was relative. To Devlin, Sarah seemed as chatty as a magpie. Compared to the rider, she was. In contrast to her sister, however, the small blonde was practically mute. The rider said precious little herself, explaining a few roping techniques to the boys and occasionally adding to the adult conversation. Devlin knew she would become accustomed to the chatter, but right now, it was definitely something new. Having anyone around her at all was relatively new, let alone the fact that these people were now family.

Devlin felt a small bit of terror in that admission. There were so many obligations and responsibilities now. Devlin had to look out for more than just herself. She had people to care for, love, and protect. She worried that the feelings would overwhelm her if she let them. Part of her felt an intense pride in the knowledge that she did have a family. These people would care for her, love, and protect her in return. Ultimately, there would be no going back from this, but the good part was that she didn't really want to.

"So, you two should have a honeymoon of sorts," Mattie announced calmly.

Devlin's fork hit the china plate and made a high-pitched clatter. Sarah tried to inhale and swallow coffee at the same time. The result was a coughing fit as the young woman tried to regain control of her breathing.

"What did you say?" Sarah finally choked out.

The blonde looked at Devlin for help, but the rider had taken that particular moment to find something fascinating about her plate. Devlin had her head bent over her food, her dark hair falling across her eyes.

"Look, you two have been through the mill in the last year. I'm not saying to take a trip to New York, just a getaway," Mattie explained. "Sarah, you keep saying you have to take a wagon over to the homestead to move your personal things here. Well, why don't you and Dev spend some time over there while I'm still here to watch the children?"

Sarah stared at her sister. Frankly, a part of her was frightened to be alone with Devlin. It was unreasonable, but Sarah feared that she would be a disappointment to the sexually more experienced rider. At the same time, part of her couldn't wait to be alone with Devlin.

Devlin watched what appeared to be a mini-war playing out within Sarah's brain. She could see the play of emotions in the expressive features on the blonde's face. Devlin knew what she wanted, but she wouldn't push Sarah.

"I think you're right," Sarah replied.

Devlin nearly choked on her food. She hadn't expected Sarah to agree without even the semblance of a struggle.

"I mean, if you want to?" Sarah looked in Devlin's direction.

"Of course. Good idea," Devlin managed to articulate.

"Well, that's settled then," Mattie declared.

Mattie looked at the two embarrassed adults at the other end of the table. She displayed a small, triumphant smile. Although they looked embarrassed, Devlin and Sarah both wore expressions of anticipation and relief. If Mattie knew her sister half as well as she thought she did, the small blonde was probably as reticent to make her feelings known as Devlin was. Mattie continued eating, happy in the fact that she could play a small part in leading both these very stubborn horses to the trough to drink.

"Don't forget Dolly, Mama." Hannah jumped up and down in front of the wagon. The younger of Sarah's two children, Hannah was now seven years old. She was a miniature version of Sarah, right down to her stubborn determination.

"I won't, sweetheart. Now, you behave for your Aunt Mattie. Okay? Matt, you look out for your sister," Sarah instructed.

"Yes, ma'am," Matt answered. The young man kissed his mother's cheek. Matthew was Sarah's oldest child. He would turn thirteen this year, but Sarah still stood an inch or two taller.

Devlin moved in front of Matt. "Keep an eye on things, boy. I talked to Hank, and he said you could ride with him for a spell each day if you've a mind. You can learn a lot from a rider like him."

"Yes, ma'am!" Matt said enthusiastically. He remembered Devlin's previous admonitions to him regarding that phrase and grinned. "Sorry, I mean, Dev."

The boy's smile was a mile wide, and Devlin couldn't resist grinning in return. She quickly tugged the brim of his hat down over his eyes and he laughed. Devlin stood towering over little Hannah. The girl stretched out her hands and jumped up and down.

"I wanna give you a kiss too, Dev!"

The rider scooped Hannah into her embrace. She lifted the youngster high over her head. Sarah and Matt covered their ears at the girl's high-pitched screams and giggles. Hannah threw her hands around the dark-haired woman's neck and planted a gentle kiss on her cheek.

"Don't forget Dolly, Dev," the youngster cautioned again.

"I won't, Princess." Devlin laughed.

The girl had been lost and unable to sleep since leaving her rag doll back at the cabin. The doll was one that Sarah herself had made when she was pregnant with Hannah. Sarah had put it in the youngster's crib when she was a newborn, and the girl carried it with her everywhere as she grew up. Now, nearly eight years later, Dolly had seen better days and Sarah had patched and repaired the rag doll many times. Still, Hannah hated the separation.

"I promise, Princess." Devlin smiled at the girl in her arms. "I will personally guard Dolly all the way home." She had meant to ride over and retrieve the treasured item more than once, but one thing or another had always prevented her.

Sarah shook her head as she watched the exchange. She wondered if the normally reserved rider even realized how tightly she was wrapped around Hannah's little finger.

"Okay!" Hannah smiled as Devlin gave her one more hug and returned her to the ground.

The trip to Sarah's original homestead cabin wasn't a very long one, and the weather decided to cooperate. Devlin drove the wagon over the hilly terrain. At the same time, she tried to calm the butterflies that kept flitting around in her stomach. She felt just like she imagined a bridegroom must feel on his wedding day. The trip afforded the two women a little time to talk about their own lives and the direction they wished for their future.

"Our lives are going to be very different, aren't they, Dev?"

"I expect there will be some things that might take a small spell to get used to," the rider answered.

"You know," Sarah began, nervously pulling at her long woolen skirt, "I wouldn't want you to stay if this was all too much. I mean, I wouldn't hold you to any sort of promises. I'm sure there are plenty– "

"Sarah," Devlin interrupted softly. "I know I'm not much when it comes to letting on how I feel about things. I can't promise that I'll ever get a whole lot better, but I do plan on trying." The rider kept her eyes trained on the horizon as she spoke. She was too nervous to see what Sarah's reaction might be. "I've spent my whole life looking for something, the kind of thing that I thought was only meant for other people. Now it seems that I've found something so close that it's damned near perfect. I may be only a rider with a little bit of dumb luck, but I'm not stupid enough to have found what I've always wanted and then keep on looking. This is it for me, Sarah, and I don't mean just for a summer or two or until it gets too hard. This is what I want for the rest of my life. *You're* what I want for the rest of my life."

"How is it that you keep saying you're not much on talking, but every time you open your mouth you cause me to fall in love with you just a little bit more?" Sarah asked.

Devlin grinned. She liked the way that sounded. Secretly,

she breathed a sigh of relief. She had hoped the words, which came from her heart, wouldn't start the young woman to laughing.

"I guess it must be the inspiration," Devlin replied.

"The women must have thought you were quite a charmer," Sarah commented.

Devlin chuckled, but she heard the hint of jealousy in Sarah's tone. She would never stop being amazed that somehow, Sarah thought of her as quite a catch. The dark-haired woman leaned over and placed a light kiss on the surprised blonde's cheek.

"That I was, darlin', but from here on in, I only plan on entertaining one woman with my charm."

They laughed, which lightened the moment enough for them to discuss their future plans in a relaxed atmosphere. In no time, they pulled up in front of the small cabin. Sarah stared at the painted design and the odd string of bones and shells nailed onto the door of the cabin. The shape was similar to a bird, but was painted a bright, sky blue color.

"Dev? Should we be worried?"

The rider smiled at the familiar marking and the fetish hanging from the door. "No, actually, it should make you feel safe."

Devlin explained that the marking was for other Indian tribes in the region. It was an unspoken warning that this *chuka*, or dwelling, and all its inhabitants, were under the protection of the Thunderbird Clan. Devlin's adopted people had a reputation in this territory for the strength of their warriors as well as the potency of their Medicine. The rider felt she might sleep a little easier at night, knowing her people watched over her family.

Sarah cleaned and aired out the cabin. The rider, in the meantime, situated the barn into supplies they could take with them, items that could be stored at the homestead, and equipment such as harnesses and assorted tack that she could send someone over to retrieve later. A loud bleating sound brought both women outside.

A very large cow moved slowly against the fence line, and the noises it made grew even louder once it caught sight of Sarah.

"Anabelle!" Sarah cried out and rushed to the animal.

Devlin moved a little more cautiously to the longhorn cow. She had a history with this particular animal. It was as large as a bull and Devlin teased Sarah about the animal being a freak of nature. It was as docile as a newborn lamb around Sarah, but according to Devlin, the cow had it in for her. In the short time since Devlin had come to work on Sarah's place, she'd had to rope Anabelle out of more situations than any ten animals. Devlin mentioned more than once that the large animal would make one hell of a barbecue, only to receive a disapproving glare from the small blonde.

The huge longhorn was a favorite of Sarah's. Its mother had died giving birth and Sarah practically hand raised the animal. Cattle were a lot like wild animals. They shied away from humans, especially the animals kept out on the range where they had little interaction with man. The fact that Sarah had raised Anabelle was probably why the animal had no fear of humans— either that or the cow's incredible size.

Devlin immediately noticed that the massive cow was even larger than usual because it was about to calve at any moment. Anabelle, by instinct, had made her way to the safest spot she could think of— home.

"She's in trouble, Dev."

The rider came up beside the animal, and as usual, it tried to kick out at her. "Oh, no you don't." Devlin quickly sidestepped the cow's rear leg. "I can't believe you even got all the way over here, you big tub of lard."

Devlin had assigned a few riders the task of driving over the few hundred head of cattle from this ranch, where Sarah had lived before her uncle's death, to the Winston ranch. Combining the herds made it easier for the riders to care for the rangelands and the cattle under their protection. There were a number of strays that got away by hiding in the hills, but Devlin made a habit of sending a couple of riders over every few days to catch the stragglers. A number of the strays were cows preparing to calve. They were the animals that usually separated as far as possible from the rest of the herd, hiding among the rocks where there was less chance of discovery by predators.

Devlin examined Anabelle while Sarah held and petted the animal's massive head. "This isn't good. Looks like her water broke, but she's bleeding, too."

Both women knew that usually meant a stillborn calf. The cow threw up her leg again, only this time Devlin understood that the animal wasn't kicking out at her but at her own stomach. That was another sure sign the calf inside was dead.

"Dev, we have to do something." Sarah had tears in her eyes.

Out on the range Devlin would have let nature take its course. In this country, only the fittest survived and it was usually for a reason. The rider couldn't stand the sight of Sarah with tears in her eyes over a cow. She quickly unbuttoned her jacket and removed her outer shirt.

"We have to keep her on her feet," the rider said.

No sooner had Devlin uttered the words than Anabelle lay flat out on the ground. Contractions rippled through the cow's large body. Anabelle made a terrible groaning sound once two tiny feet appeared. Devlin decided to give the animal a hand and gently pulled on the two feet. Anabelle grunted and tossed her large head back and forth. The cow's large set of horns came dangerously close to hitting Devlin.

"What can I do to help, Dev?" Sarah asked from behind Devlin's back. She was a knowledgeable cattlewoman, but acquiesced to the rider's superior skills in this area.

"Get up there and hold her head. Let her see you and see if that helps calm her down some."

With her head in Sarah's lap, the cow relaxed and let another contraction take over. The calf's nose appeared after a few more contractions, but Devlin knew right off that the calf was gone. Its nose was a much deeper blue than it should have been. As she eased the calf's head out of the birth canal, she could see that its eyes held no life. She plucked a long blade of grass and used it to tickle inside the calf's nose. There was no response.

Suddenly Anabelle's struggles ceased and the large animal grew quiet. Devlin, amazed at the way animals seemed to have a sixth sense about such things, figured that Anabelle knew the calf was dead.

"Dev?" Sarah called out from her position in front of Anabelle.

"It's gone. We need to help her get him the rest of the way out."

"She's sort of given up at this point," Sarah commented.

Devlin tried to pull the dead calf out but couldn't bring it any further out than to its shoulders. It seemed to be hung up on something inside the cow, which thrashed around in pain.

"Easy girl...easy." Sarah's words calmed the animal to a small extent. "Should I get some rope? We could pull him out that way."

"Nah, I'm afraid he's tangled up inside. We'd only be hurting Anabelle more."

The large animal lay flat out on the ground, growing weaker as the minutes passed. They were at a standoff. The calf wasn't coming out any further, and the large cow, her strength nearly gone, was no longer having contractions.

"Well, Anabelle, just believe me when I say that I don't like this any better than you do," Devlin said as she knelt behind the cow once again.

Devlin slipped her hand, followed by her arm, past the calf's shoulders and into the birth canal. The rider had done this before, but only when a prized cow's life had been in danger. Anabelle was Sarah's favorite and so she was valuable in Devlin's eyes. As the rider slipped her hand past the calf's body and down its back legs, she felt something further back in the uterus kick her hand.

"I'll be damned!" the rider exclaimed.

"Dev, what's wrong?"

"There's another one in here, and it's alive."

Devlin realized that the dead sibling was preventing the other calf, which was definitely alive, from entering the birth canal. The calves were wrapped around one another so neither could break free. The rider pushed the live calf off the first one, allowing her to easily pull the dead animal from its mother's body.

"Sarah, come here!"

"Drag this one over there by the fence, he's dead. Don't let Anabelle see him or she's liable to stand up. I've still got to get his twin out of there."

Once Devlin reached back inside, she quickly realized that she was feeling the two rear legs, which meant she only had minutes left before they lost this calf, too. The second calf was bigger than the first, but Devlin managed to maneuver it into the canal by using both of her arms inside the cow. Two strong pulls and the calf came sliding out. After wiping the animal's face, Devlin dragged the shivering calf around to Anabelle's head.

The large cow sniffed at the tiny, wet package before her. When Anabelle made gentle lowing sounds and Sarah started crying, Devlin knew the venture had been a success. Within minutes, Anabelle passed the afterbirth, lumbered to her feet, and started to clean the newborn calf.

"Devlin, you are wonderful," Sarah exclaimed. The small blonde made a move to hug the tall woman, but the rider stopped her.

"Don't come near me," Devlin cautioned, turning toward Sarah. "I'm covered in stuff I'd rather not even think about. Let me at least get to a bucket of water, some soap, and a clean shirt first." She grinned.

"I have to admit, though," Devlin turned back toward the sight of Anabelle cleaning her calf, "that is the strangest looking calf I've ever seen. His head's too big for his body."

Sarah examined the calf herself. "I think...well, he looks like– Dev, he looks like a buffalo," she said in astonishment.

"I told you you'd get nothing but trouble from a cow that's this big. Doesn't surprise me," Devlin said, turning to face Sarah. "I am surprised that there was a buffalo up this high, though. Seems as if your little baby has been in greener pastures." She laughed.

"Dev, look out!"

The rider turned and jumped out of the way, narrowly avoiding Anabelle's rear hoof.

"You son of a– "

"Devlin!" Sarah reprimanded the rider. "She's just an animal, Dev, she's not out to get you."

"Yeah, well, the next time she does that she's going to end up as a steak on my plate," the rider grumbled.

Anabelle loudly snorted air through her nose, convincing Devlin that Sarah was wrong this time. This cow certainly appeared to understand what Devlin was saying.

"Too damn big for a cow," Devlin muttered under her breath. "It just ain't natural."

"That was wonderful, Sarah, thank you," Devlin said, as Sarah poured them both another cup of coffee. "I hope you know that I'm gonna end up as big as Anabelle if you keep feeding me this way." She smiled across the table at the blonde.

"You're very welcome. Although, with Maria and Angelia working in the kitchen at the new place, I think you'll get a reprieve. They told me, in no uncertain terms, that the woman who owns the ranch doesn't belong in the kitchen." Sarah laughed.

"It's true, you'll have more to fill up your days than cooking and cleaning. You have wealth and power now, *sachu-kash*. That means that you can run your ranch the way you see fit, without any interference from the Association. You don't have to be afraid of what anyone will think if you want to ride the range. Just so you don't get so good that you put me out of a job," Devlin said with a wink.

"I don't think I'll ever get that good," Sarah replied.

"Well, I don't know about you, but what do you say to me heating up some water for a hot bath?" Devlin asked. "I know I sure could use one."

"I'll second that. I mean about both of us needing a bath, not just you." The small blonde laughed.

"Oh, sure, I heard what you said the first time." The rider rose from the table and leaned down to place a quick kiss on Sarah's cheek.

Devlin left to start a fire outside where the large boiling pot hung. Sarah's stomach tightened as an attack of nerves struck at her. *This is it. It's exactly what I wanted, right? Just me and Dev, the two of us all alone. So why is it that I'm suddenly scared to death?* Sarah thought, as she walked into the back bedroom.

"What is it, Sarah?" Devlin asked once she poured the last bucket of steaming water into the bathtub.

The rider watched the younger woman out of the corner of her eye as she slowly went about the task of filling up the buckets of water from the large pot outside on the fire. She could see that the small blonde watched the dark-haired woman as if she'd had never seen her before.

"Sarah?" Devlin came to the woman and gently touched her face.

Pulling the smaller woman into her arms, the rider felt Sarah's body tense. The young woman lowered her eyes and a full blush settled across her face. Devlin wasn't sure what to make of this new reaction. Sarah wasn't a woman to play at being coy. The rider tried to fathom the workings of her new lover's mind. After all, this was the first time that they would share this kind of intimacy. It was their first night together without family on the other side of the wall, a sleeping daughter lying between them, or at least one of them being fully clothed. The rider worried that perhaps she was pushing Sarah. That it was too soon.

"Do you want me to leave the room?" Devlin asked, curious to see if modesty was the problem.

"No!" Sarah looked up and both women smiled at the voracity of the blonde's reply. "I mean, no, I want you to stay," she said slowly. Sarah looked up into the eyes that held love and concern. "It's just that, well, God knows I'm no virgin, but I- I've never- I don't think I know what to do to please you, Dev." Sarah finished the sentence all in one breath, lowering her head out of embarrassment.

Devlin couldn't stop the smile that pulled at her lips. She placed two slender fingers under the smaller woman's chin to lift her face. The green eyes that looked up at her held nothing but love and anxiety. The rider's heart tightened within her chest.

"Sarah, if it's too soon for you, love, we don't have to do anything at all," Devlin said gently.

"But that's not what I want," Sarah blurted out.

"Oh?" Devlin drawled her response She looked down with a hint of amusement at the treasure in her arms.

"I mean- well, Peter was the only- I think I was his first too and...it just was never very- "

Devlin placed a finger over the young woman's lips, effectively silencing her. The rider pulled out of the embrace and led Sarah to the bed. Devlin sat down and drew the small blonde down into her lap.

"Sarah, relax, it's just me. I'm not only your lover, but I'm a woman, too. You can talk to me. You can tell me anything you need to and I'll understand. Is it because I'm a woman?" Devlin asked, unsure if she wanted to hear Sarah's answer.

Sarah took a deep breath. She wasn't used to being in such an awkward position. She didn't usually have this much trouble explaining her feelings, but the importance of what they were about to do fell on her like a load of stone. She was desperately afraid that Devlin wouldn't want a woman in her bed who didn't know what she was doing. Sarah wanted to please the dark-haired woman who had captured her heart.

"Yes and no. Peter was a very gentle lover, but I just never felt any of the sensations that I've read about. I'm afraid that lying with me- well, I'm afraid it won't be enjoyable for you." Sarah looked up at her lover tearfully.

Devlin's eyes turned deep blue as she brushed an errant tear from Sarah's face. The dark-haired woman's features displayed a mixture of emotions. "Are you trying to tell me that you've never received any enjoyment from sex?"

"I'm sorry, Dev. I was always taught that a woman had sex to have children, to please her husband. It was never about my pleasure."

"Oh, *sachu-kash*." Devlin pulled woman into her warm embrace. "It is now," she whispered.

Devlin stood and settled Sarah on her feet. The dark-haired woman began to unbutton her own shirt and Sarah could only stare.

"What are you doing?" Sarah questioned, although the answer seemed apparent.

"I'm undressing. We're going to take that bath...together," Devlin said. She moved closer to Sarah and her voice lowered into a husky alto, commanding but without any harshness. "Then I'm going to do what I've wanted to do since the very first moment I fell in love with you, Sarah Tolliver." Devlin wrapped her arms around her lover's slim waist. She bent and placed a tender kiss on the side of the small blonde's neck.

"I'm going to take you to bed and simply enjoy lying next to you, and if you want me to touch you, then I will. If you want me to make love to you, I will. And if you want me to show you what pleasure is all about, then I'll do that, too. However, if you don't want any of those things, then we'll simply take pleasure in sleeping close together until you are ready. Will that be all right?"

Sarah felt a distinct shiver run up her spine and her pulse quickened as she listened to the seductive, yet soothing tone of the rider's words. She watched as Devlin's eyes turned smoky with desire. All the blonde could do was nod in response.

Lying together in the cooling water of the large tub, Sarah was amazed at how quickly she became accustomed to the rider's body, perhaps because it *was* another woman. Many of Sarah's first jitters were thrown by the wayside once the dark-haired woman stood naked before her and helped Sarah out of her garments. Now, she leaned against the back of the tub with the length of Devlin's body stretched out in front of her. The rider's head was tucked underneath Sarah's chin, cradled between her breasts.

They lay that way for some time. Devlin eased Sarah's nerves with stories of when the rider grew up in the Thunderbird Clan of the Choctaw. All the while, the rider absently caressed

Sarah's exposed skin. Sarah could hardly take her eyes off the rider's body, and she wondered if Devlin had situated herself like this so the young woman could look without embarrassment. The rider's darker skin bore the scars of her hard life, but Sarah seemed a little more captivated by the sleek, muscled abdomen and the way the woman's breasts floated out of the water slightly, the darkened nipples tightening into stiff peaks when the cool air hit them.

"How did you get this, Dev?" Sarah asked of the small tattoo just above the rider's right shoulder blade.

"From Mantema. You met her in the Clan village. She was the old woman, very short, but very large around the middle."

"The one who laughed so much and danced with the children?"

"Yep, that's the one. Her name means To Deliver Something Sacred. She's responsible for tattooing a person's animal totem on their body when they come back from their first Quest. Tattoos are a part of the *Chahta* culture once a Clan member comes of age."

"Did it hurt?"

"I didn't feel a thing. Honest," Devlin added when Sarah made a sound of disbelief. "She does it immediately after a young person comes back from their initial Quest. I think I was so, I don't know how to explain it, but I think I still had one foot in the Spirit world. I wasn't really myself yet so I didn't really feel it. Want to know the strange part?" Devlin tilted her head to see Sarah's nod. "She doesn't have to ask you which animal came to you, she just knows."

Sarah traced the pattern of a hawk's tail feathers spread out into a fan shape. "Keeho said he saw me as a *sakli*, the salmon. If that's my name within the Clan, won't it be my animal guide, too?"

"The fact that the red-tailed hawk is my chief Power animal *and* happens to be my name is considered a special gift," Devlin answered. "It would be kind of interesting if that happened to you, too. As a *Chahta* of the Thunderbird Clan, I received nine animal totems. These animals offer me their guidance, protection, and instruction. Keeho and six other Clan Elders helped me to discover my first seven in a sacred ceremony. The last two were for me to determine alone. The red-tailed hawk spoke to me in a way none of the others had, with power. Through visions, I found that he carried special Medicine for me. When I was younger, he taught me that if I called on him, he would honor me with special talents."

When Devlin bent her knee, Sarah lost track of her thoughts and had to bite her lip not to let her fingers reach out and touch the dark patch of curls that came into view. She had no idea what she would do, but she knew she wanted to touch Devlin. Sarah knew what it felt like on the few occasions she touched herself and her mind imagined Devlin touching her in that way. Suddenly a shiver ran the length of the young woman's body.

"You're getting cold." Devlin jumped to her feet and moved from the tub. She held open a large towel and, after helping Sarah from the tub, wrapped the cloth around Sarah's body.

"Getting warmer?" Devlin asked.

"Much," Sarah said as she nodded her head. *Do I tell her exactly how very warm I am right about now?*

After Devlin placed two more logs in the fireplace, they settled onto the large bed. The rider couldn't believe how wonderful Sarah's body felt. Devlin closed her eyes and tried to slow her breathing. Her skin felt like the glowing embers of a campfire wherever Sarah pressed her body against hers.

"I've never seen you without this." Sarah's fingers traced a thin piece of rawhide around the rider's neck. The strip of leather held a small bag made by tightly tying the ends of a soft piece of deerskin. "I remember when you were shot and I tried to take it off, you held to it even in your sleep."

"It's my *ikhish bahta*," Devlin explained. "My Medicine bag."

"What does it do?"

"It protects me."

"It hasn't been doing its job." Sarah smiled as she leaned up on one elbow and touched first one scar then another on the rider's body.

"It never fails to tell me when to move out of harm's way," Devlin responded. She chuckled. "But I don't always listen."

Sarah laughed, and Devlin felt glad that she could ease some of the awkwardness Sarah had been feeling.

"What's in it, Dev?"

"You would not be any wiser if I told you," Devlin answered.

"I don't understand. What kind of an answer is that?"

"The same one any *Chahta* would give you if you asked them the same question." Devlin smiled. "It's a private thing, but even if I told you all of the contents, you would be no wiser. Some of the items wouldn't make any sense to you. They're things that have meaning only to me. Things that I alone feel will ward off evil spirits or bring me good fortune. I have a tiny piece of a red-tailed hawk's eggshell, a bit of red earth from the *Chahta* village– "

Sarah pressed two fingers against the rider's lips. "You don't have to tell me, Dev."

"I have nothing to hide from you, *sachu-kash*, I want you to know that. I would willingly tell you all my secrets."

Sarah stared down into a pair of sky blue eyes and once again wondered if she were dreaming. She bent her head and placed a slow, lingering kiss upon Devlin's lips.

"Dev?" Sarah whispered.

"Hmm?"

"Will you?"

"Will I what, *sachu-kash*?" Devlin opened her eyes and looked up at the young woman in her arms.

"Will you show me what pleasure is all about?" Sarah asked tentatively, brushing back a damp lock of ebony hair from her lover's face.

The rider gently rolled the two of them over until she leaned over her lover. Devlin didn't say a word; she simply bent her head closer until her lips pressed lightly against Sarah's. They did nothing but kiss for what seemed like forever, but neither woman was aware of time. They let their mouths and tongues tenderly explore and excite.

As their desire burned hotter, Devlin wanted so much to take the woman in her arms with all of the unbridled passion she felt. She had an uncanny notion that this small blonde would equal her fervor. For this woman, however, who had never experienced pleasure by a lover's hand, Devlin would force herself to go slow. She would make it last, until Sarah knew that every single time they came together, there would be nothing but rapture waiting.

Devlin ran her kisses down Sarah's neck and the tip of her tongue gently played with the pulse that beat fitfully through her lover's skin. Her fingertips ran down the length of Sarah's neck, in the space between her breasts, and onto her belly, which quivered under the rider's light touch. Devlin stopped when she felt the downy hairs that covered Sarah's lower abdomen.

"Sarah, may I touch you?" The request was probably unnecessary, but for some reason Devlin felt like she should ask.

Sarah felt as if her insides were ablaze. She pushed away the blanket that covered them and revealed her naked figure to the rider's intense blue gaze. "Yes, please touch me, Dev," she replied breathlessly.

The rider's fingers played in the curls that were the same light color as the honeyed tresses that fell across Sarah's shoulders. The curls grew damp as Devlin brought her tender explorations even lower, and she moaned at the feel of Sarah's arousal. Devlin placed the palm of her hand on the inside of Sarah's thigh and with gentle pressure parted her legs wider.

Devlin could hardly contain her own need now as the heady scent of Sarah's excitement assailed her nostrils. She brought her mouth to the young woman's neck and kissed her, sucking lightly at the skin to mark her. She moved her lips across the flushed skin of Sarah's shoulders, then down along her collarbone. Devlin ran her tongue through the hollow between the small blonde's breasts. All the while, Devlin's fingers caressed the soft skin of her lover's inner thighs and her index finger moved in feather light touches along her nether lips.

Sarah was unsure where she should be focusing her attention. Devlin's hand caressed her in a way she'd never even thought to touch herself, and the rider's mouth was making a feast of the upper portion of her body. A languid moan slipped from Sarah's throat when Devlin's warm lips wrapped around a hardened nipple and pulled in a soft sucking motion.

"Oh, Dev," Sarah exclaimed. Her own hands involuntarily grasped at the long raven-colored locks that spread out across her body.

"Mmm," Devlin murmured against the heated skin. "Do you like that?"

"Oh, yes," Sarah responded quickly. *My God, has there been a woman that you've done this to that hasn't?*

Sarah thought that perhaps she should be encouraging Devlin, responding in a more fervent manner, but for the life of her she simply couldn't put a coherent sentence together. All her focus was on her own body and the sensations that her lover created with every touch. She'd felt something akin to this feeling at her breast when she'd nursed her children, but it was nothing compared to the streaks of fire that ran from her nipple to the area that Devlin caressed between Sarah's legs.

Devlin felt a warm rush of liquid against her fingertips and sucked harder. She released the nipple, pressing into the hard flesh tenderly with her teeth as she did. Sarah groaned and thrust her hips against Devlin's hand as the dark-haired woman turned her attention to the other breast. Finally, Devlin brought her wet fingertips up to her lips and sucked her lover's essence from them. When the taste of her lover filled her mouth, the dark-haired woman released a growl from deep within her chest. She moved her body down the length of Sarah's and used her tongue to brand a trail of burning fire along the young woman's skin.

Sarah felt Devlin move down, and she opened her eyes and watched as the rider encouraged her to open her legs even wider. Devlin kissed and nipped the tender skin inside Sarah's thigh, running a finger along the line of her body where leg met hip. The rider continued the assault by placing gentle kisses on the damp curls between the smaller woman's legs, moving the kisses lower and lower until Sarah's hips bucked at the feel of the rider's lips on the velvety skin there.

"Dev?" Sarah called out sharply and the rider immediately froze, thinking she'd gone too far in her own haste to have the woman.

"Do you want me to stop?" Devlin asked hoarsely.

"God, no, not if you know what's good for you," Sarah panted.

Devlin chuckled against the woman's skin. This was her Sarah, the woman that had been suspiciously absent during their lovemaking thus far.

"Are you enjoying my touch, *sachu-kash*?" Devlin asked, kissing the inside of Sarah's thigh.

"Oh, Dev, yes...It's just..."

Devlin raised herself up on one elbow to see into Sarah's eyes, which were glazed over with desire. The young woman's chest rose and fell rapidly.

"Should it always feel this good, Dev?" Sarah asked with uncertainty.

"Yes, love. Every time."

Devlin began her tender kisses once again. She watched as Sarah leaned back onto the bed, a smile on her parted lips. The small blonde appeared to finally let go to the gratifying sensations of their lovemaking. The rider felt the trickle of her own arousal run down the inside of her thigh and she ground her hips into the mattress to satisfy the burning that developed there. When Devlin's tongue reached out and ran along a silky fold, both women immediately groaned. The taste of her lover caused an explosion of need in Devlin's body, while Sarah thrust her hips shamelessly at the source of her immense pleasure. The small blonde had never felt a touch so intimate in all her life.

Devlin's tender exploration of her lover's sex fell by the wayside when Sarah rocked her hips frantically against the rider's tongue. Sarah tried to satisfy a need that she didn't quite know how to express.

"Dev?" Sarah pleaded. The young woman had no idea what more to ask for, but this time the rider knew exactly what her lover desired.

The dark-haired woman wrapped her lips over the small hood of flesh and flicked her tongue against it in a quick, steady rhythm. Never stopping, she slipped one slender finger inside the small blonde.

"Oh, yes!" Sarah cried out.

Devlin slid the lone finger out and replaced it with two of her fingers. She continued the motion of slowly sliding out and then pressing in while she continued to suck at the pulsating bundle of nerves.

"Oh, yes!" Sarah groaned even louder as the sensation of Devlin's fingers filling her competed with the feeling of a firm tongue lapping insistently at her center.

Devlin felt the smaller woman's muscles tighten, then they quivered uncontrollably. Sarah arched her back and the sound that tore from her throat was like music to the rider's ears. Devlin stilled her tongue but continued the motion of her hand, eventually feeling Sarah's inner muscles pulsate strongly against the fingers buried deep inside. Sarah's body convulsed powerfully one more time as another orgasm tore through her.

Devlin moved to hold the small woman in her arms. "I love you, Sarah," she whispered, feeling the young woman's body tremble.

"Oh, Dev, how I love you." Sarah wrapped her arms around the dark-haired woman's neck and squeezed tightly. Pulling back slightly, she caressed a high cheekbone. "How I do love you."

A short time later, the rider settled onto her back, her lover nestled against her side. Sarah draped a leg across Devlin's thighs, a small hand resting on the rider's stomach. Devlin smiled to herself, realizing she had everything in life that she could possibly want. Of course, the ache between her own legs was a little bothersome, but this was Sarah's night. There would be plenty of time for the young woman to become familiar with the rider's body.

Just as Devlin voiced those thoughts in her head, Sarah's hand innocently caressed the rider's skin.

"Dev?"

"Hmm?" Devlin answered, trying not to writhe under her lover's easy touch.

"May I touch you?"

"Of course, love."

Sarah moved her hand to cup the underside of the rider's breast. "Anywhere?"

Devlin swallowed hard and closed her eyes, momentarily lost in her partner's tender caress. Opening her eyes and taking a deep breath, she looked down and used her hand to direct Sarah's chin upwards. Gazing into those emerald green eyes Devlin smiled.

"Sarah, *sachu-kash*, I belong to you as much as you belong to me. You may always touch me, wherever, however, and whenever you like."

Sarah tenderly kissed the uppermost swell of the rider's breast. The young woman explored her lover's body. She had never touched a woman this way before and at first, she acted out of curiosity. However, when her fingers casually brushed over a nipple and the dark-haired woman gasped in pleasure, Sarah realized the power her touch held. As she continued, she could feel her own excitement escalate simply from touching her lover. Just as Devlin had elicited the shameless sounds from her, Sarah wanted to be able to bring that kind of pleasure to Devlin.

Sarah's fingers lightly massaged every inch of the dark-haired women's upper body. She moved across Devlin's shoulders, lingering in the sensitive area across her collarbone, down her chest and arms, and finally across her breasts. Sarah's touch was as delicate as Devlin's had been and she wondered if the muscular woman preferred a stronger touch.

Sarah's silky smooth fingertips thoroughly enraptured the rider as they slid across her heated skin. It was arousing and maddening at the same time. She wanted to let herself enjoy the light caresses that she had never before felt from a lover, but the wetness and the pulse pounding between her legs were trying to tell her that she wanted to be taken fast and hard. Devlin took a deep breath and sighed her pleasure along with her frustration.

Sarah decided to voice her concern. "Dev," she whispered

near the dark-haired woman's ear, "show me how you like to be touched."

Devlin pulled the woman in her arms closer, until Sarah's body was lying across hers. She was just about to take the young woman's hand and press it firmly against her breast, showing Sarah that she craved a rougher touch, but she stopped herself.

This night was a first for Devlin, too. For the first time in her life, a woman who loved her was making love to her, a woman whom Devlin loved in return. The rider had never experienced the tenderness of a lover's caress before. Even when sex had been good for Devlin, it was rough and fast, similar to a sparring match. She had never once relinquished control to anyone for fear of being hurt or abandoned. Now, the woman of her heart requested that Devlin show what she liked, but how could the dark-haired woman tell her lover that she didn't know what she liked, that she'd never been touched that way either?

"*Sachu-kash*, I'd like you to touch me exactly the way you've been touching me. It feels so good– you feel so good. I want you to feel what you do to me," Devlin said a little hoarsely, taking Sarah's small hand within her larger one.

The rider slid both of their hands down her belly, pausing when she reached the dark triangle of hair. Halting briefly, she waited to see if Sarah would pull back. Instead, the strangled groan Sarah released from that first cherished contact surprised Devlin. Spreading her legs wider, she slipped both their hands into her wetness. The sensation of their hands mingling together between Devlin's legs wrenched a breathless moan from each of them.

Sarah smiled to think that her body could excite Devlin this way. She leaned into her lover and kissed her with an intensity that surprised Devlin. The rider removed her own hand from her center and wrapped both arms around Sarah, caressing the smooth skin of her back. Sarah blazed a trail of tender kisses everywhere her fingers had touched earlier. The young woman soon found that her favorite new pastime would be suckling on her lover's dark nipples. The way that Devlin moaned and rolled her hips against Sarah's hand excited the younger woman. Sarah realized that she was becoming as aroused as her lover. She pressed her fingers gently against her lover's wet entrance.

"Oh, yes, I need to feel you inside of me," Devlin moaned.

Sarah slid two fingers deeper, just as Devlin had with her. She immediately felt the warm softness envelop her fingers and moved them forward in a slow rocking motion.

Devlin groaned again and thrust her hips harder against Sarah's hand. "More," she pleaded and reached down to indicate to her lover that she wanted another finger inside her.

Feeling the fullness of three of Sarah's fingers deep inside, moving against her, Devlin gave herself up to the young woman's body. She wrapped one arm around the blonde's waist and another in her beautiful hair. Devlin rolled her hips in a gentle motion against her lover's hand. She could feel a warm wetness over the top of her thigh and realized Sarah had straddled the muscular leg, her own passions burning anew. Devlin slid her hand downward along Sarah's back until she reached the smooth flesh of Sarah's backside. She squeezed the flesh there and encouraged the motion of her lover's hips. Soon, the movement of Sarah's hips matched Devlin's as each woman came closer to her own climax.

"*Sa*," Devlin moaned into Sarah's ear. The rider had always called her *sachu-kash*, meaning "my heart," but now Devlin simply chanted this one Clan word. The rider felt the first tremors of her orgasm begin.

In response to her lover's words, Sarah pressed her body tightly to Devlin's.

"*Sa*," Devlin growled as her whole body shook with a fierce release. She groaned out the word again, muscles convulsing, feeling as if she were melting from the inside out. The Clan word that the rider continued to moan into Sarah's ear was perhaps the simplest of all words, but with the largest impact for the two lovers. Sarah was hearing it for the first time, but it would forever become her pet name. Sarah's cry of delight followed Devlin's as the younger woman met with her own release.

"*Sa*," the rider whimpered one last time, the Clan word meaning "mine."

Sarah raised her head and saw that Devlin's forearm lay over her eyes. Tears ran down the sides of the dark-haired woman's face. "Dev, are you all right, did I hurt you?" Sarah grew afraid at Devlin's reaction.

"Oh no, *sachu-kash*, I'm sorry," Devlin replied, holding on tightly to the woman lying next to her.

"Did I do something wrong?"

Devlin looked into the worried face of her lover and became overwhelmed by the emotions that filled her. "Absolutely not, my love. What you did was so very right. I've never experienced anything quite as wonderful." Devlin then admitted to Sarah that while she had experienced pleasure, no one had ever made love to her before. Sarah's gentle touches were the first Devlin had ever known from a lover. Sharing their love so tenderly simply reminded Devlin of a part of herself that she thought had died long ago. Her heart.

Both women had a night of firsts. They pulled the blankets over themselves and cuddled together to sleep, exhausted yet extremely content.

Chapter 3

Every single one of Devlin's senses was awake and alert, even though to anyone watching she appeared to be asleep. She lay perfectly still with her eyes closed, controlling her breathing so it wouldn't accelerate at the surge of adrenaline that just ran through her body. Opening her eyes a fraction, she looked around the room to confirm that nothing was amiss. She heard the sound again. It was a light footfall, almost a shuffle. It was only one person, by the sounds that filtered through the cabin wall.

"Sarah?" Devlin whispered close to the sleeping woman's ear. She was impressed at the level of alertness the small blonde displayed. "There's someone outside. Put something on and be very quiet."

Devlin slid from the bed like a shadow slinking along the ground. She silently slipped into her pants and a shirt, which she didn't bother to button. She eased her revolver from its holster and made her way into the main room of the cabin. The wooden shutters were closed over the windows on each side of the door. Placing an ear against the door, Devlin listened as footsteps moved around the other side of the cabin toward the barn.

The rider opened the wooden door without so much as a creak and her bare feet moved soundlessly in the dry dirt. She didn't follow directly behind the intruder. Instead, she went around the barn to get ahead of him. She heard scuffling in one of the empty stalls. Whoever the trespasser was, he wasn't doing much to keep his movements a secret.

Bending over so that the fencing that separated the stalls hid her, Devlin moved closer. She heard muttered phrases and what sounded like grumbling or complaining. The light from the half moon gave her enough illumination to see. It was apparent to the rider that whoever was taking up residence wasn't doing much of a job at not being caught. The right combination of surprise and menace would give her the upper hand.

The barn grew quiet as the intruder apparently settled in for the night. Devlin grinned a bit as she prepared to scare the life out of the poor soul who was unfortunate enough to have roused her from her bed. Suddenly standing upright, the rider spun on one heel, facing the open stall. Only one button held her shirt closed, and the nighttime breeze whipped her dark hair around her bronze face. Her outstretched arm held a Colt pistol.

"*Tanta kim tomi!*" the old man exclaimed, trembling in fear.

Devlin felt rather foolish. She was half-clothed and brandished her revolver, while at her feet lay a terrified old man. Actually, he was more than old. He appeared ancient. She could only imagine what the wide-eyed Indian thought, gazing up at six feet of very intimidating rider.

"*Kata chim?*" Under ordinary circumstances, Devlin would not have been so rude as to ask who the old grandfather was without first showing proper respect, but in her book he was trespassing and that's all there was to it.

"*Tanta kim tomi,*" he repeated.

Devlin tilted her head to one side, unable to make out the language the old man spoke. It sounded vaguely familiar, but she couldn't place it.

"*Chahta imanupa ish anumpola hinla ho?*" She asked if the man spoke Choctaw, hoping they could find some sort of common ground.

Now it was the old man's turn to look confused.

"Well, this is gonna get us nowhere fast." Devlin tucked her gun into the waistband of her trousers and offered the man a hand up.

"*Chisa oh,*" he said once he was standing.

The old man wasn't very steady on his feet, and his skin felt warm but dry to the rider's touch. He stood bent over slightly and simply looked exhausted.

"Yeah, *chisa oh* to you, too, whatever that means. Where do you come from, Grandfather, and what do you want in a place where you can't even speak the language?" Devlin asked the question more of herself than the old man. "Come on, let's get you inside. I've got a *tekchi* in the house who probably has a loaded Winchester right about now."

The rider motioned to the old man to follow. She slung his makeshift rucksack over her shoulder and had to practically carry him to the door. Sure enough, Sarah was waiting with her rifle. As headstrong as the younger woman was, Devlin felt better knowing that when the chips were on the table, Sarah did as instructed. The last thing the rider needed was to worry about her own wife shooting her in the middle of the night.

"Dev!" Sarah called out in concern. She leaned the rifle against the wall just inside of the cabin door and rushed out to help the rider.

The old man's eyes grew wide as Sarah came up beside him. He looked at the two women, nodded his head, and smiled weakly. He stumbled and the smaller woman helped him regain his balance. With the frail man between them, Sarah and Devlin helped their unusual guest inside the cabin.

The old man spoke in a language that Sarah didn't recognize. He mumbled on even as they helped him to the cot beside the fireplace. Hank had set up the makeshift bed when he had stayed at the cabin while Sarah and Devlin had visited the Choctaw camp. Devlin fanned the banked coals inside the stone fireplace and added some kindling, then a log. The room quickly turned warm and comfortable. The whole time, the old man muttered in his own language.

"What's he saying?" Sarah asked.

"Darned if I know." Devlin shook her head.

Sarah wrapped a blanket around the man and offered him a cup of water, which he drank greedily. She poured him another and went to the pot still hanging beside the fireplace. She dished up a bowl of their leftover dinner and brought it over to him.

"He eats like it's been a while," Devlin commented.

The old man quickly gulped down the food and Sarah refilled the bowl. Devlin knelt down beside the old wooden cot.

"*Chi hohchifo nanta?*" Devlin tried the Clan language once more, asking the old man his name. Feverish brown eyes looked at her and the old man shook his head. An ironic smile graced his features.

"*Ko sa omita?*" he asked in return. Unfortunately Devlin didn't understand the old man any more than he appeared to understand her.

"*Ak akostinincho,*" Devlin replied.

Sarah laid a gentle hand on Devlin's shoulder. "Dev, I don't think telling him you don't understand him in Choctaw makes much more sense than saying it in English." She smiled down at the rider.

Devlin fixed a sheepish grin on the young woman. "Oh, yeah. Guess I forgot."

"Maybe we can at least find out where he's from, what tribe he belongs to," Sarah said.

"Great idea. Care to give it a go?" Devlin asked the small blonde.

"Very funny," Sarah replied. She ran her fingers through Devlin's hair and rested one hand along the back of the kneeling woman's neck.

Sarah caught the old man's gaze as he watched the two women interact. Mostly she noticed the way he stared at Sarah's hand as she affectionately touched the rider. She hadn't yet prepared herself for how other people would react to her and Devlin together. Among the white men, she now had wealth, which meant power. When people were powerful, they could pretty much do as they pleased without reprisal.

The blonde pulled her hand back and took a half-step away from Devlin. The rider felt the difference as if it was something palpable in the air. She turned and looked up at Sarah. She took in the expression on the young woman's face and the way Sarah physically distanced herself from the rider. Her ire instantly sparked. She'd experienced the hurt that a man's prejudiced attitude could inflict, and she wasn't about to allow anyone to treat Sarah that way.

"Don't do that, *sachu-kash*," Devlin tenderly admonished. "Don't let him make you feel ashamed." She stood alongside Sarah and slipped her arm around the blonde's slim waist. The rider kissed Sarah's temple, and then she glared down at the man who continued to look at them oddly. "*A tekchi.*" She wasn't sure why she spoke in *Chahta*, but it felt right. She stared the old man down and repeated it then in English. "My wife." Sarah's arm went around the rider's waist and lightly squeezed.

"Ah." The old man nodded and smiled. "*Omi tu a na.*"

He slipped a hand inside his pack and pulled out a worn and

dirty piece of hide. He held it out to the rider, who knelt down so she could see the pictures painted there. Her anger flared again at the sight. She pulled the hide from his grasp and pointed to a spot on the leather.

"Who the hell are you?" she hissed.

"Dev! What's wrong?" Sarah dropped down beside her lover.

"This is what's wrong," Devlin answered in a tight voice. She passed the hide to Sarah.

"It looks like a map. There's a picture of a red-tailed hawk and a fish at the top. I don't understand, Dev, how does this man know our *Chahta* names?"

"That's what I'd like to know."

The rider abruptly grabbed the old man's sack and spilled the contents onto the cot. Part of her was ashamed for treating an old Grandfather in such a manner, but her other senses told her that this man knew far too much about them. She no longer had the luxury of thinking only of herself. She had loved ones to protect.

The old man sat calmly watching her, as if waiting for her to finish. He didn't appear to be offended by the treatment.

Devlin unwrapped the last unidentified item. She was instantly sorry she had, and she hoped it wasn't too late to make amends to whatever Spirits led the old man. She held a carved wooden bowl in her hands along with a medium-sized decorated pouch. The markings on the bowl were much the same as the ones on a similar bowl that her mother, Tima, owned.

"He's *Alikchi*, a Medicine Man," Devlin said.

"Does that explain how he knows us?" Sarah asked.

"Somewhat." Devlin turned to the blonde and smirked. "Trust me, they know things."

The rider took the hide back and quickly spoke a few words of apology to the old man. She knew he couldn't understand the language, but hoped that he could feel the sentiment behind her words. Devlin pointed to the hawk on the map and then pointed the same finger at her own chest. She repeated the action, stating her name each time she pointed to herself.

At last, the old man nodded. "Redhawk," he repeated in a halting voice.

Devlin smiled and nodded her head. She repeated the procedure, pointing to the picture of the fish and then to Sarah. The old man kept interrupting by pointing to Sarah and asking the same unintelligible question.

"What's wrong?" Sarah asked.

"I'm not sure, but he seems to think that you should be someone other than who you are."

The old man looked back and forth between the two women. His brow furrowed as if in confusion. He looked at Devlin and placed his hand upon his chest.

"*Ankahito,*" he said. He paused and looked at Devlin. "*Ankahito,*" he repeated. This time he held his hand out to Devlin.

"Oh," Devlin said. "Redhawk." She pointed a finger at her own chest.

"Na." The old man shook his head. "*Ankahito.*" He pointed to his chest, and then motioned to Devlin and Sarah with his hand.

"I think he's telling us who he is, Dev, not what his name is," Sarah said. "I think *Ankahito* are his people."

"Never heard of 'em," Devlin replied. "*Chahta.*" The rider pointed to herself.

"*Chahta,*" the old man mimicked. "*Chahta?*" He pointed to Sarah.

"Well," Devlin said, rubbing her chin, "that's a little more complicated. No." She shook her head.

The old man spoke quickly, more to himself than to the women. He looked confused, but neither Devlin nor Sarah could figure out why.

The old man rose on shaky legs and took a step toward them. "*Na Chahta?*" he asked of Sarah.

"He seems pretty upset that you're not Choctaw," Devlin commented. She pulled Sarah closer.

The old man reached out and took Devlin's hand in his own. He then placed Devlin's free hand in Sarah's. "*Tua kemli?*" he asked.

"I think he's asking if we're together," Sarah said as she looked down at their entwined fingers.

"*Omi.*" Devlin gave an affirmative answer. She looked away shyly, examining the smaller hand within her own.

The old man sat down upon the cot once more. He muttered to himself, but appeared happier. Suddenly he picked up the wooden bowl with both hands. He spoke quickly, offering up the bowl to Sarah and bowing his head slightly.

"I don't understand," Sarah said. "Why does he want me to

have that bowl?"

"It's his *ikhish itampo*, his Medicine bowl. He seems to be under the impression that you deserve it more than him. I get the feeling he thinks you're a Medicine Woman."

"It's marked on the edges like Tima's. Is Tima a Medicine Woman?" Sarah asked as she examined the bowl that the old man held in front of her.

"No," Devlin answered, her brow furrowed in concern. "Tima is a Healer. She has the healing gift, but she never trained in the ways of a Medicine Woman. Keeho is a Medicine Man." Seeing Sarah's confused expression, Devlin hurried to explain. "Medicine Men are more than Healers in the Thunderbird Clan. They're Shamans, holy men. They act as a channel between an illness and the Spirits. They use songs and rituals to heal the sick, ward off storms, bring success to a war or a hunt. I've even seen them bring rain in desperate times. Tima has a gift toward healing the physical body. She sees an occasional vision, but she doesn't have the special power from the Spirits. She heals illness with herbs and traditional prayers."

"And a Medicine Woman is different?" Sarah asked. She was still new to the Choctaw culture, particularly the Thunderbird Clan's ways.

"Oh yes," Devlin answered with a smile. "A Medicine Woman is a rare find and especially powerful. The easiest explanation is that she's part Medicine Man, part Healer. She has special knowledge and gifts, which the Spirits give to her at birth. The power is usually something that's passed on from mother to daughter.

"Tima knew of a Medicine Woman. She told me stories when I was a girl of the Medicine Woman who belonged to the Beaver Clan in the southeast. She was a young woman, but she had the ability to heal the mind as well as the body. She used dreams, visions, herbs, even stories and wildlife to heal her patients. Tima said the woman never had daughters to pass on the power to. When the old woman died, the Spirit's power had to search for another."

Sarah wasn't sure how to feel about this old man who thought she was something more than she really was. "No." She shook her head gently and pushed the bowl away. "I'm not the one you're looking for."

The old man looked as confused as the two women before him. He continued to speak softly in a language they couldn't understand."

"Dev," Sarah's voice was excited now, "maybe Keeho could translate the language. I mean, maybe his connection with the Spirits might help him understand what the old man's saying."

"Hmm, it might work," the rider answered. She rubbed her face with one hand, immediately working out the details of such a trip. "We should take the wagon. He doesn't look like he's fit enough to sit on a pony. Okay, a trip to the Clan village it is." She paused to smile at her lover. "Tima will be happy."

The women quickly helped the old man to settle in to sleep for what was left of the night. They went back to their own bedroom, their heads full of conflicting thoughts. It wasn't long before Sarah could feel Devlin's steady heartbeat. The young woman rested her head upon the rider's chest and the comforting sound, along with her deep breaths, told Sarah that Devlin was asleep.

The young woman felt uneasy. The talk of spiritual power caused an odd fear in Sarah and she couldn't understand why. She lay in the dark, Devlin comfortingly at her side, but it was long hours until she relaxed enough to finally sleep.

"Are you comfortable enough back there?" Devlin asked over her shoulder.

"We're doing fine, Dev," Sarah replied as she laid a hand on the rider's back. She didn't think the bouncing of the buckboard was too disturbing to the old man since he appeared to be sleeping soundly.

The women woke early, even after having missed a few hours of sleep last night. They discovered that their guest had begun to run a fever. He was weak but still had been able to hold down some warm broth that Sarah had prepared for him.

The rocking motion lulled Sarah into her memories of the morning. She had been preparing a thin soup over the fire when she saw the old man attempt to pull his *ikhish bahtushi* from his traveling sack. He was weak and the pouch slid from his grasp. Sarah went to him and took the small bag. She was surprised that he gave it up to her so easily, but then she remembered that he was under the impression that she had some sort of healing abilities.

Sarah examined the pouch. It was made of a single red fox skin. The head had been left attached and served as the flap to keep the *bahtushi* closed. Sarah opened the pouch and stared at the contents, individual pieces of deer hide tied into bundles. She wasn't sure why, but she lifted each hide-covered bundle to her nose. She finally found one whose smell she recognized and opened it to find six dried sassafras flowers. She took two of the flowers and retied the bundle, placing everything back into the animal skin pouch.

Sarah steeped the flowers in some boiling water to make a tea, which she held for the old man while he drank. Within an hour, his fever had lessened and he was able to sleep. He slept so soundly that Devlin carried his slight frame and placed him into the back of the wagon.

"How long will it take going this way, Dev?" Sarah asked.

"Longer than by pony. We'll have to skirt the sandstone cliffs and come up around the other side. I expect the better part of the day. Make sure you holler when you want me to stop so you can stretch your legs and such."

"Yes, ma'am." Sarah smiled in the rider's direction. The young woman had grown unaccustomed to having someone watching out for her. She was usually the one who took care of everyone else. Having Devlin in her life, and knowing the rider would always look out for her well-being, meant the world to her.

The small party arrived at the Thunderbird Clan's village in the late afternoon. After kneeling down and rubbing the red earth on the backs of their hands, Sarah and Devlin paused to greet a number of the villagers.

Tima was among the first to reach the two women and kissed her daughter's cheek. Tima pulled away from her daughter's embrace and looked up into the tall woman's eyes. The Healer saw it immediately. Actually, it was more about what she didn't see in her daughter's features. Gone was the almost haunted look of pain in the sky blue eyes. That expression was now replaced with something Tima had only prayed would one day shine from the angry girl's eyes. It was hope.

After the two young women had left the camp several weeks ago to return to the white man's village, Tima had prayed daily that the Spirits would open the eyes of the headstrong women. When Devlin sent word of the death of Sarah's uncle, the Clan sent a representative to show their respect for the young woman. For seven days after Arthur Winston died, a young Clan man kept a fire constantly burning near the gravesite. The fire was to furnish light and warmth to the old man for his journey to the Spirit world. Tima had sent Sarah a personal message, telling her that although they came from many different tribes, they were all one family. That had been the last news Tima had of her Redhawk and little Sakli.

The older woman turned and swept the small blonde into her arms. Tima could think of no better way to show her pleasure. "*Yakoke, Sakli. Himmak nitak ut achukma hoke.*"

"You're welcome, but why is it a beautiful day?" Sarah asked in confusion. She looked at Devlin's embarrassed face. Realization dawned bright. "Oh." Sarah blushed profusely.

"*Nali.*" Devlin caught her mother's attention with the pet name, which meant "smiling one," that the rider often used. "We can talk about us later. Right now we have a man with us who is ill. He looks like Clan, but we can't understand his language. I think he might be *Alikchi.*"

Tima turned to the bundle of blankets in the back of the wagon. Instantly, her Healer's skills took over and she climbed in beside the old man. The man was weak, but he attempted to speak with Tima. After a few words on her part, she gave up trying to communicate verbally and switched to hand signals. The old man nodded and shook his head a few times. Tima had apparently found a way to make him understand.

"Did he have a fever?" she asked.

"Yes, earlier, but Sarah made him a tea," Devlin replied.

"What did you use?" The Healer turned to Sarah.

"Sassafras."

"Not the root?"

"No." Sarah shook her head. "The dried flowers."

"How did you know to do this?" Tima asked.

"I, uh, I just," Sarah paused, looking from Devlin to Tima, "I thought it was common knowledge, I suppose. I don't remember who taught me."

Tima exchanged a quick look with Devlin, but neither woman said anything.

"We will take him to the Healer's *chuka*," Tima said. "I will attend to him there. Perhaps Keeho or *Miko* Kontonalah will understand his language, but Keeho is away in the hills sending up his offerings to Hashtahli." She went on to explain that the Medicine Man might possibly be away for a fortnight while he prayed to their sun god.

Tima sent a young boy to fetch her father. The white men

who came to barter for goods considered Kontonalah a *Miko*, or chief, to the Thunderbird Clan. In truth, the Choctaw didn't have just one chief for their Clan. Each different family had a spokesperson. Kontonalah was an Elder in the tribe and had been around since the age of the Old Ones. He was also spokesman for seven different families within the Clan. The white men tended to mistake Kontonalah's revered position within the tribe as a chief. The Choctaw were simply too well-mannered to correct them.

Devlin and Sarah met with a few old and new friends while Tima attended to the old man. At first the Healer had encouraged Sarah to stay with her, but when she made the offer Sarah suddenly drew back. The Healer decided to let it pass until she could talk to Redhawk.

Devlin and Sarah found their way to the Healer's *chuka* just as Kontonalah exited the dwelling. The old man greeted his granddaughter and her lover with his usual open smile and wry sense of humor.

"*Halito, ippok tek.*" The old man always called her Granddaughter when they first met. Then he would speak to her by her Clan name, Redhawk.

"Hello to you as well, Grandfather. Are you well?" Devlin said as she embraced him.

"*Omi,* I am well," he replied, offering a smile to Sarah. "You know nothing of this stranger?" Never one to beat around a subject, Kontonalah started right in by questioning Devlin about the old man. They spoke quickly and Sarah added as much information as she could.

"Do you understand his language?" Devlin asked. "It sounds familiar."

"*Keyu.*" Kontonalah shook his head. "You are right. His language does sound as if I have heard it before. He is definitely *iksa.*"

Sarah looked at Devlin in confusion. The young woman had learned to speak the Clan's language very well, but this word confused her. "This Clan?" she asked Devlin.

"*Iksa achafa?*" Devlin repeated Sarah's question to her grandfather.

"*Iksa inla,*" Kontonalah clarified.

"He means that he's from a different Clan," Devlin explained. "How can he be *Chahta,* Grandfather, and still speak with another tongue?"

"He is an Old One," Kontonalah said matter-of-factly. "The speakers of the earth. Keeho will know more when he returns." The old man looked around and breathed deeply. "It is a good afternoon to go fishing. Redhawk, I shall go fishing."

Devlin rolled her eyes in Sarah's direction. This was one of the many things about her people that infuriated her at times. They believed that everything happened for a reason and in its own time. Her grandfather was neither concerned nor curious, or if he was, he kept it to himself. The rider saw that questioning him further would be futile. His mind was already on other things.

"It's all right," Sarah said before Devlin could explain that her grandfather had just commanded her to go with him. "I'll see if I can be any help to Tima."

Kontonalah had already turned to leave when Devlin lightly pressed her lips to the smaller woman's forehead and smiled shyly. The rider didn't understand why she should all of a sudden feel bashful here in the village, but she did. Her Clan had never been reserved about expressing emotions or affection in public.

Out of the corner of her eye, Devlin saw a few young men hanging about the fringes of the camp. Some of the faces were new to Devlin and she wanted to be very sure the braves understood her relationship with Sarah before she left her lover there.

The rider looked into Sarah's face and kissed her in such a way as to leave little doubt as to the nature of their relationship. Both women pulled away feeling a little weak in the knees, but Devlin followed her grandfather with a spring in her step. She thoroughly enjoyed the deflated expressions on the faces of the young men she passed.

Sarah chuckled to herself as she turned to enter the *chuka*. Part of her reveled in belonging to the rider. Deep down, Sarah enjoyed the fact that Devlin felt so fiercely in her love for her. Of course, being the woman she was, Sarah felt just as strongly about her independence. Today, and after a kiss such as the one they just shared, the small blonde was definitely taking pleasure in the former.

Sarah pulled aside the deerskin hide that covered the opening to the *chuka* and called out to Tima for permission to enter.

"*Ant chukoa.*" The older woman invited Sarah inside the darkened abode. This was the *ikhish chuka*, the Medicine Lodge. Set apart from the other *chukas*, it was larger than other dwellings and Sarah remembered it well, having awakened there from her own illness and seeing Tima's smiling face greet her.

Sarah entered and sat down beside Tima. She looked down at the still sleeping man and wondered if he hadn't slipped into a coma. She noticed the rise and fall of his chest and his raspy, uneven breathing.

Reading the young woman's thoughts, Tima said, "He is still breathing, that is a good thing. It was smart of you to keep his fever down. I think I'll put a poultice on his chest. It may help."

"What can I do to help?" Sarah asked as Tima removed the old man's deer hide shirt.

"You can start to prepare the poultice. My *ikhish itampo* is there beside the fire. We will use *chuchupate*, I think. Will you bring my *ikhish bahta*?"

Sarah found the wooden Medicine bowl beside the fire. She picked up the animal skin Medicine bag that Tima kept her herbs and various roots in. The pelt appeared to be from a beaver, its hard, flat tail still attached to the hide. Tima had sewn the bag into an oblong shape.

Sarah sat down beside the Healer. Tima noticed that the young woman had set the Medicine bag onto the small woven mat beside the Old One. Sarah then placed the bowl upon the flat tail of the beaver pelt. Tima watched with eyes that at first narrowed in suspicion, but then went wide in surprise.

"Did I do something wrong, *Nali*?" Sarah asked.

Tima couldn't hide her smile when the young woman used Devlin's pet name for her. "You have been most helpful, Sakli. Now, would you continue to help me?" She rubbed her hands together. "These old hands feel the *hashtula* coming."

"Of course. What shall I do?" Sarah asked.

The older woman directed Sarah with each step. Tima chanted and sang as Sarah mixed the pulverized root with melted buffalo tallow. The Healer then applied the paste to the old man's chest and covered it with a soft piece of hide. Tima's healing was very physical. She sang and prayed a small bit, but it was nothing like what Sarah had seen Keeho perform on ill Clan members.

Tima showed Sarah how to soap her hands with a beige powder and a basin of water. The powder was dried yucca root, ground and stored in a red clay jar. As soon as Sarah wet her hands and rubbed the powder into them, the mixture formed a frothy soap. Then they each offered a small amount of sage into the fire. They cupped their hands and drew the smoke to them, cleansing their bodies with the Sacred smoke.

They left the *chuka* and walked away from the camp, going nowhere in particular. Each woman appeared lost in her own thoughts.

"How is it that your healing methods are so much different from Keeho's?" Sarah suddenly asked.

"Why do you ask?" Tima countered.

"Well, actually, Dev– I mean Redhawk, she tried to explain the difference between what you do and what Keeho does. She said the old man we brought in here thought I was some kind of Medicine Woman."

Tima never altered her stride, but she nodded her head, closing her eyes for a moment. "And you are confused by our differences, or do you wish to know why this Old One thought of you in such a way?"

"I'm not really sure what I'm asking," Sarah answered thoughtfully. "I know that watching you heal feels very right. It's not that I have anything against Keeho, but he frightens me. He watches me as if he doesn't trust me, but it can't be because I'm not Clan because I've seen him look at Redhawk the very same way."

"Keeho is a good man," Tima explained. "The Spirits speak through him, and the love he has for his people is great."

"I suppose it could be just me that he doesn't like."

"He cares for you very deeply, Sakli, as he does for my Redhawk. I believe he acts the way he does toward you because he fears you."

"He's afraid of me, but– "

"He fears your power, and from what I have seen, perhaps he is right."

"What power could I possibly hold over a Shaman?" Sarah asked in disbelief.

They came upon a stream and Tima led the small blonde to a group of flat sandstone rocks. The older woman sat and indicated that Sarah rest beside her. She plucked a long blade of drying grass from the ground and bit on one end. She was deep in thought as she wrestled with how much to tell the young woman. Too much could frighten, but not enough would merely serve to confuse Sarah.

"You have power in the white man's world now."

"Yes, I suppose by their standards I do," Sarah answered.

"To hold power in the Clan is neither political nor based on economics. Sometimes status and material possessions come from it, but power within the Clan comes from the Spirits and whatever destiny they have selected for you." Tima paused and noticed that Sarah was listening intently.

"Women have power simply because they are female. We are given the knowledge of fruitfulness in our ability to bear children, and we are blessed with the knowledge of blood in our cycle of the moon. In the white man's world, how do people know who you are?"

"Well, I suppose by my reputation or my name. It's my father's name, but then I married and took my husband's name, so that might be confusing."

"In the Thunderbird Clan I am known by my mother. If someone asks me who my mother was, my answer identifies me. When Tekola took me as his bride, he came to live with my mother's Clan. Most of the Clans that I am familiar with acknowledge the power that automatically lies within a woman. I have heard of a Clan which gives as equal a value to a woman who dies during childbirth as a brave dying in war." Tima watched as Sarah processed the information.

"Why do you tell me this, *Nali*?"

"Because you have power, Sakli. You have the power of a thousand generations of women in you, but you are also powerful for other reasons. You and Redhawk are *ohoyo yukpali*. It is nothing to cause shame, such as your people have caused you to think. You are unique women placed in our path by the Spirits to teach us something special. The Spirits have blessed you with a power so great that it can override that of men, and I think Keeho understands that. It is why he fears you. There is one last reason that Keeho may have found to add to his fear." Tima's forehead creased into a frown. Again, she wondered how much she should reveal. It was difficult to be less than honest with the young woman.

"What is the last reason, *Nali*?" Sarah asked with trepidation.

"He believes you hold the power to Dream."

"I'm not sure I understand. I do dream, doesn't everyone?"

"Do your dreams come true? Does the world seem to slow so that you may inspect that one moment in time more closely? Do you know things that you cannot explain, but know to be true? When you look into a man's eyes, can you see into his heart?" Tima watched as Sarah stared at the ground in silence. "Do any part of your dreams come true, little one?"

Sarah nodded and Tima waited for the young woman to continue.

"When I was a very little girl, I dreamed that my mother died. A short time later she did. I thought her death was my fault. I thought if I told anyone, they'd say I was a witch."

Suddenly, Sarah recalled recent events when she couldn't explain the odd feelings she'd experienced. She knew Peter was sick even before the cancer ravaged his body. She remembered looking into Dale Karsten's eyes just before Devlin shot him dead. At that moment, she'd known exactly what he was going to do, when he was going to draw his gun.

"Even now I have dreams, and sometimes a small piece of what I remember will come true."

"But not everything?" Tima asked.

"No, not everything. Sometimes I see things, sometimes people I don't know talk to me, but I don't always understand what they say. Every now and again, I'll dream something allegorical."

"I don't understand this word," Tima said.

Sarah had reverted to English to find the right word and now she tried to explain in *Chahta*. "It means that my dreams aren't literal. They represent some idea or something like it that will happen. It's like when I dreamed of a dark warrior who would rescue me, and then Redhawk came into my life."

"Visions," Tima stated flatly. "You have the power to Dream, Sakli. You should become *Chahta*, accept your secret name, and begin your training."

"Training for what?"

"To become *Alikchi*," Tima answered.

"Train to become a Medicine Woman? *Nali*, I don't want that kind of power. It's too big a responsibility."

"Do not look so fearful, little one. There is no penalty for not accepting."

"But what if it's my destiny and I turn my back on it?" Sarah asked.

"Your destiny is your destiny. If you do not go to it, it will come to you," Tima answered in her matter-of-fact style.

"Will the Spirits turn their back on me, or on my family, if I don't accept?"

"Sakli, you speak as though you are *Chahta*." Tima smiled at the younger woman.

Sarah chuckled nervously. "Sometimes I feel more at home here than anywhere else. I don't want to be punished. I don't want my family to suffer for something I've done or haven't done."

"Do you believe in the white man's Spirits?"

"We have only one Spirit and we call him God. Yes, I do believe. It's the religions and laws, the things that man has done in this God's name that I have no stomach for," Sarah answered.

Tima nodded in understanding. "Even among the *Chahta*, our ways have changed. We feel your white man's religions in our own ways, a little more every season. Sakli, is this the way the white man's God treats him? Punishes him for being human? Is that why you fear?"

"I suppose it's not the way God treats us. It's man's interpretation of why God does the things he does. We can't understand the mysteries of a being so great, and so we make up reasons as to why."

"The white man's reasons are based on fear. The *Chahta* do the same thing, in a sense. I learned the stories of my people that my grandmother taught me. If you become *Chahta*, then I will teach your daughter these stories. The difference between my people and yours is that the Clan bases its stories on love and acceptance. Our whole way of life exists within the Sacred Hoop."

"Is that the Medicine Wheel that you taught me to pray?"

"*Omi*, it is, but it is more than a simple prayer. It is the way we live our life. The Medicine Wheel is the circle in which our entire world exists. Our life is a circle and everything in our world– plants, animals, even the ground we walk upon– is a part of that living circle and has as equal a status as ourselves."

"I don't think I'm ready for this yet, *Nali*."

Tima reached over and brushed the golden hair from the younger woman's face. "You will know when you are ready. When you and Redhawk are ready for *itauaya*, you can speak about becoming *Chahta*. Come, it's getting late. We will make room for you and Redhawk at my *iksita*."

"Thank you," Sarah answered in relief.

They walked back to the village the way they had left, both listening to the sounds of the prairie around them. Sarah pulled her shawl a little tighter around her. The cool evening winds blew in from the north.

"*Nali*, when you said that I could become *Chahta* so that Redhawk and I might be married, was that true? Could we really be married?"

"*Omi.* You would have to become *Chahta* and a family would need to adopt you into the Clan. The ceremonies are not easy, but the Spirits smile on you, Sakli. I think your spiritual journeys will not be too hard. The Spirits will speak out to a family in the Clan and they will adopt you. Then we would perform *itauayachi* for you and Redhawk. Your warrior will have to build an *iksita* of your own, but the other warriors of the Clan will help her."

Tima never asked if this was what Sarah wanted. She could see it in the young woman's eyes. She could also see the fear of the unknown there in the young woman's face. The white man's fears. Tima knew that Sarah was a woman of determination and fierce pride. When placed in a position to choose, Tima knew the younger woman would choose wisely.

Chapter 4

Devlin met the two women as they entered the village. The rider grinned and held up a long, sturdy stick. The piece of ash held half a dozen large fish, gutted and ready for the fire.

"My daughter, I miss the food you bring to my *iksita*!" Tima exclaimed with pride.

"As long as I don't have to cook them, I'm happy to bring them to your hearth, Mother."

They enjoyed a bit of lighthearted banter while Devlin stripped down to her undershirt. "I have to wash up," she said.

Tima gave her some ground yucca root and a soft cloth. The rider turned to walk down to the stream when Sarah brought up what she and Tima had spoken about earlier.

"Dev, Tima talked to me about becoming *Chahta*," the young woman said in her enthusiasm.

Devlin stopped and threw an angry glance in Tima's direction. "It wouldn't be a good idea," she answered between clenched teeth.

"She said we could be married that way, Dev."

"Sarah, please." Devlin placed her hands on the smaller woman's arms. "Tima, why would you tell her these things without consulting me first?"

"Consulting *you* first?" Sarah angrily shrugged out of the rider's grasp. "Devlin, I am not a child." Her voice rose with each syllable.

The rider knew she was about to say the wrong thing, but she blurted out the words anyway. "Then stop acting like one."

Sarah took a step back and Devlin immediately regretted her angry remark. She had spoken out of fear and nothing more. She could barely believe that she was the one who just put that expression on Sarah's face. The young woman looked as if Devlin had slapped her. Devlin didn't wait to hear Sarah's reply. What could her lover say that the rider wasn't already saying to herself? She spun on one heel and stalked away to the nearby creek.

The sun had dipped low in the western horizon as Sarah once more helped Tima change the poultice on the old man. The younger woman hadn't said a word to Tima, but the Healer could feel anger and sorrow surrounding her. The older woman showed Sarah how to prepare the fish to roast slowly over the coals of the fire.

Neither woman made small talk as Tima taught the younger woman how to make *paska banaha*, Choctaw bread. They were more like dumplings. Tima mixed cornmeal and water, adding the water until the mixture was stiff enough to shape into small oblong balls the size of a woman's fist. She then wrapped them in corn shucks, which she tied in the middle with corn silk and dropped into a deep pot of boiling water.

Most of the women in the village used wooden *ampos*, or dishes, and boiled water by continually adding heated rocks from the fire. Sarah had remembered to bring metal pots with her on this visit and bartered with the women who would not accept them as gifts.

"You should go to her, Sakli. The meal is nearly ready," Tima said.

"She's a big girl. She knows when her supper is ready."

Tima watched the young woman and noticed that Sarah's voice no longer carried anger, only a sadness that touched the older woman's heart. Tima felt responsible for her daughter's anger and the strong words it had caused between Devlin and Sarah. "She is full of pride, Sakli, and she knows that she has hurt you with her words, but pride and shame are a strong combination. She sits, even now, and finds herself unworthy of your heart."

Sarah's heart broke at the thought that a few harsh words could make Devlin doubt the depth of Sarah's commitment to their love. In the same instant, doubt plucked at her own heart. The rider had acted so angry at the thought of Sarah becoming *Chahta*. Was it possible that Devlin wasn't as committed to Sarah as the young woman thought?

"You're right, but I don't know what to say to make it right between us."

"Sakli," Tima's gentle voice was as smooth as an eagle floating upon the wind, "when you find her, you will need no words to express what is in your heart."

Sarah offered the older woman a smile and went off in search of her warrior. Tima stopped her and suggested that she take a rabbit skin robe to combat the chill autumn air. The Healer furnished a bittersweet smile as she watched the blonde walk away. She banked the coals of the *iksita* and wrapped the food in leaves to keep it warm, knowing it would be some time before the two women would return to her *chuka*.

It didn't take long for the small blonde to find her lover. Devlin was exactly where Tima said she would be. The rider sat among the boulders that led up to the village's lookout point. She sat with her legs drawn up to her chest, her arms hugging the long limbs to her body. She was so lost in thought that she let Sarah get within inches before jumping up, her hand instinctively reaching for her pistol.

"Sarah! Hellfire, I could have hurt you!" It took only a breath of time for the rider to realize what she'd just said. "I did hurt you. Sarah, I'm so sorry."

The younger woman nearly launched herself into the rider's solid embrace. "I'm sorry, Dev, I didn't mean to make you angry."

"No, sweetheart, it wasn't you, it-it just took me by surprise is all. I don't want to see you hurt."

"It's all right, Dev. You don't have to marry me, I just thought– "

"Oh, *sachu-kash*, is that what you think?" Devlin asked as she pulled away. "That I don't want to marry you? No, Sarah, that's not it at all. Come here, love, and sit down." The two women settled on the rocks and Devlin wrapped the fur robe around Sarah's shoulders. The rider took the younger woman's small hands within her own. She didn't seem to know where to start.

"Dev, if it's not that you don't want to marry me in front of your family, then what? Do you not want me to become *Chahta*?" Sarah asked in confusion.

"*Sachu-kash*, it has nothing at all to do with me wanting or not wanting to marry you, which I happen to want to do, very much." Devlin kissed the hands in her grasp and her heart became lighter at the smile with which Sarah rewarded her.

"To become *Chahta* you have to go through a purification process. A Quest, a journey. These rituals are hard enough to get through when you've been raised with the Clan and all their teachings, but it can be torture to people who've been brought up in the white man's world. It can feel like you're being ripped in half. Part of you will embrace the Spirits, but part of you will have the white man's culture so deeply ingrained in you that it would rather suffer than be tossed aside." Devlin paused to lay the palm of her hand against Sarah's cheek.

"It's hard and painful, Sarah. I just don't want to see you go through anything that might hurt you. I know that's selfish and pigheaded of me, but it's how I feel." Devlin lowered her head, waiting for her lover's reprimand. She was surprised by the gentle kiss she felt upon the top of her head.

"Forgive me, Dev. For not understanding."

"I didn't give you much time to," the rider replied.

"True," Sarah smiled, "but by now, I know you. I should have realized that you would be thinking about my protection. That's a little new to me."

"Sarah, I love you. I loved you before we even met. I don't want to leave you, or be with anyone else, but it would tear a piece of my soul away if something were to happen to you. A Vision Quest can be dangerous; three, maybe four days without food or water. It takes a monumental commitment, too. I prayed for almost a year before I went on my first Vision Quest. I worry for you, wanting to go through this just for me."

"First off, Dev, I wouldn't be doing this just for you. I would be doing it for us, for the children, so that all of us could be one family without anything to divide us. Secondly, why do you fear me doing this, Dev? I know that you don't want to see me in harm's way, but don't you have any belief in me? I'm stronger than you like to think sometimes."

"I know," the rider muttered, lowering her head. "Too strong, maybe."

"Too strong?"

"Maybe you'll become *Chahta*. Maybe you'll learn that when we want something in our life, we have to be prepared to pay for it. You might see that I'm not a part of your path. Maybe I'll be the price you pay." Devlin whispered this last part and Sarah finally understood. It was Devlin's fear of abandonment that weighed heavily.

"Look at me, Devlin Brown," Sarah commanded, and the rider's blue gaze rose up to meet emerald green. "Hear me now. There are no Spirits strong enough, in this world or the next, to tear me away from you. Wherever my path leads, I want you there beside me."

Devlin didn't have to think twice. She leaned over and kissed the small blonde with an intensity that surprised both of them.

They pulled apart to breathe and Sarah couldn't help commenting, "Now tell me. Why would I want to leave a woman who kisses like that?" She grinned.

Devlin's laughter filled up the darkness around them as she enfolded Sarah within her embrace. Sarah enjoyed the warm, comforting arms of her lover. Suddenly all of the frightening decisions she was faced with faded into the night. She would do as Tima recommended and simply let her destiny come to her.

"Devlin!" Sarah hissed softly.

"What?" The rider mustered up an innocent-sounding voice.

"Keep your hands to yourself," Sarah reprimanded for the third time.

"I want you, Sarah." The rider teased her lover, kissing the soft blonde head.

"Oh, Dev, what am I going to do with you?"

The light of the small fire in the center of the *chuka* illuminated Devlin's flashing white smile. "I could make you a list," the rider whispered. "And it starts right here." Devlin placed Sarah's hand against her breast.

Sarah rapidly pulled her hand away. She had not yet become accustomed to the communal living of the Clan. Sarah and Devlin stayed in Tima's *chuka* beside her *iksita*. Everything came through the women of the Thunderbird Clan. When children came back to visit the Clan, they stayed at their mother's hearth. It was always possible to have more than a few members sleeping in the *chuka* at night, if not an entire family, but Sarah was having a hard enough time with only herself, Devlin, and Tima.

The Healer, like Devlin and the other Clan members, had no reservations about baring their bodies to one another. Devlin tried to explain it to Sarah, but the younger woman still could not get past her own inhibitions. Sarah politely turned away as Tima disrobed and climbed into her own *topa*. Devlin unashamedly removed her own clothes, trying to put her mate at ease, but the sight of the rider's naked body lying upon their *topa* did nothing to ease the young woman's shyness. In fact, the sight of Devlin's body caused Sarah even more embarrassment, for she was sure that everyone in the village could read her thoughts at that moment.

Now that Sarah finally lay beside Devlin in their sleeping robes, she indeed felt the same desire the rider did. The young woman couldn't seem to get past the fact that Tima was sleeping only six feet away from them.

"We'll make too much noise, Dev."

"I can be very quiet, *sachu-kash*."

"I'm not sure I can," Sarah returned.

Devlin chucked in response. "Sarah, trust me. It doesn't matter to Tima. We all live very closely in a *chuka*. I listened to my parents at night while I was growing up here. Loving one another and expressing that love is a part of life. It's natural and not something to ever be embarrassed about."

Sarah sighed in exasperation. "I'm trying, Dev, really I am," she whispered.

Devlin heard the catch in her lover's voice and realized that Sarah had reached her limit of new experiences for one day. "It's all right, *Sa*." She wrapped her arms around the body beside her and enjoyed the way the blonde head nestled easily into that perfect spot on her shoulder. "Holding you all night is high on that list of mine, too."

The next morning Sarah awoke before dawn, but she still hadn't beat Tima out of her *topa*. The Healer had already rolled and put away her sleeping robes. Devlin snored gently and Sarah smiled at how comfortable she looked lying there. It was as if a change had taken place within Devlin. Sarah knew part of it was the rider's newfound happiness with their relationship, but a large portion was simply due to being home. Devlin had confided to Sarah that it was the only place she ever really felt truly comfortable.

Sarah left Devlin sleeping soundly in the furs. She quickly dressed and made her way to the creek to wash up. By the time she was presentable, the sun was just peeking over the eastern hills. Sarah knew that Tima would be in the Healer's *chuka*. The silence of the night had been broken a few times as Tima rose to check on her patient.

The only other interruption was Sarah's dream. A confused jumble of events, some real, some imagined, had broken up her sleep. The only thing that Sarah could remember upon waking was that she had been on the ranch and there had been fire. She shook her head and wondered why her dreams seemed so vivid here in the Clan village.

The young woman pulled aside the deerskin flap and entered. Just as she opened her mouth to greet the Healer, her eyes landed on Keeho. "*Halito*," she greeted the Medicine Man with surprise.

What pleased Sarah was the fact that the old man was awake. He lay on his back, obviously ill with fever, but he had been speaking to Keeho. The Medicine Man actually appeared to be listening, understanding the old man's words.

The old man gestured in Sarah's direction and spoke rapidly to Keeho. At best, the Clan Medicine Man had always treated Sarah with a certain indifference. The expression Keeho bestowed on the sick old man appeared angry, then surprised, and finally, resigned.

"Come sit beside us, little Sakli." Keeho surprised Sarah with the cordial greeting. As always, the Medicine Man's voice was low and controlled. Devlin had told Sarah that in her years with the Clan, she had never heard Keeho raise his voice.

"I didn't mean to disturb you, forgive me, *Alikchi*," Sarah said.

Keeho smiled inwardly at the young woman. She was learning fast, and he was proud to see that she had not only become skilled in the language of the *Chahta*, but also had the grace to accept their ways as her own. He noted that she used his title in addressing him. She had respect for the Clan and what it meant, that much was obvious to him. *Redhawk has taught her well. Perhaps she needed no one to teach her.*

Sarah watched as Tima slipped from the *chuka*. The Healer left without a sound and if Keeho noticed, he gave no indication.

"*Binili*." The Medicine Man requested Sarah to sit down.

"*Achukma hoke*," Sarah answered as all the Clan members did when requested to join a conversation, or even to sit at another's hearth. The *Chahta* words meant "it is good." Sarah had learned from Devlin that it was the equivalent of saying "I am honored."

Sarah positioned herself beside the prone man, across from Keeho. She hadn't noticed before the paleness the old man's skin or the raspy intake of his breath. He raised his head slightly. He looked extremely weak, but Sarah felt the cognizance in the old man's eyes when he turned his head to gaze at her.

"His name is Taano," Keeho said. "Come sit with us, Redhawk."

Sarah looked up. A tall shadow blocked the light of the opening to the *chuka*. Devlin entered the dwelling followed by her mother. It dawned on Sarah where Tima had rushed off. She mentally thanked the woman for rousing the sleeping rider.

Devlin sat to Sarah's right. Each woman unconsciously reached for the other's hand. The gesture was not lost on the old man. He spoke as rapidly as his shortness of breath would allow. Devlin fixed a surprised look at Sarah.

"Keeho speaks his language. His name is Taano," Sarah told her lover.

The old man's voice drew everyone's attention toward him once more.

Keeho slowly translated the man's words. "Taano has traveled a great distance to bring a message to us. It is a mission that has taken his life. He has sacrificed himself at the request of the Spirits, who instructed him to deliver his message to no one but the two of you."

Sarah raised her head to Tima for confirmation of the old man's failing health. Their eyes met across the *chuka* and Tima gave a nearly imperceptible nod of her head.

Sarah took the old man's hand in her own and he smiled weakly. He coughed and then spoke.

"He says that you honor him," Keeho translated. "He has no doubt that you and the dark warrior will please the Spirits greatly. He says that you are to be commended, Mother."

Sarah gave the old man a half-smile, searching the faces around her. "I don't understand. How does he know I have children?"

"He doesn't understand. He thinks Sarah is *Alikchi*," Devlin explained.

"Perhaps it is we who do not understand," Keeho replied.

The Medicine Man exchanged glances with Devlin. The rider decided silence would be the most appropriate answer, but she couldn't help but ponder the Medicine Man's statement. Did he see more in Sarah than did the rider herself? More importantly, what would Sarah think if she knew the consequences of what might be expected of her?

"Sarah, remember once when I told you that the Clan held women in very high esteem?" Devlin asked.

"Yes," Sarah answered slowly. "Everything, a Clan member's name, their hearth, comes through their mother."

"Well, I've never known one since I was adopted into the Clan, but the term *Mother* is one of reverence. The Mother of a Clan is their Medicine Woman. She holds the highest place in the Clan, even over the Elders or chief *Miko*."

A coughing fit suddenly wracked the old man's frail frame. Tima brought some lukewarm tea for him to sip. When he spoke in low raspy whispers, Keeho bent his head to listen and translate.

"Where does he come from and why does he think Sarah is *Alikchi*?" Devlin asked. "How does he know us?"

Keeho held up one hand to the rider. He spoke to the old man in a language that Devlin was certain she had heard before, but couldn't quite remember from where.

The old man's skin appeared gray and when he paused to catch his breath, Keeho translated. "He is an Old One and comes from far to the south. It is taught that on the morning of creation, Hashtahli, the Sun Father, opened the sacred mound, *Nanih Waiya*, and from the soil grew *Okla*, the people. As they emerged from the ground, they lay themselves in the sunlight on the sides of *Nanih Waiya* to dry. The first who came out were poorly formed, some short and squatty and others too lean and hungry looking. When they had dried out, this group traveled far from *Nanih Waiya*. The second group who came out of the sacred mound was better formed, but Hashtahli had not quite yet perfected his art. These people too, when they were dry, traveled far from *Nanih Waiya*. The last group was perfectly formed, clean of limb, beautiful of face and blessed with strength and intelligence. They chose to reside in the area surrounding the sacred mound and would become the people called *Chahta*." Keeho paused, making sure he still held the attention of both Sarah and Devlin.

"Some tell of more tribes made by Hashtahli on the day of creation. It is said that only the Old Ones know where all of the tribes live. Some say there are those who live hidden to the world who have not been discovered by either the white man or the red man."

Devlin had learned all of this as a child, but she suspected Keeho related the tale for Sarah's benefit. The rider believed in the *Chahta* legends and stories. Many of them, however, conflicted with her white upbringing. It was such conflicting beliefs that had made her Vision Quest so difficult and why she feared Sarah going through the same experience.

"Taano is the *Alikchi* to one of these kin tribes," Keeho began again. "He says the *Achafa Chito*, the Great Ones, gave him a vision. The grass died two times and still they brought the vision."

"Two years," Devlin explained to Sarah.

Taano coughed once more until Keeho took the mug of tea from his hands. The Medicine Man held the Old One cradled in his own arms and softly chanted a song that Sarah found oddly reassuring. This side of Keeho, who gently rocked the frail figure as he sang, was a surprise to Sarah. Taano's skin had grown so ashen that Sarah could see through it to the complex of veins and arteries below. She watched as the blood flow grew weaker and weaker.

Taano's eyes grew heavy and he could no longer lift his own head. His breathing now came in shallow gasps. He whispered to Keeho and then turned to look at Sarah and Devlin one last time. Feeling he had accomplished his task, when he breathed his last breath, he had a small smile on his face.

In a moment of compassion, Sarah reached out for the old man, but Devlin stayed her hand. "No, Sarah," the rider said softly. "Women aren't allowed to touch the dead."

"What did he say, *Alikchi*? What was his message?" Sarah asked with tears in her eyes.

"The buffalo must run free. He said that a calamity of great proportions was coming and that only if the buffalo ran free would the land be able to continue. Taano believed that the Spirits led him to you, that only *Hasimbish humma* and *Sakli* held the power to protect our lives."

"The buffalo? They're already free," Sarah said. "What does it mean?"

"The Spirits do not always speak in the same language as

we, little Sakli," Keeho answered. "I must meditate and pray to the Sun Father for guidance. You may join me if you wish."

Devlin nearly fell over in shock. Suddenly the old man's death, and the sadness it brought, had disappeared from her mind. She realized she was sitting there with her mouth hanging open, but Sarah's expression mirrored her own. Actually, the look the small blonde wore seemed to be a combination of surprise and fear.

To the rider's knowledge, Keeho had never even invited Tima to partake in meditation and prayer with him. If there had been another Holy Man in the Clan, Keeho would have strengthened himself with the other man's help. Most Medicine Men, even the ones that Devlin had met from other Clans, never allowed women in their circle. Women were too powerful, especially women who were still young enough to experience their cycle of the moon.

"I...I would be honored," Sarah stammered.

"After Taano's burial, we will send up smoke," Keeho replied.

Tima indicated that the three women should leave Keeho to prepare the body. As soon as they were free of the *chuka*, Sarah and Devlin bombarded Tima with questions regarding the Medicine Man's behavior.

"Come with me." Tima stopped the women from both talking at once.

Tima led the women into her *chuka*. "*Binili*." She indicated that they should sit down.

They sat in a circle around the small fire. Tima moved about the *chuka* quickly and prepared a tea. Devlin took note that it wasn't an everyday drink, but rather a more formal, ceremonial tea. The Healer handed each woman a shallow bowl with a generous amount of tea. Tima then unwrapped a doeskin-covered package to reveal a small pipe. Devlin had never sat in on a woman's council, but she recognized this as one.

"Does your Sarah understand the way of women in the Clan?" Tima asked Devlin.

The rider understood that this was her mother's way of asking Devlin to explain. "The *Chahta* are a matriarchal society," Devlin said to Sarah. "What most outsiders never realize is that the women of the Clan make the majority of the decisions, sitting around a council like we are now. Women are the givers of life and are the most powerful members of the Clan. They decide what the rules will be, but it's the *Miko*, or the Clan's spokesperson, that announces the decisions, hence the outsiders' idea that men rule the *Chahta* Clans."

Devlin and Sarah watched as Tima set tobacco into the smooth sandstone bowl of a short, thin pipe. The Healer lit the sacred tobacco and its sweet smell filled the *chuka,* tendrils of smoke drifting lazily upward. Tima offered a silent prayer to the four directions, the Mother Earth, and finally up to Hashtahli, the Sun Father.

"The pipe has great power," Tima said as she pulled on the pipe and blew the smoke into the air. She handed the pipe to her daughter and Devlin took a draw from it.

The rider handed it over to Sarah. "Have you done this before?"

"Mattie and I used to sneak Father's corncob pipe. Is it the same?"

"Yes." Devlin quietly chuckled in reply.

Sarah took her turn and then returned the pipe to Tima and the Healer drew from it once again, holding out the palm of her hand as if urging the smoke upward.

"The *hakchuma ashuka* is made of two separate parts. There is the bowl, and there is the stem. Without one another, they are nothing more than parts. Together, they unite to provide a way for us to communicate with the Spirits. Together, they are one spiritual entity." Tima drew from the pipe one final time.

"Tobacco is sacred to the *Chahta*. The white man offers tobacco without knowing its special meaning to us. They have taught the red man how to misuse the tobacco, corrupting the gift from Mother Earth. It is up to the Clan Mother to preserve the way."

Sarah suddenly felt something more than three women sitting in a *chuka* smoking. There was a bond there, something natural yet unspoken between them. It had nothing and everything to do with blood. It was not the blood of kin, but the sacred and powerful blood of women. Sarah had no idea that at that moment, Devlin was feeling much the same thing.

"The Spirits are calling the two of you. Do you feel it?" Tima asked.

Without knowing exactly why, Sarah and Devlin nodded their heads. They could feel something, had felt it since the night they first met the old man. It was as if something was pulling at them.

"Sakli, it is time for you to come into your power."

"But I thought you said there wasn't any hurry, that I could just let it come?" Sarah replied. Her voice rose in pitch.

"It has arrived. I feel the winds of change already. Now there is an urgency and I can feel it deep inside," Tima answered.

Devlin had silently followed this exchange, but she was now to the point of confusion. Somehow, Taano had followed his Vision and, since he was an Old One, Devlin believed in the old man's spiritual power. The Spirits were calling her and Sarah. Perhaps it was a test, or it could simply be that she and Sarah were the best suited for the job. What the rider hadn't been able to fathom was why Keeho had been willing to accept Sarah into his private ways. Now, as Tima spoke again of Sarah's power, it dawned on the dark-haired woman. *Did the Old One know all along? Is Sarah more than she appears?*

"They want you to become *Alikchi*?" Devlin turned to Sarah and asked with a surprised whisper.

"I don't understand it either, Dev." Sarah brushed golden bangs from her forehead in her customary gesture of impatience. "*Nali* says that I have power and that it has something to do with my dreams."

"You Dream?" Devlin asked. "Do they– "

"Come true? Yes, bits and pieces of them."

"*Nali*," Devlin turned to her mother, "is this why Keeho wishes Sarah to communicate with the Spirits along with him? Does he see her destiny, does he know?"

"We have both seen her destiny, but it is for Sakli to choose if she will follow this path," Tima answered.

"But she's not *Chahta*."

"It would be as arrogant for us to think that the Clan's Mother should be one of us as it would be for the white man to think that he is the rightful heir to the soil beneath our feet," Tima replied. "She can become Clan."

"What if she doesn't want to?" Devlin could hear the rising pitch of her own voice.

"She already said she did."

"For us to be married, not to become a Medicine Woman!"

"I do hate to interrupt this mother-and-daughter conversation, but you both do realize I'm still here, don't you?" Sarah's voice increased in volume to make her presence known.

"I'm sorry, *Sa*, but I want to make sure you're not being

talked into something that you're not prepared for." Devlin reached for Sarah's hand. "What they're asking of you—"

"Is not something I would ever do without discussing it with you first, Devlin," Sarah replied firmly, finishing the rider's sentence. "Besides, *Nali*," Sarah turned to the Healer, "I can't believe that I'm the only one who has an occasional dream come true. Surely there must be someone more...well, more qualified."

"You haven't even seen any proof, *Nali*. How can you be so certain that Sarah is the one?" Devlin asked.

"She knows the way. She passed the test," Tima replied in her customary offhanded manner.

"You took a test?" The rider looked at Sarah in surprise.

"No, I swear," Sarah exclaimed.

By this time, both women were staring at Tima. The Healer sighed deeply, bowed her head, and stared at her hands. She stretched her fingers, rubbing the stiffness from the joints. Sarah and Devlin exchanged inquisitive looks over the older woman's silence, but they patiently waited for the Healer to explain. The quiet persisted for a few moments more.

"Sakli helped me to prepare the Old One's Medicine yesterday. I instructed and she made."

"Sarah, you made the old man's Medicine?" Devlin asked.

"Well, yes, but Tima told me what to— oh, dear God!" Sarah exclaimed. "I killed him, didn't I?"

"No, *Sa*, no." Devlin tried to keep a straight face in this serious situation, but given Sarah's expression it was extremely difficult.

"You did no such thing," Tima added.

"Relax, *sachu-kash*. I was surprised is all. Tima doesn't usually let anyone help her when she heals." Devlin arched an eyebrow at her mother, who met her daughter with an equally intimidating gaze. "Sarah, tell me what you did, exactly as you remember it, every step."

Sarah pondered the reason for the rider's question, but she related the event to the best of her recollection.

"What root did you use?" Devlin asked.

"*Nali* called it *chuchupate*. I always called it osha root; at least it looked and smelled the same. Kind of like really strong celery."

"How did you know?"

"I...well, I...I guess I just knew."

"And when you placed the Medicine bag and bowl beside

Tima, where did you set them?"

Sarah scrunched her eyes closed for a moment in an attempt to relive the moment in her mind. "I placed the Medicine bag on the mat, right next to Tima. I laid the bowl down right next to it. Oh, yes, I remember I put the bowl on the flat part of the beaver's tail."

"Why there?"

"It seemed to make sense, I suppose. I'm not at all sure why I did it that way. I guess I thought that if I did it wrong, Tima would say something."

Devlin squeezed her lover's hand before giving her mother another sidelong glance. "You should have told her what you were doing, *Nali*, that wasn't fair. Sarah, that was Tima's test. She gives it to all women she thinks might have the gift of Healing."

"*Tasa*, it would not have been a proper test if she had known. You should remember. You took the same test," Tima answered.

Devlin gave her mother a sort of half smile, partly at the sound of her pet name, which her mother rarely used anymore, and partly in remembrance of the test. Hearing her pet name softened the tall woman's rising annoyance with her mother. It was a nickname, a shortened version of the word *tashka*, meaning "warrior." Tima had known the very moment she met Devlin, as a young girl, that the child was a warrior.

"Dev?" Sarah called for the rider's attention. "You're a Medicine Woman?"

"I took the test and failed," Devlin replied. "I didn't know which root was which. I didn't know where to place the Medicine bag or even the fact that a beaver's tail is sacred and an excellent spot to mix the healing herbs. I didn't know any of that and so Tima stopped me and told me to leave the *chuka*. If someone unfamiliar with the Healing Spirits mixes *ikhish*, or Medicine, we believe that the Spirits will grow angry and take the patient's life to show up the false practitioner."

"Oh, Dev," Sarah's hand flew to her mouth, "but that's what happened. The old man died."

"No, little Sakli," Tima said in a soft voice. "The Old One heard the Spirits calling him, yet your Medicine allowed him to finish his journey. Your Healing gift woke him long enough for Keeho to speak with him. Without you, he would have gone to the Sacred Land with his task unfinished."

"Let me get this straight, then," Sarah began. "You want me to go through the rituals to become *Chahta*, then train to become a Medicine Woman, all simply to understand the old man's message?"

"There is more to it than that," Tima replied. "The message is only a small piece. In exchange for the Spirits imparting their knowledge, you will become the Sacred Mother to the Clan. It is a great honor as well as responsibility."

Sarah brought her fingers to her head and massaged her temples. She jumped up and paced the roomy *chuka*. "I can't do this. I'm a cattlewoman. I deal with what I can feel and touch, not in what I can't even see. It's too much. I can't, I just can't–"

"It's all right, *sachu-kash*, you don't *have* to do anything. Besides, this isn't something you can do right now anyway. I'm sure they mean when you're older."

"What do you mean? Tima and Keeho both say they see it as my destiny." Sarah stopped her pacing.

"You're too young, Sarah," Devlin explained. "A woman can't start her training in the Medicine Way until she stops having her cycle. As long as she bleeds, she's considered too powerful. So, you see? Tima and Keeho must be seeing something in your future."

Sarah looked down at the seated rider and tears filled her eyes. The small blonde looked over at Tima and found an expression of compassion on the older woman's face. It was that look of understanding that caused Sarah's last reserves to finally crumble. Suddenly, she turned and ran from the *chuka*.

"Sarah!" Devlin called after the young woman. The rider sat where she was, stunned at Sarah's emotional departure. "What did I say?" she asked.

"You should go to her, *Tasa*. She will need gentle words from you," Tima answered.

"But what– "

"Go to her now," Tima said firmly.

The mother watched as her daughter left the *chuka*, confusion in the rider's expression. Tima shook her head. She hoped the little one would open up to Redhawk. It would be bad *fahpo* to begin their life with secrets from one another.

Chapter 5

"Sarah? Sarah, wait!" Devlin called out.

Sarah stopped but didn't turn around. By the time Devlin caught up with her, Sarah had gotten her emotions under control, but not her tears.

"*Sachu-kash*, what is it? Is it something I did, something I said? Whatever it was, I'm sorry. I can fix it if you give me a chance."

Sarah took in the tall woman's expression, which was equal parts remorse and pain. It seemed out of place for the rider to be standing there looking so contrite. Just a short time ago, Sarah knew this woman before her to be intimidating, angry, and full of fire. Now Devlin's apologetic behavior touched Sarah's heart. She couldn't hold back the innocent laughter that bubbled forth.

"You're very cute when you're not sure what it is you've done," Sarah said through her tears.

Devlin grinned and pulled Sarah into her arms. The smaller woman wrapped her arms around the rider's lean waist and buried her head against her chest. Devlin kissed the top of the blonde head. "You do know that you completely own me, don't you?"

Sarah looked up and tears glistened on her cheeks. "It's the best investment I ever made," she whispered.

Devlin wiped away the younger woman's tears and kissed her forehead. "*Sa*, talk to me. Tell me what caused you to run away like that."

Sarah nodded her head and they walked hand in hand through the village, heading toward the open prairie. Finding a spot under a large hickory tree, the women watched in silence as the squirrels busily carried nuts back to their nests.

Devlin leaned back, stretching her long frame along the ground. She lifted herself up on one elbow and placed a gentle hand on Sarah's back. "What made you run away back there, *Sa*?"

The winter winds swirled around the women and Sarah pulled her rabbit skin robe tightly around her shoulders. "Fear, I suppose. That and the fact that I don't ever want you to be disappointed in me."

"Sarah, you should know by now that I don't think you could ever do anything that would disappoint me. What are you afraid of, *sachu-kash*?"

"Of what Tima and Keeho know about me. All of you rely so much on these Spirits, what you can't see. It frightens me."

"That's why I was so worried about you becoming Clan. It's hard, Sarah. Hard to change your belief system in the middle of your life."

"It's difficult to believe in things I can't see, to think that I have gifts that make me special. This," Sarah pulled up a chunk of grass, "this I know how to deal with. I can plow in it, plant in it, and use it as feed. I can shape it into what I want."

"I know exactly what you mean, Sarah. For me, this was what I believed in." The rider laid a hand on the pistol at her hip. "This is what was real for me. It was strange thinking that no matter what I did, there were powers that had control of my life. I think that was the hardest part of all, realizing that I wasn't in complete control of my life's path."

"How did you get past it?" Sarah asked.

"I simply accepted the fact that there is a solid world and a Spirit world, and that it's possible to live within both. I finally came to believe that I wasn't in charge of my own destiny and that there wasn't anything wrong with taking help when the Spirits offered. Sometimes, *sachu-kash*, there's nothing wrong in depending on someone else."

Sarah tossed the chunk of earth away from her. She realized the truth in Devlin's words. They were from Devlin's experience, but they could very well have applied to Sarah. She feared few things in life, but depending on someone was high on that list. She remembered the expression on Tima's face just before Sarah had run from the *chuka*. What frightened Sarah the most was that the older woman knew. Sarah could tell by the look in Tima's eyes.

"I don't think it was a vision of the future, Devlin, the one that Tima and Keeho saw. I think what they see in me is right here, right now," Sarah admitted.

"But– "

"I can't have any more children, Dev," Sarah said as tears again filled her eyes. "I haven't had my cycle since Hannah was born."

Devlin pulled Sarah back against her and held the younger woman there. "I'm sorry, *sachu-kash*. Is that what made you so sad?"

"Yes, plus it scared the blazes out of me. Once you explained that a woman doesn't start her training until then, I knew that Tima had seen my future. Besides, Dev, it means there'll be no more children for the two of us."

"Well, I think at least one of us is lacking the means to make that happen anyway." Devlin grinned and kissed the back of Sarah's neck.

"I know that, silly. I've heard, I mean I know that in some cultures if a man can't father a child, his wife sleeps with someone they know, a trusted friend..." Sarah trailed off, her embarrassment complete.

"Would you want that, to be with someone else?" Devlin's voice raised in pitch at her lover's surprising admission, even though the rider tried to hide the jealousy she instantly felt.

"No!" Both women laughed at the strength of Sarah's exclamation. "I mean, well, I thought that you– "

"*Sa*, I love the children we have now. I couldn't be any happier or feel any more complete than if they were truly a physical part of me. We have what we have and frankly, this is more than I ever thought the Spirits would bless me with. We don't need a child of our blood to bond us together. Our hearts couldn't be closer, *sachu-kash*."

"Is it true, Dev, that the *Chahta* believe once you're married in the Clan way your hearts belong together forever, in this world and the next?" Sarah asked.

"Yes, it's true."

"I love you and I want to be a part of your world, Dev. I don't know if I'll pass their tests, but I want to go through with it. I want to belong to the Thunderbird Clan. I want to be your wife, even though you haven't asked me yet." Sarah turned her head and smiled at the rider.

"The ultimate honor a lover can bestow on a *Chahta* woman is to respect her with an offer of love and marriage. When you become *Chahta*, I'll ask you to marry me in the traditional Clan way. You can bet on that," Devlin answered. She placed a gentle kiss on Sarah's lips.

"Come on." Sarah unexpectedly jumped to her feet and held her hands out. "Let's go tell Tima."

Devlin laughed at the young woman's enthusiasm. The rider knew that once Sarah put her mind to something there would be no stopping her. She rose and obediently followed her lover back to the village to find Tima.

Tima smiled when she gave permission for the two women to enter her *chuka*. She could tell by Sarah's demeanor that the young woman no longer carried her burden alone.

"*Nali*, I hope you'll forgive my poor behavior before. I can offer no justification or explanation. The *Chahta* beliefs are so different from the ways of my people that I grew frightened at the thought of having no control over my own life. I've never been the kind of woman who has lived her life in fear, and I don't intend to start now. I'm not certain I'll ever pass your tests, I admit to letting my fears get the best of me sometimes, and I am fully expecting to kill the first person crazy enough to let me heal them, but if you feel like I have what it takes, I'll give it a try."

Tima's smile grew larger and she nodded her head. "If you felt any differently you would not have the gift."

"I need to admit something else," Sarah looked up at Devlin. "I was frightened by the feeling that you knew I no longer had my monthly cycle."

"Sarah," Tima rarely used the name Sarah had been given at birth, but she felt that in this instance, the young woman needed to hear it, "you forget that I helped heal you just a short while ago. A Healing Woman looks not only into her patient's body, but also into their soul. I saw into your *chukash*, into the center of your being where you hold all your secrets. A patient cannot hide anything from their Healer's eyes." Tima paused and watched her daughter, who only had eyes for the beautiful young woman beside her.

"It is because a Healer can see within a person that I wish to explain something to the both of you. If you wish to become *Chahta*, Sakli, then I must extract a promise from you both."

"Sit, both of you," Tima said gently. Once Devlin and Sarah seated themselves, the Healer continued. "*Tasa*, you know that your grandfather has no sons, and you are the warrior of his heart."

"*Omi*," Devlin replied.

"He will someday ask you to become *Miko* for our family. The Clan respects you, in heart as well as strength. I see the men voting to make you chief *Miko* someday. If you accept the position, you know there will be things that cannot be discussed outside the Elders' Council, even with your mate."

"Yes, *Nali*, I understand that," the rider answered.

"Sakli, it will be the same with you. If you pass into the ways of the Medicine Woman, you will accept the position of Clan Mother. There will be Visions given to you that you will have to bear alone. You may be commanded by the Spirits to speak of these Visions to no one." Tima looked from her daughter to the young blonde. "You may become privy to the secrets of those you heal. Can each of you do this? Can you promise to obey the ways of the Clan if these situations arise?"

"That will be hard, not being able to share with Dev," Sarah admitted.

"I agree," Devlin added. She looked out of the corner of her eye and her serious expression disappeared. A small grin formed. "I bet you crack before I do."

"I bet ya I don't," Sarah replied within half a heartbeat.

The two women laughed and joined hands. In that instant the atmosphere within the *chuka* changed. Tima felt it even though the oblivious young women did not.

"Children." The Healer shook her head, her own light laughter joining in. "Go, leave my *chuka* and make yourselves useful. I have two strong children at my *iksita*, yet I have no meat for a meal and my water jars are empty."

The sound of their laughter carried through the village and for some reason, it seemed to make the day lighter for the people of the Thunderbird Clan.

Sarah wrenched herself free of her dream. She pulled herself into a sitting position and Devlin moaned softly in her sleep as she felt the loss of her lover's warm body. When Sarah's eyes adjusted to the dim light of the *chuka* she slipped from the *topa* she shared with the rider and fed some small pieces of kindling into the fire set in the center of the lodging. The young blonde's eyes met Tima's, as the older woman watched her from across the *chuka*.

"Your dreams woke you," Tima whispered.

Sarah nodded, wondering why she always felt as if Tima could read her mind. She supposed it had more to do with the way the Healer phrased her statements than any mind-reading capability.

"I have had dreams the last three days," Tima continued. "Do you dream of fire?"

"Yes," Sarah replied. "Did you see it, too?"

Tima nodded and her eyes held a faraway expression. "I wish I knew the meaning. I only feel that it is of great import, that our very existence might depend on the outcome. I lack the training to understand my dreams completely. The Spirits have been unwilling to reveal the truth to me."

"It's coming on winter, though, so it really couldn't be grass fires. It's been a dry fall, but the snows this winter and the spring rains should remedy that. Let me ask you, *Nali*," Sarah whispered so as not to wake Devlin, "if I should complete this training successfully, to become a Medicine Woman, will I know the meaning of my dreams then?"

"I believe so. You have to understand that I cannot remember a time when our Clan had a Medicine Woman. I learned the Healing ways and knowledge that my mother before me knew. So you see, I cannot say what you can expect exactly."

"Then how can you train me if you haven't been through the training yourself?" Sarah asked.

"The Spirits will guide me. Besides, Keeho will teach you also. He knows many spiritual ways that I am not privy to. I believe our combined methods of instruction will be enough to set you on your path. The actual journey, however, will be up to you."

"Do you think Taano's prophecy has anything to do with our dreams of fire?"

"I believe they both come too close together to be coincidence," Tima answered.

"I wish the Spirits wouldn't be so cryptic with their visions," Sarah huffed in exasperation.

Tima chuckled lightly. "You must show as much patience with them as they do with you. It has been many, many snows since the Spirits walked in our reality. They tend to forget that we do not have the same understandings as they. When you begin the first moon of your training, you will go on a Healing Quest. During this time, when the Spirits decide to accept you or not, you will receive visits from one of the thirteen Clan Mothers. These will be your Holy guides and they will intercede on your behalf with higher powers. If the Clan Mothers do not visit you, then you have not been accepted as a worthy candidate for our Clan."

"I see so many different scenes inside my dream," Sarah explained, "and I feel that if I only had the power to piece them all together, they would tell a story."

"If you desire, we will go before Kontonalah and the Elders in the morning. If you pledge your desire to become *Chahta*, he will begin your acceptance into the Clan. Acceptance is a simple ceremony where you learn of the history of our people. Once that is complete, you may vow to give yourself up to be trained in the way of the Medicine Woman. When these steps are accomplished, you may join with Keeho and the Elders in prayer."

"Seems like a lot just to be included in their prayers," Sarah responded sleepily.

"Sakli, no woman of our tribe has ever been a part of the Elders' prayer and meditation circle. They have never allowed a woman to take part in the Sacred Prayer Lodge in this way. The power of women can be a fearful thing to a man, but our Clan is trusting in Keeho's word that you will use your power for the good of the Clan."

"I hope I can live up to their expectations of me," Sarah whispered as she slipped under the fur robe beside Devlin.

"You will," Tima reassured the young woman with her customary frankness.

The rest of the night passed quickly for Sarah and the two other women sharing the *chuka*. A cold front had come through in the night. Sarah shivered slightly, now standing outside of *Miko* Kontonalah's *chuka*. Devlin went in first to go through the formalities involved in pleading Sarah's case.

The process entailed gaining the chief *Miko*'s approval, but more importantly the approval of Sarah's adoptive parent. Devlin had explained that before a newcomer could become a part of the tribe, the Spirits had to speak to an existing member, who had to accept the calling from the Spirits as an adoptive parent to the new initiate. If no one within the Clan felt compelled to come forward for the newcomer, then the Elders would deny the request.

Devlin peeked out of the large *chuka* that belonged to Kontonalah and motioned for Sarah to enter. She gave the younger woman a smile and formally introduced Sarah to the Elders and *Miko* Kontonalah, even though the Clan already knew her. The elderly chief *Miko* directed Sarah to sit before the semicircle of men. Devlin sat beside her.

"*Na hollo ohoyo,*" the Clan *Miko* began. Even though he knew who Sarah was, he addressed her as simply a white woman. Sarah had a Clan name, but that was highly unusual. Keeho had seen the vision of the Salmon and named Sarah *Sakli* before she had even decided to become *Chahta*.

"You come to the Clan with a request?" Kontonalah asked, already knowing the answer.

Sarah was frightened beyond reason to be in this room full of the most important men of the Thunderbird Clan. She didn't want to give her fear away, however, by looking at Devlin for support. She tried to imagine the Clan Elders as the men of the Cattleman's Association, the men with whom she'd often had showdowns. That thought gave her back a little of her old courage.

"Yes, I do. I wish to be *Chahta*. I hope to learn and I wish for my children to know the Clan way," Sarah answered, as Tima had instructed her.

"Sakli," Kontonalah now addressed Sarah by her Clan name, "listen to the story of our people."

Sarah watched as Devlin's uncle, Kaylan, stepped forward. The brother of Devlin's adoptive father, Kaylan had been responsible for much of Devlin's training as a warrior within the Clan. He carefully unrolled a large deer hide. Inside, on the smooth skin, someone had painted many pictures. As Kaylan spoke, Sarah realized the hide was actually a storybook of sorts.

"Too many snows ago to be counted easily there were no *hatak isht atia*, or humans, in this world. Hashtahli lived alone with our brothers, the animals. They were no comfort, as they only wanted to play *toli* all day long. Hashtahli asked Hushi Ninak Aya, his wife, the moon, why she shone so bright at night.

"'See my children, they play and hunt in the woods at night. They keep me happy.'

"Hashtahli thought about this. Then Hashtahli decided that he should have children, too. First, he built a great mountain. He placed the seeds for the idea of man deep inside the sacred mound. Then Hashtahli sat down to await the birth of his children.

"First born were the *Creeks*. When they came out of the cave, they climbed out of the sacred mound and lay down on the warm rocks under Father Sun to dry themselves. They slept for the night, but grew cold when Hashtahli's light left them.

"When Father Sun came again, they said to themselves, 'Let us travel to the land where Father Sun dwells so we will not be cold.' Therefore, they traveled east.

"Then were born the *Chalakki*. When they came out into the sun to dry themselves, they found the woods all around them had burned to ash. They lay on the side of the sacred mountain, and when they were finally dry, they could not locate the trail of their *Creek* brothers. They walked all around the mound.

"Finally someone said, 'Let us leave this place and find a spot to be a family.' They traveled north and there they found the home for their Nation.

"The *Chiksa* emerged from the mountain next. As they lay upon the warm ground, drying in Father Sun's light, they saw the *Chalakki* walking away to the north. They followed their brother *Cherokee* and settled close to the *Cherokee* Nation.

"The *Chahta* came last from the sacred mound. The *Chahta* walked all around their Mother, the sacred mountain, and finally climbed upon the rocks to dry under Father Sun. When the *Chahta* were dry, they gathered into a circle and met together, each man having a voice. When each man had his say, they formed a tribe, and then they broke up into smaller Clans, thirteen in all. They decided they would not leave their Mother, the sacred mountain, alone. They would stay within the mountain's sight where she could watch them and her power would protect them always.

"This is the story of our people as it was told to me by my *moshi* and how I will tell it to *saibaiyi*."

Kaylan finished the tale and Sarah had to shake her head slightly to bring herself back to the moment. The storyteller had immersed the young woman so thoroughly in his tale that she actually believed she had just witnessed the birth of man as the

Choctaw saw it.

The silence in the *chuka* persisted for long moments and Sarah's nerves, combined with the heat from the fire, caused a lone bead of sweat to trickle down the side of her face. No one moved or made a sound as they patiently waited to see if the Spirits had granted Sarah's wish.

Once more, Sarah dared not look at Devlin as she waited to see who within the Clan had received the calling to adopt her into their family. She worried at first who it would be, since she hadn't yet gotten to know many of the Clan on a personal level. Now, as the awkward silence in the *chuka* persisted, her heart fell as she realized that no one at all would come.

Although Sarah's back was to the entrance, she saw a slice of outside light brighten the *chuka* and a chill breeze swept through the lodging. Sarah had thought she was the only nervous one, but Devlin's sigh of relief told the young woman she was not alone in her feelings.

Finally, Sarah allowed herself to glance at the rider. Devlin had looked back to see who the mystery parent was, and she didn't even bother to hide the expression of astonishment on her face. Sarah shuddered to think who could cause that reaction from her lover. Suddenly, she felt the weight of a hand upon her shoulder. When she turned her head, she was sure her expression matched Devlin's.

"I have received the call."

Keeho's voice rang loud and clear through the *chuka*. If Devlin and Sarah were amazed that the oftentimes cantankerous Medicine Man came forward as Sarah's *Chahta* parent, then the Elders were equally surprised.

A strong looking man jumped up from his seated position. Sarah recognized him as Nitushiabi, or Young Bear Killer. He was the youngest *Miko* in the circle. His expression was angry and he pointed a finger at Keeho.

"I will not say I do not believe you, *Alikchi*, but are you certain that the Spirits speak to you with a Vision?"

"Do you question a Holy Man's Vision?" Kontonalah asked.

"I do not accuse, I only ask. Is Keeho certain that he felt the calling or was it simply a wish to make his clan go strong?"

Devlin listened to the surprising exchange. She had never expected Keeho to become Sarah's *Chahta* parent, but she never anticipated there would be outrage or debate over it. Her fists clenched and unclenched as she tried to bite down her anger at

Nitushiabi.

Young Bear was in the Hunter clan of their village. The Clan included everyone within this tribe of *Chahta*. There were also clans, meaning the many families who made up the village. Young Bear's family had always been successful hunters. Because of this, they were a strong clan and had much say in the way the Elders ran the village.

Keeho came from a clan of Healers and Medicine Men. They were also very powerful within the Clan structure. Devlin understood what drove Nitushiabi to speak. Gossip had obviously already spread about Sarah's possible gift as a Medicine Woman. Devlin was certain that Nitushiabi feared that since Keeho was already a powerful Shaman, adopting Sarah and bringing her to his *iksita* would shift the balance of power in the village to Keeho's clan.

The rider had always known Keeho to be a man of few words, and this moment was no exception. The Medicine Man snorted at Nitushiabi's comments. "Do you accuse me?" he asked impatiently.

Young Bear found himself standing alone. If he made further trouble, it would border on an accusation. In the eyes of the other Elders, a *Chahta* Holy Man was not the person to offend. The young Hunter might possibly find himself without allies or honor after the confrontation. Nitushiabi weighed his options carefully and chose to take his seat.

The Elders bent their heads together briefly, whispering among themselves. Finally, it was Kontonalah, as the chief spokesperson, who looked at Sarah and said, "*Achukma hoke.*"

Sarah looked up. Devlin was already standing. The rider motioned Sarah to exit the *chuka*.

"*Yakoke*," Sarah hastily offered to the Elders.

Once they were outside, Sarah turned to the dark-haired woman. "That's it?"

Devlin smiled. "I told you not to worry, didn't I? Besides, it will be the tests of your conviction to become *Chahta* that will be difficult, not this part."

"Keeho? All this time I thought he couldn't stand me," Sarah commented.

"I just think he's not used to being around women much, along with the fact that most Medicine Men aren't fond of the natural power that women possess."

"Still and all...I guess I expected it to be just a little harder than that," Sarah responded.

"It will be," Devlin answered ominously.

Chapter 6

The next morning found the first frost of the season on the ground. Sarah shivered, even with a heavy horsehair blanket and Devlin's arms wrapped around her. The young woman wore only a deerskin wrap as she prepared to enter the Prayer Lodge. Keeho and the other Elders had gone in before her wearing only their breechclouts. The heat would be intense and the lack of clothes necessary, but Sarah still felt quite naked with only the hide wrapped about her.

"I sent Talako down to the ranch with a message for Hank," Devlin whispered to Sarah. "Just so Mattie and the kids would know where we are and that we're okay."

Talako, Gray Eagle, was Devlin's childhood friend and had been happy for the opportunity to go down to do a little trading. The rider wasn't sure why she brought this up just now. Perhaps it was simply something to say. Devlin felt weak and inadequate at that moment. She was not familiar with the ways of Medicine Men and Women and she could offer little in the way of protection for Sarah.

Sarah had spent the previous evening, and most of the time she should have been sleeping, listening and learning from Tima. The Healer taught Sarah what she knew of the Prayer Lodge and the cleansing sweat ritual, but she admitted that she had only experienced the ceremony with women. The *Chahta* men believed that a woman's natural power became too intense during the sweat ritual for the men and the women to share the same space. Even the women of the Clan refused to let a menstruating woman join them for fear of her power at that time of the moon. Keeho had promised he would teach Sarah as well as let her experience the ceremony.

"In a way, I'm kind of jealous of you," Devlin once more whispered into Sarah's ear. "I've always wanted to see what they do in there."

"Okay," Sarah replied nervously, "you go in there and I'll go home."

Devlin squeezed the small woman tighter. "You'll be fine, *sachu-kash*, Keeho won't let anything happen to you." Sarah noticed that her lover's expression wasn't nearly as confident as her words.

The small blonde pushed the negative thoughts from her mind. Tima had told her that it would be a mistake to enter the Prayer Lodge with anything but positive thoughts in her mind. If Sarah went into the lodge believing she didn't belong there, the Spirits wouldn't come.

They watched the fire keeper tending the great fire pit outside of the Prayer Lodge. The fire was at the end of a pathway that led from the lodge to the fire pit. The fire keeper had filled the pit with large stones, each about the size of a man's head. Tima had explained that when Keeho called for a round to begin, the fire keeper would cart a load of hot rocks into the buffalo hide-covered structure and place them into a pit in the center of the lodge.

Keeho came to the entrance and indicated that it was time for Sarah to enter. The rider kissed Sarah's forehead and took the blanket. The Medicine Man looked up just as two red-tailed hawks floated in a lazy circle in the sky, high above the lodge.

"A good sign," he said.

Sarah entered the lodge and narrowed her eyes in an attempt to see. The Prayer Lodge was already hot from the fire in the center pit. She was depending on Keeho to tell her all she would need to know to complete the ceremony. Tima had told the young blonde not to ask questions, to simply listen to all the Medicine Man said. She said there would be time enough for questions later. Sarah wished that she'd had more time to prepare, but this was an emergency in a way. Since Taano's prophecy was too cryptic for Keeho to solve alone, the Elders seemed to think that they needed Sarah's power. She still didn't know how to tell these people that she felt as powerless as a newborn baby.

Keeho positioned the hide flap to the entrance so that it spared Sarah enough light to see. She knew that once the lodge was sealed, the slight illumination would disappear completely. The Medicine Man stood directly behind Sarah as she entered. True to his word, he instructed Sarah with each step.

"When you enter the Prayer Lodge, always move with the arc of the sun," Keeho said. "You see how the lodge is shaped like brother Turtle on the outside. Always remember not to step over Turtle's neck." Sarah realized that he meant she should move in a clockwise direction, always to her left.

"Did Tima teach you the proper words of respect?"

Without answering, since Tima had told her not to speak if she could help it, Sarah demonstrated. She went to her knees, touching her forehead to the ground. "*Akanohmi moma*," she said aloud. Tima had loosely translated the words to mean "to all my relations." The words were not only an acknowledgement that all living things– plants, rocks, water– were her brothers and sisters, but also to honor the materials that would be drawn upon for this ceremony.

"Sit here," Keeho instructed. "Beside me, Sakli."

Sarah sat down on the bare ground. The grass had worn away to the dirt. The earth felt cool when she sat, in complete contrast to the heat of her skin. She watched as the fire keeper brought in two large earthen bowls filled with water. He placed one beside the center fire pit and the other beside Keeho.

Sarah thought it odd the way her mind trailed off. The ladle in the bowl mesmerized her. It was a long piece of river cane, and the cup looked to be woven grass. It made her think that she would someday like to learn how the women here worked their art of basket weaving.

Keeho ordered the fire keeper to bring in eight rocks for the fire pit. As the fire keeper performed the task, Keeho explained to Sarah what was happening.

"There will be four *folotas*, or endurances, for our prayers today. After the fire keeper brings the stones in, we will begin with the Smudging ceremony and the Prayer stick will go around the circle. Once those ceremonies are complete, I will call for the end of the *folota*. If the experience overcomes you, then you must wait until I end the endurance to leave the Sacred Lodge. If you leave the Lodge, you must wait for the start of the next *folota* to enter again."

Keeho pointed to the fire keeper. "Shanafila is the fire keeper. It is an honored position. He is strong and will do much work to carry in the hot stones."

Sarah watched as the man known as Blue Hawk brought in the rocks one at a time. He carried them in a many-layered hide sling to keep the glowing rocks from burning his hands or body. When he passed Sarah the first time, she could feel the heat flow from the large stone.

"The Holy number of the *Chahta* is *ushta*, four," Keeho told Sarah. "The most sacred of things come in fours: the family—mother, father, brother, sister. There are four elements to our physical world: earth, water, sky, and all living things. There are four seasons and the four directions to which we offer our prayers. Because of this number, I tell Shanafila to bring in stones four at a time."

Aside from Keeho's voice, the only audible sounds were Shanafila's grunts and heavy breathing as he carried out the laborious task of bringing in the heated stones.

"That is the last stone Shanafila will bring in for now. When he leaves, he will seal the door. The women outside will sprinkle cornmeal all around the Prayer Lodge. This will help to keep the bad spirits away."

Sarah watched as Shanafila left the lodge and carefully sealed the entrance. They were immediately plunged into an inky blackness. The sounds of breathing, the popping of the glowing embers from what was left of the fire, and the hiss of the heated rocks were the only sounds. The combination of oppressive heat and complete darkness felt a hundred times more claustrophobic than Sarah could have imagined. She concentrated on the feel of her own hands running along her legs in an attempt to fight down her rising panic. Suddenly, she could hear her own anxious breathing echo loudly within the confines of the lodge. She was one heartbeat away from bolting when she felt comforting hands on her shoulders.

"Do not be afraid, Sakli."

Keeho's voice came from close behind her. In her fright, Sarah's first instinct was to shake the man's grasp off.

"Close your eyes, Sakli."

Sarah wanted to laugh aloud. Why should she close her eyes when it was blacker than pitch already?

"Relax, Sakli, close your eyes."

I can do this. I'm stronger than this, dammit! Sarah screamed in her head. She closed her eyes tightly.

"What do you see?" Keeho asked.

"Dark," Sarah answered.

"Dark is a state. Tell me what you *see*."

"I– well, I see nothing. There's nothing *to* see."

"Now, open your eyes." Keeho's grip on her shoulders had loosened slightly. "Tell me what you see now."

"I don't see any more than I did with my eyes closed. I see nothing."

"Then why do you fear nothing, little one?"

Keeho's voice was so low that Sarah barely heard it, but she was embarrassed at her own frailties. She smiled in the dark.

"This is the beginning, Sakli. This is Mother Earth's womb, a source of power for all women. You lived here for nine moons before you saw the outside world. You were not afraid then and you will not be afraid now."

She thought about the Medicine Man's words. The dark, close quarters could indeed substitute for a mother's belly. The sweat that dripped from her body fell onto the ground, making the earth around her warm and damp. With a little thought, a mother's womb was exactly what Sarah could imagine.

She felt the hands leave her shoulders and saw the shadow of Keeho's body walk before the fire. She briefly saw a flame appear by the fire pit and again recognized Keeho's form. She thought she saw a bowl of some sort in his hands. After a moment, the Medicine Man's voice came to Sarah from the opposite side of the small lodge.

"My bowl holds the leaf of the sage. The first step is to cleanse and purify."

The sound of Keeho's voice moved within the circle. Sarah pictured the Smudging ceremony as she had seen the man perform it previously. Finally, he paused before Sarah. She imagined him gently waving his feather over the smoking earthenware bowl, the smoldering herb wafting in her direction. The sweetly intense odor of white sage blew across her face and she invited it in to her senses with a deep breath.

"I use a feather from brother Hawk today. He will help us to see Visions, to gather inspiration." Keeho's movement stopped. "We have now entered Sacred Time. This is a time for your mind to open and be still."

Sarah felt Keeho move away from her, but she couldn't tell

whether her eyes were open or closed. She thought to raise her hand and touch her eyelids just to be sure, but felt as if she were floating in the blackness. Her brain couldn't give the command to her arm. She couldn't move. She was simply there, floating.

More odors filled the lodge. Keeho sprinkled sage, cedar, and sweetgrass on top of the glowing hot rocks. Sarah recognized each in turn. She listened as Keeho thanked the rocks for their part in the ceremony.

A loud hissing noise broke the silence, but it didn't startle her. She could hear Keeho's voice inside her head, or was he beside her? For a moment, she thought that perhaps she was only *feeling* the Medicine Man's voice. The hissing grew louder and Sarah could feel the steam spreading into the lodge as Keeho splashed cool water onto the red-hot rocks. The steam billowed in enormous clouds that reminded Sarah of thunderheads over the prairie. She listened to the voice inside her head that she recognized as Keeho's. She heard the Medicine Man call out to the West power, the first of the four directions. She knew that the first *folota* had begun.

"The West power will open us up to the Spirit's world. We name ourselves so the Mighty Ones will know us. I am *Keeho Naksika binili.*" Keeho announced his Clan name as He Who Sits Apart.

One by one the Elders declared their full Clan names, along with their secret names. Even Sarah felt an odd strength as her turn came and she declared her identity. She never paused to wonder how she knew it was her turn in the circle, but suddenly she no longer feared the dark or the mysteries of the Prayer Lodge. An unusual peace came over her and she refused to let her common-sense self fight against it.

Somewhere in her mind, soft like the last waves of a dying echo, Sarah heard the words *I am Ankahito...I have always been Ankahito.* They reminded her of Taano, the Medicine Man whom she had tried to save. She felt similar words grow in her heart.

I am Chahta...I have always been Chahta.

"The Prayer Stick goes around the circle," Keeho explained to Sarah. "We pray to the guardians of the Four Directions. We ask their power to infuse us."

They went through this process for each of the Sacred Four directions. Keeho commanded every aspect of each round. He entreated the Spirits, led the Prayers, initiated the songs, and controlled the amount of heat and steam within the lodge. Sometimes the singing and chants were loud and boisterous, and at other times they were soft and low.

Sarah lost track of time and, very nearly, who she was within the dark facsimile of Mother Earth's womb. She couldn't even remember the ending of the last two endurances, and now it was time for the fourth and final *folota*.

A drum sounded and Sarah wondered why she hadn't heard it before. Suddenly, the intense heat of the lodge disappeared. A gentle spring breeze cooled her body. Sarah laughed aloud, realizing that she still had her eyes closed. She opened them and met a breathtakingly beautiful blue sky. She knew that she was still in the lodge. Part of her could hear the Elders chanting and Keeho praying.

Sarah stood and turned in all directions. She was in the lodge, but at the same time, she was standing out in the open prairie. Every one of her senses felt ten times more acute. She could smell the loamy earth under her feet and feel the tall grass as it brushed against her hands. The prairie was alive and Sarah was a part of that life. The vista changed and the spring grass dried. Leaves fell from the trees and nuts and berries fell to the ground. It was fall.

Her newly heightened senses picked up an unmistakable odor.

Smoke.

Suddenly there was a feeling like panic rushing through her. Everywhere she turned animals ran in different directions. Sarah clapped her hands over her ears to shut out the sound of thunder. It was as if she were right on top of a thunderhead. The sound grew so loud it shook the earth. Her eyes opened wide when she realized that the sound wasn't thunder.

Looking in all directions, she saw walls of burning hot flames. They quickly spread across the range, feeding on everything in their path. Just ahead of the flames came the source of the deafening sound. It was cattle and buffalo, hundreds of thousands of them. Mixed breeds of cows, longhorns with their dangerous horns, and massive buffaloes the size of which she'd never seen before. They all rushed away from the red-hot evil nipping at their heels.

Sarah watched helplessly as the animals all vied for escape, but suddenly wires sprang up before them. Barbed wire and tall fencing, just the sort the cattleman used to mark their land. The animals had no way to escape. The fire ran at them from the rear and the wire halted their progress. It didn't matter to the crazed animals. They pressed in and strangled the animals in the front with the deadly wire.

Sarah screamed again and again. She shouted and yelled at the beasts to stop their stampede, but there was nowhere else for them to turn. The white man's wire blocked their only route of escape. Thousands of animals trampled one another as still more were cut to shreds by the razor-sharp wire. Sarah could do no more than weep at the sight, crumpling to the ground in her fatigue and anguish.

When she looked up again, the Clan surrounded the dying animals. Now the cattle were all gone and only the scores of buffalo remained, huge beasts that lowed, snorted, and tore at the ground in their anger and frustration. Soon, even they succumbed, trampled underneath their brothers' hooves.

Sarah saw Tima and the others of the Clan that she had grown to love so well. She thought that perhaps they would help her save the animals. It soon became apparent that the *Chahta* had no knowledge of how to save the buffalo. The great beasts supported the people of the Clan, but the *Chahta* could not undo the white man's power.

Sarah watched and with every buffalo that fell, a member of the Clan disappeared in the mist that surrounded them. She felt a voice inside her head again, but this time it wasn't Keeho. The voice told her that once the buffalo were gone, the *Chahta* people would pass away also.

"No!" Sarah screamed out when, one by one, the buffalo dropped to the ground.

"Help us, Sakli." Tima raised one hand to Sarah as the white mist engulfed her body.

"No!" Sarah screamed one last time.

She thought she had already been lying on the ground, but how could that be, she wondered, as her legs crumpled underneath her. The last thing she remembered was the feel of the moist earth below her cheek and the oppressive heat as the flames swallowed her.

Devlin had paced the same patch of ground for hours. She was on the verge of being punished by her grandfather for her earlier behavior outside of the Prayer Lodge. Now, she risked banishment by interrupting a Medicine Man's ceremony, but the only thing on the rider's mind right now was Sarah.

"Do not," Tima warned as she spied Devlin eyeing the entrance to Keeho's *chuka*.

"I need to know how she is. What could be taking so long?" the rider hissed.

Tima didn't answer, but Devlin didn't need to hear one. The rider could see by the expression on her mother's face that Tima was worried as well. It had taken three men to hold the strong rider when she had heard Sarah scream the second time. Devlin had tried to cling to her beliefs, but the idea that her lover needed her pushed every other thought into second place.

Tima had tried to calm her daughter, but it was nearly impossible for the men to hang on to the nearly hysterical rider. When at last the fire keeper opened the Prayer Lodge, two men carried Sarah's limp body out and straight to Keeho's *chuka*.

"Redhawk, Tima, come," Keeho ordered from inside the *chuka*. His voice was hoarse and he looked as if he'd just run the footrace of his life.

Devlin rushed into the *chuka* and would have burst into tears at the sight before her had she been alone. "Sarah!" she cried out as she dropped to her knees and crushed the young woman with a fierce hug.

"It's all right, love," Sarah whispered. "I'm okay."

She didn't feel okay. In fact, Sarah felt as if all the energy in her body had been wrung out of her like a dirty shirt on washday. Sweat and grime covered her, and her golden hair was plastered around her face. The acrid odor of herbs clung to her hair and skin.

"How is she really?" Devlin asked Keeho.

"She has seen much." Keeho looked at the young woman with something like admiration evident in his gaze. "She is drained and needs to eat and rest, but she will be fine. It was the intensity of the Vision and no malady that struck her."

Sarah sat up slowly, as if it were a great effort to move. "I know what Taano's message means, Dev," she said in a tired voice.

"Later, *sachu-kash*," Devlin responded. "You need to get some rest first."

"No, Dev, it can't wait, it's too important." Sarah looked at Keeho, Tima, and then into the eyes of her lover. *How can I tell them that with the end of the buffalo comes the end of the Chahta?* Sarah remembered that Tima had told her that, as a

Medicine Woman, Sarah would be privy to information that might possibly have to be kept from the Clan. Sarah knew she wasn't a Clan Mother, but she made the decision anyway.

"There's going to be a prairie fire— in the fall, I think. Hundreds of thousands of cattle and buffalo will die because of the ranchers' wire fences. That's what Taano meant when he said the buffalo must run free. I saw them, Dev. It was horrible. The way they died was just hideous."

Sarah leaned into Devlin's embrace. The rider didn't even need to look into Keeho's face as the Medicine Man nodded his head, confirming Sarah's Vision as truth. She could see it in Sarah's eyes, feel it in the way the young woman's body trembled. It was as if she were reliving the horror of that moment once again.

Sarah pulled away from the rider and ran a hand through her long hair. She looked at her arm, covered in sweat, dirt, and bits of dried grass. "Good Lord, I'm a mess."

Sarah smiled weakly at Devlin and the rider felt better. The young woman was becoming more like herself again. Devlin continued to hold the blonde, needing to be in constant contact with her lover.

"I will speak with the Elders. I will tell everyone of your Vision, Sakli. Now that we know the riddle, perhaps the Spirits will bless us with the answer. Go rest, little one. You have done well," Keeho said.

Tima stayed to speak with the Medicine Man, but Devlin helped Sarah to her feet. Keeho wrapped an extra blanket around the small blonde's shoulders before sending her from his *chuka*.

"Are you okay with walking?" Devlin asked with concern.

Sarah had to admit that she had been a bit unsteady when she first stood, but was now feeling stronger, although mentally exhausted. "I have to clean up. I need a bath," she said, turning toward the creek.

"It's pretty darned cold."

"I think I'm too filthy to care. I feel like I'm entirely covered in dirt. Tell me the truth, Devlin," Sarah stopped to look up at the taller woman, "how do I look?"

"Not too bad..." Devlin slowly trailed off.

Sarah chuckled as they reached the water and she laid the blanket on the bank. "So diplomatic of you. I know I look— "

"Absolutely beautiful," the rider interjected. She suddenly realized that Sarah was removing her wrap. "What are you doing?" she asked in surprise and turned to eye one of the young men with a fishing spear who stood in knee-deep water a short way off.

"I'm going to bathe."

"Well, why don't we go downstream a ways? It's quieter and— I thought you didn't like bathing in front of other people?" Devlin tried to say in a low voice.

"I'm just too tired to care, love," Sarah responded as she dipped her body into the cool water. She scrubbed her face and body, working on her hair next.

Devlin tried to use her own body to block anyone's view of her lover. She could have sworn that the young man fishing had snuck an eyeful. By this time, Devlin was standing in the water up to her knees, and the brave sat on the bank removing a fish from his pronged spear.

"What are you looking at?" Devlin growled in warning.

"Uh, nothing," he answered.

"Haven't you got anything better to do?"

"No," the brave responded in confusion.

"Then find something!" Devlin hissed and the young man quickly scuttled backwards like a crab. The brave didn't know what he'd done to earn Redhawk's ire, but whatever it was, he didn't want to compound the problem. He grabbed his gear and moved off to the deeper part of the stream.

"Dev?"

"Hmm, what?" Devlin finally came out of her watchdog stance to look at her lover.

"Are you taking a bath, too?" Sarah asked.

"What?"

Devlin followed Sarah's eyes in the direction of her own legs, all the way down to her boots, which were underwater.

Sarah laughed and the sound was so precious to the rider's ears that she was quite willing to look the fool. Devlin grinned and walked to the bank. "I was just cleaning my boots off," she muttered.

Sarah didn't understand why, but for the first time in a long while her laughter felt completely free. She finished her bath, much to the rider's consternation and, shivering, wrapped herself tightly in the warm blanket. They shared an afternoon meal with Tima within the Healer's *chuka* and spoke of only inconsequential things.

"I have many things to do yet today," Tima announced. She

touched each woman as she left the *chuka*. Devlin suspected her mother understood the need for Sarah and the rider to share some time alone.

"Come here, *sachu-kash*," Devlin requested.

Sarah needed no further coaxing. She lay down beside the rider, feeling a strange energy within her own body. She knew she should be tired. She had been absolutely devoid of strength when she left Keeho's *chuka*, but right now, it was as if there was something humming inside of her.

"We need to go home, Dev," Sarah said. "We need to talk to people, see if the Association will help us. We have to get the ranchers to take down their fences."

"It won't be easy, *sachu-kash*," Devlin replied.

Sarah leaned up on one elbow to look at her lover. "You believe me, then?" She sounded a little surprised.

"Of course I do. Did you think I wouldn't?"

"I don't know. Dev, what happened to me in that lodge, it was the strangest, oddest thing I have ever experienced, but for some reason it all felt...I don't know." Sarah brushed her bangs from her forehead. "It felt perfectly natural. I was afraid at first, but once it was happening it felt right somehow. I know I'm explaining it badly, but– "

"Sarah," Devlin interrupted. "This is the way my people live. None of it seems strange to me. I'm happy and surprised that you're able to accept it so willingly. I've never spoken of these things because I thought it might disturb you. The Spirits are talking to you, Sarah. It's a great honor. It's almost as if you were already *Chahta*."

I am Chahta...I have always been Chahta.

The words that had come unbidden into Sarah's mind at the Prayer Lodge called to her again.

"There was more to my Vision, Dev." Sarah moved herself into a sitting position beside the rider. "More that I didn't tell the others." She guiltily revealed the rest of the Vision to her lover.

"Maybe I'm interpreting it incorrectly." Sarah attempted to rationalize her feelings.

"No, I think your first impression was correct." Devlin looked up at the young woman with sad eyes. "This isn't the first time I've heard this. Anyone who knows the land, and how it was before the white man swept west, feels the same way. For thousands of years mutual need has tied together the buffalo and the tribes on the plains. Our Clan's been blessed. Our village still stands where it was when I met them. Most of the Indians on the prairies in the west are nomadic. They go where the buffalo go." Devlin paused to touch Sarah's face.

"I think you're right, *Sa*. Your Vision tells us of a great disaster, but I think it says so much more. If the buffalo disappear from this land, then I think so too will the Clan. As a people, they'll still exist, but I think their way of life will fade. That will be the real loss. These people, all the tribes across the land, knew this earth thousands of years before the white man got here. Now, the government reduces them to nothing more than slave status. They have to go where and when the government tells them."

Sarah felt an incredible sadness for a race of people who had suddenly learned that they were no longer the captains of their own fate. "If people like me had never come west, we wouldn't be having this problem," she said tearfully.

"*Sa*, there has always been enough for all. It was never the white man's entry into this land that brought about destruction. It was what he brought with him, his mentality and his thought that he had the right to take what he could. The Indian people look at the land as if they themselves are a part of it. They are just one point in a circle that includes everything that has life. The white man looks at it as something he needs to own, to bend to his will."

"Why? I don't understand why it had to be that way." Frustrated, Sarah balled her hands into fists.

"Who can say why one man has certain instincts and another doesn't? The *Chahta* believe that all men came from the same original tribes. Somewhere along the line, for whatever reason, they separated. I've heard stories that tell how most of the tribes went east, and a smaller portion of them traveled west. Suddenly, they didn't all learn the same ways. Grandfather tells a story that describes the people who came west across this land as Indian tribes. He seems to remember that his grandfather told him that the tribes which traveled east became the white men."

Sarah settled herself back against Devlin, her body finally having grown tired. It was almost as if she had the energy to have only this discussion with her lover and no more than that. She thought about all the mysteries of life surrounding her in this *Chahta* village. She wondered how differently she would look at all the happenings in her life now.

"Tell me one of your grandfather's stories, Dev."

"A story?"

"Mm hmm. Something to make me forget bad thoughts."

Devlin wrapped the fur robe around Sarah and kissed the top of her still damp hair. The rider suddenly grinned and knew what tale she would tell her lover. "This is a short story, but when I was younger it always made me think. It still makes me smile because it reminds me to always be thankful for what I have and not to worry so much about what I don't have." She crossed her ankles and placed her arm around Sarah's shoulder.

"I asked my grandfather how the raccoon and the opossum could be brothers when they looked so different from one another. He sat down with me and said that the raccoon's beautiful fur coat had always been a source of envy for brother opossum. He said that at one time, the opossum and the raccoon both had thick furry coats.

"One late summer day, raccoon and opossum met and stopped to speak to one another. As they relaxed and spoke, opossum looked at his brother's finely colored coat, but most especially his exquisite tail. You see, the opossum and his brother had always shared the same plain coat, just as Hashtahli had made them.

"'Halito, brother, are you well?' asked raccoon.

"'Halito, brother, yes, I am well, and you?' opossum asked right back.

"'Yes, I am well too,' raccoon replied.

"Now the opossum was admiring his brother's fine tail so much that he couldn't think of anything else to say.

"'Where are you off to this morning?' raccoon asked.

"'I'm on my way to the forest,' answered opossum, all the while staring at raccoon's tail.

"'What for?'

"'For persimmons. I love persimmons and I hear they're almost ripe.'

"'Well, I just passed a persimmon grove and the trees are all full, so you're just in time,' raccoon explained.

"'Where are you off to then, Coon?'

"'I'm going down to the creek to look for crawdads.'

"'Oh, I just came from the creek. There are crawdads everywhere!' opossum exclaimed, as his eyes drifted to his brother's tail once again. 'Your tail is so beautiful, Coon. How did you get it that way, with the rings all around?'

"'I took hickory bark, wrapped it around my tail, and then singed it. That's the way I got the colored rings.'

"They took leave of one another, each going off in a different direction. Opossum couldn't keep his mind on anything else for the rest of that day. The days turned into seasons, but opossum's admiration turned into envy, and finally into jealousy.

"It got so bad that opossum refused to speak to his brother, angry for what his brother had. One day opossum decided that he too was good enough to have a colored tail.

"He got some hickory bark and wrapped it around his tail. He built a fire, but opossum wasn't very used to building fires. It turned out to be a very large fire, much larger than he needed. When opossum went to singe his tail, the large fire burned all the hair off his tail.

"Because of opossum's inability to be happy with the gift that the sun god gave him, Hashtahli had his close friend, Luak, who we know as Fire, take off all the hair from opossum's tail.

"That is why opossums, to this day, have no hair on their tails. They are embarrassed by this and still sulk over it a bit so they travel at night."

Devlin wondered if Sarah had heard the entire story. The rider could feel the relaxed, heavy breathing of her lover in sleep. Devlin thought she should rise and find something to help her mother or the villagers with, but at that very moment, she couldn't imagine anything that could take priority over this.

The rider smiled into the silence of the *chuka*. That story always made her smile. It made her think of her mother. Devlin had avoided the truth when she told Sarah that her grandfather had always told her that story. She hadn't lied. Kontonalah had sat her down to tell her that tale, but she hadn't the heart to tell the old man, whom she had grown to care for, that it was one of the few tales she remembered from her mother. Devlin had never thought about *not* telling Sarah. The rider swallowed hard to hold back tears, which instantly appeared over thoughts of her mother. She realized that when she explained her story to Sarah, it would be an emotional discussion. Devlin didn't like feeling out of control and she knew that's what a talk about her real family would do.

Devlin could hear the sounds from outside. There were children playing and some women singing as they worked to shuck corn. If she listened closely, she could hear a few young men as they bragged of their latest hunt. She could hear her mother's pleasant voice in her memory. Devlin had laughed whenever she heard the story of coon and opossum.

"But what does it mean, Mama?" Devlin asked.

"It means not to worry so much about what you don't have and to always be thankful for what you do have."

Devlin held her lover in her arms and thanked anyone who would listen for the blessing of this woman and her children in the rider's life.

Chapter 7

The Elders decided that the best course of action would be to trust in Sarah and Devlin. Taano had traveled a great distance and even gave his life to deliver the message. He had told the Clan that the Spirits indicated that Devlin and Sarah alone would be able to solve their dilemma.

Sarah wished there could be an easier way, but there certainly didn't seem to be one. She and Devlin discussed the idea of talking the cattlemen into taking down their fences. While that prospect appeared slim, they both knew they had to do everything in their power to persuade the ranchers otherwise. With Sarah's new wealth came a larger voice among the Indian Territory ranchers. She and Devlin hoped it would be enough.

Sarah was sad that she could not stay with the Clan and go through the rituals to become *Chahta*. Although frightened at first by the mysticism surrounding the ceremonies, she now wanted nothing more than to be married to Devlin in the eyes of the Clan. She promised Tima they would return with the children in the spring as soon as the weather allowed. She promised to communicate with the Clan if their circumstances should change.

Sarah let the heavy curtain fall back over the window. The bulky cloth prevented the cold winds from filling up the room. The fireplaces in every room also helped to keep the large ranch house warm. Sarah plopped back into the soft chair beside the window. She felt lonely now that her sister had gone back home and the sound of screaming children no longer filled the house.

Devlin was out on the range. The rider took an enthusiastic Matthew with her whenever she could. Hannah was fast asleep during her afternoon nap, and Sarah now wandered the house aimlessly. Maria and Angelia shared the household duties and Angelia did most of the cooking. Since cooking and cleaning were a big part of the day, Sarah felt a little lost in her own home. It was more than the isolation the cold weather brought. She had been depressed for the last two days about the situation with the cattlemen.

They explained most of the story to Hank one night. At first, the easygoing rider wasn't sure whether his friends were pulling his leg or not. After examining the serious expressions on their faces, Hank realized that if Sarah and Devlin believed the whole thing was true then chances were that it was. He pitched in and promised his help wherever they thought best.

Two months had gone by since they left the Clan village. It was nearing the end of February, but Sarah and Devlin had discussed how best to approach the problem from the moment they returned home from the village. The idea of calling a meeting in town held no thrill for either woman. The Cattleman's Association of the Indian Territory was composed of men, with two exceptions– the widow Henley and Sarah. To the town's populace, Devlin was just a hired hand. Even the people who knew what Sarah and Devlin's relationship was all about weren't going to accept them as a couple. It simply wasn't done. Sarah considered herself and Devlin as equal partners in life and business, but she agreed with Devlin that the others wouldn't see it that way.

No one had seen the widow Henley in quite a few years. Next to Sarah, the widow owned the largest ranch in the Indian Territory. Sarah and Devlin were unable to get the old woman to listen to their story because they could never talk to her. William Hennessy took care of everything from the widow's legal affairs to her personal business. He relayed the message to her, but the answer he returned was that the widow didn't care anything about anybody. The feisty old woman herself had run off the few people who had actually ever visited her house.

Devlin and Sarah decided that Sarah should be the spokesperson. Calling a town meeting had been her idea, but it had been a complete disaster. Any credibility she had with the townspeople dropped considerably after that humiliation. The men laughed so hard that it took every bit of Devlin's restraint not to unload a few rounds over their heads just to quiet them down. Sarah, a naturally strong and intelligent woman, became tongue-tied and frustrated at the men's jokes. The more she tried to explain without making herself look like a complete lunatic, the more the men jeered and ridiculed her thoughts. Finally, she had no other choice other than to give up.

The winter had been a cold one so far, but with very little precipitation. Usually the late fall was rainy leading right into the winter snows. There had been no rain or snow this season, only bitter cold and blowing winds. This turn of the weather didn't sit well with Sarah. The drier the land grew, the closer she felt they were to her Vision becoming a reality. The hardest part to accept was that they were no closer to a solution than the day she had her Vision.

Sarah detested failure. Inequalities were a part of life, and the small blonde had set some high goals for herself over the years. She was one of the lucky ones. Through determination and hard work, she had accomplished everything in life that she had set her mind to, even though at times the odds against her had been enormous. She didn't like not measuring up, and in her opinion that was exactly what was happening now. She was at her wit's end and a disastrous deadline was drawing near.

She hadn't meant to sit there and feel sorry for herself, but when Devlin returned home a short while later that was how she found the young woman. The sight of Sarah with tears running down her face was enough to alarm the rider.

"Sarah! Are you okay?" Devlin rushed over to kneel in front of the young woman. "Is something wrong with Hannah?"

Sarah's heart melted at the rider's worried expression and her words of concern. "No, really, I'm sorry. There's nothing wrong, Dev." She brusquely wiped the tears from her face. "I hate crying like this."

"Don't feel that way, *sachu-kash*. Your tears are part of your compassion. It's a part of you."

"Well, it's a part I can do without so often, I guess," Sarah replied. "Whew, you smell," she added with a smile.

"I ought to," laughed Devlin. "I've been working hard."

"You need a hot bath."

"Nah," said Devlin, standing up. "I can wash in cold water."

"Dev, you'll catch your death. I'm going to put some water on to heat. If you promise to wait for some warm water, I'll scrub your back for you," Sarah said with a gleam in her eye.

"Now that sounds like a good reason for a bath." Devlin watched Sarah leave the room. "That woman's moods change quicker than the weather," she exclaimed to herself.

Soon after that the rider was enjoying her bath, although it was difficult for her to stay focused. Sarah began by helping the rider to wash her long hair and continued with the promised back washing. Her hands tended to wander a bit, which made concentrating on speech that much harder for the rider. Finally, promising to behave, Sarah sat on a small stool beside the tub. Devlin leaned back and closed her eyes, luxuriating as the warm water relaxed her sore muscles.

"Why were you crying, *Sa*?" Devlin asked softly. Her eyes were still closed, but she peeked one open to gaze at the small blonde.

Sarah sat with her chin cupped in both hands, her elbows resting on her knees. "I'm frustrated and angry. I don't know what to do, Dev, or who to turn to for help."

The rider knew that her lover referred to the task they had of somehow getting the ranchers to tear down their wire fences. The reaction from the cattlemen at the town meeting had devastated Sarah. So far, the women had been searching for allies, people to help them spread the word and get the job done. Something Sarah said, however, made Devlin think that perhaps they were going about it wrong.

"Why do you think Taano gave us that message? I mean, why would the Spirits send an old man across the country like that?" Devlin asked.

"I guess because we must have some sort of abilities that others don't have. Something unique that will get the job done," Sarah answered.

"I agree. If that's the case, then why do we keep trying to find others to get the job done instead of just doing it?"

"I'm not sure I understand," Sarah said slowly. "We don't use wire fences on our ranch."

"Then maybe it's time we just went out to every rancher personally and used some of these unique abilities the Spirits give us credit for. Sarah," Devlin sat up out of the water and her voice grew stronger as a plan of action took shape inside her mind, "you may not know it, but you have an incredible gift for persuasion. It's not always in the way you speak or even in what you say. Sometimes it's just the way you carry yourself or the expression on your face. Those kinds of things have to be experienced one on one, not in front of a crowd."

"And you think something like that will work?" Sarah asked.

"It's how you got me."

Sarah looked into Devlin's smiling face and remembered the day Devlin decided to ride for her brand. She had always assumed her uncle Art had forced the rider to accept.

"I think we need to go see every rancher within a day's ride. Talk to them individually. Work some of your magic on them," Devlin added.

"And just where are you going to be while I'm working this magic?"

The rider leaned back and entwined her fingers, cracking her knuckles. "I'll be using my unique abilities."

"Which are?"

"Keeping you out of trouble." Devlin laughed.

Sarah reached forward to splash the rider. She then moved in and kissed the woman passionately.

"Hey, don't kiss me like that unless you plan to keep going," Devlin commented after they broke apart for air.

"And if I do?" Sarah questioned.

Devlin's heart fluttered. "Then go lock the bedroom door," she answered in a husky voice.

Without another word, Sarah rose and Devlin heard the key turning in the bedroom door's lock. The fluttering moved into the rider's belly as she eased her body from the water and made her way into the bedroom.

"Make sure Hannah goes down for a nap, Angelia. She'll try to talk you out of it if she can," Sarah said.

Angelia and Maria had become trusted members of the household. Sarah's uncle had hired the sisters to cook and clean when Maria's husband, Alejandro, brought them from Mexico and started work on the ranch as a rider. Sarah had offered the family a small house on the ranch. She felt more comfortable with two other women around to talk to and Hannah enjoyed playing with Maria's little girl, Nelli. Sarah didn't know what she would do without the sisters.

"*Sí, Señora*. I know how that little one can be." Angelia laughed.

"Where are they all this morning? Dev and I are getting ready to leave."

"Hannah is playing dolls in the kitchen with Nelli. Maria is cooking and has an eye on them. Matthew is in the barn with *Señor* Hank. He shows him how to care for something they called tack."

"Well, we'll be back by supper-time. Just let them be. If you need anything at all, call for Hank; he'll be here at the ranch house all day."

"We will be fine, *Señora*. Be safe."

Sarah and Devlin took the smallest wagon. The back had already been packed with supplies should they need them and a large picnic basket for their lunch. It was a quick ride and even though it was the end of February, the breeze was already infused with springtime's warmth. The widow Henley had quite a bit of land to the south, but her ranch house was only a two-hour wagon ride from the Double Deuce.

Devlin pulled the wagon up to a stop some thirty feet from the house. It looked quiet enough, which was how the widow liked it. Her riders, bunkhouse, and nearly all of the ranch's activity were situated on land further south. The large two-story house was in the middle of nowhere and seemed perfect for the antisocial old woman.

Devlin jumped from the wagon first and walked around to give Sarah a hand. Sarah just stared at the quiet house from her seat in the wagon.

"*Sachu-kash*, she's not going to eat you."

"You don't know this old woman, Dev. She shoots first and asks questions later." Just as her feet hit the ground, Sarah heard the distinctive sound of a little girl's giggle.

Devlin tilted her head and furrowed her brow at the small blonde. "Sarah, did you hear the same thing I just heard?"

"Oh, that's impossible," Sarah replied.

Once again, they heard the muffled laughter.

Sarah stepped to the back of the wagon and removed the canvas covering their supplies. "Hannah Marie," she exclaimed.

"I wanted to s'prise you, Mama," the little girl quickly answered in an attempt to remove the stormy expression from her mother's face.

"Uh oh. Sarah, come up here and count to ten." Devlin waved the small blonde to the front of the wagon.

"Dev, I– "

"Honey, there's nothing we can do about it right now. Let's just make the best of it and– "

"Make the best of it?" Sarah's voice was a high-pitched whisper. "Dev, you've never met this old woman before, have you?"

"Well, no."

"The summer I was ten I lived out here with Uncle Art. Mrs. Henley's husband had just died and I came out with Uncle Art to offer condolences. She shot at us, with a rifle and not a peashooter, I might add. She's as ornery as– as– "

"Okay, okay, I get the picture. Let's just get Hannah, go back home, and hope the old woman didn't see us."

The women agreed with a nod of their heads and Devlin went to the back of the wagon to get Hannah. "Um...Sarah?"

Sarah followed the rider and looked into the bed of the wagon where moments before the young girl had been hiding. "Oh my God," she cried out as she did a double-take at the empty wagon bed. "Dev!"

"Well, who have we here?"

"Hannah Marie Tolliver," Hannah answered proudly. She walked up the back porch steps and sat down on a small keg.

"Well, just make yerself at home," the old woman said.

"My mama's got one of those an' she shot a fox an' bam! Right here." Hannah placed her finger between her eyes. "From a long way aways, too."

"I guess I'd best not shoot you then. I wouldn't want yer mama after me with a Winchester."

"You shouldn't shoot me anyway." Hannah looked up at the old woman with a serious expression. "Mama says people shootin' each other don't make sense. She shot that bad man, though. We should only shoot when we hunt. You should be careful where you point that thing. That's what Mama tells my brother Matt a lot. He's a boy and you know how boys are. He never listens to nothin'."

The old woman chuckled. It had been a long time since she had heard her own laughter, but this little girl was a regular chatterbox. She leaned the rifle against the wall beside the door. "Reckon it wouldn't do to be shootin' you then, considerin' yer not much bigger'n a prairie dog."

"I am so bigger'n a prairie dog." Hannah puffed out her

chest.

"Was that you makin' all that ruckus out in front?"

"Nope." Hannah absently kicked her heels against the wooden keg. "That was my moms."

"You got more than one mom?"

"Uh huh."

"Well, come on, little prairie dog. I wanna see these two moms of your'n. Easiest way to get to the front is goin' through the house." The old woman held out her hand and Hannah obediently slipped her own small hand within the withered yet strong grasp.

"Okay, okay, let's not panic. I mean it's not like she's really lost." Devlin kept telling Sarah not to panic, yet she could feel her own voice rising in pitch with every word.

"I swear, Dev, if that old woman shoots my little girl—"

"We are not going to let that happen. I haven't seen any movement from inside the house, so chances are the old lady's taking a nap or something. Let's work our way, very quietly, to the back of the house."

Sarah and Devlin crouched down slightly, using hand signals to communicate as they crept around the west side of the house.

The widow Henley and Hannah were walking through the parlor. Lace curtains covered the windows, making it difficult to see in but easy enough to see outside. The old woman paused, watching the women outside creep around as if they were characters in a penny novel.

"Are yer moms slow-witted or something?" the old woman asked.

"Huh?" Hannah asked.

"Never mind. Let's go sit on the porch. I reckon it's warm enough for it. Bundle yer coat up there, prairie dog, or you'll catch yer death." She checked on the progress of the women outside and shook her head. "I expect they'll find us on the porch sooner or later. Gotta say though, they sure don't act like the two sharpest ears of corn on the stalk, that's fer sure."

Finding the back of the house deserted, Devlin turned to Sarah. "I hear voices."

"Me too. Up front?" Sarah asked.

They didn't waste any time rushing back the way they'd

come only moments before. The sight that met them rendered both women speechless.

Hannah sat in the lap of a woman who looked to be at least eighty years old. The youngster was relating how Devlin had saved Dolly from a fate worse than death by retrieving her from the jaws of Rupert, Art Winston's old hunting dog. The old woman was listening intently, interjecting the appropriate responses.

"Hannah!" Sarah cried out.

"Mama!" Hannah smiled from her comfortable perch in the old woman's lap. "I found you."

"Oh, you found us, did you?" Sarah tried not to smile, but she could rarely stay angry with her daughter for long. The youngster was simply too much like Sarah had been at that age to hold it against her.

"Come here, you," Devlin said. She stepped onto the porch and moved to lift Hannah up when she promptly got her knuckles rapped. "Ow!"

"She seems pretty comfortable where she is," the old woman snapped.

"Mrs. Henley, I'm– " Sarah began, holding out her hand.

"Sarah Tolliver. And you're Devlin Brown. Yep, I know who ya are, but what I don't know is why you come callin' when yer not welcome."

"Look, Mrs. Henley, we– " Devlin started.

"And bringin' a hired gun with you don't help yer case any," Mrs. Henley added.

"Now you wait just a minute." Sarah stepped forward to confront the woman. "Devlin is not a hired gun."

"No? Then what is she to ya?" The old woman's eyes gleamed with mirth as she set the trap.

"She's my– "

"Look, we don't want any trouble," Devlin interrupted. She gently held Sarah by the shoulders. "If you don't want us here we'll just be on our way. I don't see any reason to get into name-calling."

"Oh, don't go gettin' your tail feathers ruffled," Mrs. Henley replied. "You're here now, might as well stay a spell. You hungry?" she asked Hannah.

Hannah smiled and nodded her head. "My tummy says feed me, please."

"Me too." The old woman gently settled Hannah on her feet

and led the way into the house. Pausing at the front door, she turned slightly. "I reckon ya expect me to feed you, too. Well, come on then. Two moms indeed." She chuckled.

"Do you have any idea what just happened here?" Sarah turned to Devlin to ask.

"Nope." The rider shook her head. "I say we don't look a gift horse in the mouth, though."

Sarah had a thought, ran back to the wagon, and grabbed their picnic basket. She and Devlin cautiously entered the house. It was a beautiful home with furniture and glassware that had obviously come from back east. Old portraits hung on the walls and a spinet stood in one corner of the parlor. The house looked expensive to Devlin and she was afraid to touch anything.

"We have lunch." Sarah held up the large basket. "Would you like to share it with us?"

"I reckon that's about the best idea you had so far, little lady," the old woman answered.

It was a short, uncomfortable meal for Devlin. If Hannah hadn't carried the bulk of the conversation the two sides probably wouldn't have spoken at all.

Mrs. Henley rose and walked into the kitchen.

"Sarah Tolliver, come on in here and make your young self useful," she called out.

Sarah rolled her eyes at Devlin and rose to follow the sound of the old woman's voice. When the small blonde returned, she was carrying a tray with a coffeepot and three delicate looking china cups. She poured the coffee, which didn't get an argument from the old woman.

"Rider, open that door just a ways behind you." Mrs. Henley indicated a side door near the entrance to the sitting room.

Devlin complied and looked back at the old woman. The door appeared to lead into a small storage closet.

"There, that small chest, the one on the top shelf. Bring that one down for the young 'un."

Devlin pulled down the chest, quickly becoming annoyed that this woman was ordering her around like some hired hand. She placed the lightweight box on the table before the old woman.

Mrs. Henley unbuckled the leather strap that kept the lid closed. "Come here, little prairie dog." She opened the top to reveal assorted rag dolls with tiny little outfits, all in different colors and patterns.

"Dollies!" Hannah exclaimed. Sarah smiled at her daughter's response. She could never understand why something so simple as dolls delighted Hannah so much.

"Now, Rider, you take these and put 'em on the rug in the sittin' room. You can play with them in there," she said to Hannah.

"They're too nice to play with, I don't want her to—" Sarah began.

"Nonsense. No sense lettin' the moths make a feast of 'em. Go on," she ordered the rider.

"What do you say, Hannah?" Sarah asked.

"Thank you, Missus...I don't know your name," Hannah blurted out.

The old woman chuckled. "My name is Cordelia Leander Henley." She laughed again as Hannah tried to wrap her tongue around the name. "Why don't you just call me Cordy? That's what my friends use to call me."

"Thank you, Cordy." Hannah beamed. She happily followed Devlin into the next room.

"Oh, you'll have trouble with that one. She's a charmer, she is," Mrs. Henley commented.

"The face of an angel and the ways of a devil." Sarah blushed when the old woman looked up with an odd expression upon her face. "It's— well, it's what my father used to say to me."

The old woman found that most amusing and laughed loud and long. "I bet this one found that out the hard way, eh?" She indicated Devlin, who had just taken her seat.

"Did I miss something?" Devlin asked.

"Just an old woman's friendly bite is all. So, Sarah Tolliver and Devlin Brown, now that little ears are out of the way, what say we lay our cards on the table? I'll tell you right off. My fences come down over my dead body."

"That could be arranged," Devlin muttered in a low voice.

"What's that?" Mrs. Henley asked.

Sarah kicked the rider's shin under the table.

"Ow! Um, it's a nice day on the range," Devlin answered.

"Mm hmm." The old woman raised a skeptical eyebrow at the dark-haired woman. "I'm old, Rider, I ain't deaf."

Devlin at least had the good sense to blush at her error. "Sorry, I didn't mean—"

"'Course ya did, but that's neither here nor there. Now,

word is you want ranchers to take down their wire. I can partly see the sense in it. My husband never put up fences at all, even wood. In those days, a rider's salt was if he could keep his herd in check. Times are different, though, and I got a hundred times the size of the herd we started with here. If'n I hired all the riders it would take to keep my herds in check, I'd soon be a poor woman. Now, suppose you start by tellin' me why I should want the fences down."

Sarah looked at Devlin and the rider's face changed. Mrs. Henley watched the amazing transformation. The pale eyes turned a warm sky blue and the hard line of the rider's mouth curved into a slight smile. It was as if something lit the rider from within when she looked at the small blonde.

After an almost imperceptible nod of encouragement from the rider, Sarah turned back toward the old woman and told the story. Sarah knew that she was opening herself up to humiliation and ridicule by relating her Vision, but she and Devlin agreed on one thing. If it didn't feel right, depending on who they were talking to at the time, they wouldn't tell more than they had to. Even though the widow was an ornery curmudgeon, Sarah and Devlin both felt as if she might be receptive to the whole truth.

Nearly an hour later, Sarah leaned back in her chair. The old woman just stared at Sarah and Devlin.

"And you expect me to believe this?" Mrs. Henley asked.

"Well, all I can say is that it's true. As for you believing, I guess that's another matter," Sarah answered.

"It's so crazy I reckon it must be true. Who else have you told this to?"

"You're the first," Devlin replied. "We tried to tell the Association, but we didn't get very far. We haven't told the whole story to anyone else yet."

"Well, don't. They'll think you're nuttier than a hickory grove and it won't get ya nowhere."

"But how will we get the ranchers to join with us?" Sarah asked.

"Young woman, I look at you and I see you know a fair piece 'bout cattle. I know this rider's 'bout as good as they come, too. I been on this land since the only other woman in the Territory was an Indian squaw. There's only one thing the ranchers in the Indian Territory respond to and that's money. You can tell all the stories and make all the predictions you want, but there'll be only one reason them men'll follow you and that'll be 'cause there's somethin' in it for them."

Sarah and Devlin listened to the woman in rapt fascination. The widow had been here before any of them, and there was one thing that Devlin and Sarah weren't too proud to admit– this old woman was smart and she had experience dealing with ranchers as well as with life. If Mrs. Henley had a way to work this out, the younger women were more than willing to listen.

"You say that this big fire's supposed to come in the fall?" Mrs. Henley asked.

"As near as I can tell," Sarah answered, "but that's not for sure. I mean, I could be wrong. It could be in the summer even."

The old woman seemed to consider this. "What were you gonna do with yer stock? You got an awful lot of beef on the hoof at the Double Deuce."

"We planned to sell just about all of them at market price. We'll drive them into the stockyard in the spring. That's only forty miles away," Devlin explained.

"And what'll that thief Charlie Roberts give ya up at the yard?"

"Three, maybe four dollars a head," Devlin replied.

"You'd get nearly forty dollars a head in Abilene. I hear they got a new cattle market up there."

"I suppose we would," Sarah responded, "but it's a long way between here and Kansas. We'd be talking about a cattle drive we just don't need to make. Sure, we'd make a small fortune, but we don't need the money."

"You don't, but a lot of other folks do. Take a listen to my proposition. Next to you, I got the biggest ranch around. If'n I spread the word, say I'm puttin' in with you, then you can bet there won't be a rancher who'll stand against us."

"In return for?" Devlin asked.

"You put together the drovers to drive all their cattle to Abilene in the spring or early summer, with you as trail boss," the widow said, pointing to Devlin.

"Are you crazy?" Devlin raised her voice. "Do you know how many cattle you're talking? No one's ever driven that many. Most I ever trailed at one time was five thousand head. You're talking forty, maybe fifty thousand head of beef!"

"It's too dangerous, a drive of that size. It'll take all summer," Sarah added.

"I'm just tellin' ya what kind of a deal we can make. It's up to you to think out the particulars. All I'm sayin' is if you tell these ranchers you can get them ten times what their beef is worth around here, then you'll have a deal. Money is the bottom line."

"And what's your bottom line?" Sarah asked. "What do you want out of this?"

"More money. Look here. I'll give you my cattle to sell in Abilene and I'll give you every man on my ranch that wants to go. I got fifty good men you can count on and I'll pay 'em from my share. When the deal's done and yer rider gets back home, I'll sell you every acre of land I own at thirty cents on the dollar."

"I don't understand. Why would you sell us your land?" Sarah asked.

"In case ya haven't noticed, I'm gettin' on in years." She smiled. "My mother met her maker at 102 years old. My grandmother was 116 and her mother before her was 109 when she passed. We're a bunch that likes to stick around some. I think I'd like to take my fortune and buy one of them fancy houses in Kansas City. Have servants and such to fetch and carry for me. I figure I want my last days to be easy ones. Plus, I wouldn't give ya a plug nickel for even one of them ranchers in that Association. I ain't about to leave one acre to any of those idiots."

Sarah and Devlin smiled at the old woman's wish. "Dev?" Sarah asked.

"It'll be one hell of a trail ride." Devlin grinned before her face turned serious. "I don't see much way around it. Maybe this is the way it was meant to be." She shrugged her shoulders.

"Then I suppose we have a deal, Mrs. Henley." Sarah offered her hand to the older woman.

"I reckon since we're business partners you best call me Cordelia."

They shook hands and spoke for a while longer about how best to let the other ranchers know of their deal. Cordelia smiled and told the two women to let her take care of the others. Devlin grinned, imagining that this old woman had a way with ranchers.

Devlin scooped up the now sleeping Hannah and stopped to shake the old woman's hand. Cordelia insisted they take the chest of dolls along for Hannah. Sarah carried the chest just ahead of the rider holding the sleeping child. The small blonde paused and then turned back to Cordelia.

"You know, Cordelia," Sarah began, "my Uncle Art and I came up here to visit when I was a girl. You shot at us."

"Did I hit ya?" The old woman had that familiar gleam in her eye.

"No." Sarah chuckled.

"Then I wasn't shootin' *at* ya." The old woman's laughter carried a long way out onto the late afternoon prairie.

Chapter 8

"What do you mean I'm not going?" Sarah's voice rose slightly with each word.

"Tell me which part you don't get and I'll go over it again," Devlin answered.

"Don't treat me like the men you work with."

The exchange had only been going on for a few short moments, but already the men on the ranch knew when to step out of harm's way and look busy. It wasn't the first time they'd seen the two women butt heads during the stressful roundup, but it usually ended with a joke or an apology. Everyone on the Double Deuce was aware of the urgency to get the spring chores taken care of so they could begin the difficult task of putting together the largest cattle drive in which any of them had ever taken part.

Devlin lowered her head and took a deep breath. "I'm sorry, Sarah," she looked up, her hands on her hips, "the trail is the most god-awful place there is on earth. It's brutally hard. If you think you've lived with men, you haven't lived with them at all until you've spent two months with them like this. It's too dangerous."

"But not for you."

"Sarah, be reasonable," Devlin pleaded. "I've been doing this for a hell of a long time."

"And all I do is play cattle queen all day? I do own most of the beef that's going."

"So you want to pull rank on me?" Devlin asked in a low voice.

The two women were toe to toe, hands on hips, staring one another down. Sarah flinched first. She looked up into the wounded blue eyes of her lover and realized how her last words must have sounded.

"I didn't mean it like that."

"That's sure how it sounded," Devlin replied.

Sarah thought she detected a note of hurt to the rider's voice. "I know. I'm sorry, Dev."

Green eyes filled with remorse as Sarah instantly regretted allowing her bad humor to speak for her. Sarah's temper created more problems than anything else on some days, yet the rider had become somewhat accustomed to her moments of fire. The incidents were usually short-lived and burned out in a hurry.

"It's just that– " Sarah began.

"*Sachu-kash*," Devlin interrupted the small woman with a touch of her hand, "remember how upset I was at the thought of you going through the rituals to become *Chahta*?"

Sarah grinned. "Hard to forget your reaction."

"But I agreed to stand behind you. I had to let you be the person you are. You may scare me half to death with your headstrong ways, but I would never ask you to be less than you are. *Sa*, don't ask me to be less than I am. I don't mean to say it like this, but I do know more about this than you do. Let me do what I do."

Sarah immediately felt any residual anger flow from her like water from an overturned bucket. She leaned forward, her head hitting Devlin softly in the chest. "I'm such an old shrew some times."

"You're not old," Devlin replied. She laughed and engulfed the smaller woman in a hug at the expression on Sarah's face. "*Sachu-kash*, you're the woman I fell in love with. I wouldn't want you any other way."

"Dev, are you sure I can't just ride along as far as– "

"Sarah," the rider drawled in warning. She took a step back and arched an eyebrow at the younger woman. "There is no way I'll be able to do my job properly if I'm worrying about you. And," Devlin held up a hand just as Sarah opened her mouth to speak, "don't tell me that you can take care of yourself and I shouldn't be worrying. It just happens to be something I'm good at and I do it whether you're with me or not."

Devlin held Sarah's face in her hands and kissed her lips. "*Sa*, I know it may drive you *loco* most of the time, and this may sound plumb crazy, but it feels good to have someone to worry about that way. Only this job is going to be the biggest thing I've ever done, and I'm going to need every last bit of concentration for it. Whenever you're around nothing else gets my full attention."

Sarah chuckled and covered the rider's hand with her own. "Well, if you're going to get all charming on me, I certainly can't be mad, can I, my *tashka*?"

"*Tashka*, eh? And is that the way you see me, as your warrior?"

"Absolutely. My charming warrior."

"I was kind of hoping you'd think that."

"Oh, you!" Sarah gave the rider a gentle slap in the ribs that caused Devlin to grab her and hold her close.

"I love you, Sarah," the rider whispered.

Sarah smiled into the kiss. "Love you, too."

"'Cause I'm so darned charming, huh?"

"And humble," Sarah added. "Dev," she made as if to push the rider away, "the men are looking at us."

Devlin looked over her shoulder to the nearest group of men and then back to Sarah. She kissed the young woman again. "I don't care. Let 'em get their own girls."

"Go on," Sarah responded with laughter as she pushed the rider back. "You and all that charm best get back to work."

Devlin was grinning from ear to ear when she returned to the fire where Hank and Matthew were branding and castrating spring calves. Every tenth bull calf that came through was released after branding, intact, to become a range bull. Matt had turned out to have quite some talent as a roper. He skillfully tossed ropes around the calves and dragged them over to one of the many fires where the men had branding irons ready.

Hank paused to wipe the sweat from his face with a large bandana. The heavily muscled rider hadn't been able to avoid overhearing the heated exchange between the two women, who had stood only a short ways off. He always laughed to himself because he figured it to be a kind of romantic justice that Devlin had finally met a woman that was as stubborn as she was.

"You talk her out of comin', did ya?" Hank asked.

Devlin stood up and tipped her hat back on her head. "Yep," she answered with a superior air, rocking back on her heels.

Hank knelt down beside Matt and winked at the boy. "Must have been a lot of bowin' and scrapin' on your part, I reckon."

Devlin eyed the two, who were kneeling on the ground and trying hard not to laugh. She burst out laughing herself. "You betcha," she exclaimed.

Donning her leather gloves, Devlin took one look at Matt's face and ruffled his hair. "Don't ever forget, boy, out here I'm in charge, but in there," the rider jerked a thumb back in the direction of the ranch house, "she's the boss!"

Sarah sat back in the soft leather chair. She closed her eyes and could still smell the faint aroma of cherry tobacco that her uncle used to smoke in this room. She didn't know if it was in her mind or if the odor still clung to the fabric of the curtains. The den had been the central point of operations for the ranch. Sarah remembered watching many an evening as her uncle worked at the very desk she sat at now.

With her eyes still closed, she heard nothing outside but the lowing of cattle as they settled to the ground for the night. They surrounded her ranch for nearly as far as the eye could see, penned within the temporary rail fences the men had built. Men came from as far away as Texas when they heard about the undertaking at the Double Deuce. There were jobs to be had doing just about anything. Thousand of rails had to be split for the makeshift fences. Devlin had insisted they use rail fences. She had explained to Sarah that if anything happened prematurely, charging longhorns would be able to stampede right through a rail fence.

Sarah had just finished writing the last of the bank drafts to their many creditors. Just the everyday operations on a ranch this size were expensive, but with the enormous task they were preparing for, expenses were colossal. She knew their ultimate goal couldn't be measured in dollars, but as she saw their bank account balances dwindle, she feared what would happen if Devlin couldn't make it to Abilene. She shook the negative thoughts from her head. Even if Devlin made it to Abilene with only half their stock, the price the railways were paying for beef would set the Double Deuce up for the rest of Sarah's life and then some.

True to her word, Cordelia Henley had persuaded every

rancher within a hundred miles to pitch in with them. Devlin had been right with her first guess; the entire stock came to about fifty thousand. Sarah had heard of a trail boss who had led fifty-two thousand head on a drive up the Chisholm Trail, but taking that many was almost unheard of.

In exchange for trailing their cattle to Abilene, each of the ranchers agreed to provide enough provisions and riders for one herd. That was considerable, since one herd would trail over three thousand head of cattle. That meant each rancher would provide at least fifteen to twenty riders, extra horses, a cook, wrangler, and all the supplies for the chuck wagon. Sarah was astonished when Devlin told her what they would need for the three chuck wagons her ranch would supply. She had no idea that many men could eat five hundred pounds of salt pork and two hundred pounds of beans, or that it would take nearly two hundred pounds of coffee to keep them going. After Devlin hired the cook, Sarah deferred to the knowledge of the man Devlin introduced as Mexican Bob and simply ordered the supplies he requested.

It took the better part of a month to round up the cattle from the various ranches after calving season. The Double Deuce had the largest acreage and the temporary corrals, so they herded the animals into the makeshift holds there. Devlin called the next process confused chaos. The riders herded small groups into a long narrow chute. As the cattle went through, one man called out the brand, one man counted, and one put a road brand on the animal just behind its left shoulder. The Double Deuce used a bar as its road brand, a sign to identify all the cattle as belonging to this drive. All the shouting took place at once, while at the same time some of the cattle panicked and tried to climb out of the confining chute. Matt earned his salt, as the riders liked to say, by being one of the information recorders. Since many of the riders could neither read nor write, a man who could cipher and knew his letters was invaluable during this process.

Everyone's temper ran a little shorter as riders worked with men they didn't know, each riding for a different brand. Each day after Devlin read the tally books, her expression grew a little more somber. As the numbers mounted, so did the rider's concern.

Sarah looked up and realized she'd dozed off.

"Caught ya," Devlin said with a grin. She lowered herself onto the soft couch, leaned her head back, and released a sigh.

"Yep, now you know what I do all day, just sit in here and nap," Sarah answered sleepily.

"I always suspected as much."

Sarah moved to one end of the couch and encouraged the rider to stretch out her legs. Devlin lay with her head in Sarah's lap as the blonde ran her fingers through the long dark hair.

"You're working awful hard," Sarah commented.

Devlin gave a half smile in agreement. "This won't feel like a thing compared to what I'll feel like on the trail." Sarah massaged her temples. "Mmm, you're gonna put me to sleep," Devlin muttered.

"It's okay, you need it," Sarah countered.

"No, not before I talk to you about some things." Devlin opened her eyes wide and sat up beside the younger woman. "I want to ask you how'd you feel about staying in the Thunderbird Clan's village while I'm gone. Now just hear me out before you say anything," she added, as Sarah was about to speak.

"But, Dev, I– "

"Please, Sarah."

"Okay, speak." Sarah gave in with a smile.

"I know you've run a ranch with a lot less resources than you have now, so that's not what I'm worried about. There'll be plenty of men we trust staying to work the small herd that we're leaving behind. I keep thinking about your Vision and what might happen if fire breaks out before I get back. I'd feel so much more comfortable if you were with my family. Besides," the rider grinned, "if you go through the rituals to become *Chahta*, I can marry you when I get back."

Sarah took a moment to let the rider's last sentence sink in. "Is that a bribe, Devlin, or a proposal?"

"That's a promise, *Sa*. Look, Sarah, I know– "

"All right."

"– you're independent and– "

"I said all right."

"What?" Devlin finally stopped to listen.

"Dev, I said all right. I agree." Sarah smiled in that way that made Devlin's tongue tie up so she couldn't speak. "I've been thinking about it myself and I think it's a good idea."

"Oh," the rider muttered. "Oh!" she exclaimed, a wide grin on her face. "So you and Hannah will stay with Tima. You'll be okay without me there?"

"As long as Tima doesn't throw me out for being too mule-headed, then I guess we'll be okay." Sarah laughed.

"Nah, remember, she raised me. She's used to a stubborn daughter. I have a feeling she's going to love spoiling Hannah."

"Will you be okay with me going through the ceremonies without you there?"

"I have to admit, if I was there, I'd probably do something to get both of us banished from the Clan. It's just something in me, *Sa*. I can't stand the thought of you in any sort of pain, physical or mental."

"It's okay, Dev, I understand." Sarah touched the rider's cheek with her fingers. "I may not show it the way you do, but I do feel the same way. You know there wouldn't be a safe enough place for *any* man to hide from me if he hurt you in any way."

"I know, *Sa*." Devlin kissed Sarah's forehead. She immediately flashed back to the look on John Montgomery's face when he looked down at the spreading crimson stain and realized that Sarah had just shot him in the chest.

"Do you think Matt will be okay with staying in the village?" Sarah interrupted the rider's thoughts.

"What? Oh, um, that's another thing I want to talk to you about, Sarah..." Devlin ran her fingers through her long hair. It had become an unconscious habit when approaching a delicate subject. "I sort of promised Matt that he could come on the drive. I mean, I told him only if you agreed, but he's got the smarts and..." Devlin's voice faltered as she looked at Sarah's stricken expression.

"But he's just a boy, Dev. It's too dangerous."

"Sarah, you're looking at Matt like a mother."

"How else am I supposed to look at him?" she responded with tears already forming in her eyes.

"He's going to be thirteen tomorrow. Hell, half our riders are only sixteen. He's a young man, Sarah. He's smart, respectful, and a hard worker, everything you taught him to be. Only now it's time to let him learn some lessons that aren't taught by you."

Sarah couldn't very well fight Devlin on that point. It was hard to run far from the truth, and she knew that every word Devlin said was absolutely true. It didn't stop her mother's heart from breaking, though.

"What would he do? Would you watch out for him?" she asked softly.

"Of course I would, *Sa*." Devlin sat back and opened her

arms for Sarah to nestle in. "I'll make him the wrangler for the herd I'll be leading. He'll drive the *remuda*, the loose horses. After he ties off the horses for the night, he'll help the cooks, wash dishes, gather firewood, things like that. He's not going to be doing a rider's job, I can promise you that. He'll start out at the bottom. I guarantee you that by the time he's done with one full day, going back east to college and getting a sit-down education will start looking mighty good."

They both laughed and Devlin wiped the tears from the corners of Sarah's eyes. "I'll look after him, *Sa*, I promise."

"I know you will, Dev, that's why I'm agreeing. Is that why you talked me into getting that quarter horse for him and why you bought him that fancy saddle for his birthday?"

Devlin grinned sheepishly. "Well, it's a wrangler's saddle, and he'd need a good strong horse, but I would have never said anything to him directly without talking to you first, Sarah. He's your son and– "

"He's our son, Dev," Sarah interjected. She bowed her head and took a deep breath before continuing. "Peter was a wonderful man, and I don't ever want either of the kids to ever forget he was their father, but you have qualities I want them to learn from, too."

"Me? I have ways you want the kids to take up?" Devlin asked in astonishment.

"Absolutely. You're smart, Dev. You know this land and you know people. You know how to deal with them. You work harder than any two people I know. You're a loyal friend and you have integrity. I want Matt to grow up knowing all those things."

Devlin didn't know what to say. She was sure that if she opened her mouth to speak she would start crying like a baby. No one had ever placed that much faith in her before and she was determined to be worthy of Sarah's trust. "I won't let you down," she whispered.

The exhausted women felt as though they had just gone to sleep when it was suddenly time to rise again. There was still much left to do before Devlin led the cattle out on the following day. At the noon meal, they had a small party for Matt's birthday, but Sarah and Devlin decided to wait until later in the day to give the young man his presents.

The rest of the day was filled with last minute details and organizing the herd. Devlin wanted to leave just after the herd had quit grazing in the morning, a few hours after sunrise. She ordered the men who would ride in the drive to camp with their herds that night, standing watch just as though they were on the trail. She didn't want any cattle spooked after dark. She told the rest of the riders to stand watch and all the men who were going on the drive to meet up at the ranch house in one hour.

Sarah walked into the corral just as Devlin quickly sidestepped a massive set of horns.

"Anabelle," Sarah chastised the large cow. The longhorn snorted air from its nostrils and stood still when it saw Sarah approach. "What are you doing to her?" she asked, knowing the dislike rider and cow had for one another.

"Anabelle's going on the drive," Devlin answered.

"Oh, Dev, you're not going to sell– "

"No, but don't think I didn't ponder it some." Devlin raised her voice and Anabelle snorted once again. Sarah thought the cow really did understand the rider.

"She's going to lead this drive," Devlin explained. "We don't have any steers who've made the trip before. As cantankerous as she is with me, Anabelle's the most unflappable longhorn I've ever met. I figure since she's the size of a buffalo, the herd will follow her anywhere."

"But what will you do with her when you come home?"

"Hank, Alejandro, and some of the other men said they'd herd her back, since Matt and I will be traveling by train. They'll take care of her at the stockyards until we decide what to do here."

"Okay, but don't get mad at her halfway there and sell her off, Dev," Sarah said in a warning tone.

Devlin grinned wickedly at the woman leaving the corral. "That all depends on how much fuss she causes me between here and Abilene." She laughed as Anabelle snorted and grumbled low in her throat.

Later, when Devlin finally stood up in the back of the buckboard wagon to speak to the men, she had to swallow down a bit of nerves. Sitting on the fences and generally milling about were all the men involved in the drive. She had a foreman, cook, wrangler, and nighthawk for each of the fifteen herds. In addition, there were a total of two hundred twenty-five riders. Although Devlin had personally hired every one of the men before her, she wanted one last chance to speak to the group that she'd be riding with on the trail. Sarah stood on the front porch, along with Cordelia Henley and a number of the other ranch owners.

"You all know me and what I'm about. You know what I can do, too. I don't tolerate laziness and I make quick work of troublemakers." She didn't have to explain the last statement. Any number of eyes quickly glanced at the gleaming six-shooters resting on each hip and understood her meaning.

"As you probably already guessed, this is one of the biggest herds to ever hit the trail. It's going to take a hell of a lot of work to make it to Abilene with them, but I don't have to tell most of you that. We've got some fifty thousand beeves out there. I've split them up into fifteen herds. You already know I'm the trail boss, but each herd's got a foreman who reports directly to me. When I'm not there, your foreman speaks for me. Each herd has also got a cook and two wagons. I happen to know a few of those chuck wagon cooks myself and they'll cook you up grub so good you won't even miss home. Of course, if any of 'em aren't so good I sure ain't gonna be the one to tell 'em." Devlin chuckled and the group of men laughed heartily. It was well known that even if a trail cook's biscuits were as hard as lead, eating hard biscuits was better than eating none at all.

"I plan on driving the herd pretty hard the first few days. I'm hoping that will tire them some by nightfall. They should be road broke in about three days' time. Remember, we're taking a mixed herd, not just steers, so we might end up with late calves. I don't want to hear of anyone shooting them in the mornings. We've got plenty of wagons, so if they can't keep up, toss them in a blattin' cart till the noon stop and do the same thing for the afternoon run. Try to keep your herd from widening too much, no more than a hundred feet across. Last thing, every rider gets his wages, forty dollars a month, plus a bonus when we get the beeves to Abilene. Anybody here have questions about what's expected of him?"

The group was silent as Devlin looked them over. "Then I suggest you make your way to your camps and settle in for the night. No music, no liquor. We start work at sunrise."

There were a few yee-haws from a couple of the Texans in the group, but the men were generally quiet as they headed for their assigned herds. Devlin accepted congratulations and good wishes from the ranch owners until she and Sarah finally found themselves alone on the front porch.

"Matt, come on over here," Devlin called.

Sarah put her arms around the young man and kissed him on the cheek. "Dev and I got you something special for your birthday, Matt."

Devlin whistled through her teeth and Hank led a muscular sorrel quarter horse from the barn. Matt's eyes lit up when he saw the mare and he rushed toward Hank and the animal.

"Mine?" He turned to look at Sarah and Devlin.

"All yours, son," Sarah answered. "Her name is Smokin' Molly. Although I don't even want to know why they gave her that name."

Matt looked the horse over, stopping to give her a scratch under the chin. "Dev, why's her saddle have a double cinch on it? I've never seen one like that before."

"Well," Devlin began, with a look at Sarah. The blonde nodded her head and the rider continued. "When a wrangler ropes a horse, he ties off his lariat to the saddle horn. 'Course, some of those horses are barely broke, so they still pull plenty hard. The double cinch on the saddle keeps 'em from pulling your saddle clean off your mount. I'm going to be pretty busy on this drive. Don't think I'll have time to be pullin' you out of every prickly pear patch between here and Abilene."

It took the young man a moment to grasp the rider's words. "For real?"

"For real," Devlin answered.

Matt rushed forward and threw his arms around the tall woman, which surprised Sarah just as much as the rider. After a moment's hesitation, Devlin returned the boy's affection wholeheartedly.

"Oh yeah, thanks, Mom, for letting me go." Sarah, unable to keep from teasing, stood with her arms folded across her chest watching the unexpected display.

Matt looked at Sarah with the same sheepish grin that Devlin usually wore. Somewhere along the line, the young man had begun to emulate the rider's charming grin. He gave his mother the same hug.

"Oh, yeah, thanks, Mom," he teased right back.

Sarah realized the young man was nearly as tall as she was. It seemed like such a short time ago that she'd been at least two inches taller than Matt. She smiled and stood on the first step of the porch. "There, that's better." She smiled and put her arms around her son's neck. She kept the tears from streaming down her face, but she wasn't able to keep them from forming in her eyes. "Okay, no growing taller than your mother."

"I'll see what I can do about that, Mom." Matthew laughed.

Sarah's face suddenly grew serious. "It's dangerous business out on the trail, Matt. You have to promise me that you'll do everything Dev tells you, exactly as she tells you."

"I promise. Don't cry, Mom."

"She'll be all right." Devlin stepped up behind Sarah.

The small blonde looked up into the rider's gentle blue eyes. "Dev's right. I'll be fine." She took a deep breath and smiled. "You better find out what you'll need to bring and where you need to be tonight. Sunup will come quicker than you think."

"Yes, ma'am."

"Hank's in the barn," Devlin said. "He'll be the foreman in our herd. He'll tell you enough to get you started and I'll sit down with you tonight. Okay?"

"Sure thing, Dev." Matt started to run toward the barn, but turned back. "I mean, boss," he added with a grin.

"Come on." Devlin put her arm around Sarah and started toward the house.

"Where are we headed?"

"I'm going to take a very hot bath and I was hoping you'd join me in our very soft bed," Devlin said in a low voice.

"Oh you did, did you?"

"Yep." Devlin pulled Sarah closer and whispered in her ear. "It's going to be quite some time before I get to see either of them again and I want to make tonight count."

Sarah smiled. "You promised to meet with Matt later this evening," she reminded.

"Yes, but that leaves an entire afternoon free." The dark-haired woman turned a sultry smile on the younger woman.

"I like the way you think," Sarah responded. "Let me check on Hannah."

After the two women ducked their heads into Hannah's room and assured themselves that the child was sound asleep, they made their way, arm in arm, toward their own room.

"Promise me one thing, Dev." Sarah walked with her head on the rider's shoulder.

"Anything, *sachu-kash.*"

"Promise me that even when our lives are filled with chaos and time is pulling us in about fifty different directions, like it is now, promise me that we'll always make time for things like this."

"This?"

"You know, stopping in the middle of the day to...to be together. To make love," Sarah admitted with a blush.

Devlin paused to run her fingers along Sarah's cheek. "I think," she reached out with her other hand to close and lock the bedroom door, "that will be the easiest oath in the world to keep. I promise," she whispered just before her lips met Sarah's in a kiss filled with a lifetime of such promises kept.

When the sun rose over the eastern horizon, anticipation dawned along with the new day. Even riders who were seasoned drovers felt the energy in the air. The cattle had been grazing for about two hours and Devlin took one last ride back to the ranch house before setting out.

"I was hoping you'd get back one more time," Sarah said. She stood on her toes to wrap her arms tightly around the rider's neck. "I love you, Dev."

"I love you, too, *sachu-kash*. Besides," Devlin bent down and scooped up the youngster who tugged at her pant leg, "how could I leave without saying good-bye to my two best girls, huh?"

"I'll miss you and I will be sad with you gone, Dev," Hannah pouted.

"I'll miss you, too, Princess," the rider replied with a catch in her voice. "I'll need you to help your mom not be so sad."

"Will you be sad, too, Mama?"

"Yes, sweetheart." The small blonde met the rider's eyes. "I'll be sad, too."

"Then I will help." Hannah smiled.

Devlin chuckled and shifted the girl into one arm, wrapping the other around Sarah's shoulders. "I want you to try and behave for your mama, okay?"

"Okay, I'll try, Dev, but it's hard sometimes."

"I know, Princess, but as long as you try," Devlin winked at Sarah, "then I'll be happy."

"'Kay. I love you, Dev." Hannah threw her arms around the rider's neck.

It took everything the rider had not to break down at the small girl's display of emotion. Devlin knew she would think of this later as the first time she'd actually felt like a part of this family. "I love you, too, Princess." She returned the strong embrace. "Now you run up to the porch. It'll take us almost all day to leave, so if you sit in the swing there, you'll be able to see everything. Okay?"

Hannah offered an enthusiastic smile and ran to the porch swing as fast as her seven-year-old legs would carry her.

"Don't you even think of not coming back home to me, Rider." Sarah tugged on Devlin's leather vest.

"Wouldn't dream of it," Devlin responded. "My heart will be with you, *Sa*, remember that. I'll always be watching out for you wherever you are." She held Sarah tighter and whispered into her ear. "Remember that I am Redhawk. I can float on the air and see for miles. Wherever your path leads, I'll be there alongside you. When you need me, *sachu-kash*, I'll be there."

Sarah nodded, fighting back tears. "If you don't go this very minute, I'm not going to let you leave at all. I love you, *tashka*."

Devlin smiled and held Sarah closer. She kissed the smaller woman just once, but it was filled with a fierce intensity. Just as the first kiss they shared, standing in town out in the rain, had brought them together, so this kiss reinforced that relationship. Each woman felt the arms of eternity embrace her as she looked into a future filled with a lifetime of the other by her side.

Chapter 9

"Line 'em up!" Devlin shouted back to Hank and the point men, who in turn passed the word along.

The swing men on the side of each herd shouted back to the flank men near the rear, and they alerted the drag men, who rode dead last and ate most of the dust from the trail. For the first week, extra riders would accompany them. The extra hands would then turn back once the herd was trail broke. With a combined herd this size, Devlin expected that to take about a week.

Devlin had ordered each foreman not to start his herd out until the tail end of the herd in front of him had been gone at least a quarter of an hour. She planned to move them fast at first. It would move the beeves away from their customary ranges and serve to tire the animals out until they were road broke. They'd be more tired at night and less likely to spook easily. Fifteen minutes could put a decent bit of distance between herds. She'd never trailed a drive this size, but she expected their herds would spread out for at least ten to fifteen miles, a fair piece on the prairie.

Yells, shouts, whistles, and the crack of cow whips filled the early morning air. Devlin had encouraged most of the riders to learn to use the whips as opposed to their six-guns for rousing the cattle. She knew it would cut down on accidents and save ammunition. Many men she rode with used their guns too often.

Her personal feeling was that it made it all that much easier for the rider to draw his gun on another man when disagreements arose. Devlin's cow whip was almost twelve feet long. She'd seen some men wield whips that were at least twenty feet in length. Made of tightly plaited rawhide, the whip ended in a wooden handle. She kept it well oiled and hung it on the pommel of her saddle.

Once the herds were moving, Devlin circled back to check on Matthew. The young man concentrated so much on the task before him that he never saw Devlin far off to one side watching him. His only task while the cattle herd moved was to drive the *remuda*, the herd of all their spare horses, two extra for each man. Devlin had hired a wrangler for each of the fifteen herds, knowing it would be a difficult job. Matt and his own horse worked well together, considering they only had one day to get to know one another. The rider watched a few moments longer before heading over to the nearest chuck wagon.

A team of four mules pulled the chuck wagon. As opposed to a farmer's wagon, the chuck wagons had wide wheels for better traction in open country. The wagon had bows over it, to which a canvas sheet could be tied to keep out the sun or bad weather. Since there hadn't been a drop of rain in a long while, the cook had packed the canvas away in the bed of the wagon.

Mexican Bob was the cook in Devlin's herd. Devlin was no fool. She liked good food and Bob had been a cook with Art Winston's trail drives. She'd heard Art say once that "Bob made biscuits so light, if he didn't put blueberries in 'em, the mosquitoes'd carry 'em off." Like other cooks, Bob made the rules around the chuck wagon, and even Devlin wasn't foolish enough to get on his bad side.

"Bob, I want to try to get a few miles away from the Washita before we break for dinner at noon. We can cross the river and go another six miles before we camp for supper. Have your nighthawk pass the word to the foremen and the other wagons."

"Okay, boss."

Devlin turned away from the moving wagon. She would have to get used to the men calling her boss. Whether they were serious or just having some fun, she was the trail boss and that meant that no one did anything on the trail without her approval. It was her job to ride ahead, scout out the best route, and intercept any possible trouble the herd might encounter. She also had to let the cooks know where to set up camp. The chuck wagons had to be at the intended campsite hours before the herd. Nothing made a saddle-tired rider forget his weariness faster than a good meal that was ready the minute he jumped off his horse.

After notifying Hank that she'd be traveling on ahead, Devlin set off north. The trail they followed wasn't that old, but the wagon ruts were visible enough to follow easily. Thousands of hooves had eaten the grass away as they tramped by on their way to Kansas. The best beef prices were in Abilene, and the only way for the Texans to get there was to come through the Indian Territory along the path that some riders called the Chisholm Trail.

There was nothing but prairie for hundreds of miles in any direction. Tall grass blew gently in the warm breeze. Patches of bluebonnets and Indian paintbrushes added color to the prairie. Usually, green grass would have been everywhere, but the rain had been scarce over the past spring. There was enough to last the herd until Abilene, but Devlin knew that if a bit of rain didn't ease the summer heat, Sarah's Vision might take place sooner than expected.

She rode all the way to the Washita river and marked the spot where the herd would noon. Having crossed the river, she made her way north into the Washita Valley and marked a similar place for the evening camp. The cooks would easily spy the red bandannas that she had tied to an Osage orange tree.

Carefully avoiding the two-inch thorns, Devlin searched the branches for any signs of leftover fruit. The horse apples, or hedge apples as the homesteaders called them, usually ripened to a bright green color in the late fall or winter. She slashed away at the surrounding branches to reveal a dried fruit still hidden away from the squirrels that voraciously ate the seeds nestled inside. This would probably be her last chance to find one of the fruit bearing trees along the trail.

In days past, the rider had never seen a tree like it outside of the Red River Valley in the southern part of the Territory. Nowadays, unscrupulous suppliers charged settlers nearly fifty dollars a bushel for Osage orange seeds. New wire was expensive, so farmers planted miles of the thorny hedge trees. The branches grew together and made a wall that divided the land and contained their livestock. The wood was the hardest thing Devlin had ever come across and she'd spent many a day earning a dollar by cutting the trees up for fence posts.

The rider sighed as she felt more than urgency and fear in

Sarah's Vision. She felt a sadness surround her. She realized that a way of life was disappearing for the Indian peoples within the Territory and for the cattleman. The settlers and the trains brought more people west every day, people who had no idea how to live on wild land. They came west looking for a land to tame. Devlin shook her head as she tucked the fruit into her saddlebag and rode away. *As if man could tame something as unbroken and wild as the land.*

Some of them were willing to learn that if they gave back to the land, it would share its secrets with them. There was plenty for all. That was the harshest pill for the rider to swallow, the fact that there were far fewer of these kind of men than the other– the men who felt that the land was merely a thing to be owned, to be bent to one's will; the men who believed that the world was only meant for those strong enough to take and hold it.

A bout of melancholy so soon? What will I be like after I've been away from her for a month? Devlin asked herself as she spurred Alto into a canter. She set out further north to scan the area where they would camp later. The most difficult task was deciding upon a decent bed ground for fifty thousand beeves to spend the night.

By the time Devlin reached Mexican Bob's chuck wagon, the first shift of riders was just sitting on the ground with plates full of biscuits and bacon. Their noon meal would usually be light, but suppertime was something the riders looked forward to with enthusiasm. One thing supper always included on the trail was beef.

The rider rode up the hill to where Matt had already set up a temporary rope corral for the *remuda*. Devlin paused before dismounting, watching the young man readying fresh horses for the first group of men who had come in to eat. A couple of the riders smacked the young man on the back as they handed over their mounts' reins.

"How was dinner?" Devlin asked.

"Good." Matt grinned.

The rider knew the nighthawk and wrangler ate before anyone else. To pay for the pleasure, they did just about every small, thankless chore there was on the trail. The nighthawk took care of the *remuda* at night. During the day, he washed dishes and drove the second wagon filled with the riders' bedrolls. When he and the cook arrived at the evening camp sometime in the middle of the day, the nighthawk found a quiet spot under a tree, if there was one, spread out his bedroll, and went to sleep.

"Did you give Bob a hand with the firewood?"

"Yep. I brought in firewood and told him I'd dig the trench for the fire at night camp."

"You're gonna wear me out just watching all that energy you got, boy." Devlin laughed. "Pace yourself, Matt. It's a long way to Abilene."

"Yes, boss," the young man replied with his customary grin.

"Keep Alto's saddle on, I'll be taking her back out." Devlin tucked the mare's reins into the empty stirrup. Alto wasn't a wild range pony. She would come when Devlin whistled for her.

"Okay," Matt replied. The novice wrangler was back at it as a few of the first dinner shift of riders strolled up the hill.

"Hey, partner," Willie Abbott, the left point man, called out to Matthew. "I need Belle. She's the white mare right over there." He pointed toward the back of the makeshift corral.

Devlin turned back to watch Matt. The fresh trail horses in the *remuda* were nothing like Alto. Those horses had quite a bit of rough left in them; they weren't about to come when called. What's more, they never let a man stroll up to them and put a rope around their neck. The feeling was that if a range horse allowed a man to get too close, it would be too easy to steal.

The rider watched as Matt twirled his rope a few times and effortlessly captured the dun mare. The horse pulled back by raising her head, but Matt had already braced his feet and begun to reel in the fresh animal. The young wrangler gave the horse to the rider to saddle and immediately hustled up his rope to catch the next animal.

Devlin turned and made her way to the chuck wagon and her own dinner. She couldn't help the somewhat uncharacteristic smile that graced her features. She would continue to keep a good eye on Matt, but at least she wouldn't have to worry so much about him. Matthew was shaping up just fine and Devlin felt suspiciously like a proud parent.

"You finally get hungry, boss?" Hank popped another sourdough biscuit into his mouth when Devlin sat down on the ground beside him.

"You too?"

Hank laughed, his brown eyes twinkling as he did so.

"Don't tell me you're missin' home already? We ain't even one day out."

"I was missing home the minute my butt hit the saddle this morning, my friend."

"Yeah, but just think of the homecomin' you two'll have." Hank waggled his brows.

"You got a filthy mind. Is that all you ever think about?" Devlin responded.

"Pretty much. And don't tell me you won't be missin' it. Every rider in the bunkhouse can hear you two when ya get goin' at night." Hank rose and dumped his dishes in the wreck pan by the chuck wagon.

Devlin's face turned into a look that Hank could only describe as sheer embarrassment coupled with extreme terror. He passed by the seated woman on his way back to the herd.

"Is that– " The rider nearly choked on her biscuit. "Is that the truth, Hank?" she asked quietly.

"Nah. I just wanted to see that look on yer face." The beefy rider tipped back his head and laughed loudly.

Devlin could never admonish her friend for his teasing, since his affable manner and laughter were always infectious. She laughed out of utter relief. "You're ridin' drag tomorrow, you son of a bitch," she called out, which caused the man to laugh all the louder.

Devlin swallowed the last of her food and tossed the dirty dishes into the wreck pan. The pile of dirty dishes awaited either the nighthawk or the wrangler's hands to wash them before the cook could move on.

"I marked a good spot for ya, Bob, plenty of brush for firewood. You need Matt for eatin' irons detail?"

"No, boss, Francisco will help."

Francisco was not only the nighthawk, but also Bob's son. He was a friendly enough young man, about Matt's age, whom the riders called Frankie. Devlin remembered the day she had hired the young man. At first, she'd been hesitant. She took one look at the scrawny youngster and shook her head. After Bob had his son demonstrate his talent with horses and his skill at driving a bed wagon, the rider changed her mind.

Once mounted, Devlin rode by the herds checking the cattle. When she saw some of them lying down, she knew they had grazed enough. She stopped and spoke to her foreman with instructions on crossing the Washita River.

Willow trees lined the red clay banks of the river. This would probably be the most uncomplicated crossing of the entire drive. Rain could quickly flood the river, but since there hadn't been any substantial rainfall in months, they would easily be able to ford the Washita.

Devlin led the way to a spot called Rock Crossing. The river was extremely wide, but halfway across, the riverbed changed from sand to hard rock. The cattle had few problems crossing the shallow water and Devlin ordered the men to slow their pace to almost a crawl to let the beeves drink their fill.

Six miles later, in the middle of a rolling prairie, Devlin sat astride Alto atop the highest hill. She took her hat off and circled it high over her head. Two miles away the point man saw her and gave the signal to Hank. The large rider waved until he was sure Devlin had seen him. Then he directed his men to drive the cattle to their bed ground for the night.

Devlin watched the herd below and breathed an uneasy sigh of relief; one day gone and probably forty-five more to go. She thanked the Spirits that watched over her for a first, very uneventful day.

Hours later, she watched as the men once again split into shifts to eat their dinner. The tempting aromas coming from the various camps made her mouth water, but the dark-haired woman rode around the encampments to check on the herds and the men before she stopped for her own supper.

When the exhausted woman rode into her own camp, she once again checked on Matt. Supper was the one meal the wrangler didn't eat before anyone else. Frankie was off somewhere curled up in his bedroll, catching what sleep he could before the cattle were bedded down and he would have to take over the *remuda*. This meant that once Matt had arrived at their campsite, a few hours before the cattle, he had a lot of work to do. He had to gather firewood, dig a fire trench for the cook, help to unload the chuck wagon, and if necessary, grind the Arbuckles coffee.

Devlin smiled to herself and wondered if the young man would have as much energy this evening as he did at noontime. She dismounted and unsaddled Alto before Matt drove his *remuda* into the rope corral. The men took turns getting their night horses. They saddled the animals and picketed them by wherever they threw their bedrolls.

Willie Abbott had just gotten a fresh horse at noon, but he had Matt place his white mare, Belle, back in the *remuda*. The rider saddled a different horse for the night. The drovers were superstitious when it came to white horses and lightning. Devlin had learned on her very first cattle drive that most of the men believed that white animals attracted lightning. She had openly scoffed at the notion until one night during a thunderstorm, while riding guard, she saw a bolt of lightning hit a white steer, and then jump to another white cow almost twenty-five yards away. It killed both beeves and set off a stampede that lasted most of the night.

"Well, you hungry yet?" Devlin asked Matt as Frankie took over the *remuda*.

"You know it!" the young wrangler replied.

"Me too, let's see what's on the menu."

Devlin had seen Bob butchering a steer earlier in the day, so she already knew what supper would consist of. For at least a couple of days after a fresh kill the men would eat son-of-a-bitch stew. Devlin had no idea where it got its name, but most said it had every part of the cow in it but the tail. It was a mixture of tongue, liver, heart, and all the rich parts that the cook had to use that day. Bob used only the juices from the meat, so it was the richest, most flavorful stew a drover ever ate.

During their supper, Matt and Devlin sat slightly apart from the other riders. It wasn't uncommon for the trail boss to remain somewhat aloof, and most of the riders already knew Devlin's reputation as a woman of few words. Devlin tried to take the time when she and Matt were alone to answer the young man's questions and teach him lessons that would help him on the trail.

After finishing the hearty meal, Matt helped Bob with dishes and cleanup. Devlin mounted her night horse and took off to check the herds. The rider gave directions to bed the cattle down on the high ground to take advantage of the breeze. She also set up teams of riders in each herd to be on stampede watch. These men didn't have to actually watch the beeves all night, but they would be the ones to jump in the saddle at the first sign of trouble. Devlin had learned years ago that it was easier to stop a stampede with only a few well-coordinated men than with a dozen yelling riders, all moving in different directions. She said a quick prayer that they saw no such trouble on this night or any other.

Devlin looked at the gold watch she always held tucked into her vest pocket. She could have guessed it was near nine o'clock when the first, or cocktail, guard rode out and all the other men rode into camp. By the time Devlin made it to camp, most of the men were either sitting around the wagon talking or spreading out their bedrolls. She watched as the cook turned the tongue of the wagon toward the North Star.

"Thought you'd be sound asleep already," she said to Matt.

The young man had placed his bedroll near the spot where Devlin put her own blankets earlier. "Guess I was too excited, ya know?"

"Yeah, I think I was the same way on my first drive. Feels like a hundred years ago, though."

"Do you mind? I mean, is it okay if I bed down here?" Matt indicated the area near Devlin's blankets.

"Sure, make yourself a space there." The young man sank down onto the blankets with a sigh. "Sure feels good at the end of the day, don't it?"

"You know it," Matt replied. He sat up and began to take off his boots.

"Sleep with your boots on for the first few nights," Devlin commented. "Till the beeves are more trail broke. The first few nights are when they're the touchiest. If they come runnin' over us in the middle of the night, at least you'll be ready to jump in the saddle."

The rider pulled a long-handled blade from a sheath on her leg and cut up the Osage orange fruit that she'd gathered earlier in the day. Since it had dried, it was tough to cut. "Here," she handed a few chunks to Matthew, "put these in the bottom of your bedroll. Make sure they don't fall out when you roll it up in the morning. It'll keep the bugs out of your blankets."

"Great. Thanks, Dev."

"You did a good job out there today, Matt. You got a real feel for the rope."

The sounds of the night guards mounting up and riding out of camp interrupted their conversation. Devlin flipped open the top case on her watch and noted the time.

"Do all the riders have watches like that, Dev?"

"No, this one belonged to my father." Devlin snapped the lid closed before Matt could see the inside. "Most of the men use the stars to tell time." She watched the young man's confused expression. "Look," she explained as she pointed into the sky, "there are some times the men always want to know during the night. First is ten o'clock. At ten, the first guard goes out, they ride herd for two hours before trading places with the next man.

It's ten o'clock right now. See the Big Dipper over there and the North Star in the Little Dipper?" She turned to look at Matt as he nodded.

"At ten o'clock the Big Dipper's handle is up and the dipper is down, like if you had anything in the dipper part, it would all run out. It's just northwest of the North Star. By four in the morning, the Big Dipper has rotated until it's horizontal, or like it was sittin' on a table. Then it's southwest of the North Star. Eventually, you get kind of good at splitting it up into two hour shifts. You already know the position at the beginning and the end. All you have to do is put two more spots in the middle."

"Swell," Matt said as he looked up at the stars.

"*El reloj de los Yaquis.*" Alejandro had been listening from his own bedroll and he turned to smile at Matt and Devlin.

"What's it mean?" Devlin asked the young rider.

"It is my language for your Big Dipper. In English, it means 'the Yaquis' watch.' It is what we use to tell the time." Alejandro once more offered up his customary amiable smile and rolled over to sleep.

"The Yaqui are the tribe he's from. They lived in Mexico, so I reckon they speak Mexican. You could learn a lot from him." Devlin nodded her head in the sleeping rider's direction. "Where he comes from they're not called riders. They call themselves *vaqueros*. I'll tell you, they are some of the toughest bunch of cattlemen I ever seen." She watched as Matt stretched his youthful frame out onto his bedroll.

"You may not know it, but longhorn aren't native to the Territory, not even Texas," Devlin said.

"Hank says they come from Texas. He says God created 'em there 'cause Texas was the only place big enough to handle 'em," Matt responded.

Devlin chuckled before responding. "That's 'cause that's where he was born. I never knew a Texan yet that didn't believe that God created everything bigger'n 'better in Texas. Truth is, before the white man was even in this country, back when the Indians where the only ones to tramp across the land, men from Spain came to this part of the country. Your ma ever teach you about Columbus and Coronado?"

"In 1492, Columbus sailed the ocean blue," Matt replied.

"Yeah, my mother taught me that one too," Devlin laughed. "Those Spanish fellows brought the longhorns here with 'em. 'Course hundreds of years later, the Mexicans and the Texans didn't think too much of keeping the longhorns as stock cattle. They were ornery creatures and lived in the brush, and I ain't talkin' about the brush we got at home. I've seen a full-grown bull hide in a patch of thicket and cactus that would make a starvin' bear think twice about goin' in to get him. Those *vaqueros* sure went in after 'em, though." Devlin removed her hat and settled into her own blankets.

"I spent some time down in old Mexico. I watched those riders down there work at night capturing them longhorns, but they called those wild ones mossy horns. They worked in the moonlight and they called it brush popping. First, they'd capture some wild mustangs to ride. Those brush ponies are about as fearless as the longhorns they were after. They loved to chase longhorns. Then the riders would get all dressed up, covering themselves from head to toe. They wore big, heavy chaps, a jacket, gloves, and even leather gauntlets to protect their arms from the thorns. They sewed on *tapaderos*, leather stirrup coverings, just to protect their feet." Devlin looked over to see Matt hanging on her every word.

"The *vaqueros* would take a tame herd of cattle and set 'em up as decoys. Pretty soon, they'd be able to hear them wild longhorns crashing through the brush. Then those wild brush ponies would go right into the thicket, tearin' after those cows. I saw men hanging on for their lives once those ponies took off. It was all a rider could do to stay in the saddle. Lot of men, ponies, and longhorns got killed that way. When they were successful, after they rode back into their camp, I watched those men pull thorns as long as your thumb out of those pony's hides. Now those were tough riders," Devlin whispered.

She turned to Matt and wondered how long she'd been talking to herself. The young man was now sound asleep, no doubt dreaming of being a rider. Devlin clasped her hands behind her head and listened to the sounds of the cattle. It would most likely be midnight before the beeves settled down and lay on the ground to rest. She looked into the night sky and thought of Sarah. She wondered if Sarah was asleep or if she was looking at the same stars at which Devlin gazed.

"Good night, *sachu-kash*," the rider whispered before she rolled over and went to sleep.

Chapter 10

Sarah stepped from Tima's *chuka* and raised her head to stare at the stars. She felt as she always did when looking into the night sky, as though she were rather small and insignificant in a world so large. She thought of Matt and Devlin, hoping they were safely asleep by this time.

Sarah sat upon the dry grass beside the *chuka*. The ground was still warm from the heat of the day. She brought her knees up to her chest and rested her chin there. Almost all of the cook fires around the village had grown cold. It was quiet, apart from the nighttime noises from the prairie. It had been too hard to sleep without Devlin lying next to her. It hadn't even been one full day since the rider and Matt rode off toward Abilene. Sarah already missed them both.

Sarah felt the gentle weight of a hand on her arm and jerked away, startled. "Goodness, *Nali*! You're going to have to clear your throat or something so I can hear you coming." She placed a hand over her heart in an attempt to return it to a more regular rhythm.

"I may move silently, but this time you looked as though you were miles away from this place."

"I was." Sarah smiled. "My mind is where my heart lies."

"And do I need to ask where that would be?"

"That's easy. Wherever Devlin is."

Tima squeezed Sarah's arm as a way of reassuring the young woman. "Perhaps you should give yourself some time, Sakli. Maybe tomorrow will not be a good day to begin your lessons."

"No, I don't want to wait." Sarah brushed her fingers through her hair and the unconscious gesture reminded the older woman of her own daughter's mannerisms.

"It's not that I want to rush anything. I know that you and Keeho have both explained that I need to work on developing patience. I'm trying, really I am. It's just that I want something to do, some way to move forward and tax my mind as well as my body. If I don't have something like that to focus on, I'll just worry and see monsters lurking in every shadow."

Tima nodded her head in silent agreement. She understood the young woman's reasoning. It had been many seasons past, but she remembered the first time Tekola went away with the warriors on a hunt. A full moon passed before she saw her husband again, and Tima had to keep herself constantly occupied for fear of giving in to her fears and worries.

"I'm a little worried about Hannah, though." Sarah voiced her concern about her daughter because she knew that Tima would have an answer for her fear. "Will she be all right while I have to be doing all this training and learning?"

"She had no problem seeing the Clan as family today, did she?" Tima asked.

"No," Sarah smiled, "she didn't." Hannah had refused to leave Tima's side once the youngster learned that the older woman was Devlin's mother. By the end of the day, Hannah was calling Tima "*ipokni*," or Grandmother. Tima seemed just as thrilled. She introduced Hannah to the women and other children of the village with great pride. Sarah was secretly delighted that Tima so readily accepted her children as a part of Sarah and Devlin's relationship.

Sarah and Hannah had arrived in the village earlier that day. Sarah had driven the large wagon full of supplies and items with which she wanted to trade with the Clan. The *Chahta* believed that a good trading technique was a mark of good character. Sarah was learning, even if on some days it came slower than on others.

Sarah also tied her new pony, Coal, to the wagon. He was a spirited gelding whose coloring was as black as pitch, hence his name. Sarah fell for the animal instantly. He reminded the young woman of her beloved Telemachus, whom she had to put down after he broke his front legs in a fall that nearly cost Sarah her life as well.

"Hannah is a good girl and very pleasant to get along with. She will enjoy having other children her own age to play with. When I am teaching you, Oka kapassa will watch over Hannah, as she does all the girls. When you are with Keeho, or away from the village, I will see to Hannah. When she is with me, it will be as if you have never left her side."

"Thank you, *Nali*."

A slow smile spread across Tima's face. "You have given my daughter something she has dreamed of all her life. You have taken her family into your heart and you have encouraged the children of your body to become the children of her hearth. It is you who deserves thanks, Sakli."

Sarah lowered her head, overwhelmed by the older woman's words. They sat together for a few more moments in silence until Sarah finally spoke. "What will we do tomorrow? How will we start?"

Instantly Tima became the teacher. Her face was a study in neutrality, her emotions well hidden. She patted Sarah's arm and then rose. "What will happen tomorrow is best left until tomorrow. Come back in and rest, Sakli. Your new life will begin soon enough."

Tima pulled aside the deerskin flap and entered the *chuka*. Sarah watched the retreating figure with a smile on her lips. One moment Tima could be the loving mother, and the next moment she turned into the plain-speaking Healer.

"She's right. I can't go all summer without sleeping just because Dev isn't here." Sarah sighed deeply, closed her eyes, and lifted her face to the warm summer breeze. "Good night, my *tashka*." She gazed once more at the stars in the sky and went inside. Although it was a long time in coming, sleep eventually captured the young woman.

"I already know how to braid, *Nali*," Sarah complained. "Is this a part of my training?"

Tima and Sarah sat outside the Healer's *chuka*. Tima also had a personal *chuka*. Medicine affected people as well as their lodgings. The Spirits and their powers could affect even inanimate objects.

It was an accepted practice among the Clan not to interrupt a Healer unless they called out to the passerby. Whenever Sarah sat with Tima beside the cooking fire of the Healer's personal *chuka*, there was much happening around the village. People stopped to talk, children played, and old women would occasionally nap in the afternoon. Now that Sarah and Tima sat beside the Healer's lodge, no one spoke to them or even came close. Sarah realized that this behavior was what she could expect for her future. She was now learning how to become *Chahta* and if she succeeded, to train as a Medicine Woman. Whether Sarah saw it that way or not, the people of the Thunderbird Clan looked on her as special.

"Even when we are learning there is still work to be done," Tima replied.

"So, am I working or training?" Sarah asked in confusion, her brows knit together.

"Is there a reason you must make a distinction?" Tima asked.

"Well, I– " Sarah didn't finish her thought. She knew what she sounded like– *Na hollo ohoyo*. She sounded like a white woman. Everything had to have an answer instead of simply being. Sarah mentally chided herself. She knew that the *Chahta* looked at the world differently than her people did. Daily Clan life was much more relaxed. Tima's matter-of-fact personality was similar to Keeho's; the Medicine People looked at life with even more of an accepting style. They realized that there were things in life that they could control and things they could not. They found no sense in worrying, expending energy, on matters that were beyond their reach.

Tima, satisfied that Sarah had found an intelligent answer to her own question, answered her. "You are not simply braiding," she said. She spread long, thin bundles of sweetgrass on a straw mat. "You are working *and* training. As a child, you learned to crawl before you began to walk. Now, you must learn to be *Chahta* before you can train as a Medicine Woman. You must learn our ways before you can hope that one of the Clan Mothers will choose to take you under her wing and teach you her Way."

Sarah nodded to show her understanding.

"Some of this grass we will leave in long lengths to dry. Later, we will use the dried grass to weave baskets to store clothing. Some of the grass we will use to fashion small baskets, or bundles, in which we place a newborn baby's navel cord."

Sarah worked with her hands and listened to the older woman. Tima hoped this technique would become a first step in focusing for the younger woman. Tima had learned as a young child that basket weaving could be soothing, almost meditative.

"You have heard me talk of the Sacred Hoop. Everything we do as *Chahta* has its place within in a circle. Today we create totems that we will use in ceremonies later. We braid the length of sweetgrass while it is still pliable. We tie it into a circle and hang it in the *chuka* to dry. These will be used to burn for purification." Tima took a few moments to show Sarah how to tie and tuck the ends of the braided length of sweetgrass. In no time at all, they had a small mound of braided sweetgrass hoops lying on the ground beside them.

"All of life exists within the circle," Tima said as her fingers worked without pausing. "The circle has many names, but it is most often called a Medicine Wheel. It is difficult for some to see. It is a way of thinking, thinking in circles. We humans are not the only objects to exist within the circle. Plants, animals, water, and fire, they are all a part of the Wheel. Every living creature, even the rocks beneath your feet, the four winds that blow in your face, and the seasons that change every few moons, these are all a part of the circle of life. Everything has a purpose and a reason for being. One cannot exist without the other. When one ends, another begins. Where there is death, there will always be life. Nothing ever ceases to be when all the parts of the Wheel take care to work together. We do not live in straight lines, but in circles.

"The Medicine Wheel can be a complex tool for the Holy Ones, but its concept and use are very simple to those of us who think of it in terms of our daily lives. We all enter the Wheel at different points at birth and spend the rest of our lives traveling around it. A cross divides the circle, which indicates the four directions– north, south, east, and west. Each direction of the Wheel governs a time span of three moons. The phase of the moon you are born under will determine those aspects of your life that the Medicine Wheel will dominate. For ages, we have used the Medicine Wheel to share Mother Earth's power. Through the Wheel, we find that we have certain strengths within us based upon our time of birth and position on the Wheel."

Neither Sarah nor Tima stopped their work, but Sarah listened intently as the Healer spoke. "We live in a world that is filled with opposites. For the darkness of night, there exists the brightness of day. There is fire and water, the sun and the moon. They are opposites and yet they exist together. The key to this harmonious existence between Mother Earth's elements is the same thing we strive for within ourselves. The Wheel reminds us of this concept. Through balance we achieve our ultimate goal of a perfectly natural existence as a part of Mother Earth."

"So, I spend my life trying to become as balanced as everything I see in nature?" Sarah asked.

"It is a concept the white man has found difficult. They wish to master the world around them. In reality, they should be learning how to master themselves. A woman strives to achieve balance within the circle by coming to know the warrior that exists within her just as well as she knows the feminine side of her being. The only way to change the world around you, Sakli, is to first change yourself."

Sarah nodded thoughtfully. She thought about herself and her personality. She'd always wondered where some of her traits had come from. Had it been a whim of creation or her place in the Wheel? She also knew that she indeed lacked balance in her life. She had been a victim many times in her life. When she met Devlin, she wished that she were more like the strong, fearless rider. After hearing Tima's words, Sarah realized that she could do with a few additional warrior-like qualities. Perhaps that was the reason she and Devlin made such a good match. Though they were opposites in many ways, there was a certain balance about them as a couple.

"Come, Sakli, we have as much learning as working yet to fill up our day." Tima smiled at Sarah, whose head appeared to be in the clouds.

"Yes, *Nali*," Sarah replied dutifully.

The teasing look in the young woman's eyes reminded Tima of her daughter. *Yes, they are truly a good match.* The older woman's smile turned into a worried frown as she walked away with her sack of sweetgrass braids. Thoughts of Redhawk reminded the Healer of the difficulties her daughter had experienced upon her own Quest to become *Chahta*.

Tima shook her head and bid the negative thoughts to flee. She would teach Sakli all she would need to complete her entrance into the Clan. It was up to the Spirits and Sarah's own strength to prevail.

For over a fortnight, Sarah worked alongside Tima. At night, she spent time with Hannah and rocked the youngster to sleep. Then Sarah's lessons would start in earnest. Tima would tell Sarah stories, and within each story would be a lesson. Tima explained what it was like to be *Chahta*, to grow up within the Thunderbird Clan. She told of their daily life and the beliefs that separated *Chahta* culture from other Indian tribes. Everything the Healer had spent years living out, she tried to teach to Sarah in only a short amount of time.

The Healer thought that at times she went too fast. She felt the urgency in her dreams. The Spirits told her to go as fast as Sarah could manage. Just when Tima would think that she had pushed too much on her, Sarah would smile as if ready for more. The young woman's nature allowed her to grasp the concepts and beliefs of the *Chahta* with amazing ease. If Sarah struggled with any of the *Chahta* traditions in comparison with her own people's ways, she kept it to herself.

Happiness as well as labor often filled Sarah's days. She was accustomed to daily hard work for her family's survival. Her adult life on a cattle ranch had taught her that, but on the prairie, she had been alone. Here in the village, the men and women shared their respective areas of work with the other men and women of the Clan. Groups of women gathered water, they tended crops of corn, beans, and squash, and they even took turns watching the children. Oka kapassa, one of Tima's sisters, had never married, but she loved children. She kept a watchful eye on them and told stories or taught basket weaving. Even though different women led group child care at times, all the children ran to Oka kapassa for special hugs or stories.

Oka kapassa made Sarah feel uneasy, but the blonde couldn't understand why she felt that way. The older woman was tall, thin, and strikingly beautiful. Sarah thought of Devlin the first time she met Oka kapassa. Even though Sarah knew that Tima and Tekola had adopted Devlin, she found a remarkable resemblance between the rider, Tima, and the Healer's other sisters.

Oka kapassa was a basket maker. While all *Chahta* women could create baskets, her work was exceptional. Her baskets told stories within their weave. Sarah spied Oka kapassa watching her on occasion. When Sarah caught the older woman's eye, Oka kapassa would simply look away. The woman's gentle manner and her loving actions when caring for Hannah were a paradox compared to her relationship with Sarah. When Sarah had to grind corn or make drying bundles from the plants she and Tima had gathered, she made a habit of doing her chores near where Oka kapassa was telling the children stories. The storyteller always filled her tales with laughter, love, and a lesson for young ears. Sarah couldn't have been happier with the way Hannah fit in with the people of the Clan. Sarah credited much of Hannah's good behavior to Oka kapassa and the woman's quiet strength. Still, there was always something in the older woman's actions toward Sarah. It was nothing overt, but it was enough to confuse her.

Finally, Sarah's special day arrived. This would be the day she would make her Quest to become *Chahta*. She would spend as much time as necessary at the Clan's sacred place. It was high up on the cliffs, among the ancient cedar trees. There she would make her pledge and offer prayers to the Spirits who led the *Chahta*. She would not to return to the village until she had received a sign of acceptance from the sky, where Hashtahli, the Sun Father lived.

Sarah awoke that morning full of nervous energy. By the time she finished feeding Hannah breakfast, she had developed a sick feeling in the pit of her stomach. She was worried how long her Quest would last. She remembered Devlin saying it had taken her a year of prayer and four days without food and water before she saw her Vision of acceptance.

Then there would be the doubts; *Keyuachi* was the word Tima used. The older woman explained that even the Sun Father had his enemies just as the *Chahta* had their adversaries. The *Keyuachi* were enemy Spirits of Hashtahli and therefore enemies of the *Chahta* people. They would come to Sarah as doubts. They would use whatever means they could to draw her from her path. Tima warned that they would tempt her to walk away from the *Chahta* Way, and their temptations would always be enticing.

Stay focused. Stay strong. Sarah repeated Tima's words like a mantra in her head.

"How do you feel today?" Tima asked the pale young woman.

"Like I'm going to throw up," Sarah replied.

"Good." Tima smiled and tenderly touched Sarah's cheek. The young woman cast an unpleasant glance at the Healer. "If you felt too good, I would think you were overconfident."

"I'm sorry, but I don't consider *not* feeling as though I'm going to lose my breakfast at any moment feeling *too* good."

"Here, drink some of this, it may help." Tima handed the young woman a warm cup of tea.

"Mmm, mint," Sarah responded. She murmured what she'd learned. "Mint is harvested in the summer when– "

"Sakli," Tima interrupted, trying hard not to laugh at the younger woman's grave expression, "it's not a test."

"Whatever it is, I'm going to fail. I'm going to do something wrong just like I always do."

"No, Sakli. There is nothing that can be done wrong. This is a Quest. You go to search. Answers may come to you, or they may not. There is no right and wrong. You are thinking like *Na hollo ohoyo* when you believe there is only right and wrong, black and white. Open your eyes and see the way Hashtahli intended for you to see, with the light of many colors."

"I'm afraid, *Nali*. I've never really said that before. I always pretend that I'm not." Sarah bit her lower lip.

Tima sat down beside the young woman and took one of Sarah's hands within her own. "Sakli, I will not promise you that there will be no pain associated with your Quest, but have you ever experienced something truly worth having that was easy to accomplish? You will walk from us today as *Na hollo ohoyo*, but you will return as a *Chahta* woman." She reached out and smoothed Sarah's hair away from her eyes.

"To fear something so important in your life is natural. I would think one weak and foolish who felt no fear at all. Your Quest today will be as if your old self has died. It will be painful as you experience the passing of old ways, but the result will be worth the pain. You will go through a life-altering process, but there is always pain connected with birth. You will be reborn and your fear will be forgotten in your happiness. Tell me, on the day when Hannah came into this world, were you afraid?"

Sarah couldn't help but smile nervously as she nodded her head. "I'd done it before, but when you're miles from nowhere with only a nervous husband for help...yes," she admitted. "I was terrified."

"But the fear you felt, this thing that had the power to terrify you, it could not last. Did it equal the feeling you had the first time you held your daughter in your arms?"

Sarah shook her head.

"Neither will your fear overwhelm you today. Fear is not bad, Sakli. It tells us when we have things that need to be brought into the light. They are as yet unknown to you, and the fear of the unknown is what terrifies us all. Deliver those fears to the Spirits, Sakli, and have courage. I have faith that your strength will carry you through."

"How will I know if Hashtahli accepts me?"

Tima smiled. "Your sign will come from the sky."

Sarah sat in the middle of the large Healer's *chuka*. The council of Elders sat around her in a semi-circle, three men to the left of *Miko* Kontonalah and three women to the right. Behind Sarah was the warm fire, its orange glow making strange shadows on the faces of the men and women who surrounded her.

The Elders gave Sarah instructions for her first Quest. They repeated much of what Tima had already taught her, but even so, Sarah listened intently. A trickle of sweat rolled down the skin between her shoulder blades. She wore a traditional *Chahta* dress, which fell to well below her knees. It was made of soft deerskin and dyed a deep reddish-brown color. Upon Tima's recommendation, Sarah wore men's leggings under her dress for the climb up the cliffs. Heavy knee-high moccasins completed her outfit, which was growing uncomfortably damp in the well-heated *chuka*.

Mantema came forward and sat down directly before Sarah. The older woman was quite short, but what she lacked in stature she made up for in girth. The young woman had rarely had an occasion to speak with the old woman, but she remembered that Devlin had said Mantema was responsible for the first tattoo a *Chahta* youth received. Sarah always thought about the pain associated with the marking, but today, that pain was the furthest thing from her mind. Devlin had told Sarah that Mantema knew, without anyone saying a word, which animal had selected a young person to be their guide, their chief Power animal. As soon as Sarah returned to the village from her own Quest, Mantema would place a tattoo symbol on her back, provided the Sun Father accepted Sarah as one of the *Chahta*.

Mantema brought out an old pouch made from some sort of hide. She had nearly worn the bag smooth with years of constant use. Sarah could still see the faint outlines of some sort of power symbols that had been painted on it at one time. The old woman gave the pouch a few shakes and untied the piece of rawhide wrapped around the top of the bag. She opened it and held it out in front of her.

Sarah paused and took a deep breath. She bowed her head and asked the animal Spirits to guide her hand to the totems of the creatures that would be good Animal Medicine for her. She reached one hand into the bag. Tima had instructed her to reach in and, without conscious thought, pull out the first item that her fingers touched.

She pulled out the first item and handed it to Mantema. One at a time, Sarah pulled seven icons from the bag. Some were claws and pieces of hide to distinguish the animal that the totem represented. Others were simply tiny carved fetishes. The old woman took each item and placed it within a coiled sweetgrass bowl.

When Sarah was finished, she sat back and watched as Mantema picked up each item. She held some for long moments while she quickly placed others on the skin side of a small buffalo robe. The hide was small enough to have come from a buffalo calf, but on the skin side, someone had painted the *Chahta* version of the Medicine Wheel. Like a compass, there were points indicating north, south, east, and west. Three more spots were marked with symbols that Sarah knew meant above, below, and within. Finally, when Mantema had laid all the items on the hide, she looked up at Sarah and smiled. She moved to one side so the Elders behind her could see. Some murmured a few words that Sarah couldn't make out. Others nodded their heads appreciatively.

"From the east, we receive vision and illumination. It is good fortune indeed to receive Owl Medicine. The owl can see in the dark and is a silent hunter. He represents wisdom because he can see what others cannot."

The old woman went on to describe the other animal Spirits that had elected to be Sarah's teachers, guides, and protectors. She explained each as if the Elders had never heard the information before. One by one, she pointed out the prairie grouse, swan, mountain lion, turtle, and ironically enough, the salmon. Lastly, Mantema held up a long object that appeared to be a bird's beak.

"The Within animal instructs you on how to find your heart's desire. This totem helps to protect the you that no one sees, the Sacred and Holy beliefs that you hold deep inside yourself. The hawk is your animal Within." Mantema paused as if to give her words time to have an effect on Sarah.

Sarah felt herself smile. She could have told anyone that this was true. Devlin's Clan name was *Hasimbish humma*, Redhawk. The rider's Power animal was the red-tailed hawk, and now Mantema was telling Sarah that the young woman's protector was the hawk. It made perfect sense to Sarah. Suddenly she didn't feel as though she was play-acting anymore. Sarah felt it now, felt the connection to the beliefs these people held so dear. She could never again count the occurrences of stepping into the Sprit world as coincidence. That belief elated and frightened her.

"The hawk Within will serve you well, Sakli. Heed its cry, for when the hawk cries out, there is danger at hand. Be aware and listen for its message." Mantema scooped all her items together and placed them once more into her bag. Before she rose, the old woman looked at Sarah. "We will see one another again– very soon. *Inola*, Sakli," she added, to wish Sarah good luck.

Sarah sat upon the rock ledge feeling somewhat disappointed. She had left the village determined to receive her acceptance into the Clan within moments of setting out. That had been almost five days ago. She was hungry, thirsty, sweaty, dirty, and extremely tired. Perhaps she should have been none of these things. After all, although she was forbidden to drink water from the stream, Tima had taught her how to collect the dew from the morning leaves and to chew on the pulp of the prickly pear to quench her thirst.

Even though she couldn't eat any of the plants or animals in the forest around her, she did have a small supply of *banaha* left. Of course, they weren't Tima's, which made them somewhat less appetizing. Sarah had learned to make the Choctaw bread, but her first efforts had been horrid. If she boiled the cornmeal inside the cornhusk for too long, once they hit the air, they dried into something akin to musket balls. Sarah had made the *banaha* she carried with her on this Quest. They were not as light and fluffy as Tima's, but her *Chahta* culinary skills had improved considerably since those first attempts.

She never did understand why she couldn't bathe, but as her mind wandered, she reminded herself to ask Tima about that. The leathers she wore smelled as if they'd just been stripped off some poor animal.

The forest was chilly, so Sarah sat in the sun, high upon a

ledge. She lay on her back and dangled her feet over the edge of the rock-face. She thought it odd that she should have feared heights before this. She rolled onto her side and peered over the cliff. The feeling of dizziness that used to accompany heights was no longer there. She absently flicked bits of rock and twigs off the rock ledge.

Lying on her back once more, Sarah looked up at the ancient cedar trees that surrounded her. Devlin had once told her that some of the trees up here in the Sacred Place were hundreds of years old and had never seen a white man before. Sarah nibbled on an oblong piece of *banaha* and kicked her heels, enjoying the sound her leather moccasins made as they scuffed the surface of the rock. She looked at the bits of green herbs in her half-eaten bread, wondering what kind of plant they had come from. Tima simply handed her the herbs and told the young woman to mix them into her bread. Whatever the mixture was, Sarah felt it helped her to stay focused. Immediately after she ate she would grow sleepy, but after only a few moments of sleep, she not only felt revived, but energized and able to think much more clearly. She was amazed at the ideas and problems she had sorted out during that time after she ate. The energy would last for hours, but then the depression would return.

Sarah tried to be strong against the *Keyuachi*. The doubts were strong and they loved to tease and tempt her. She had seen what they looked like. At first, she simply thought Tima's *Keyuachi* were an analogy of sorts, but yesterday Sarah convinced herself of their substance. She thought she could see them in the shadows. Sometimes they would offer a tempting meal or a cool cup of water, but Sarah stayed strong. When she thought of Devlin, it became difficult to remain committed.

"I will not go back. They'll have to come and bring my bones home because I'm not giving up," Sarah said aloud. Her brows knit together and she wondered how long she'd been waiting on the cliffs. "I wonder if they'll come and get me? Maybe they already forgot about me. Maybe Dev has too," she added softly.

She thought of Devlin and remembered the rider's strong arms around her. She remembered the pleasure of making love and the blue fire that seemed to light up the rider's eyes from within. It was during her thoughts of Devlin that she heard the music.

It started out soft and light at first. It was flute music, low and mournful. It sounded as if it came from somewhere high atop the cliffs. Sorrowful at first, the rhythm changed and the flute lightened. To Sarah's ears, the music sounded like it was now something happy and light, a dried oak leaf floating on billowy currents of air. Suddenly she felt herself as that leaf, blown into the water. She bobbed and fluttered, but remained atop the surface. She passed by smooth rocks rounded by the water's passage over time. She finally gave in and allowed the water to carry her along the top of the swiftly flowing creek.

Sarah opened her eyes again and realized she must have slept. She strained her ears to listen for the music. At first, she thought it must have been a dream, but there it was again. It wasn't as strong as before, but the unmistakable rhythms of *Chahta* flute music drifted down on her from higher up the cliff.

"Sarah..."

The young blonde sat up and looked around. She heard her name spoken in a familiar tone.

"Sarah..."

"Dev?" Sarah knew that was impossible, but she couldn't possibly mistake her lover's voice.

"*Up here, Sarah.*"

She looked around and caught a glimpse of a warrior walking up the path to the top of the cliff. "Dev?" she shouted after the familiar voice.

"*Follow me, Sarah.*"

She rose and hurried along the path, never quite able to catch up. The warrior was dressed as no one Sarah had ever seen. The outfit, even the paint disguising the warrior's face, was black and white. Eagle feathers and pure white buckskin contrasted starkly against the colorful autumn foliage of the forest.

Sarah had to scramble over the last few rocks to reach the top. She stopped short as she took in the sight. She stood upon a flat plateau of rock. It appeared as though it was another Clan's village. People went about their daily routines and Sarah looked high up another cliff wall to see that there were lodgings hewn from the face of the rock.

I am Ankahito...I have always been Ankahito.

The thought came to Sarah unbidden, and in her mind, she knew what the statement meant and why she said it. In her waking mind, however, she couldn't quite grasp where she had even heard such words.

The people of the Clan paid her no mind as they went about

their chores.

"*I am here, Sarah...*"

She spun around to find no fewer than twenty of the black-and-white warriors. They were all dressed and built alike. Broad shoulders tapered into narrow hips. Sarah couldn't tell whether they were male or female in their ornately beaded leathers. Long ebony hair fell to their shoulders and their faces were painted diagonally, half black and half white.

Sarah just now realized that the flute music had changed once she began climbing up the path moments ago to the pounding rhythms of drums. The beat grew more powerful and all at once, the warriors moved in a group dance. They moved in perfect synchronization. Not a step or a jump was mistimed. The dancing grew more frenzied and acrobatic as the drums beat out a wickedly intense rhythm.

"*Can you feel me, Sarah?*"

She wanted to turn around and look for the voice that seemed to come from just behind her right ear.

"*I want to be with you, Sarah. Come with me.*"

It was Devlin's voice, and just the thought of the rider caused Sarah's body to hum with the same pulsating rhythm as the music of the drums.

"*One more day...surely you can put aside this journey for one day...*"

Louder and more urgent, the music matched the way Sarah's body felt.

"*...to be with me.*"

"I– " The music hit a deafening crescendo. Sarah whipped her head around only to find empty space behind her. She returned to scan the dancers and before her, inches away, stood her warrior. The warrior stood with head bowed and even had Devlin's distinctive scent.

"*Tashka?*" Sarah asked.

Eyelids painted black slowly rose to reveal cornflower-blue irises. "*Give up your fool's journey, Sarah. Come be with me.*"

Sarah watched as a strong arm extended forward and an open hand reached out to her. She became lost in the beauty of those blue eyes. She knew in that instant that she would give anything up for her warrior. She reached out her hand and the warrior smiled as Sarah drew closer.

Give up anything? Give up? Sarah thought.

Sarah jerked her hand back, but the powerful pull of the

warrior's eyes had her trapped. Suddenly there was a high-pitched keening sound and Sarah covered her ears in pain. When she looked into the warrior's eyes once more, they were no longer the deep blue she had remembered. She took a step back in shock and fright. The warrior's eyes had turned completely yellow with a reptilian slit in the middle.

From somewhere above her she heard a scream. It was deafening to her sensitive ears and she looked up. When Sarah craned her neck, she looked into a blue, cloudless sky. High above her a large hawk circled. It swooped toward her and cried out again.

Looking around, Sarah found herself completely alone on top of the cliffs. Gnarled old cedar trees, whose trunks looked as though they had been pulled and twisted like soft molasses candy, surrounded her. She dropped to the ground, unable to stand any longer.

The hawk screeched loudly once more. It was perched in one of the old cedar trees whose top had been sheered off by wind, ice, or both. The hawk hopped from the limb and easily opened its wings to take flight. It soared high into the sky until Sarah had to lie on her back to see it. She heard the hawk's cries as it appeared to fly all the way into the sun. The brightness of the light blinded her and she held up a hand to ward off the glare. In the shadow caused by her hand, Sarah was able to see what she would come to think of as the first of many miracles in her life. It floated down at her slowly and steadily. A few moments later, a beautifully pristine hawk's feather wafted down onto her chest.

She held it in her hand and examined the reddish-brown side in contrast with the white side. It appeared to have lines waving through it. Sarah rolled over on the smooth rock, unable to keep her eyes open. She would have to examine the trap, which she had narrowly avoided, later. She had only averted her thoughts at the last moment due to the warning cries of the hawk. Otherwise, she would have given in to the *Keyuachi's* trick. Within her hands she clutched the red-tailed hawk's gift, her sign of acceptance from the sky, where Hashtahli, the Sun Father, lived. Devlin's parting words came to Sarah as she fought to keep her eyes open.

Remember that I am Redhawk. I can float on the air and see for miles. Wherever your path leads, I'll be there alongside you. When you need me, sachu-kash, *I'll be there.*

"Thank you, *tashka*," Sarah whispered. She smiled as her eyes closed.

Chapter 11

Devlin rolled over and spied the last two guards waking the cook before they headed towards their bedrolls. They didn't even bother to remove their hats, knowing they only had another hour or two before breakfast would be ready and they would be back in the saddle again.

Devlin closed her eyes and attempted to ease herself back into sleep. They had been on the trail for a little over a fortnight now and she had yet to spend a night sleeping well. She hadn't really expected it to be any different. Hadn't she anticipated dreaming of Sarah every night? Last night's dream, however, had seemed frighteningly real. Devlin grew up around people who took dreams very seriously. Wondering whether Sarah was in trouble, and being unable to do anything about it, made the rider surly.

Being the trail boss did have its advantages. At least Devlin didn't have to wake up in the middle of the night to ride herd for two hours at a time. Still, while others lay snoring in their bedrolls, Devlin heard every rider come into camp during the night. She was a light sleeper at the best of times, but since the drive started, she was aware of everything that happened around them, especially at night. She had come to recognize the sounds particular beeves made as they situated themselves on the bed ground and she could differentiate between the various riders by the sounds they made when they rode back into camp.

She lay there, staring into the dark sky. She watched as the darkness faded into a light, predawn gray. She ran through the trail in her mind and what she would run into with the coming dawn. Every day that passed without running into hostile Indians was a good day for the rider. Two men had been trailing them for a couple of days, and she expected a Comanche party to ride up any day now.

The trail so far had been routine and every drover felt blessed because of it. After crossing Walnut Creek, they'd ridden through at least ten miles of barren prairie before coming to the South Canadian. Oak and cottonwood trees lined the river, and the south bank had afforded them a good camping ground. Mexican Bob had found an immense thicket of wild plums. He and Matt gathered enough of the ripe fruit to make fried pies, which encouraged the men greatly. Thirteen miles later, they crossed the North Canadian River, which was when they had picked up the two Comanche scouts.

There had been plenty of grass for the beeves and firewood for the cooks. The riders were able to add a little variety to their mostly beef diet by doing a little hunting along the way. The upland plains leading to the Cimarron River yielded prairie chickens, deer, and an occasional antelope. The morale of the men had been relatively good, but Devlin knew they were still a long way from their goal. A lot could go wrong between here and Abilene.

"Come a-runnin', boss, there's bacon in the pan," Bob called out.

This first shout meant that Devlin, Hank, and the point men could eat breakfast. The other riders moved slowly, getting dressed, cleaning up, and picking up their bedrolls. Devlin tied her own bedroll and dropped it beside the chuck wagon. The wrangler or nighthawk would gather the bedrolls and load them onto the cooney, a cowhide suspended by its corners and slung under the chuck wagon. Most of the time it held firewood or buffalo chips as an emergency fuel supply.

Usually Frankie, their nighthawk, would have carried the bedrolls in the second wagon, but just as Devlin had predicted before starting out, they had to turn the second wagon into a blattin' cart. The blattin' cart was filled with only one thing during the day— newborn calves that were too little to keep pace with the herd.

Devlin sat in silence and ate her breakfast as she watched the riders load the calves into the wagon. They had to take care, as Devlin had instructed Matt and Frankie the day after they started out. Cows often gave birth to late calves, and when the beeves rose from the bed ground in the morning, there the little ones would be. Devlin had been on a few drives where the trail boss ordered the calves shot and buried, so the cows couldn't find them. It had become a common trail drive practice, but she could never see the sense in it.

Each morning as the beeves were grazing, a rider roped the newborns and carried them off to the blattin' cart. There weren't too many of them, maybe five or six. Frankie, who drove the wagon during the day, kept a burlap sack marked with each calf's nickname or a number, something to identify them. A good rider always knew his cattle, and when he rode up to the wagon with his package, he called out the calf's marker. They would wrap the burlap sack around the calf and toss the little one into the wagon. The sack was an important step. A cow wouldn't tend to her calf if it had another calf's smell on it and that was unavoidable in such a small wagon, so each day the rider wrapped the calf in the same sack. At noon and again at the end of the day the riders brought the calves to their mothers to feed.

Matt woke with the other riders and stuffed his hat over his unruly hair. He gave Devlin a sleepy smile and went off to relieve Frankie of the *remuda*. The nighthawk would then sleep for a few hours before driving the second wagon. Devlin, Hank and the point men, Willie and Jake, finished their meal and went out to watch the herd as they rose from the bed ground. While the riders ate their breakfast, Devlin and her group kept an eye on the grazing herd.

Over the next few hours, Devlin rode around the herd, checking on the beeves that she could now recognize by sight. Out of a few thousand, she could easily identify the troublemakers, the slowest, even the most aggressive. Then there was Anabelle. To the dark-haired rider, it was as if the massive cow snorted and feigned swinging her wide set of horns at Devlin whenever she passed by. Devlin would grumble and curse the cow under her breath and Anabelle would snort so hard that dust blew all around her.

The point men positioned themselves back quite a bit from the lead steers so that the cattle could spread out and graze at their own pace. Devlin pulled every trick that she could think of out of her hat to keep the beeves happy and content, and she saw that the other foremen did the same. She wanted to get to market with as many of her original fifty thousand head as possible.

The riders finished their morning meal and took their places in the herd. The point men always stayed the same. They were trusted hands who knew the ways of cattle and who could act as if they had a brain in their head if trouble started. The swing men and the flankers rotated position every day. The drag men, unfortunately for them, always rode in the same spot.

The draggers rode dead last, waiting for the slowest or injured among the herd. All of them wore large bandannas across their faces, covering mouth and nose. They ate the dust created by thousands of hooves. When the herd stopped and the drag men came into camp, at least an inch of dirt and dust covered them from head to foot. The draggers were only one step above the wrangler on the pay scale, but they took pride in calling themselves riders all the same.

Devlin rode back into camp once the drovers eased into place around the herd. She shook her head at Matt, who was up to his elbows in soapsuds. He washed dishes for the cook with the same enthusiasm with which he rode herd over his horses.

"You wear me out every time I watch you work, boy," Devlin said as she passed.

Matt looked up, grinning as he wiped some foamy soap from his chin. He knew it was a compliment when Devlin teased him like that. The rider gave out little praise and never falsely. When she did, it meant a great deal to the recipient.

Devlin felt a particular pride at the flattering remarks she received about Matt. The riders gave him a little grief, but that was because of his age. It was a rite of passage among riders, but they were the first ones to answer Matt's questions, teach him how to do something new, or watch his back when trouble arose.

Devlin dug into her war bag, as the riders liked to call their meager bag of personal possessions. She pulled out her light canvas jacket and an old cotton shirt, then removed the tight-fitting leather vest and shirt she wore. Clad only in her light cotton undershirt, she removed her hat and sat down to braid her ebony hair into one single braid that hung flat down her back. She then put on the cotton shirt, which was baggier than the shirts she usually wore. Finally, she put on the loose jacket and placed her Stetson upon her head.

Matt met the rider with Alto saddled and ready for the day.

"You gonna ask why I'm dressed this way?" Devlin asked.

Matt shrugged his shoulders. "Figured if it was important, you'd tell me."

Devlin wondered what Sarah would think of her son now. She realized the boy was becoming more like Devlin every day. His mannerisms and the silent way he worked by himself made Devlin feel as if she were watching her own flesh-and-blood son.

"There've been a couple of Indians trailing us since we crossed over the Canadian. I can't tell what kind, they never get close enough. I expect Comanche or Kiowa."

"What do they want?"

"Probably just some beeves. Look, Matt, I've got a strange feeling they might approach today. It would be a good spot for them to cause trouble if they've a mind to. We're a few days away from the Cimarron River and there's a lot of trees and thickets over this prairie."

"Will they start trouble? Are they hostile, Dev?" The young man tried not to let the news affect him, but there was worry in his eyes.

"No way to tell if they're friendly or not until they're right up on you. I guess we'll know the answer to that question if they try to steal our cattle instead of ask for some."

"Why don't they just bargain like the *Chahta* do?" Matt asked.

"They got nothin' to barter with. This," Devlin motioned with one hand, indicating the area around them, "the Indian Territory, was all supposed to be their land once, but now the government says that the Indians have to stay in small areas called reservations. It's hard for them to change their way of life. Hell, it's not just a way of life, but there's pride involved. They're used to following the buffalo herds and living as free as the Spirits intended them to live. Now the buffalo have moved on, but the Indians aren't supposed to leave the reservations. The government treats them like children, not men. So some of them, mostly the young ones with short tempers, they took off and left the reservations." The rider checked her pistols, seeing to it that the six-guns were fully loaded.

"It's hard to know what they want anymore, Matt. I used to know a fair amount of them. I think most just want to feed their families. I can't say as I'd do any different. Some of them, though, want to make everyone pay for the white government's actions. These people have been lied to, cheated on, stole from, and damn near exterminated." Devlin sighed deeply. "It doesn't make killing women and children right, but it gives you a small look at why they're so angry. There are some of them, though, that are way past talking reason. Those are the ones I'm the most worried about."

"Dev?" Matt asked.

"Yep?"

"So, why are ya dressed that way?"

Devlin hopped into the saddle and grinned. "I'm gettin' like your ma, all chatty and going on and on. I figure today, at the latest tomorrow, we'll have a party of riders approach us. The Kiowa and Comanches are pretty similar when it comes to the way they look and dress. If they're Kiowa, chances are they'll have hair plates on. You'll be able to see a long rawhide strap, sometimes hanging all the way to the ground, tied to their scalp lock. It'll have silver disks tied to it, kind of like the belts some of the *Chahta* wear. Sometimes the Comanche go in for the hair plates, but not like the Kiowa do. The one sure way to tell a Comanche is by the way he dresses. A lot of them wear white man's clothes now, but the one thing they always have on is a breechclout. Even if he's wearing pants and a shirt, like you are now, he'll still have on a breechclout."

Devlin looked down from her vantage point atop Alto into Matt's intent face. "You just leave it to me to recognize who's who. Okay?"

"Okay, Dev."

"You only have to remember a couple of easy things and that's it. Think you can?"

"You bet," Matt answered.

"First off, even if they're hostile Indians, they're not going to go up against as many guns as we have. Their tactic is to usually ask for what they want. If you aren't fair with them, and they think they can get away with it, they'll come back at night and stampede the herd. While we're out chasin' beeves, they'll cut out the cattle they want and take off. So the first thing is not to cheat them, but that doesn't mean I aim to give 'em the whole store.

"What they'll want more than anything is stuff they can only get from white men— horses, guns, whiskey, and tobacco. What I expect they'll do is do come up on the *remuda* first. If they're Comanches, then they'll be the most talented horse thieves and shrewdest traders around. Don't get frightened, even though the looks of some of them are enough to make you want to piss your pants. You won't understand what they're saying unless they have someone who speaks English with them. It doesn't matter, though. No matter what they say or how much they point to the horses, you only do one thing."

"What's that, Dev?"

"You point to me. You're probably wondering why I don't just come and help you– "

"I'd look weak," Matt replied without missing a beat.

Devlin smiled at the boy. *Yep, he's coming along.* "Yeah, that's part of it. If they think I'm the one they have to deal with, well, we want them to come to me. It's just one of those little things you do when you're dealing with people. It kinda gets the power goin' in your direction." Devlin winked. "Most importantly, we want them to think I'm a man."

Matt's eyes lit up with understanding. "Oh," he drawled, "that's why you're dressed like that."

Devlin winked again. "It makes things easier sometimes, if you know what I mean. No matter what they say, just point to me and call me a man or even use the *Chahta* word. You remember what that is?"

"*Nakni*. Yep, I get ya, boss."

"You think you can do this on your own, Matt? You know, there's no shame in saying you can't. I'd rather have you tell me now– "

"You can count on me, Dev," Matt said quickly.

Devlin looked at the fierce determination in the boy's eyes and knew immediately where she'd seen that expression before. Even though his face was beginning to lose some of its boyish chubbiness, he had his mother's eyes. The hard, angular chin that he was beginning to develop and the way his nose crinkled up when he smiled only added to the resemblance. At that moment, he had the same firm set to his jaw that Sarah took on whenever she set her mind to a difficult task. Devlin rather doubted that she would ever tell the boy that, but there was something comforting about the fact. Something secure in knowing that a little piece of Sarah rode with her.

"The second thing you do is under no circumstances do you draw that rifle." Devlin pointed to the rifle that lay flat in a cowhide case near Matt's saddle. "Not even if it looks like they're ready to attack. If someone aims an arrow or a gun at you, dive off your horse and use the animal's body to protect you. If a commotion breaks out, then you hightail it over to me. Got that?"

"Sure, Dev, but I'm a good shot." Matt was proud of the skill that his mother had taught him and the prized Winchester she'd given him for the trail.

"You may be good, boy, but they'll be better. I guarantee it. When a man holds a weapon in his hand, it puts a big target on his chest. The longer you can go through life without drawin' a gun, Matt, the longer you'll live. Are we clear?"

"Yes, boss," Matt answered with a resigned tone. He had promised his mother he would do everything Devlin told him. Matt may have been young, but there were two truths that he had already grasped in his young life: a man doesn't break a promise to his mother, and he never, ever crosses Devlin Brown.

Devlin wondered what Matt was thinking as he walked back to the chuck wagon to help the cook with any leftover chores before rounding up his *remuda*. "Probably cussin' me good," the rider mumbled as she rode north.

They had watered the herds at Kingfisher Creek earlier in the day. Devlin thanked whoever needed to be thanked in the heavens above her for keeping the land dry. When she thought about it, though, the lack of precipitation was why they were in this fix in the first place, but rain on a trail drive could be disastrous. The creeks heading up to the Cimarron and all the way to Nine Mile Creek had banks made of quicksand. In the rainy season it was almost impossible to water a herd, let alone cross.

When they'd reached Kingfisher Creek, Mexican Bob watered the chuck wagon's mule team first. He filled the water barrel, then made way for Matt and the *remuda*. Finally, the drovers allowed the cattle in, a little at a time. Always last on the list, of course, was the trail crew.

Right after the noon meal, just when the herds had been underway for a mile or two, Devlin's anticipation became reality. She watched from a high sandstone summit as the scouts who had been trailing the herd joined up with a small band of their friends. They took no notice of Devlin, and she waited patiently until the band split into three groups. When they moved in the direction of the cattle, Devlin quickly ate up the distance back to the first herd.

"I hate bein' right," Devlin said to Hank as she rode up.

"Been watchin' the closest two for quite a spell," Hank answered. "I wondered when you were gonna join the party."

"Wouldn't want to miss all the fun," Devlin answered in a distracted voice as some of the Indians headed straight for the *remuda*. She cursed herself for leaving Matthew alone. Even though he'd said he could handle it, Devlin was beginning to second-guess her earlier decision. She had wondered early on if bringing the boy would affect any of the decisions she would need to make. She was about to find out.

Devlin watched out of the corner of her eye even as the small party approached her from the front on horseback. She could see Matt warily shaking his head and pointing her way. He never made a move that could be mistaken as hostile and the three, whom Devlin now identified as Comanche, made their way to where she had stopped her horse. The herd kept moving but Hank and the point men, along with one or two of the flankers, pulled away from the cattle to mill about behind Devlin.

Devlin fixed a disdainful scowl upon her face and waited in her saddle. She rose up slightly, placing her weight on the balls of her feet. Two younger men flanked the brave that approached her, who appeared to be around Devlin's age. She easily recognized the signs of anger and wariness in the Indian's expression. He wore his hair separated and tied into two braids on each side of his head. His shirt was made of heavy buckskin, fringed sleeves coming to a v-shape at the back of his neck. Typical of Comanche dress, the brave's shirt was long, falling nearly to his knees. His leggings were fringed and tightly fitted and a breechclout hung from his waist, under the shirt.

Devlin wondered at the party's style of dress. Usually the Comanche, Kiowa, and Apache wore everyday or plain shirts, when they wore them at all. This band all wore what the *Chahta* would describe as dress shirts. Painted symbols or intricate quill and beadwork adorned all the outfits. The leader's shirt bore yellow jagged lines along the front. Devlin recognized the symbol from Shoshone outfits. For some reason, this Comanche owed some respect to lightning, having paid homage to it upon his shirt.

The leader made a sign with his left hand, holding his palm out and moving it forward and back. Devlin, through her association with the Shoshone, knew a small number of hand signals and words that the Comanche would understand. The leader was beckoning her to stop.

"*Yatahe*," Devlin said. She purposefully lowered her alto into a more powerful bass pitch.

The leader squinted his eyes as if he recognized Devlin. He gazed at her for a full minute before appearing to accept her as the leader of the massive herd. The Comanche leader didn't speak, but once more raised his hand to her. He held his palm outward, moving his hand back and forth.

"*Chahta*," Devlin answered. The hand signal was an easy one, asking who she was, and she was relieved. "*Hasimbish humma*." Devlin added the name "Redhawk" in Choctaw.

They stared at one another and Devlin prayed the drovers behind her remained patient. She could hear the soft sound as their horses tossed their heads and stamped their hooves in the dirt. Obviously, the Comanche leader wasn't one for small talk.

"*Seemote*," he requested forcefully.

"No." Devlin shook her head at the man's request for ten beeves. She was, essentially, on their land, but she was also aware that if this small raiding party felt that she was a soft touch, they would be by every day for more cattle. She would have given them a hundred head of cattle if she thought it would feed their women and children, but the time had passed for such charity.

"*Wahatehwe*," Devlin said as she held up two fingers.

The leader looked as if he would have liked to bargain further, but he risked a glance behind Devlin. The heavily armed riders made an impressive sight. Not wishing to risk using the few bullets his small party had left, the Comanche leader nodded his head once. He motioned with one hand to his fellow braves, who swiftly headed toward the front of the herd to cut out their payment.

It was obvious they had done this before. The young men knew that the biggest, strongest steers were at the front of the herd. That was the funny thing about cattle on a drive like this. The strongest of them stayed in front, setting the pace. If they became sick or injured along the way, they slowly moved toward the back of the herd. Once they were feeling in shape again and able to pick up some speed, they made their way back to their original place in the herd.

Devlin heard the high-pitched bleating of a cow and looked over her shoulder. The braves were trying to cut Anabelle from the herd. They were having a hard time of it, but seemed determined to take the largest beeve of the lot.

"Not that one," the rider shouted over the din. The warriors looked over at her and she realized that they spoke English. "Leave that one be." Devlin pointed at Anabelle, who was dangerously close to goring one of the Comanche horses.

The warrior closest to Anabelle ignored Devlin's shouts and pulled his bow from across his back, swiftly notching an arrow onto it. Devlin instinctively reached for her six-gun. The entire time her hand was moving, she kept reminding herself that going into an offensive mode might spell the end for all of them, but she couldn't get Sarah out of her mind. Devlin could only see the look of disappointment on the blonde's face as she explained how she had let a few Indians butcher Sarah's beloved Anabelle.

Devlin could hardly believe it herself as the report of her Colt rang out and the flint head snapped from the arrow's shaft. Immediately, Indians and riders drew their weapons. It was a testament to each side that neither party seemed willing to begin the bloodshed.

Devlin quickly holstered her pistol and jumped off Alto's back, rushing to Anabelle and the Comanche warriors. "No, no, no," she shouted, waving her hands. "No fight...just not this cow."

The leader urged his horse closer to Devlin and glared at her. He seemed unable to discern whether Devlin was trying to cheat him or if she was simply unbalanced.

Devlin, in the meantime, knew these Comanche spoke English better than they were letting on. "It's not my cow," she said. The leader shrugged. It was hard to tell whether he hadn't understood or was simply expressing his indifference. Swallowing her pride, Devlin looked up at the Comanche leader. "It belongs to my woman," she mumbled.

There was complete silence for a few long moments until the leader chuckled lightly. He turned to the men behind him and made a few unintelligible comments, then they too laughed. Devlin could feel the tips of her ears burning as she admitted her weakness to these men, but when her eyes connected with the leader's, she felt more than embarrassment. The man nodded as if he completely understood her predicament. He wasn't about to let her off that easy, however.

"Two in place of big one," he said.

"You got a deal." Devlin grinned and nodded her head. "Ura," she said in thanks to the leader.

It took only moments for the small band of Indians to capture their payment and ride off. When the leader looked back at Devlin he called to her. "*Puha*," he said. As close as she could figure, it was the Comanche word for power. The leader pointed to Devlin as he repeated the word and then rode out of sight. The Comanche language was almost identical to Shoshone, but still the rider couldn't fathom why the man had used that word for her.

"Good save, boss." Hank grinned as he rode past Devlin. The rider was aware of the humorous grins on the rest of the drovers' faces as some of the men tried to hold back laughter at Devlin's admission.

"Who wants to ride drag?" Devlin cautioned the men. Instantly, worried frowns replaced the riders' smiles. She picked up her hat, which had fallen to the ground during her hasty jump from Alto. At that moment, Anabelle snorted loudly, and the rider jumped quickly to avoid the longhorn as it attempted to step into her.

"You owe me, cow," she exclaimed, smacking the cow's rump with her Stetson. "And if I don't start seein' some admiration pretty damn quick, I'm givin' you to the next raiding party we see. Keep it up and you'll be Comanche barbecue."

As usual, Anabelle snorted and acted as if the rider wasn't even there.

"I wish there was rain." Devlin gazed into the sky as lightning flickered constantly on the horizon.

They had camped for the night without incident, but just before the evening meal was ready the weather had turned. The air became still and tasted like a copper penny. Devlin and Hank rode herd so the men could eat their dinner and jump back into their saddles. The rider had an uneasy feeling that it would be a long night.

"Me too," Hank answered. "I'd rather face a five-day downpour than an electrical storm with a herd this size."

"You and me both. Looks like it's moving fairly fast. I say maybe two or three hours."

"Yep, that'd be my bet. Maybe we'll get lucky and it'll move more to the east."

"Maybe," Devlin agreed distractedly. Turning to her friend, she readjusted her hat. "If ya catch any shut-eye, though, I'd wear my boots to bed."

Both of the riders chuckled at the thought, but they knew it was no joke. Cattle stampeded for the strangest and simplest of reasons. On Devlin's first trip north with Art Winston's herd, there was a young drover who loved his pecans. Since it was fall at the time, the trees were full of pecans and the young rider always had his saddlebags full of nuts. One night, when the evening was so quiet he could hear frogs in a pond a mile away, young Pete decided a snack was in order. He pulled out a handful of nuts. He usually just cracked them open with his bare hand, but that night, the cracking noise resounded through what seemed the entire Indian Territory. It took three days to round up that herd after the stampede.

Devlin rode back into camp just as the second group of riders headed back to the herd. "Get rid of your long metal. It's gonna be a hot one tonight," she told them.

Most riders didn't need the reminder. On nights when electrical storms threatened, drovers knew better than to ride around with rifles tucked behind their saddles. They'd all seen at least one rider laid flat by a bolt of lightning that had gone straight for the long metal barrel of the rider's gun. On this night, all the riders stopped by the chuck wagon and gave Mexican Bob their rifles for safekeeping.

"You ever been in a stampede, boy?" Devlin asked Matthew.

"Nope. You think we'll have one tonight, Dev?"

"You never can tell. I can feel something in the air, though. I bet your horses were acting kind of skittish this afternoon, weren't they?"

"Yeah, they were." Matt remembered that the animals had become downright moody as they made camp.

"Well, sleep with a saddled horse by you tonight. If all hell breaks loose, jump on his back and ride away from the herd. If your horse bolts before you can get on him, then jump up that tree over there," Devlin said as she nodded to the one straggly tree around them.

"Dev?" Matt called out as he was about to lie down to sleep. "Should I keep my clothes on?"

"I sure would. 'Less you want to show up in Abilene in your long johns." Devlin winked as she walked away.

The rider joined the rest of the men riding watch around the herd. Less than two hours later, intermittent white flashes filled the sky. There was nothing but blackness, the sound of restless cattle, and the calming voices of the riders as they tried to soothe the herd. The flashes of light grew more frequent, bathing the landscape in a false daylight.

Devlin patted Alto's neck. The mare shook her head back and forth as if trying to hide from the eerie shadows the lightning caused. The rider was merely thankful for small favors. In some electrical storms she'd been in, the thunder cracked like the report of a rifle. Tonight it rumbled, deep and low.

They all rode in circles around the herd, usually in opposite directions from one another. They walked their horses slowly and tried to keep their mounts as calm as possible. The storm might last an hour or three; there was no way to tell. Some of the drovers sang songs. They didn't particularly have good voices– Devlin thought a few were actually painful to listen to– but it helped the herd. Like babies in a cradle, the beeves were restless but stationary. Only a few of the cattle had settled to the ground for the night. Typically, one of the prone cows was Anabelle. Devlin couldn't help but shake her head as she passed the cow. Anabelle never seemed to have a care in the world, nor did she ever appear to be concerned with what went on around her. The rider could only surmise that a longhorn as large as any buffalo probably didn't have many natural enemies.

It started quickly, which is the way things always seemed to happen on the trail. One moment Devlin was in her saddle, quietly contemplating life's little idiosyncrasies, and the next minute she was in the middle of chaos. Off to her right, she saw Willie Abbott's horse rear up as the beeves bunched into a tight knot around him. The horse let out a few screaming neighs and continued to rear. The cattle were spooked, but not yet out of control. Devlin rode directly into the herd, kicking steers to loosen them up from around Willie's terrified horse.

By this time, the cattle at the back of the herd decided to join the restless group in the front. The constant flashes of lightning caused everyone's timing to slip. There would be two or three seconds of pitch black, then the sky would turn white for a second. The surreal effect panicked the milling herd. Their sounds became higher in pitch, and suddenly the cattle went into full-blown anxiety mode. They all tried to run away at once from Willie's bucking horse. The cattle from the back pushed in against Devlin and she realized that she had to get out of the middle of them before Alto reared up in fright.

She tried to turn, but there was no space to maneuver. She

immediately loosed her whip and cracked it over the heads of the advancing cattle. They shoved back a small ways, enough for her to turn Alto around, but the space where she had been moments before was now filled with cattle. Some of the riders had joined the fray, but they stayed on the outer fringes of the herd. They cracked their whips and pushed and shoved cattle out of the way to clear a path for Devlin to break free. Suddenly Hank was there, but he couldn't urge his horse into the sea of tightly packed steers. That's when the inevitable happened.

Willie still clung onto his saddle, but just barely. Something had spooked his horse and at this point it was just plain crazed. It bucked as if a swarm of hornets were under its hide. Devlin could see the fear on Willie's face each time the lightning lit up the area. Even though he was an experienced drover, the man apparently feared for his life enough to make a critical mistake. She watched as the rider reached for a pistol tucked in the belt of his pants.

Devlin shouted out a warning in the hope that Willie would hear her over the sounds of the terror-stricken cattle, the screaming horses, and the rumbling thunder. She could only watch helplessly as the rider drew his pistol and fired it into the air. Two shots immediately brought Willie's horse under some semblance of control. He looked up at Devlin and they both seemed to breath a sigh of relief. The reprieve was short-lived, however.

Perhaps only five seconds passed since Willie had fired his pistol, not even enough time for the echoes to completely die out. The cattle in the back pressed forward again, except now the steers in front were just milling about, not moving to expand the area the herd covered. The surging cattle from behind now seemed spooked by something, and the rear beeves attempted to leap over their milling brothers. Others imitated the acrobatic steers and soon the small area that Devlin and Willie were both caught in was a swarming, milling mass of panicked cattle.

Devlin tried to keep her seat as Alto stumbled and faltered when the cattle pressed into them. The leaping and charging animals' horns came dangerously close to the horses trapped within the herd. Alto tripped again and as much as Devlin dreaded it, she felt that if she didn't loosen up the herd, she and Alto would end up dragged to the ground by the hysterical creatures around them.

Devlin threw her arm up in an arc over her head and let fly with her whip. She laid the leather down on the backsides of the steers at the front of the herd. The high-pitched screams of the cattle that received her stinging blows prompted the other cattle into action. The herd loosened, but before the rider could break for the outside edge, she found herself with at least two hundred head of cattle racing across the prairie.

Devlin's biggest fear became reality when she turned and saw the rest of the herd stampede right along with the small rogue herd that she and Willie were caught in the middle of. There was nothing to do now but to try and outrun the cattle, get in front of them, and turn them. When cattle turned into oncoming steers, they naturally slowed down and milled into one another. It was Devlin's only hope at this point.

It was easier than she anticipated to get to the outside edge of the stampeding cattle. Willie obviously had the same thought because he was already there. His horse was lighter than Alto and already had adrenaline flying through her. They made a speedy pair and were perhaps two hundred yards ahead of Devlin and her mare. The crack of whips from behind Devlin grew fainter. She risked a quick look and the next flash of lightning lit up the landscape behind her. She saw the majority of the stampeding herd turn as the riders all rode along the right edge and pushed the leading cattle left.

Devlin snapped her head back to focus on her own position. Alto slowed slightly and the herd seemed to be responding to Devlin's whooping sound, along with the cracks of her whip. Staring ahead, Devlin tried not to flinch as every few moments the lightning filled her vision with split-second daylight. A long moment of electric brilliance showed that Willie was racing along in front of her. The next time the lighting lit up the sky, Devlin had to blink in disbelief. She believed that if she had blinked a third time, her life would have been over.

In one instant, the storm illuminated Willie Abbott. He was still at least a hundred yards ahead of Devlin when he, his mount, and the cattle surrounding him appeared to hover in mid-air for an instant.

Devlin didn't need to hear the screams or see that man and animals were no longer there to realize what had happened. Instinct took place of thought as she pulled Alto's head hard and to the left, her gun hand already wrapped around the ivory-handled Colt. As Devlin forcibly turned her horse, she shot the three closest steers. The sudden gunfire, coupled with the bodies blocking their path, caused the bulk of the herd to turn left along with the rider and her mare. To keep them moving that way, Devlin fired her remaining bullets.

With no more fanfare than that, the cattle milled together into a small group, minus nearly half their original number. Perhaps another few minutes passed before Hank and four other riders caught up with the breakaway herd. Devlin sat in her saddle breathing hard and feeling her heart pound against the wall of her chest. Her mouth had gone dirt-dry and she realized the cause was fear.

"Dev!" Hank held a lantern high in one head as he approached her. "You okay? What happened to Willie?"

Devlin could only point ahead of them until she finally found her voice. "Up ahead. Careful...you'll need the light," she warned.

Hank's horse took a few tentative steps forward and the large man held the lantern aloft. "Good God!" he cursed. The terrain ahead of him disappeared into nothing. The ground simply stopped, dropping sharply into a crater at least two hundred yards below them.

Devlin collected herself quickly and began shouting orders. "Get these beeves back with the rest. A couple of you ride to camp and bring back some long coils of rope and some lanterns." The rider dismounted and found her legs a bit shaky. She walked up beside Hank, placing her hand on his mount to steady herself. "We need to get down there and see if Willie's still alive."

"Don't be crazy, Dev. There's no way he could have survived."

Hank's voice was gentle and filled with concern, but Devlin was the trail boss. "I have to be sure."

The rider's dispassionate tone was back in place as she walked over to an outcropping of sandstone and sat down wearily. Ironically enough, the storm was moving past them now. Hank came over and sat beside his friend. Neither spoke, which wasn't much different from the way they usually acted, but something had changed for Devlin.

In that brief space in time when Devlin saw Willie plunge to his death, she had felt fear. She had felt a fear of dying, of loss. Even now, her heart beat erratically at the idea of never seeing Sarah again. Devlin couldn't remember a time when she was afraid. When had it been last? When she was a child? Perhaps she had feared for someone else, but never for herself.

The rider removed her hat and ran slightly shaking hands

through her hair. That's what made her so good, wasn't it? Hadn't that always been her advantage over other people? Hadn't it always been because she knew the truth? The truth, as Devlin saw it, was that men didn't really want to die, most men anyway. Her power had been that she never once cared whether she lived or died. She cared now. As she sat gazing into the dark shadows, Devlin Brown had to wonder if she'd finally lost her edge.

Chapter 12

"Dev!" Sarah hissed as she bolted upright, pulled from her own nightmare. The young woman looked around the *chuka* to see Hannah still tucked into her sleeping robes. Tima, as always, looked completely at peace as she slept.

Sarah crawled to the center of the *chuka* and added some small pieces of kindling to the banked fire. Her heart was beating rapidly, as though she had been in a race. She took deep breaths to try to calm her nerves, shaking her head to clear away the last tendrils of sleep and to remember the dream. She couldn't recall the visual images, which was unusual for her, but the residual feelings remained. At first, she felt that Devlin was in danger. Sarah could sense that the immediate threat had passed for the rider, but now there was a sense of despair associated with her. Sarah closed her eyes tightly, but try as she would, she couldn't grasp any more of the feelings.

Sarah adjusted the blanket that had slipped down to reveal the small tattoo on her right shoulder blade. Mantema had fixed the tattoo upon Sarah's skin as soon as Sarah had returned to the village on the last day of her Quest. The old woman, along with Tima and the Elders, had worried for the small woman when four days had passed and the small blonde had not returned. On the fifth day, Sarah came back to the Clan village.

Mantema found it surprising that the young woman was able

to walk back. As soon as the older woman prepared Sarah for her marking, she fell asleep. She slept for two more days and when she awoke, the Clan had a feast to mark her naming. From that day on, no one in the village used her given name of Sarah. To the *Chahta* people, Sakli was now a true member of the Thunderbird Clan. She was now *Chahta isht ia*, Choctaw blood. Keeho had also announced to the village Sarah's secret name. This would be a name known only to the Thunderbird Clan and which Sarah would only use when she introduced herself during Ceremonies. From that moment on, the Clan knew Sarah as *Sakli Alakofichi,* "She Who Heals."

Sarah moved a little closer to the fire. For about the hundredth time, she wished for Devlin's warm body lying near her at night. She squirmed as the sleeping fur rubbed against her tattoo. The marking had grown a scab, and as the dried skin fell off to reveal the new skin underneath, it itched. Her Power animal symbol looked out on the world fiercely from Sarah's back. She was unable to see the tattoo, even when she craned her neck as far as possible. Mantema had finally solved the problem by showing her a small piece of hide onto which Mantema had painted the design.

Sarah rubbed absently at the skin on her back. As she looked into the embers of the small fire, Sarah thought about her Power animal design. She had never raised the question as to how Mantema knew about any part of her Quest. The small blonde may have had doubts about the mysteries and *magick* of the *Chahta* people, but her first Quest silenced many of those thoughts. She hadn't said a word when Mantema handed her the image that was now a part of her body. A hawk's head stared full on with eyes that appeared fierce and gentle at the same time. The uniqueness of the tattoo was that the hawk didn't have the usual reddish-brown markings. Its face was half black and half white, in a diagonal design exactly like the warrior in Sarah's Vision.

She hadn't discussed any part of her Quest with Tima or Keeho. The Clan respected her actions and no one ever brought up the matter. The *Chahta* considered Visions private, and only when villagers needed interpretation did they go to see Keeho for answers. Sarah was fully aware of the fact that the *Keyuachi* had visited her in hopes of turning her away from her Quest of becoming *Chahta*. She knew that she would tell Keeho of her vision at some point to hear what wisdom he could shed on it, but now was too soon. Sarah's way of accepting everything that was so different to her previous beliefs was simply not to examine them too closely just yet. She acknowledged what had happened to her as easily as if it had occurred at her ranch house. It was the only way for her to believe right now.

I am Ankahito...I have always been Ankahito. I am Chahta...I have always been Chahta.

Sarah pushed her hair away from her face and wrapped the fur more tightly around her shoulders. A strong chill passed through her and her body shuddered in response. She would have to ask Keeho sometime soon why these words kept popping into her mind. She wasn't even sure who the *Ankahito* were, except that the dead Shaman, Taano, had called them his people. She felt warmer now as her thoughts of the mystical transformed into thoughts about her lover.

Sarah didn't know if she had imagined the fear she felt for Devlin or if the dream had been real, but in keeping with all she had come to believe of late, she chose the latter. She placed her hand upon her chest and felt that the beat of her heart had returned to a more regular rhythm. She took this as a good sign. Her earlier turmoil had disappeared. Now she experienced an odd feeling of resolution. While it wasn't exactly peace, it was a form of calmness. At any rate, perhaps it was enough to allow her to sleep the rest of the night.

"I need to learn what?" Sarah asked Tima in astonishment.

"Do I need to speak louder for you, Sakli?" Tima asked seriously.

"No, but I– "

"Then why did you ask me to repeat what I said?"

"It's more like disbelief than being unable to hear," Sarah explained.

"Oh," Tima replied. The older woman had understood her, but she found it hard to get Sarah to verbalize her thoughts. Because of that, Tima treated Sarah much as she had Devlin when the rider was a young girl.

"But, Tima, basket weaving?"

Tima stopped what she was doing and fixed an exasperated look on Sarah. She didn't have to say a word. Sarah breathed deeply and closed her eyes.

"I know, I know. I promised that I wouldn't question your

training methods." They had reached this agreement once Tima decided to teach Sarah. The training was a preparation of sorts for Sarah's Healing Quest, during which the young woman would appeal to the Spirits for a Spirit guide. Hopefully, one of the Clan Mothers, Medicine Women who came before Sarah, would accept Sarah's request and direct her in her Medicine Way.

"Sakli, some of the strongest Healers in our Clan have been basket makers. Hashtahli has given this craft to women alone. Some say it is a reward for the faithfulness that *Chahta* women have shown to their Clans. Others say that that it is a way for women to excel, to show their imagination and power. I believe that it has a direct connection to the path you wish to follow. You are *Chahta* now, Sakli. This skill will teach you much about the ways of the *Chahta* women."

Sarah gave Tima a defeated look. "Why does it have to be with Oka kapassa? Why can't you teach me?"

"Because Oka kapassa is the best one to learn the craft from. She has the same natural ability with weaving as you do with healing. Why do you not want to train with Oka kapassa?"

"I...I–" Sarah paused and bit her lip nervously. "She scares me," she murmured almost silently.

"What?" Tima chuckled and Sarah found the action reminiscent of something Devlin would do.

"I said she kind of scares me," Sarah said more forcefully as she placed her hands on her hips.

"Why would you fear Oka kapassa?" Tima asked.

Sarah sat down beside the Healer. "I feel like a foolish child, actually saying the words aloud like this."

"Often what frightens us in the shadows of the night looks foolish in the light of the day."

"She watches me, Tima. It's unnerving. Am I crazy? You must have noticed it when she and I are near each other."

Tima wanted to scoff at Sarah's accusations, to tell her that this was all foolishness built up in her mind. The Healer wanted to reassure the young woman, but she had seen it, too. She understood her older sister's looks, but how could she explain the truth to Sarah without breaking her word to Devlin?

"Sakli, you are not crazy. I have seen the way Oka kapassa gazes at you when she thinks no one sees her, but it is not to try to frighten you that she does this. She can't help herself, I suppose."

"I'm not sure I understand, *Nali*. Why can't she help herself?"

The Healer sighed and looked upward. Why hadn't her daughter told Sarah the truth? Devlin had promised Tima before they left the village the last time that she would explain the story of her mother and father to Sarah. The Healer suspected her fearless daughter had blanched at baring her emotions, even to her mate. She could not go against the pledge she'd made to her daughter, however.

"Oka kapassa cares for Redhawk very much. I believe my sister worries for my daughter. She worries that something will take Redhawk from the path of good that she has so recently committed to."

"And she thinks I'll be the one to do that, to lead Dev astray in some way?" Sarah was genuinely surprised at Tima's explanation.

"I think," Tima paused, searching for a way to phrase her feelings, "I think that Oka kapassa's worries are not so much about you and your commitment to Redhawk, but because your world is down in the valley. She fears that your world will become Devlin's world instead of the other way around."

"But haven't I proved my love for this world, the *Chahta* way?" Sarah asked.

"Sakli, you have never had to prove anything to me. You have earned my love and my respect simply because you are the woman of my daughter's heart. I need nothing more to convince me."

"But Oka kapassa does." Sarah looked off into the distance and thought for a moment. "I need to show her who I am. I need to show her that I'm *Chahta*, in here," Sarah placed her hand over her heart, "and that no matter where we live, the *Chahta* ways will always be a part of our family."

Tima smiled at Sarah. The young woman had such a way of examining the world around her. *She will be an excellent Medicine Woman.* "You will become a basket weaver, then?" she asked.

Sarah returned the Healer's smile. "*Nali*, I'm going to become the best damn basket weaver I can!"

"Welcome to my *chuka*, Sakli."

"I'm honored that a weaver of your talent has agreed to

train me, Oka kapassa," Sarah replied.

The two women sat outside Oka kapassa's *chuka* in the sparse shade of a small cedar tree. A mutual respect existed between them, but nothing more. Oka kapassa was determined not to allow herself to be swept away by the young woman's charm. She had seen how the small blonde's natural charisma, something Sarah wasn't even aware of, drew in others of the Clan. Oka kapassa could see what the others had seen, but she steeled her heart against it. She resisted the temptation to open herself to Sarah. She had to be sure. She couldn't let history repeat itself.

Sarah felt as if she were studying under her childhood schoolmaster. Back in that one-room schoolhouse in Kentucky, she'd learned many a lesson at the end of a stiff hickory switch. Her rebellious nature caused her to clash with the schoolmaster until they'd finally called a truce. It wasn't until Sarah had swallowed her pride and treated the man with a little respect that she opened up to the lessons he taught.

Sarah tried to take the same hard-learned approach with Oka kapassa. Days went by as Sarah bit her tongue at the older woman's remarks, some of which she knew were meant to bite. The one thing that kept her going back for more was the way the older woman treated Hannah. Her transformation from aloof instructor to loving caregiver when Hannah came into view was amazing. It was obvious that Oka kapassa's troubles were with Sarah alone. Although the older woman was naturally quiet and reserved, she seemed to hold back her sting for Sarah alone. Sarah, on the other hand, was determined to prove herself to this woman, to prove that Devlin had made the right choice in a mate.

"Well, it didn't turn out quite the way I had in mind." Sarah looked at the design on the basket that she had just completed. "I just don't think I'm good enough yet. What am I doing wrong?" she asked in exasperation, looking almost longingly at the beautifully shaped baskets in Oka kapassa's *chuka*. Small and large, platters and bowls, the detailed work was flawless. Displayed in a place of prominence was a large oval platter. The design actually told a story. The weave of the center of the platter was so decorative and detailed that Sarah was convinced she could never duplicate it.

Oka kapassa held Sarah's platter. Her fingers caressed the coils of plant fibers like a Healer examining a patient. She searched the platter and felt each imperfection. They were not always visible; some were in the spirit of the object. The older woman smiled approvingly at her student. The young woman's technique was sound; she had learned the fundamentals well. Oka kapassa knew that it was time to move on to the next step.

"It is not your ability that prevents your vision of the weave to come through, Sakli. To weave the everyday items that we *Chahta* use, the materials we have in store are appropriate. For a basket maker to create something that they see within their own mind's eye, the weaver must harvest the materials themselves. You need to approach the plants and the trees with this vision in your mind, with the knowledge that they are as much a part of the Sacred Hoop as you are. Then, you wait for the spirit of the item to speak to you."

"The materials that *want* to a part of my basket will tell me?" Sarah asked.

At first, Oka kapassa thought the young woman was patronizing her. It would not be the first time someone scoffed at her for her belief in the ways of the Medicine Wheel. The children who had yet to go on their first Quest, who did not yet know of the *magick* within the Clan, did not often understand the complexities of the circle. Oka kapassa stared hard at Sarah, who looked intently at her. The expression on Sarah's face took the older woman by surprise. Oka kapassa saw a genuine belief for the *magick* in the small blonde's eyes.

"Yes, Sakli, that is precisely what they will do. Each living thing, even plants and trees, have a spirit and a place within the Sacred Hoop, just as we do. Even knowing this is not enough. Until you come to the place where you believe that no spirit is greater than another, you will be unable to hear other Spirits calling to you."

"But I do, Oka kapassa. I have learned to believe this way," Sarah answered. "Will you show me how to harvest for the baskets?"

Sarah seemed to have forgotten the natural animosity that existed between herself and the older woman. So caught up in her desire to learn this new aspect of *Chahta* life, she willingly put aside her own pride in order to take advantage of Oka kapassa's wisdom.

"Then tomorrow morning we shall begin," Oka kapassa said. The old woman found herself smiling at Sarah's enthusiasm and delight.

Sarah kissed a sleeping Hannah good-bye before the sun rose the next morning. She shared a warm mug of tea with Tima before leaving the Healer's *chuka*.

"You seem very excited with basket weaving now," Tima teased Sarah.

Sarah grinned in embarrassment. "At first, I didn't want Oka kapassa to know she was bothering me. I didn't want her to win. Now there's something in what she's teaching me, something so much more that I'm willing to set aside my personal feelings. I can't really explain it any better than that."

"You have come very far in so short a time, Sakli. You have changed much. I think Redhawk will be very pleased."

Sarah had a moment of doubt. "Are you sure? I mean, you don't think she'll be displeased with the ways in which I've changed, do you?"

"Sakli, Redhawk is *Chahta*. I truly believe that she would love you no matter what, but to know that the woman she already loves has become a *Chahta* woman— that is a gift without price."

Sarah's smile returned and she squeezed Tima's hand. "Loving Dev has not only given me what I've always dreamed of, but it's also brought me a family and a people. I think I'm the one who has been given the gift."

Later, just after sunrise, Sarah sat in Oka kapassa's *chuka*. The basket maker offered prayers to the Spirits as she tossed sage and then sweetgrass into the fire. "No life-force means more than another or is more valuable. We ask the Spirits to give themselves up for our use. They all fit together, along with our essence. We are all a part of one another within the Sacred Hoop. We depend on one another for survival. It is not our right to use the materials of Mother Earth simply because we are faster, or stronger. She gives these things to us as gifts. The *Chahta* people accept no gifts from anyone, other than the Spirits."

Some time later, Sarah trailed along behind Oka kapassa. The woman was twice Sarah's age, but her legs were as long as Devlin's and the small blonde had to hurry along to match her stride. So far, Oka kapassa had spoken to Sarah about the spiritual aspect of harvesting the plants. Now, as they walked slowly along the edge of the woods, she explained some of the more universal aspects of basket making.

"As a Healer, what has Tima taught you of the use of sweetgrass?" Oka kapassa asked.

"We use it for purification. We burn it to send up smoke in

many of our *Chahta* ceremonies," Sarah answered dutifully.

Oka kapassa nodded her head at the small blonde's concise reply. "Do you know why we make baskets of sweetgrass?"

"I– " Sarah stopped short. She wasn't sure and something told her not to guess. She shook her head and Oka kapassa couldn't help but smile in reply.

"There are many reasons, but no one reason is any more important than another. Because of its ceremonial use, we reserve sweetgrass for the baskets in which we place a newborn baby's birth cord. Because of its sweet smell, we store clothes and furs in baskets made of sweetgrass. Because it dries extremely light, yet sturdy, we are able to create long-lasting storage."

"I honestly never realized all that. I suppose I've grown up taking certain things for granted, just like I never thought about how much we use baskets."

"It's true, Sakli. We use the many shapes of our baskets for gathering, harvesting, storing, and cooking. You are not alone. Even many *Chahta* people take their daily lives for granted. They think that what we have now will always be. We buy blankets in the white man's store instead of weaving our own, we trade for guns to replace our bows, and we take mates outside the Clan. They do not realize that every time we go outside the Clan, we lose a piece of ourselves."

Sarah didn't know how to respond to the older woman's reasoning. She could understand and agree with Oka kapassa's response to the inevitable change to the *Chahtas'* way of life. A heartbeat later, she realized what the woman was trying to say. Oka kapassa thought Sarah played a part in changing the Clan ways. The young woman had no words to refute the subtle accusations until she remembered who she was.

I am Chahta...I have always been Chahta.

Sarah tried to shake off the feelings of anger and self-doubt. She knew that Oka kapassa said things like this to get a reaction from her. She remembered the words that Keeho had spoken to her during one of their many discussions. He'd told Sarah that she held great power within her being. To allow others to make her feel certain emotions such as anger or jealousy only gave away her power needlessly.

Sarah bit back the words that lingered on her tongue. "What aspects of life do I need to be aware of to become a basket maker, Oka kapassa?"

The older woman turned and looked down at Sarah. She didn't know what to expect after her biting remark to the young woman. She hadn't expected any response at all. When she examined the small blonde's face, she saw the will behind the patient demeanor. Oka kapassa could sense the war that Sarah had within herself. To feel and not to speak was a hard thing. The basket weaver was unable to prevent the small nod of her head. If Sarah was as intuitive as Tima gave her credit for, she would recognize the older woman's apology. Sarah looked up at Oka kapassa, patiently awaiting a reply.

"It takes many winters to learn the skills of a master weaver," Oka kapassa finally answered. The two began walking and the older woman was teacher once more. "You must be accepting of Mother Earth and what she provides, as well as what she holds back. You need to be in tune with the seasons and when the Mother will provide what you need. Lastly, you need to learn all you can of the plants and the trees a basket maker will use. Just as you are learning from me, it is important that you teach your daughter in the same manner. This way, the knowledge will never be lost or forgotten."

"There's so much to know. How arrogant I was in thinking I could become a basket weaver." Sarah shook her head, her earlier ire forgotten.

"You will do well at whatever you work hard to achieve, Sakli."

Sarah looked up in disbelief at the basket maker's words, as the old woman turned and walked away.

An hour later, Sarah and Oka kapassa were beside a shallow creek. "It is not enough, Sakli, to know where to find the plants you will need. You must identify the plants; know what parts to use and how to prepare them. In this respect, gathering items for basket weaving is similar to harvesting plants to use in Healing."

"Oka kapassa, do you have to depend on finding the colors that you want? What if you want some part of your weave to be a particular color?" Sarah asked.

"We can use materials from Mother Earth to create any color scheme that exists in nature. For instance, we use the sedge grass root for white areas and new shoots from the redbud tree for a reddish brown color. If we soak dried bulrush root in wet ashes, we can use the dried grass for black weave. We create yellow with the wood of the hedge apple, red with sumac berries, blue using larkspur, and green with fronds of the evergreen."

"How do I make the dyes?" Sarah asked as she stripped the bark from the black willow limb in her lap.

"Different techniques for different materials. Walnuts, pecans, and hickory nut hulls can all be boiled in water. Then, the material is soaked in the water. Most wood is handled in the same manner."

The day went on in much the same way. Sarah would ask a question and Oka kapassa would answer. The older woman pointed out plants or areas of interest to Sarah as a basket maker. After some time, Sarah began openly equating the balance of plants and animals to life within the Medicine Wheel. Near the end of the day, Oka kapassa said very little. The older woman simply watched and listened as Sarah displayed a profound skill for recognizing plants and herbs. On occasion, the small blonde appeared to identify plants and their uses that she could not remember having learned. It was apparent to Oka kapassa that the young woman possessed powerful Medicine.

Sarah spent every day learning with Oka kapassa. She completed projects, both large and small. She paid special attention to the art and *magick* of Oka kapassa's craft. It would be many years before the young woman's skill equaled her teacher's, but her innate talent shone through in her work.

Eventually, Sarah began her training with Tima and Keeho. It would take her many more years to become a seasoned Medicine Woman than it would to be an expert basket maker. Before she could begin, she would have to experience a Healer's Quest. Therefore, Keeho and Tima worked together to prepare the young woman for her next Quest.

Sarah still spent her mornings and an occasional evening with Oka kapassa. Despite the older woman's reserve and stubborn reluctance to accept her as a *Chahta* woman, Sarah was determined not to give up. One evening Sarah, Tima, and Oka kapassa shared one another's company outside around the fire. The warm summer breeze felt good on their heated skin. Many of the Clan women avoided the heat of the day by saving their chores until the coolness of the evening.

Hannah appeared from within Tima's *chuka*, rubbing sleepy eyes. "I'm thirsty, Mama."

"Then you may have a drink of water, but then it's back inside," Sarah replied.

Hannah walked over to a large water container that looked like a clay pot, but was actually a basket woven of sumac and thickly coated inside and out with hot piñon pitch. The coating waterproofed the basket, and, with its birch bark lid, the container kept the water cool for hours.

Hannah took her drink, then sat down beside her mother. "It's hot, Mama," she complained.

"Yes, I know, love. Come here." Hannah slipped into her mother's lap and Sarah wiped the girl's forehead with a cool cloth. "How does that feel?" She kissed the top of Hannah's head.

"Much, much, much better," Hannah answered with her customary smile. Suddenly the smile turned into a frown. "I miss Dev," she said, slumping against Sarah's chest.

"Me too, sweetheart, me too." Sarah hugged Hannah. "You know, Dev told me a story before she left and it made me smile. I bet it would make you smile, too. Wanna hear it?"

"Uh huh." Hannah nodded her head and snuggled into her mother's embrace.

Tima and Oka kapassa watched with a smile, exchanging a surprised glance as Sarah told Hannah the story of brother opossum and brother raccoon. By the time Sarah finished, Hannah had forgotten what had made her sad in the first place.

"What's this for, Mama?" Hannah ran a finger around the tiny leather pouch that Sarah wore around her neck.

"This is my *ikhish bahta*," Sarah replied. She then explained to Hannah what the Medicine bag stood for and how Tima had shown her how to make it after her Quest.

"Will I get one?"

"Yes, but not until you're older." Sarah went on to tell Hannah some of the things she could expect as a young woman growing up *Chahta*. Hannah seemed to accept the knowledge unconditionally. Sarah talked and rocked the young girl in her arms until she was fast asleep. Sarah closed her own eyes and tilted her face up to the sky.

While mother and daughter shared their exchange, Oka kapassa watched them with a critical eye. She was taken back by Sarah's words. In all of the time Oka kapassa had spent with Sarah, she had refused to accept the small blonde as an acceptable mate for Redhawk. Oka kapassa had seen what had happened to Redhawk's mother. She had fallen in love with someone outside the Clan and because of that, her daughter had grown away from her people. It had only been through the Spirit's graciousness that Redhawk came back to the Clan.

Oka kapassa had been successful in removing the memories of Redhawk's true mother from her thoughts. While not victorious every day, the basket weaver was at least able to put the pain in its proper place. Sarah's entrance into the Clan had brought all the old emotions to the surface.

Oka kapassa could see the past happening all over again. This was exactly what the older woman had feared. That Redhawk's love for the small blonde would not only take her from the Clan, but that any family that came of such a relationship would never know the *Chahta* way. The curse would go on and the Clan would take one step closer to extinction.

There was something different this time, though. The small blonde was teaching her daughter, teaching her the Clan way. Sometime during that evening, Oka kapassa felt her heart melt. With one small action, Sarah had dispelled the notion that the Clan teachings would not be a part of her family's life. The basket maker realized that she had fallen into the very trap against which she had tried to harden herself. Completely against her better judgment, or at the very least her will, Oka kapassa had finally let the small blonde into her heart.

The next morning dawned bright and beautiful as always. The summer sun rose into a sky streaked with magenta and blue. Tima walked into the *chuka* just as Sarah finished dressing.

"The Spirits have been good to you, Sakli."

"What do you mean?"

Tima indicated that Sarah should look outside and lifted the hide flap covering the *chuka*'s entrance. Lying on the ground was a package. Sarah lifted the cloth-covered parcel up and looked around as though expecting to see someone. She examined the red cloth. Painted in black was the outline of a jumping fish. Tima had been right when she said the gift was for Sarah.

Sarah brought the package into the *chuka* and carefully unwrapped it. The people of the Clan didn't believe in gift giving. They believed that all the gifts they would ever had need of would be given to them by the Spirits. Even the *Chahta* knew, however, that there were times when only a gift could say what was in one's heart. That was the case as Sarah simply stared at the woven platter in her hands. It was the beautiful piece of work from Oka kapassa's *chuka* that Sarah had looked at with such longing. In fact, its spectacular design made the platter the envy of every woman in the village.

"I don't understand, *Nali*. What does it mean?" Sarah asked in confusion.

Tima chuckled as she shook her head. "You have such knowledge, Sakli. You know things about the *Chahta* that make me wonder how you could have acquired such knowledge, but when it comes to people, you can be rather blind. I think you have just treated your first patient."

"My first patient?"

"Yes, my child. I believe that you have healed my sister's heart."

Chapter 13

They'd found Willie's body at the bottom of the deep ravine. Mercifully enough, his neck had been broken and he'd died instantly. Devlin ordered the men to put all of the fallen cattle out of their misery. She herself had gone back to camp. Matt had become quite fond of Willie. The older man used to sit by the fire at night and teach the boy everything from knot tying to how to pull off a good practical joke. Devlin had wanted to break the news to Matt herself. He took it like a man, but she heard him crying once they all settled into their bedrolls. She had reached out a hand to comfort the young man. That night was a very long one for the rider, and she waited for sleep that never came.

At sunrise, Devlin passed the word that they would stay camped for another day to butcher the dead cattle and disperse the beef among the fifteen herds. They'd have to cut up the animals in the ravine and rope them up by hand. It would take the better part of the day, but the drovers would all eat three-inch steaks that night. They ended up filling two wagons with the leftover meat. Devlin said that they would either give it to the first Indians they met or drop it by the nearest settlement. The hardest job of this morning would be burying Willie Abbott.

Devlin pulled off her hat and nervously held it in her hands.

Her fingers rubbed against the velvety soft brim as she fought for the words she needed to say. She was the trail boss, and along with all the accolades from a successful drive came the tasks that were not quite as pleasant.

"I'm not sure if Willie was a God-fearing man, but I reckon he was," Devlin began.

Most of the men gathered around a shallow grave that had been covered with flat pieces of sandstone. A couple of the men had carved Willie's name and the date onto one of the slabs as a grave marker. Another had fashioned a crude cross from two sticks tied together and stuck it into the ground. Matt stood next to Devlin and she spied the youngster wiping his eyes and using his sleeve to wipe his nose.

"Willie was a real good man and he was a good rider. He didn't have any family to speak of, so I guess we'll just have to think that he went to his maker with a smile on his face." Devlin paused as a number of riders nodded in agreement. "I figure he's in a place now where the ponies never get tired, the trail's never dusty, and where God doesn't allow creatures as dumb as cattle. Good luck to ya, Willie." The riders nodded their heads at Devlin's parting words to their friend. Most of the drovers admitted that they shared the same dream. A dream where cattle were smart or there were none at all.

Devlin gave a few orders for the day and walked away from the gravesite. Hank found her high up on a grassy knoll that overlooked the prairie, her back against a sandstone ledge.

"Hey, hope I didn't scare ya," Hank said.

"I heard you comin' ten minutes ago. You make more noise movin' through the brush than a rogue bull."

"Well, I figured with the mood you're in it might keep me from gettin' shot." Hank sat down beside her. "How ya feelin', Dev?"

"Lousy."

"Yeah, well, I reckon I'd be feelin' the same way, but look here, Dev. There wasn't a thing you could do to save Willie. It was a damn miracle that you didn't go over that cliff right along with him."

"I know," Devlin answered sadly.

"Oh. Then what are you lookin' so long in the tooth about?"

"It's nothing." She leaned back against the rocks with a sigh.

"Nothin', huh? You sure maybe you don't feel responsible

for Willie, 'cause if that's the case—"

Devlin sighed again, louder this time. "You are not going to leave me in peace about this, are you?"

"I figure that's what friends are for."

"What?" She opened one eye and glared at the large man. "To give you hell until you cave and spill your guts?"

Hank grinned when he caught Devlin's amused look instead of anger. "Yeah, somethin' like that."

She sat up straighter and folded her long legs in front of her. "I was afraid last night, Hank."

"Damn right you were! That was a hell of a drop—"

"I've never been afraid before."

Hank just sat there and stared at his friend. "Ever?"

"I don't know, sure, when I was a kid, I guess. I only know that nothing ever caused me to feel the way I did last night, like I had so much to lose."

"You do."

"Thanks, that makes me feel a lot better."

"Well, hellfire, Dev, you do, but that ain't cause to worry. If I had everything waitin' at home for me like you do, I'd be afraid of spoilin' it, too. That's just life, though. I go through most of my years afraid I'll never find something as special as you and Sarah have. When I do get it, I'm sure I'll spend the rest of my days fearin' that I'll lose it. I once heard you tell someone that only fools and little children don't know fear. You thinking you're better'n the rest of us now?"

Hank pushed against her with one shoulder. Devlin wondered how the man kept his constant good nature. "It's made me feel like I'm gonna second-guess myself. Like maybe I'll make a mistake 'cause I'm holdin' on too tight."

"That's 'cause you got a naturally doubting air about you. Instead of always thinkin' somethin' great is around the next corner, you always think there's disaster. I reckon you're thinking that you're afraid now because you got something worth living for all of a sudden."

"Pretty much. I never had it this good, I don't want to lose it."

"Then maybe you ought to start thinkin' of fear as your friend. There's a good side to it, ya know. Instead of lookin' at fear like it's gonna make you do something stupid, look at it like it just may save your hide. Us ordinary folk use fear to keep us from doing things that just might get us killed. Maybe you could try to start looking at it that way, my friend."

"You ought to quit the cattle business and become a preacher." Devlin laughed. She understood what her friend was saying, and she'd honestly only looked at it from one perspective.

"Nah, I like to sleep in on Sundays."

The two laughed and Hank was happy that he could help his friend a small bit. He suspected Devlin's mood might have had something to do with missing Sarah, too.

"Well, I'm headin' back down. You comin'?" Hank asked.

"I think I'll sit for a spell longer. Might be the last time I get to just sit and do nothing for a long while. Thanks, Hank."

Hank smiled at his friend before he turned and went down the hill, leaving Devlin alone with her thoughts. He ran into Matthew sitting under the shade of the chuck wagon. The youngster had taken Willie's death perhaps harder than the drovers.

"Hey, partner," Hank said.

"Hey," Matt returned.

"Ya know, I just came from talkin' with Dev. She's up there." Hank motioned to the rocky path. "I think she was feelin' poorly over this whole thing. It might help if you were to find your way up there, maybe to cheer her up a bit."

"You think I could help?" Matt asked seriously.

"Sure. Sometimes all ya need to make you feel better is somebody you know kinda bein' there for ya."

Hank smiled to himself as he watched the young man head off in Devlin's direction. He hoped he'd done the right thing. Those two were both hurting and he figured they might be of some help to one another. Besides, he'd seen the look of pride that Devlin wore whenever someone praised Matthew's work. It nearly had knocked the large man over the first time he saw it. A few years back, he would never have guessed an outlaw like Devlin Brown could even have feelings. What he discovered was that after someone had been beaten down enough times, they simply buried their emotions where others couldn't get to them. It wasn't that Devlin didn't have feelings; she just got better than most at hiding them.

"Hey, Dev."

"Hey there, Matt. Why don't you sit a spell?" The rider ran her fingers through her hair and replaced her hat as Matt sat down beside her. "How're you holdin' up?"

"Okay, I guess. I reckon I'd feel a whole lot worse if it was you we buried."

"I have to admit, I'd be a tad upset about that, too." Devlin smiled at the young man. She knew what he was saying to her, but she wasn't sure how to respond. She understood that Matt looked up to her, but she wasn't exactly certain what that meant. Devlin, Matt, and Hannah had yet to examine the boundaries of their relationship. She knew both kids liked her, but as what did they see her? What role did they see her as fulfilling in their lives?

Matt scratched his cheek and looked out onto the prairie. He liked being around the rider, but sometimes he felt awkward, not really sure she wanted to be a real part of his life. At times the two of them could talk easily and other times the words were sparse. When his mom was around, Devlin was different. The rider laughed and joked a lot more naturally. Then again, Matt was different with his mom around, too. She had a way of making him laugh.

Matthew thought of his father and how much he missed him. He and his dad could talk about anything; his dad was just that way. Matt wondered if Devlin had always been this quiet, even when she was his age. He wondered if she'd always worn men's clothes or if she had ever dressed as his mom did. The young man decided to give conversation a chance.

"Was your pa tall?" It wasn't much, but it was all Matt could think of to ask. He saw the rider's long legs stretched out on the rock underneath her.

"Well, I recollect that he was pretty tall, but I guess everyone looks tall to a little kid," Devlin answered. "How about your father? Was he tall?"

"Nah, not really. I mean, I don't think he was as tall as you."

"Well, you've grown some since your pa passed. I reckon everything looks a bit smaller when you're the one gettin' bigger. I guess you must miss him."

"Yeah," Matt bowed his head and mumbled. "We used to talk a lot."

"Reckon that ain't my strong suit, huh?" Devlin asked in embarrassment. Somehow, she thought she was letting Matt down.

"Well, you're good at other stuff, Dev."

An uncomfortable silence replaced their speech and Devlin reached into her vest pocket and pulled out her pocket watch. She looked at the time and out of the corner of her eye, she glimpsed Matthew leaning over. He stared at the picture pressed under the lid's glass case. Devlin snapped the watch shut with an impatient click just as Matt realized she'd caught him.

"I-I'm sorry, Dev, I didn't mean to pry." Matthew hung his head, afraid that he'd ruined the growing trust between them.

Devlin couldn't help but feel sorry for the boy. What was she hiding, anyway? She had wanted to tell Sarah before they parted, but there simply wasn't time.

The rider fingered the ornate design embossed on the watch's hinged lid. She carefully unclipped the watch from the chain anchored in her vest pocket and handed it to Matt. "If you press that little knob in front, the lid pops open," she instructed. Matt held the heavy object in both hands, treating it as though it were a priceless work of art. "Go on," the rider reassured him.

Matt flipped open the pocket watch and took in the beauty of the design. "I never saw anything like this before," he said. He examined the photograph. It was like some of the photographs he'd seen that belonged to his mother. She had one of her father in a uniform that she kept in an old chest.

Matt looked at the portrait of a young couple. The man looked big. He wore a wide brimmed hat and wore a sheriff's badge on his vest. Matt figured these must have been Devlin's parents because the rider appeared to favor both of them. The man had eyes that were so light in the picture that they must have been the same color blue as Devlin's. The woman was very slender, but didn't seem frail. She was very beautiful with her dark hair pulled back and cheeks that looked just like the rider's. Her skin was very dark, much darker than Devlin's.

"Are these your folks, Dev?" Matt asked as he handed the rider back her watch.

"Yep. My pa was a sheriff in Sedalia, Missouri. That's where he got killed," Devlin added softly.

"Your mom's pretty."

Devlin smiled to herself at some half-forgotten memory. "Yeah, she was beautiful all right, in her heart as well as her face." She waited to see if the boy would ask, but she should have known better. Sarah hadn't raised him to be anything but a gentleman. "My mother was a Choctaw Indian."

Matt looked relieved that the rider had brought up the issue.

"I thought you were just adopted by the *Chahta*, Dev."

"I was adopted by the Thunderbird Clan, but my mother was already a part of that village. She left them to live with my father after they were married. After my parents died, when I was pretty close to the age you are now, I ended up in a scrape close to my mother's home. The people of the village took me in and when they discovered who I was, they welcomed me. When I decided to stay, Tima and Tekola adopted me as their own."

"Is it a secret, Dev? I mean, who your mom and dad really are?"

"No, Matt, it's not a secret. In fact, I meant to tell your mom, but things got a little busy before we left. I guess— well, I became sort of quiet about the fact as I grew older. People can be pretty mean about some things, ya know?" Devlin wondered if Matt would understand what she was saying. She didn't even begin to know how to explain the way she'd felt the first time someone had called her a half-breed. She never forgot that Dale Karsten, the man she'd killed not too long ago, had called her Breed whenever he wanted to get a rise from her.

Matt felt bad now that he'd brought the subject up. Devlin had the saddest look he'd seen on her face, and he had never meant to bring up any bad memories. He was old enough, however, to imagine the kinds of things that people could say and do to those who were different from them.

"It's a swell watch, Dev," Matt said.

Devlin turned to look at the boy and cupped his cheek in one hand. She smiled, but it was a smile tinged with pain. "My grandfather gave it to my dad. I guess I was supposed to give it to my son." She chuckled lightly. "I reckon I didn't quite turn out like my father thought his little girl would, huh? I suppose I'll leave it to you, if you've a mind to have it that is. It's not much, not even real gold, but I— "

"I'd be proud to own it someday, Dev. Real proud."

"You would, huh?" Devlin stared into his eyes and discovered the truth. The reason that Matthew's expressions reminded her so much of Sarah was that deep down, they were the same. Not simply because they were of the same blood, but deeper still, in their beliefs, in their heart. Sarah had a pride and strength about her, but she was also the most compassionate soul Devlin had ever met. Devlin finally saw what every parent hopes to see in their own children— a piece of themselves staring back at them. Only the luckiest parents saw the best of themselves;

Devlin would have to remember to tell Sarah that she was definitely one of those lucky ones.

"Okay, it's a deal. I'll depend on you to keep the tradition going. That means you keep the watch until you have kids and then you hand it down to one of them. Not till I'm gone, though." Devlin winked at the boy and hooked the watch back onto the chain. "And I hope you won't be too disappointed if I don't go givin' it up right away. I figure I still got a few years left anyway."

Matt laughed and dropped his head in reply. The silence enveloped them before Matt chimed up again. "Does this mean I'm like your son too, Dev?"

The rider coughed and cleared her suddenly dry throat as an eternity floated by. In truth, only seconds had passed. She wasn't sure how to answer, or even what Sarah had planned to tell the children. The youngsters had both simply accepted that Devlin was now a part of their lives.

"Well, I guess kinda like that..." she trailed off, at a loss for additional words. Matt merely looked up at her and smiled. "You okay with that?" she asked.

"Uh huh." Matt's smile grew as he nodded his head.

"Of course, that doesn't mean you have to call me anything special, ya know. Or– "

"*Ishki toba*," Matt interrupted.

"Where did you hear that?"

"It's right, isn't it?" Matt asked with concern. "It means second mom, right?"

"Yeah, stepmother, or second mom. Who taught you that *Chahta* word?" Devlin asked again.

"Oh, I think I might have heard Mom say it." Matt lowered his head until the brim of his hat hid his eyes, but Devlin could see the boy's cheeks were pink.

"Your mom, huh?"

"Maybe."

"Or maybe it was Talako and his oversized mouth."

Matt shrugged his shoulders. "Maybe," he replied softly.

Talako, Devlin's childhood friend, had jumped at the offer to leave the village and help with the cattle drive. Lately, he had been teaching Matt the *Chahta* language in order to describe the game of *toli* to the young man. The rider certainly wasn't angry at her friend for teaching Matt such a special word, but she wanted to be certain that the boy knew its intended meaning.

"I'm honored that you would call me that, Matt, but there's more to it than just a name." Devlin watched as Matt looked up in relief and waited for her to continue. "When a woman becomes *ishki toba* to a child, it's a voluntary sort of thing. I mean, it's sort of– well, exceptional. The bond that a mother and a child share is special. You and your mom will always have that distinctive tie. Even after you've grown to be a man and you're no longer under your mother's protection, her heart will still look at you the way she did when you were born. It's hard to describe, but it's different from any other kind of relationship there is. So, when a woman comes along who can make a child feel those same feelings, then she's called *ishki toba*. Do you understand?"

"I think so," Matt answered tentatively after a few moments of silence. "Yeah." His smile returned and he nodded his head. "I get it, Dev, and I think it fits. I think you're *ishki toba*."

Devlin decided to do something completely uncharacteristic. She hugged the boy. Matt had grown up expressing affection, so the display seemed perfectly natural to him. Devlin prayed that the boy didn't laugh at her. When they broke apart, however, Matthew's smile appeared so genuine that the rider wondered why she had been worried in the first place.

"Did ya find a decent place to cross?" Hank asked Devlin as she rode up.

"You're not gonna like it," Devlin answered.

"Damn! I just knew that river would be trouble."

"Well, just think what it would have been like if we'd had a rainy summer. They sure must have been gettin' plenty of rain in the Rockies this summer."

"So, what's the word, boss?" Hank asked, although neither rider felt quite like joking now.

"Not much we can do. It's gonna take us another month to get to Abilene. We can't afford to wait for swollen rivers to go down. We'll have to do the only thing we can do. Spread the word that we'll have to spend most of the day crossing. Take it real slow and a little at a time."

Devlin cut her horse and rode away from the herd. Hank understood his friend. They had been on the trail for almost one month, with another to go. Progress had been slow with a herd this size, but they hadn't run into near the problems that they could have.

"It was supposed to be the Cimarron, not this one," Devlin muttered to herself. She remembered the days when most folks called it the Red Fork of the Arkansas. Even though the river wasn't flooded, there was always the danger of quicksand. They'd been lucky, though.

They had reached the Cimarron about three days after Willie died. The beeves crossed the river with hardly a misstep. Six miles farther north came Turkey Creek. Wood got scarce. Matt and Frankie had helped the cooks in finding firewood or a suitable alternative. Sometimes they used dried buffalo chips, and once they'd resorted to the dried stalks of sunflower plants.

For miles and miles, they traveled across flat prairie. They ran into a prairie dog town, its tunnels dotting the turf for at least six miles. Occasionally a steer would get its hoof caught in one of the holes and fall to the ground. With every passing day, Devlin grew more worried as the herd's numbers dwindled.

They watered at Hackberry Creek and had to stop the herd for nearly three hours as a buffalo herd passed them by. Devlin thanked the Spirits that the buffalo weren't coming at them. When buffalo wanted the right of way, they usually got it. In this case, the buffalo simply galloped past, seemingly unconcerned with the cattle. Hackberry Creek offered clear water and plenty of grazing area, but still no firewood.

At Shawnee Creek, nine miles farther on, the riders had to keep the herds away from the water because poisonous gypsum deposits filled the river. The place put Devlin in a bad humor simply by its nickname. The drovers called it Skeleton Creek because the bleached bones of Indians who had died during a cholera epidemic lined the treeless banks.

After protecting the herd from the creek's contaminated water, the riders watered the beeves at Nine Mile Creek. There had been good camping just east of the trail at the edge of the timber. Devlin heard Mexican Bob praise the Lord at one point for the firewood. The cook had been tired of the rider's constant joking that his food tasted of buffalo dung, which it did. Of course, everyone smelled like it, too. Buffalo chips were all they'd had to burn for the last few days.

Once more Devlin stood in front of the Salt Fork of the Arkansas River. Along with the South Canadian and the Cimarron, this stream was one she had marked on her map as having the potential for trouble. The rider had assumed that since the drought had made the previous two passable, this river would be the same. She was wrong.

"It's movin' fast," Matt said from behind her.

Brought out of her thoughts, Devlin turned and placed an arm around the young man's shoulder. "I've seen a lot worse. We'll get 'em across over there, see?" She pointed to a spot where the bank dropped down steeply, but the river seemed at its shallowest. The water was moving swiftly. Branches and other debris bounced atop the churning surface.

"We'll take one herd at a time. We'll get the chuck wagon and the *remuda* across first, then move the cattle in. If we keep them moving, we'll all be okay." Devlin spoke with a confidence she didn't actually feel. She saw the potential for a myriad of disasters. The first thing she wanted to do was to get Matt and his horses safely across; then she knew she'd feel much better about the situation.

"Okay, Bob," Devlin shouted. "Get that wagon up here."

The wagon and its steady mule team crossed the river slowly. Devlin and Matt each took a side and hustled the horses down the steep bank and into the water. The animals could practically smell dry land on the other side and they were in a hurry to get there. The river ran from somewhere high up in the hills, making the water frigid. It was nothing like the warm, slow-moving pools they had crossed thus far.

"Where do you think you're going?" Devlin asked when they reached the opposite bank.

"Well, I thought I could help with the cattle, kind of– "

"No, Matt."

"But– "

"Matt, who's in charge of this drive?" Devlin growled.

"You are, boss," the boy answered in defeat.

"Then just do as I say, all right? Keep an eye on the *remuda* and move them off a ways so the cattle don't get spooked. Okay?"

"Okay." Matt kicked at the dirt with the toe of his boot and mounted his horse.

"When you get a little bit bigger, Matt. Right now, I just don't have the time to be pullin' you out of the river if something happens. Understand?"

Matt nodded his head and Devlin led Alto back into the freezing water. She allowed the mare to move at her own pace, avoiding the debris that rushed down stream. Devlin pressed her tongue against her front teeth and signaled Hank with a shrill whistle to bring the herd down the bank.

Cattle, as any rider would gladly tell a person, were perhaps God's dumbest creatures. They didn't have the stubbornness of a mule, to simply dig in their hooves and stay. Instead, although their fear was palpable, the beeves allowed the men to cajole them down the slippery embankment. Even worse, the riders had to continue wheedling the animals into movement or they would mill right in the middle of the stream, drowning themselves and anyone who got close to the panicked animals.

Anabelle led the beeves into the water. The massive cow wasn't distracted in the least by the freezing current. The first few steers to reach the opposite side must have given incentive to the others. The herd moved a little faster and that made Devlin happier.

Without warning a submerged tree branch, perhaps ten feet in length, shot to the surface of the water. The nearest steer jumped back from the object and fell against Alto. The horse screamed in fright and tried to keep its balance. Failing, she landed in the water on her side, unseating Devlin in the process. Hitting the surface of the icy water flat on her back knocked the wind out of Devlin. Before she could come to her senses, she lost her grip on Alto's reins. The moment she released the leather, her body began moving downstream.

"Dev!" Hank shouted and pointed to Devlin's body in the water. Standing on the other side of the cattle, he raced around the herd. The other riders couldn't stop their task for fear that the entire herd would stop in midstream.

Devlin fought to keep her head above the surface, but the river was full of uprooted trees and brush. Her flailing hands caught in the branches and her waterlogged clothes pulled her beneath the surface. It felt like hours, but in reality was seconds before she hit something in her path. She first felt the impact to her left shoulder, then her face slammed into it and a red stream of blood filled her vision. Suddenly, the object that was floating with her in the churning water rolled over. Devlin realized it was a huge tree, uprooted by the rushing torrent. She figured she could hold onto it and at least not drown. As the tree rolled again, she realized that her leg wasn't free, but tangled among the lower branches. There was no way for her to stay on the water's surface.

The log rolled once more and Devlin's upper body came

clear out of the water. In that moment, the rider felt something hit her. She quickly discovered that a rope had settled over one of the tree's branches and around her chest. An instant later, her forward momentum slowed, then stopped altogether. The water continued to move against her, but now she could see that not only did the rope have her secure, but the tree was now wedged behind two large boulders.

"Dev! Dev!"

"Matt?" Devlin couldn't believe his voice was so close to her. She craned her neck to see behind her and watched as Matt crossed the water hand over hand. He looked like a rag doll with the river pulling him downstream, but he held tight and was able to scramble across in record time.

"Are you crazy? Go back," Devlin shouted. If Matt heard her, he gave no indication.

Hank could only watch, since he was too late to reach his friend. Matt had come out of nowhere, racing his horse along the riverbank as tree branches and brush scratched at him and his mount. He saw his opportunity when Devlin popped to the surface, and he roped the tree and Devlin with one try. The weight immediately pulled his horse into the water and Matt dismounted, swiftly tying the rope off onto one of the massive willow trees beside the river.

Matt could hear Devlin shouting at him and he knew he would be in some big trouble once she made it to shore. He didn't even stop to think about the danger of the situation when he scrambled across the rope and out onto the tree. The water was freezing cold and Matt's teeth were already chattering. When he reached Devlin, she was holding onto the rope and a branch on top of the tree trunk to keep her head out of the water. By this time, Hank had called for help and given orders for the men to keep the herd moving across the river.

"What in the hell are you doing? Get back to shore!" Devlin yelled at Matt.

"Not 'less you can get there, too." Matt stared defiantly at the submerged woman until he saw something change in her expression.

"I can't, Matt. My leg's caught." She tugged with more force this time, but her foot and ankle were completely trapped in the tree's dense branches.

"Hank could use an axe. Mexican Bob has one in the chuck wagon."

Devlin shook her head. "It would be impossible to get under here with the way this water is moving. Besides, even if he could, he wouldn't be able to see a thing in this muddy water. He might end up chopping off my foot."

Matt listened to the woman as she spoke calmly about her own rescue. She didn't show it, but Matt knew she must be freezing. He knew he was, and her lips were almost blue. "Then we'll pull you and the tree to shore."

Devlin hesitated, wondering if that plan had a chance. She had her doubts, but she was quickly running out of options. "It might be worth a try, but I want you on dry land first. I don't– "

"No, Dev. I'm not gonna leave you."

Matt spoke the words with such an authoritative finality that Devlin found herself unable to come up with an argument. She nodded her head silently and listened as the boy shouted to Hank. She craned her neck to see the herds moving across the river without further mishap.

Hank and two other riders took hold of the rope that held Devlin and the tree. They put their backs into it as they pulled, but even with Hank's enormous strength, they could barely budge the tree trunk against the rushing water. Devlin sighed, but opening her mouth caused her teeth to chatter.

"We just need a few more guys," Matt said upon seeing Devlin's defeated expression.

"Matt." Devlin tried to come up with a way to get out of the mess, but the cold water was making her sleepy. She tried to shake off the sluggishness. "Matt, I think we'd need a dozen men to pull this thing out."

The boy's eyes filled with tears. He looked at the rider and then at the shoreline. His face suddenly creased into a smile. "How about just one thing that's as strong as a dozen men?"

Devlin turned her head. There, by the riverbank, stood Anabelle. The longhorn remained impassive as ever as she stood near the shore, apparently disregarding the icy water swirling around her legs. For a moment, it looked to the rider as if the animal was watching the entire scene.

"Are you crazy? That animal hates me, Matt. She'd let me drown just to be ornery."

"No, she can do it, Dev, I know she can." Matt blew on the fingers of each hand in an attempt to keep them warm. Then he once again grabbed the rope and the boulder blocking the tree's path. "We don't have another way, Dev."

Devlin looked back at Anabelle, who continued to absently watch as the river swept by. Cold and fatigue were taking their toll on the rider. She figured that had to be the case since she was about to go along with the insane plan. "Okay, but you get back to shore first."

"Okay." Matt smiled and Devlin wished that she had as much confidence in Anabelle as the boy did.

Through Matt's shouts and pointing to Anabelle he made his plan known. Devlin imagined that if the situation hadn't been so serious, Hank would have been lying on the ground laughing his ass off. The men tossed another rope out to Matt, which he and Devlin managed to secure all the way around the tree. Then, once Matt was safe on dry land, they secured the ropes around Anabelle.

Devlin felt the log shift as the pressure built up behind her. She didn't doubt for one minute that the cantankerous side of beef was simply going to stand there and let her flounder. Much to Devlin's amazement, Anabelle looked up at her and snorted. It was that loud grumbling sort of noise the cow seemed to make around no one but Devlin. As everyone held their breath, Anabelle began a slow and steady ascent onto the riverbank.

The water spilled around Devlin and she could barely expand her lungs enough to take in a breath. The pain in her ankle intensified as Anabelle laboriously tugged the massive tree to shore, along with Devlin's trapped body. They were nearly halfway there when the rider felt the wood shuddering beneath her. A loud ripping sound filled her ears just as she was dragged beneath the water's surface.

She felt her leg tug free and instantly bobbed to the surface. She strained to take in a gulp of air and saw pieces of the tree all around her. The rope around her chest was still attached to one large section of the tree trunk. In one swift movement, the tree rolled forward and Devlin was pitched head first into the frigid water.

The rider tried to fight her way to the surface, but the branch kept rolling back onto her. In the meantime, Matt and Hank cajoled Anabelle to move faster. When she was within ten feet of shore, the men held onto the ropes and ran into the water. Their combined strength was enough to move the tree off the pinned rider. When they pulled Devlin to shore, she was unconscious. Hank wasn't even sure she was breathing. He slapped her face and pressed the palms of his hands against her stomach in attempt to force out the water she'd swallowed.

Devlin was still for what seemed like forever to the men standing by helplessly. Someone ran up with blankets and another rider brought Devlin's war bag filled with dry clothes. Finally, she coughed, expelling several mouthfuls of water.

Devlin wasn't quite herself yet. She knew she'd blacked out, but right now all she could think was how good the sun felt beating down on her skin. That's when she smelled the horrid odor and felt something warm and slimy rub against her face. Opening one sky blue eye, she saw Anabelle's tongue heading straight for her face.

"Son of a–" The rider jerked her body up into a sitting position and pushed the longhorn's face away.

"She's just tryin' to say she's glad you're alive, boss." Hank laughed out of sheer relief.

The rest of the men laughed for the same reason as Devlin pushed the cow away from her for a third time. "All right, all right! Thank you, Anabelle. Matt, get her off me."

Matt grinned pulled the longhorn, who'd obviously had a change of heart regarding the rider, back up the riverbank. No one knew why, but some suspected the cow understood that Devlin had saved the longhorn from becoming a meal for the Comanches.

"How are ya, Dev? Can ya get up?" Hank asked.

"I ain't that easy to kill," Devlin grumbled and Hank gave her a hand up. "Ankle's a little sore," she commented as she gingerly placed her weight onto her foot. "But I'll live." She looked at all the smiling faces around her. "What the hell are you all gawking at? Get to work! You think that herd's gonna find its own way to Abilene?"

The men realized that their trail boss was back and quickly scrambled to find their mounts and their places tending the herd. "Never seen a luckier woman in all my born days," one of the riders muttered under his breath. Even with the sarcastic remarks, Devlin, as well as the other riders, knew what had happened. One of their own came close, and it made every man there just a little more conscious of his own mortality. In the blink of an eye, everything they were, everything they had, could be taken away. The outcome had been good this time. Next time, they might not be so lucky.

"And you." Devlin pointed to Matthew, who was returning after leading Anabelle to her position at the head of the herd.

Matt prepared himself for the lecture he was sure was next. He braced himself for Devlin's fury. The tall woman surprised him by grabbing the neck of his shirt and pulling him into a strong hug. Looking up from the embrace, Matt was completely taken back by the affection that shone down on him from sky blue eyes.

"You listen to me about as well as your mother does." Devlin ruffled the boy's wet hair. "And I'm damn glad."

"I saved your hat." With a smile, Matt offered up the crumpled Stetson.

"Oh, well, all is forgiven then." Devlin reshaped the wet felt and placed it on her head. "It's hard work breakin' in these things." She would have especially hated to lose this one, since it had belonged to Sarah's father. Life was unpredictable on the plain, whether in a house, *chuka*, or even on the trail. Becoming attached to material possessions only led to heartbreak. She flipped open her pocket watch and water dripped from its insides.

"Is it ruined?" Matt asked with concern.

"Nope, not to worry. I know a gunsmith in Abilene that can fix it up. You get some dry clothes on before you get back on your horse," Devlin said. "If we both go home with pneumonia, your mom'll never let us have this much fun again."

They both laughed as Hank watched them. He knew that Matt's change in attitude was mostly due to the new relationship that he and Devlin shared. The young man had never really been sullen or temperamental, but he was prone to a certain quietness. Since Matt and Devlin had gone from friends to more of a parent-child relationship, Matt seemed more at ease. It was as if knowing his place in the pack helped the young man to relax.

Hank walked along with them and hoped that this bit of scariness would be the last, for a while anyway. He knew that was an improbability, but he wished for it just the same.

Chapter 14

Sarah couldn't concentrate on any of the Prayers or Ceremonies that Keeho had been teaching her over the last few weeks. She found herself continually drawn to Oka kapassa's *chuka*. The older woman had gone out of her way in a seeming attempt to avoid Sarah. They hadn't even spoken, with the exception of an occasional friendly greeting, since Sarah found Oka kapassa's gift outside the *chuka*. The small blonde thought about giving in to the basket weaver's obvious wishes, but Sarah's Clan name was Sakli for a reason. The salmon that constantly swims upstream against the flow, never giving up until it reaches its destination, fit Sarah's personality precisely.

One afternoon Sarah sat along the edge of the prairie. She looked into the valley below and watched the bison move in huge herds. She thought about Oka kapassa and the older woman's change of heart. She wondered why Oka kapassa cared so much for Devlin. If Devlin had been so special to the woman, how was it that Tima was the rider's adopted mother? Sarah knew that *Chahta* law did not preclude single women from adopting children since uncles, and not the father, provided much of the instruction for warriors. Suddenly a thought popped into Sarah's head and rolled around and around until she couldn't stand it any longer. How could she have been so blind, and why hadn't Devlin ever told her? The resemblance was amazing. Of course, Sarah being Sarah, she had to know the truth.

"May I speak with you, Oka kapassa?" Sarah went right to the source, whether the older woman wanted to see her or not.

"You are always welcome in my *chuka*, Sakli. What is it that you wish to speak of?" Oka kapassa behaved as though there had never been any sort of animosity between them. She sat on the floor of the lodging sorting dried roots, barks, and grasses into separate bundles for future use.

Once Sarah settled herself beside Oka kapassa, she blurted out the words that had been on her mind for days. "You're Redhawk's mother, aren't you? I don't mean like Tima, I mean her real mother."

Oka kapassa didn't look surprised in the least, which caused Sarah to believe she had hit the mark. It was Sarah, however, who was about to be surprised.

"No, Sakli." Oka kapassa smiled gently at her. "I am not Redhawk's mother, but you are not far from the truth."

"I was sure, I mean– I didn't mean to– I just thought..." Sarah stammered. "Forgive me," she finally said in embarrassment.

"Sakli, there is nothing to forgive. As I said, you came very close. Redhawk's mother, the woman who gave birth to Redhawk, she was my sister. Okshakla was my twin sister. Do you know what my name means, Sakli?"

"Cool Water," Sarah replied.

"Correct. My sister's name, Okshakla, meant 'Deep Water'. I was quiet and reserved. Okshakla was quiet, as well, but when she did speak, it was always something profound. We grew up to fit our names."

All of Oka kapassa's words and actions now made sense to Sarah. She understood everything, each harsh word the older woman had ever uttered. The physical similarities between Devlin and Oka kapassa made sense also. "I'm not sure I understand, Oka kapassa. Why is Tima Redhawk's adopted mother? I would have thought, given the love that I hear in your voice for your sister, that– "

"My pain was very great when my sister left the Clan, Sakli. I knew that she was very much in love, but I felt that no good would come from her giving up her people. When Redhawk returned to us and told us of her parents' deaths, I grew angry. So angry that I refused my birthright, refused to adopt Redhawk as my own. I turned my back on the child because I thought of her as part of the reason my sister had died." Oka kapassa paused to wipe away the tears that now ran in a steady stream down her cheeks. "I blamed my beloved sister's death on her leaving the Clan. I blamed her husband for allowing her to give up who she was."

"So that's why you disliked me so much," Sarah added in a whisper. It was clear to the young woman that Oka kapassa saw Sarah and Devlin's relationship as history repeating itself. "You only saw me as someone who Redhawk would give up her people for."

Oka kapassa nodded her head. "I was wrong. I was wrong back then and I was wrong to have treated you so. It is not the *Chahta* way. Forgive me, Sakli." She hung her head in shame.

Sarah placed one hand on Oka kapassa's shoulder, unsure how to take away the pain that had been a part of the older woman's existence for so long. Sarah said the only words that she might have wished to hear under similar circumstances. "There is nothing to forgive, *akana*."

The word *akana*, which Sarah chose carefully, added so much more to the comforting statement. To accept someone as simply a friend was done often, but to accept someone as *akana*, or "my friend," was like saying they were as close as family. Sarah did not yet consciously realize that every day she spent in the Clan village caused her family to grow a little larger.

Sarah had spent the early morning helping the elder women of the Clan as they taught the younger women and girls how to prepare *nita nipi itaba nusi*, acorns and bear meat. The dish was one that the *Chahta* traditionally cooked in a large pot in a central location of the village. Sarah received nods from the Clan women for her foresight in bringing one of her large iron pots to the camp.

It was unusual for the hunters to come across a fat bear this time of year. In the heat of the summer, the men usually had to be happy with squirrels and rabbits as an addition to their diet of buffalo meat. Because of its fatty flesh, they needed to cook the bear meat right away. They reserved a small portion to cut into strips and dry to use later for making pemmican. The Clan had been provided with the means to have their favorite feast meal on the eve of a village celebration. The Elders looked on this occurrence as a very favorable sign from the Spirits. It only served to remind Sarah that the Clan expected so much from her. It was the following day's start of her Healer's Quest that they celebrated.

Most of the acorns in the woods around the village, while quite plentiful, were bitter to the point of being inedible. One of the older women, Shinkak, explained to Sarah how they would remove the bitterness. "You can tell the difference because white oaks have rounded leaves and the black oaks have pointed leaves. The white oak acorns are less bitter. We must be fair to our four-footed brothers, however. Squirrels hunt for the white oak acorns, too. We aren't the only one of Hashtahli's creations who do not care for bitter nuts. Black oak acorns will make you pucker up just like when you take a bite from an unripe persimmon." She laughed along with the young women when she puckered her lips as an example. "We must leach them to remove the sharp, bitter taste."

The youngest girls spent the morning gathering hickory sticks for the fire. The women and girls cleaned off a spot on top of a large, flat piece of sandstone. They made a small fire with the hickory wood and when it had burned down, they gathered the ashes. The women spent quite some time shelling and picking off the red skin from the acorns. They then split them into halves and placed the pieces into a large, loosely woven basket. Shinkak directed them to place a second basket containing the hickory ashes above the basket holding the peeled acorns.

Finally, they dripped water slowly through the basket of hickory ashes and down into the basket of acorns. The combination of the water and hickory ashes created a mild form of lye, which would remove the bitter taste from the acorns. Sarah helped to wash off the acorns and placed them in the large iron pot. Lastly, they added chunks of bear meat and some of the pungent wild garlic that grew in the forests around the village. The stew boiled until the meat and the acorns were tender.

Now Sarah and Tima sat outside of the Healer's *chuka* under a lean-to made of brush. The shelter provided necessary shade on hot summer days such as these. As the end of summer rapidly approached, many households were slow-drying meat over hickory wood fires, as well as laying in stores of other cold weather supplies. Sarah breathed in the wonderful aroma of the cooking stew, which had already brought a number of people to the area of the cook pot.

It was early yet for the Clan to harvest many of the nuts from the trees, but some were gathered green. Hickory, black walnuts, and pecans were abundant in the nearby forests. Tima taught Sarah the *Chahta* way of storing the nuts so that worms and insects would not infest them. They smoked the nuts over a hickory fire and then gathered them into clusters. Tima covered each cluster of nuts with mud, which when dried served as a hard outer shell for the fruit inside. The *Chahta* learned this technique from watching the *tekhanto*, the mud dauber. The insects placed food for the next season's hatchlings inside sealed mud containers. Even years later, the *Chahta* could crack or soak open the mud balls to reveal crisp, smoked nuts inside.

As they worked, Tima explained some aspects of Sarah's upcoming Quest. "When you go on a Quest," Tima said, "you are searching for something. We may Quest many times during our lives, but always it is because we are seeking answers. The first Quest a *Chahta* youth experiences is the same one that you underwent. Its purpose was twofold. First, for acceptance to the Clan; secondly, to receive the Power animal that will always be with you. Tomorrow, you undertake a Quest that few *Chahta* go on. It is called the Healer's Quest."

Sarah had heard most of this before, but she still listened intently to Tima's words.

"You will not stay as long as you did before. It is forbidden to stay more than four days without food and water. I have known of Holy Ones to go on Quests for nearly a fortnight, but you are very far away yet from communicating that closely with the Spirit World. On the fourth day, if you do not receive your guide, you must return to the village. Do you understand that, Sakli?"

Sarah nodded her head. She knew why Tima stressed that. The older woman was aware of Sarah's stubborn streak. Tima must have suspected that her first willful thoughts would be to do it her way.

"Women of the Clan go on many Quests during their lives just as men do, searching for truths. They will ask answers to many questions. The questions we ask in life will change as we grow older and our focus broadens. Young women sometimes are very narrow in their searching. Perhaps they wish for wisdom, a husband, or children. Some look for the path they are to follow. Older women become selfless in their Quests and oftentimes search for assistance for the ones they love most. The Elder women of the Clan become introspective with age. They seek answers to who they are and where they fit within the Creator's world. It is the *Chahta* way, however, to forbid women to enter into Vision Quests. They may Quest for other reasons, but not to seek Visions."

"But Redhawk– "

"Redhawk is looked on as a warrior to the Clan. The laws for the *Chahta* female do not apply to her."

"But won't I see Visions on every Quest?" Sarah wondered if she should tell Tima about the black-and-white warrior she'd met during her first Quest.

"Not at all," Tima replied. "Some Quests are simply a way to separate us from the busy day-to-day activities that encompass our lives. You will learn, Sakli, it is not always necessary to go to a Sacred Place to obtain wisdom from the Spirits. Many times, we find that the answers we sought during a Quest were inside of us all along."

"I understand that, Tima, but what happens if I do experience a Vision while on a Quest? Am I supposed to keep quiet about it?"

Tima smiled. Sometimes Sarah emitted an aura as powerful as the Old Ones. Other times, the young woman exuded the innocence of a child. Tima felt blessed to teach her Way to one so open to the world around her. "In future generations, I believe many of our ways will change, Sakli. For now, we must let the men of the Clan harbor their small insecurities."

"I don't understand them most of the time, *Nali*. I thought maybe *Chahta* men were different."

"In many ways they are, but in small ways all human beings are the same. I am a young woman by Clan standards, but still, I have seen much. I have met white men and women who had the essence of the *Chahta Okla* in their hearts. I have also known people of the Clan who acted with the same petty fears and jealousies as the white man. There is no one Clan better in Hashtahli's eyes. He sees each of us individually and when it is time for us to go to the Sacred Place, he will bless each of us according to the way we led our lives as earth walkers."

"*Nali*, I've heard the tales of how Hashtahli created the *Chahta*, but the stories say nothing of men being created separately from women. The tales of the Creator that the white men worship, at least the men I grew up with, tell of the Creator making man first, then woman. They use this concept to teach women that they're less than men."

Tima chuckled at the thought. It wasn't the first time she had heard that white man's notion. "I will tell you the way I see the difference in beliefs. When I was very young we made the Long Journey from our homeland to where we live now. A white *aba anumpuli* spoke with my father. I remember that my mother was beside Kontonalah and some of my sisters were listening. My sister, Okshakla, was older than I and she sat beside the white soldier who would become Redhawk's father. His name was John Devlin Brown."

Sarah smiled. She had often wondered how Devlin had received such a name.

"The missionary told us how his God had created man, then created woman from a piece of the man's body. I don't believe my mother was amused with the man's tale. Artamicha was a woman of some status within the Clan. Her mother's clan had all been powerful women and had married powerful warriors. Kontonalah received much of his status in the Clan by marrying Artamicha."

Tima paused and from the expression on her face, Sarah was aware that the Healer was remembering a pleasant time in her life.

"The white missionary only spoke to the men in our family. He looked at my father and John Devlin and asked them if they were glad that the Creator remembered to create a woman as an afterthought. John Devlin spoke up first. He said that he was very glad. He asked the missionary who would cook, clean, and give him children if not for woman. My father said that he too was glad. He asked the missionary who would he hunt for? Who would he go to war to protect? Who would he build a *chuka* for? Who would he dance for during harvest? I remember my mother seemed very pleased with my father's answer."

Sarah nodded her head in understanding. "John Devlin felt the loss of a woman because of what she could do for him. Kontonalah felt it as though his existence revolved around what he would do for her."

Tima nodded, still smiling. "We have some beliefs simply because that is all we know." Her smile grew larger. "John Devlin changed much before he married Okshakla. Now, let us speak more of your own Quest tomorrow. You will experience what few women of the Clan have. Yours will be a Healer's Quest."

A Healer's Quest was the last step in preparing Sarah for

the years she would spend studying to become *Alikchi*, a Medicine Woman. She would return to the high cliffs that she had visited before and would go without food and water until her Spirit guide accepted her into the ways of the Medicine Woman. A Healer's Quest was specific in that Sarah would wait for one of the thirteen original Clan Mothers to offer to become her *ikhananchi*, or teacher.

"Will I be okay if I have to stay there for four days without food and water?" Sarah asked.

"It will be difficult," Tima answered, "but what good is victory that is not earned?"

Sarah understood the truth in those words. She bowed her head and stared at her hands as they rested in her lap. She had fought her entire life to live the kind of life that *she* wanted, not what others wanted or expected of her. It had never been easy, but the rewards had been great.

"I hope we are not pushing you, Sakli; going too fast." Tima wondered if Sarah's silence meant she was feeling overwhelmed. "I prepared for a full year before my Healing Quest. I worry that I have not done enough to prepare you."

"Not so, *Nali*. I've understood the urgency of my training from the start. I know that it will take me many years to learn all I need to know, whether it's as a basket maker or a Medicine Woman. I also know that if I hadn't agreed to begin now, we might never have known about the fire or the damage the cattlemen's fences would do. Since the beginning, though, I've felt a rightness about it all. You've been a teacher, mother, and a friend to me, *Nali*. These gifts give me strength."

After the celebration feast, Sarah went inside the Prayer Lodge to take part in a purification ceremony before starting her Quest. She slept for a few hours, which felt more like minutes, in Tima's *chuka*. Even if she'd had the whole night to sleep and let go, she wouldn't have been able to. Her restless mind couldn't relax its nervous wandering.

Sarah bathed as the sun rose and donned the same leathers she had worn during her previous Quest. Keeho and Tima met the young woman and walked with her to the edge of the forest. They paused before entering the woods and Keeho drew an object from his pack.

"Sakli, I wish there were words I could speak, a spell I

could conjure to make this journey easier for you. It matters not whether the Mothers select you. Remember that I have adopted you to my hearth, and I will be proud of you no matter what. To have family is everything, and the relationship that we now share binds us as tightly as blood." Keeho placed the object in Sarah's hands. "This knife belonged to my father. I have rebound the handle and sharpened the blade many times over the winters. I give it to you now to carry with you and to remind you that my bloodline will continue through you. It was because of the Spirits that you became the daughter of my hearth. It is because of who you are that you became the daughter of my heart."

Sarah didn't know what to say to Keeho. His honest and heartfelt emotion surprised her. She had grown much closer to the old man in the past weeks. They studied and prayed together, and although Sarah felt the same way about her adopted father, she didn't dare speak the words in case the feelings weren't mutual.

Keeho, in the meantime, wasn't accustomed to such displays of emotion. Sarah's silence embarrassed him and he turned to leave. "I go," he said quickly.

"Keeho," Sarah called out. She held him back with one hand on his arm. "I will always feel honored to be at your *iksita*."

The old man smiled, which was something he rarely did anymore. He squeezed Sarah's hand and nodded in Tima's direction. He walked back toward the village, leaving the women to finish the journey to the cliffs by themselves.

Sarah helped Tima to make a small camp at the bottom of the large rocks. The older woman would stay there until Sarah returned. Tima's job as Sarah's mentor was to pray and offer spiritual strength during the time Sarah was engaged on her Quest. Tima and Sarah finally sat beside one another and offered up smoke from Tima's pipe. Sarah presented the older woman with a small pouch of tobacco tucked inside a cane basket. The basket was far from perfect, but it had been Sarah's first creation. The misshapen object reminded Sarah of the gifts her own daughter had given on occasion.

Tima pulled a flute from her own pack of supplies and played a tune. Sarah listened in wonder. "You never told me that you played the flute."

"You never asked," the Healer responded. "A good Healer demonstrates the need to create. I learned to play the flute from my grandmother. That is why I sent you to Oka kapassa to learn basket weaving."

Sarah nodded, but then her brows came together in a frown. "After all I put up with from Oka kapassa, do you mean to tell me that I could have learned the flute instead of basket making?"

"Of course."

"Why didn't you say that then?" Sarah's voice rose until she saw Tima's knowing smile. "I know, I know. Because I didn't ask," she added wryly.

"No, Sakli, because we already have a flute player in our family. We have no one who makes good baskets, though."

Tima returned to her music after the casual statement. Sarah opened her mouth to offer a retort, but stopped before she could utter a word. She could see the Healer's eyes crinkled up at the corners as she held back her smile. Sarah understood that the older woman was teasing and realized that it was as close as she would ever come to outright joking with Tima.

Sarah was tired after her climb among the trees and rocks, but she immediately began collecting the stones she would use to make a circle all around her camp. Tima had told her to select rocks that felt right. Whenever Sarah lifted a rock from the ground, she placed a bit of cornmeal in its place. The cornmeal was her offering, a way of thanking the earth for its use. She had searched the area until she found a spot that made her feel strong and powerful, and she piled the rocks in the large flat clearing. She would not make her camp until first thing the next morning when she created the circle of stones, a version of the Medicine Wheel. Sunrise would add a particular energy to the stones.

Sarah built a small fire away from the area she intended to use for her camp. Once she made her circle, she would create a hearth within its protection. Throughout her entire Quest, she would sit up at night and feed the fire. During the day, she was to sleep. Keeho had taught Sarah that the Spirits enjoyed the cloak of darkness and were more apt to visit during the night. Besides, predators like bobcats and pumas did the majority of their hunting at night.

Sarah prepared herself for the evening with a Smudging ceremony. She would use this to remove any negative Spirits from her camp, while inviting the positive Spirits to stay. Keeho had demonstrated and explained the ceremony in detail to her a number of times, and she was now able to perform it easily from memory.

Sarah gathered up some coals from the fire and placed them in a clay bowl that Keeho had given her. She tossed sage and sweetgrass onto the glowing embers so the herbs would smolder and not burn up right away. To keep the embers hot, she fanned the bowl with the hawk feather she had received on her first Quest. She fanned the smoke toward her chest and then over her head. This way, she drew out and away any negative feelings within her heart. Finally, she offered up the bowl to the four directions.

She sat for a while and absently fed small sticks into the fire. She thought and prayed, and then she thought some more. She took advantage of the chance to walk around, wandering along the top of the sandstone cliffs and around the ancient cedar trees with their twisted and deformed trunks. Once she built her circle of stones, she was only supposed to leave when absolutely necessary. She was surprised that the afternoon turned into night so quickly. What surprised her even more was when the first rays of the sun peeked over the horizon and she was still awake.

Sarah offered up more smoke and went about building her camp. First, she arranged the large circle of stones. Near the north end of the circle, she made a hearth for a fire. In the middle, she built a small lean-to of wood poles and cedar fronds. She set an opening in the stones to the east so she could leave the circle when necessary. Every time she re-entered the circle, however, she replaced the stones as if closing the door to a cabin. Without another thought after the camp's completion, she curled onto her fur blanket and promptly fell asleep.

Sarah awoke a number of times during the day. The bright sun and the constant chatter of the birds nearly kept her awake, but she refused to budge from her sleeping robe. She knew that she would need every bit of rest to stay alert at night and feed the fire. Finally, as late afternoon passed and the sun dipped low in the horizon, she made a trip to the bushes. She was refreshed and prepared for her journey. The growling in her stomach was annoying, but not painful. She hoped that she would return to the Clan village before the growls turned into pangs.

Sarah heard movement in the brush in front of her. She carefully slipped her hand around the handle of the bone knife that Keeho had given her. She watched, not moving at all, as the branches quivered. Suddenly, her breath caught in her throat as an animal burst through the dense thicket. A large deer, a buck with a heavy set of antlers on his head, looked at Sarah. He stopped a dozen feet from her circle and sniffed the air suspiciously. Sarah found it odd, since deer usually didn't go anywhere near fire. The animal acted as if she wasn't even there. There was additional movement in the bushes. Sarah watched as eight does came from the same thicket and followed the buck down a narrow path into the trees.

"Well, that was good to get the heart beating." Sarah laughed aloud. She released her grip on the knife and fed some more wood into the fire. She wondered how long it would be before one of the Clan Mothers came to her.

She made herself comfortable, sitting cross-legged before the fire. She was supposed to think of nothing, empty her mind and call to the Mothers. This was supposed to signal her willingness to learn the Medicine Way. She found it difficult. Clearing her mind of the things she thought about every day was quite a chore. She knew that people depended on her and the outcome of this Quest.

Sarah didn't have any real expectations regarding this Quest. She had many hopes, however. She believed that the future of the *Chahta* people depended on her in more ways than simply opening up the prairie and predicting a fire. True, she had found a way to convince the cattlemen to remove their fences, but the Vision she'd had that day in the Prayer Lodge felt like so much more. She remembered every detail. How, with each buffalo's death, a member of the Clan disappeared. She also recalled Tima's plea for help in the Vision. She felt the weight of responsibility for these people who were now her people.

Sarah felt her head nod and she jerked it upright again. "Okay, looks like meditation with my eyes closed could be trouble."

She settled herself again and stared into the orange flames. Now she knew why Tima had suggested that she collect small twigs and sticks to constantly feed into the fire. The large limbs would have lasted longer, but then she would have nothing to do. Tossing the twigs into the fire kept her focused and awake.

A noise in the brush pulled her mind from its empty wandering once more. "Not you again," Sarah said. She chuckled until an animal popped into view.

Sarah froze and was afraid of even taking in another breath. A large, muscled puma stood before her exactly where the deer had been. The cat sniffed, its nose raised high in the air. The puma came to the very edge of her circle, its large paws barely making a sound as they padded along on the soft earth. Its muzzle was coated in blood and she thought that was why the cat hadn't attacked. Perhaps it had just eaten.

The animal stood there looking at Sarah, then sniffed the stones that she had carefully put into place that morning. It opened its mouth and gave a sort of yowl. The sound wasn't similar to the loud cries Sarah had heard big cats make. This was soft, as if the puma had yawned. It plunked down on the ground, the dirt rising up around it as it settled comfortably in place.

Sarah could only assume that the animal wasn't hungry right now. She realized that there was nothing to stop her from becoming next on the menu. She slowly reached for her knife again. It was right beside her, but the cat looked up at her as if knowing what she was doing. It growled under its breath, licked its paws, then rubbed them across its face. The cat repeated the whole procedure until its face was clean of the blood.

Sarah held the sharp knife tightly, but she knew that even if she managed to surprise the cat, it was too large for her to fend off with only a knife. She watched as the puma cleaned itself and looked around, apparently surprised to find Sarah still there. It made the soft yowl again.

Sarah tried to remember everything that anyone had ever taught her about dealing with predators. She couldn't seem to come up with anything that would help her in this situation. The cat stared hard at her again and licked its muzzle. It appeared to Sarah as though the puma was considering if she would make a good meal or not. She decided to try the one thing that had worked for her when people were involved– reason.

"Hi there," Sarah said. The cat's whiskers twitched at the sound of her voice. "I bet this part of the forest belongs to you, huh?" she asked, already knowing the answer.

The cat jumped up, causing Sarah to jerk back in response. The cat walked around the perimeter of Sarah's camp and lifted its nose into the air once more, then returned to its previous position, lying outside the circle of stones. The expression on the cat's face looked like a question to Sarah. *Why shouldn't I eat you?* was what Sarah's mind heard.

"You can see how very small I am," Sarah began. "I wouldn't make much of a meal for a bobcat, let alone a big puma such as yourself." She searched her brain for some better reasons, and the perfect one hit her. She hoped those deer took their position within the Sacred Hoop seriously.

"Besides, human flesh isn't really very healthy for you. From what I hear, a nice fat deer would be much better than little, stringy me. Don't you agree?"

The cat blinked in a bored fashion and Sarah, inside her head, heard *Go on, you said something about deer?*

"You know, a herd of deer came through this very spot not too long ago. They followed that path over there." Sarah pointed nervously to the path that led into the trees. "They're still around, I bet, and in the circle of life, there are so many more of them than of me."

The puma licked its muzzle two or three times and Sarah had a feeling it was thinking of dinner. The cat rose and looked around the camp, then back at Sarah. She swore the look said, *Now, in which direction did they go?*

Sarah lifted a shaking finger toward the path and the puma looked in that direction. It offered up another soft yowl and padded off silently into the underbrush. Sarah quickly threw some more wood into the fire until the flames were high and then she fell back onto her sleeping robe. She was sure the chattering of her teeth echoed back and forth across the cliffs.

Sarah sat before her small fire in a very dejected mood. She always became discouraged when things didn't happen the way she expected them to, though her disappointment never lasted long. This was the last night of her Quest. She would have to return to Tima empty-handed, in a way. Sarah had sat, her mind clear, waiting in the stillness. Still, none of the Clan Mothers had appeared to her. Now it was difficult to keep from thinking about how thirsty she was. The hunger wasn't so bad. After the second day, she hadn't felt very hungry at all.

Sarah sighed and tossed a few more sticks into the fire. She had chanted some of the old words that Keeho taught her, but still there was only silence around her camp. The puma had never returned, but the deer had. She felt guilty when the herd passed by her camp again, minus one of its number. The buck looked at her the same way as the large cat had, as if it understood. He had lowered his massive set of antlers in her direction as if to say his people were aware of their place on the Sacred Hoop.

Sarah dropped her chin into the palm of her hand and stared

at the fire. She closed her eyes and fought back tears. "Please, Sacred Mother, show yourself," she muttered in exasperation.

"Finally!" A voice sounded in front of Sarah.

Sarah opened her eyes as her mouth formed the shape of an O.

"Sakli, I am The One Who Keeps The Wisdom. The Clan Mothers have sent me as an emissary to offer you inclusion into the Way. You have kept me waiting, little one."

"But I've been here for days!" Sarah said. "I've stilled myself, and cleared my mind, and I–" she stopped abruptly. The soft sound of laughter met her ears and immediately she covered her face with both hands. "I forgot to ask you to come to me," she admitted at last. "All this time I was waiting for you to come to me and– "

"I was waiting for an invitation." The old woman finished the sentence. "But we are together at last and we have much to accomplish."

"But I have to return to Tima's camp by midday tomorrow," Sarah said.

"Have no fear, little one. You will find that time moves differently for those who walk in the Spirit World than it does for the earth walkers. You have made a declaration to learn the Way for the sake of your Clan. I am only one of the Medicine Women from the original thirteen Clans. Over the course of your life, I will visit you often, as will the other Mothers. It will take many winters to attain the knowledge necessary to be a true Medicine Woman."

"When will I learn all I need to know?" Sarah asked.

"On the day that you pass over to the Sacred Place, then you will have learned all you need to know."

Sarah smiled. "So, what you're saying is that I'll never really stop learning. I'll never know all there is to know about being a Medicine Woman, even until the day I die."

"You are an intelligent young woman, Sakli. This *Chahta* Clan has chosen well. Now, we have work to do. Are you willing to accept the sacrifices necessary to follow the Way?"

"I suppose I would want to know what kind of sacrifices we're talking about," Sarah responded.

"In order to become a Mother to the Clan you will be expected to give up your all to the original Mothers."

"And what will I receive? What will the Mothers do for me in return?"

"We will teach you to see," the old woman replied.

"I don't know." Sarah smiled. "I think I've been able to see pretty well for some time now all on my own."

The older woman chuckled at Sarah's humor. "Sakli, the Mothers will teach you to see what is beyond the ability of an earth walker. We will teach you to see truth and beauty, as well as ugliness and lies. We will always be there to comfort you in your own pain and not least of all, we will teach you to see and heal the pain of others."

Sarah thought for a moment. "I understand and I accept your offer."

"Good. Now we shall begin."

Suddenly Sarah and the old woman were standing before a wall of rock. They were high up on a cliff face and Sarah looked down to the ground below. She could just make out her own little camp with its circle of stones and bright campfire. The outer rock ledge upon which they now stood glowed orange as the sandstone captured the light from a torch in the old woman's hand. Sarah looked before her to see an opening, like a doorway, carved into the rock. She raised her head and saw many such dwellings carved into the rocks.

The old woman indicated the entrance and handed Sarah the torch. "The Mothers see in you, Sakli, the heart of a Medicine Woman. It is important that we also know what you see in yourself. Travel through the *kiva* and I will be waiting for you on the other side. If you turn back to exit through this door, then you cannot be accepted into the Way."

"What's in there?" Sarah asked as she strained to see into the darkened opening.

"Friends...enemies...family. To see the end of any journey, one must simply see the truth. Hurry now. It will take you many days to find the truth."

Sarah turned to face the old woman once more, but found herself alone on the rock ledge. She realized there was nothing to do but go forward. She clutched the torch in her sweaty grasp and stepped into the dark lodge. The same orange glow appeared when the coppery flames from her torch danced upon the walls. Her ears picked up a soft sound, low like the beat of a drum. She turned in a circle to find the source of the sound.

"It is the heartbeat of Mother Earth." The voice was a deep alto that Sarah knew well, but when she turned to look, it wasn't Devlin's face. The black-and-white dancer now whispered in her ear. "The *chuka* reminds you of a womb. This is your rebirth, Sarah. Happiness mixes with pain. If you accept the joy, you must be able to stand the pain. Can you truly face all that the truth might show you?"

"Yes," Sarah answered with an intense confidence she didn't entirely feel. When she looked again, the dancer had disappeared.

Sarah kept moving through the maze of rooms. She saw images of those whom she loved and faces from her past. Some of the Spirits spoke to her, but most of them simply watched with lifeless expressions as she passed them by. She spoke to some, but she knew that she would never repeat the words, this Vision, to anyone. There were numerous times when she thought to turn back. Some of the Spirits she saw there hurt her soul deeply. It was only her will, the unshakable drive that had been with her since birth, that prodded her into placing one foot in front of the other to keep moving forward.

Sarah also saw herself at different ages and in many different circumstances. She was the child who thought her dreams had killed her mother. Later, she was the young woman whose will couldn't save her father's life. She was child and adult, happy and sad. The dancer had been right. Birth was a thing of joy and pain mixed together as one emotion.

Sarah felt the maze of earthen rooms ending. She looked at the torch in her hand and watched as the flame popped and burned weakly. The material wrapped around the head of the torch had almost burned away. She saw one last obstacle ahead of her. A figure stood before the opening to the outside world, blocking Sarah's path.

"Who are you?" she asked at last when the figure did not speak as the others had.

"I am the truth, Sakli. I am your best friend and your greatest enemy. I have the power to lift you up and the ability to conquer your very soul. Come closer if you wish to face the truth."

Sarah paused before taking one hesitant step. The figure was dressed as the black-and-white dancer had been. Instead of black and white face paint, however, a black cloth masked the figure's features. The stranger beckoned Sarah forward with one hand.

"You are *Keyuachi*," Sarah said to the figure. "You are doubt."

"Look again, Sakli. I do not exist if you do not wish it so.

Do you hide from the truth?"

Sarah took another step forward and quickly reached out with one hand. She ripped the black cloth from the stranger's face. She gasped as the dying remains of the torch sputtered in her hand. She stood frozen in place, her breathing accelerated as if she were unable to take in enough air. What the stranger had told her now made perfect sense, as Sarah stared into her own silent reflection.

"We are one, Sarah. Don't let these people convince you that you are what you are not. You will never be special."

A look of pain flashed across Sarah's features as she remembered her mother saying something very similar when she had been a small child. Her mother knew that Sarah could Dream, and the woman had discouraged her from believing in such nonsense, believing that she might be special. Sarah felt like crumpling in on herself. She felt like a pretender in a fantasy world inside her own mind. For so many years, she had stifled the anger and resentment she felt for her mother. It wouldn't have been kind to think badly of the departed. She finally realized it had been that thinking which had led her to give up so many times in her young life.

Sarah's brow creased together and her jaw tightened. "You are wrong. There is one difference between us, *Keyuachi.*" She lifted her hand and shoved what little remained of the failing torch into her mirror image's face.

The *Keyuachi* screamed in pain and flailed in agony until it dissipated into nothing. The *Keyuachi* turned into a ghost-like wraith and screamed as it flew around the room, circling the ceiling above Sarah's head.

"The difference is that I don't give up," Sarah shouted over the screams of the wailing *Keyuachi.* The wraith circled the room once more and flew out the door it had once guarded. Darkness surrounded her, but Sarah followed the *Keyuachi's* glowing light trail out of the room.

"Congratulations, little one." The Clan Mother stood before Sarah in the middle of her camp as if they had never left. "It took you many winters, but ultimately you saw in yourself the same strength that we see."

Sarah stared in confusion. She was not only in her own camp, but her campfire still burned strongly. She remembered the Mother telling her that she would be in the cliff maze for days. Looking around, she realized that only moments had passed.

"You look unsteady, Sakli. Sit down." The older woman sat on the ground with Sarah. She offered the young woman some food and drink. "Go ahead," she said in response to Sarah's reticence. "Your Quest is over, Sakli. You are now a Medicine Woman."

"I don't feel any different," Sarah said between mouthfuls of water and *banaha*.

"What did you expect?" The older woman laughed.

"Well, I don't know. I guess I thought you'd suddenly fill me with all sorts of wisdom or something."

"But we have, Sakli."

"I don't know anything different than I did before," Sarah replied slowly.

"When the time comes, little one, you will know. It will take time for all of the knowing to work its way into your waking mind, but in time you will understand. Learning the Way must be a slow process, Sakli, for anything with the power to heal has just as equal a power to harm. Remember to always act, not react. And when you act, never let it be out of fear."

"Thank you– all of you."

"You are welcome, little one. The honor is in the giving. Now, Sakli, you are responsible. In your Clan's language, you are now *isht ahalaia*. It means that you are not only responsible for your own health and spiritual development any longer. Just as you are mother to your physical children, so must you be mother to your Clan. You are responsible for the welfare of the children of your body, just as they are similarly responsible for the care of their aging parent. As Medicine Woman, you are responsible for every person in your Clan. They will also protect and care for you as a parent. You must now look to the needs of your *Chahta* Clan no less than you look to the needs of yourself and your own family. This is parallel to the Clan's interconnectedness with all people and the world around them. It is also a way of saying that we should treat others as we treat ourselves."

Sarah yawned deeply.

"Sleep now, little one. Your future begins at first light."

Sarah and Tima embraced when the young woman found her way into the Healer's camp the next day. Sarah winced and Tima quickly turned her around to examine the source of the pain.

"Did you know this was here?" Tima asked.

Sarah scrunched up her eyebrows and pulled at the leather on her shoulder. She grabbed at a part of the buckskin that appeared cut away. Through the opening, she could see part of a gash on the top of her shoulder. "I must have cut myself on the rocks last night," Sarah remarked absently.

Tima smiled as she examined the mark. "When this heals, you will have a scar," she said. "It will look like this." She took a stick and drew a mark in the dirt for Sarah to see.

Sarah smiled at the older woman. Her scar would resemble a feather, the mark of a *Chahta* Medicine Woman.

"I admit, *Sakli*," Tima began with tears in her eyes, "last night I saw the *Keyuachi*."

Sarah smiled to herself. "I know what you mean. I'm getting sick of them myself. I'll tell you about it someday. Right now, I'm starving. Do you have anything to eat?"

Tima laughed at the young woman and they sat down together. Tima brought out fruit, bread, and a jug of water that she'd recently filled. She listened as Sarah related parts of her Quest. She knew that the young woman left gaps in her story, but that was her right.

Finally, Sarah spoke up with a question of her own. "*Nali*, would it be ill-mannered of me to ask why you're not a Medicine Woman? Didn't the Clan Mothers select you?"

"I was selected to train another." Tima smiled and placed her hand over Sarah's. She had never told anyone, aside from Keeho, what the Spirits had said to her as a young woman. "The Clan Mothers did come to me during my Healing Quest. They gave me a choice that day. I could become *Alikchi*, or I could train another. They told me that some day, someone would come who had no knowledge of the Clan ways. This one would have no mother from whom to receive her training or even status in the Clan, but she would possess the power to save the *Chahta* ways. I chose the path of responsibility instead of the path of recognition. I have never been more happy about my choice."

Chapter 15

Three miles after the incident at the Salt Fork, the herd crossed Pond Creek. There was a large pond on the south side just east of the trail, which gave the creek its name. More prairie dogs, Indian parties, and buffalo crossed their paths. When they reached Polecat Creek, Devlin knew they were in Kansas.

They crossed the flat prairies of Kansas, riding through fields of sunflowers and goldenrods. They saw an increasing number of Osage orange trees planted in rows. That was a sure sign of farmers, or nesters, as the riders called them. The farmers called the fruit hedge apples and they planted the trees as windbreaks and natural fencing. Herds of buffalo still crossed their trail, but their numbers dwindled the further the drovers pushed north.

Just after they crossed over the Chikaskia River, a group of Osage warriors approached them looking for tobacco and a steer. Devlin gave the small party two steers, but refused to give them any tobacco. Some of her men had some and she knew that Mexican Bob even kept a store of it on the chuck wagon. It saddened her that what once was Sacred to these people had become so commonplace. She herself had even enjoyed a cheroot or two, but on those rare occasions, a small part of her could always see Tima's scolding glance.

On day number fifty, Devlin and the Double Deuce drovers

reached the Arkansas River. They forded the clear water without having to swim. The water was shallow, making the six-hundred-yard width easier to cross. They rode on past the village of Wichita. It was a growing place on the site of an Indian camp. Jesse Chisholm had built a trading post at the mouth of the river and little by little, the village grew. Wichita had a few stores, a saloon, blacksmith, and saddle shops. There couldn't have been more than twenty or thirty families there, but Devlin was mistrustful enough to steer the herd clear of the village.

After crossing the Arkansas, there was a change in the drovers surrounding the herd. Devlin even felt it herself. For the first time since they had started out, she allowed herself to believe they might actually make it. They crossed flat prairies grown high with mesquite grass and more Osage orange trees, heavily laden with hard green fruits.

On day number fifty-three, they reached Elm Springs. The cool springs joined the Smoky Hill River and flowed directly past Abilene. They were now only twenty-seven miles south of their destination. They had shelter, firewood, and water in the area surrounding Elm Springs. Devlin ordered the herds to find some good campground and settle in for a day or two. She and a few others would now have to complete the task of selling the herd.

This last bit would be the easiest of the drive. Although Devlin didn't relish the thought of dealing with the men who sold beef to the railways, at least she wouldn't have to haggle. The price had been set and Sarah had telegrammed Abilene before the drive left the Territory.

Devlin brought Hank and two other men from her own herd along with her into Abilene. She didn't want the drovers too close to town just yet, at least not until they'd moved the herds into the stockyards. It didn't take long to settle with the men of the Kansas Pacific Railway, and a day later she and her party were on their way back to the herd.

The following morning, on day number fifty-eight, they drove the herds to camp on the Smoky Hill River. They were two and one-half miles away from Abilene. The men who ran the railway market had told Devlin it might take a thousand cars to ship all the beef, so she had agreed to bring in two herds a day. Most would be shipped east to the slaughterhouses. There had been a shortage of livestock in the west, so a number of each herd would go in that direction as farm stock. The *remudas*, minus the drovers' personal mounts, were also sold to go west. Seven days later, Devlin rode into Abilene with the last of the herd. She accepted bank drafts from the three railway companies and immediately headed toward the town's bank.

Devlin dreaded this part. Hank and Matt came along as moral support. Actually, it had seemed more like an order to them. They prepared to be within the bank's four walls for most of the day as they counted and separated each ranch's take for the drive. Devlin's bonuses and shares that belonged to her simply for leading the drive had to be parceled out from each rancher's share. Lastly, there was the pay for the men. While Devlin handled all the other monies using bank drafts and wires, she paid the men in cash. She realized that, unfortunately, by the time they left Abilene, most of the drovers would have spent their hard-earned wages on food, drink, and entertainment, usually of the female variety.

The trio sat inside the cramped offices of Malcolm E. Sanders, an officer of the bank. The young man wore wire-framed lenses and spoke in a rapid clip. Devlin thought that was mostly because the bookish gentleman kept glancing at the six-guns she and Hank wore.

Matt, sucking on a hard candy he'd bought at the general store, leaned over Malcolm's desk and watched the man add columns of figures. The bank man kept looking up as though he wanted to request that the boy move back a bit, but then he would look at Devlin and Hank and get back to work adding numbers. He repeated each figure aloud as he read it from the book in which Devlin had carefully detailed all the herd numbers. As Malcolm added the sums on a piece of ledger paper, Matt watched him write and Devlin silently tapped her fingers together.

When Malcolm revealed the total figure, Devlin arched an eyebrow. "You're off by five hundred sixty-three dollars and thirty-seven cents," she pointed out.

"Well, I-I certainly don't know how— I mean, I— " Malcolm stammered. He was usually very accurate in his sums, but this group unnerved him. He wondered how a woman like this had amassed so much wealth and most of all, how she knew so quickly that his figures were off. Her expression looked like one of amusement rather than anger, but Malcolm was disturbed nonetheless.

"You have to carry the two here." Matt pointed to the man's

ledger and smiled amiably. His teeth were tinged pink by the candy he'd been eating.

"Uh, yes...I see. Honestly, I wasn't trying to– "

"Calm down, Malcolm," Devlin said as she removed her hat and ran her fingers through her hair. "We don't shoot people for bad math. Well, not the first time anyway." She winked at Matt. "Just relax and do your job."

"Yes, ma'am."

The young man finished the rest of the figures and filled out the information necessary to wire the monies to the appropriate people. Cordelia had been right. The cattle drive made them all rich, that much was certain. Devlin had never had so much money in her whole life.

"And this one, Miss Brown?" Malcolm indicated Devlin's money.

"Wire it into the same account as Sarah Tolliver's." Devlin couldn't think of much use for the money beyond her new family, so she figured it might as well all go into the same pot. "Wait a minute. I reckon I'll have fifty dollars in cash."

Malcolm smiled. It was the first time he did so that day. The soft-spoken rider, who didn't seem to put much stock in the enormous wealth she now controlled, genuinely affected the young man. "Will you need to hire guards to pay your men?" It seemed a ridiculous question given the rider's gleaming pistols, but it was his duty.

Devlin grinned at the young man. "I don't think we'll find anyone foolish enough to try to take it away from us, do you?"

"No, ma'am." Malcolm returned the pleasant smile.

"What about me, Dev?" Matt asked as he looked at the cash the rider tucked into her pocket.

"You're the hired help, son. You get paid when the men get paid." Devlin laughed at the anxious boy. "Malcolm, it was a pleasure doin' business with you."

The next day Devlin gave the men their pay and their bonuses. Out of nearly fifty thousand head of cattle, they'd lost fewer than four hundred. The men who planned to return to the Double Deuce as riders allowed Devlin to bank their bonuses. Most of them realized that if they had the money in their pockets in a town like Abilene, it wouldn't stay there long.

The order for pay was riders first, then came the cooks and finally, the nighthawks and wranglers. When Matt stepped forward for his pay, Hank looked at Devlin.

"You made thirty dollars for the drive. Plus, you get a bonus just like everyone else. Your total wages are a hundred and thirty dollars. Give him ten in cash," Devlin told Hank.

"Aw, Dev," Matt complained. The others who had stayed around camp laughed at the boy's disappointment, since they all knew what kind of a taskmaster the trail boss could be.

Devlin considered it and gave the young man a smirk. "Okay, twenty, but I best see you in new clothes when we get on that train day after tomorrow."

"You got it, boss."

When the metal cash box was empty, Hank closed it with an air of finality. "Looks like you did it, Dev. Sarah's gonna be awful happy with ya. You done good, my friend. Real good."

Devlin smiled one of her genuine smiles. She knew Hank was one of the few people to realize what an accomplishment the drive had been for her. He also realized how much she had been missing Sarah.

"You think there's anyway to get home in a day?" Devlin asked.

Hank laughed at his friend's lovesick expression. "If there was, Dev, I know you'd be the one to find it."

Devlin went to town early the next morning. She promised Matt that she would come back to camp and take him into town for a spell. In all honesty, she had wanted just a bit of time to herself. First thing she did was to send a wire back home in hopes that it would reach Sarah at the *Chahta* village. Then she headed over to the store and bought a new set of clothes— not everyday clothes, but a real dressy suit. She decked herself out all in black except for a gold brocade vest and a white shirt. She even bought a pair of black boots. She felt a bit like one of the poker-playing gamblers who hung around the saloon's gaming tables. Once she had her new clothes tucked under her arm, she made her way straight for the first place that offered a hot bath in private. Once she arrived back in camp, her good humor faded fast.

"What do you mean he went to town? Alone?" Devlin raged at the men left in camp. She had been looking for Matt for an hour before someone finally spoke up to tell her where he was.

"Well, no, boss. He went with Sparks and Jimmy One-eye."

"He went with those two mutton-heads. What for?" Devlin

looked around at the men who suddenly found the dirt at their feet filled with interest. "I said what for?" She was shouting now and she saw one or two of them flinch.

"Well, ya know, he's a guy and he has...guy kinda needs." Buster had ridden drag for Devlin's herd and now she knew why it was the only position he could handle.

"Tell me you didn't," she said taking a step closer to the man. "Tell me you didn't send my son to get laid in a whorehouse in Abilene!"

Buster swallowed and tried to muster up some nerve. He looked around, but he didn't find any support from the other riders. The men simply hoped that Devlin wouldn't single out any of them to vent her wrath upon.

"Well, I figured— I mean, he's a guy and— "

"He's a boy!"

"I did it when I was his age," Buster made the mistake of saying.

"That's because you're an idiot!" Devlin shouted as she mounted her horse. "You better hope I find him in time."

"Well, what if he's already done it, boss?"

"Then I'm comin' back and breakin' both your legs," Devlin yelled back as she rode off in the direction of town.

Devlin now found herself in the part of town south of the railroad known as Texas Abilene. She went to every bar and dance hall she could find in search of the two half-witted riders and Matthew. She looked in the Bull's Head, the Elkhorn, the Pearl, the Old Fruit, and finally Tom Downey's. She was growing worried as she entered the Alamo.

The Alamo was one long room with a forty-foot front on Cedar Street, facing west. The bar had an entrance on each end. The front had three double glass doors, which always remained open. A bar with sparkling brass fixtures and rails ran the length of the back wall, and behind that were large mirrors. Large paintings of nude women hung on the side walls. Devlin searched the spacious floor area, but even though they had an orchestra playing, the floor was taken up mostly by gaming tables.

Devlin looked through the glass doors out onto Cedar Street. There, across the street, stood Matthew. The young man looked up at one of the many two-story buildings, but he didn't move. Devlin didn't have to be told what the building housed. She quickly left the Alamo and came up behind the unwitting youngster.

Just as Matthew rubbed his sweaty palms along his new pants and took a step forward, his momentum was stopped by a hand around his collar. He knew he would recognize that steely grip anywhere.

"Aw, Dev!"

"Just what in hellfire are you doin', boy?" Devlin didn't have the heart to say anything more.

Matt stood there with his hands thrust deep in his pockets and his cheeks tinged pink. "Don't matter. I was too afraid to go in anyway," he mumbled.

Devlin put an arm around the boy's shoulder and gently directed him out of the street. She instantly remembered how terrified she'd been her first time. "I learned a little something about fear the last couple of months, Matt. You wanna hear what it is?"

Matt shrugged his shoulders as they walked. Devlin still had her hand on the boy's back when she noticed something she hadn't before. The top of his head came up past her shoulder. Sarah stood just shoulder high to Devlin and the last time the rider had seen mother and son together, Sarah had been a bit taller than Matt.

Devlin paused and leaned against the wooden railing in front of one of the many stores in town. "Sometimes fear is our brain tellin' us that we're doin' somethin' mighty stupid."

"Yeah, but I thought you said that sometimes you have to just go ahead and be afraid; that sometimes you just have to push yourself."

"Sometimes you do. You're right, Matt. However, you have to take the time to look at each side, to decide if what you're doin' is gonna help in the long run or if it's just gonna hurt or, even worse, get you killed. A smart man makes decisions after thinking about the consequences of his actions."

Matt simply stood there, apparently processing the information the rider was giving him. This was one of the many reasons she took pride in the boy. He always seemed to listen to her and take her words to heart. Whether he believed them or not was another matter.

"You ever been to places like that, Dev?"

Devlin sighed. She didn't understand all the specifics of how men felt about this particular rite of passage, but she'd lived closer to men than most women ever would. She lived in their world as an equal. She saw them in ways many of their wives never would. "Matt, I grew up different than you. Different rules applied back then. Yeah, I visited places like that one, but you got a chance to live your life better than I did. Do you know what I regret most about givin' it up to calico queens in sportin' houses like that one?"

Matt shook his head, wondering if he should be embarrassed about having this conversation with the woman he had begun to think of as another mother. He liked that she talked to him like an adult instead of simply ordering him around. Most of all, he knew she had always been honest with him. He questioned whether the tall woman actually understood all that he felt.

"I missed out on something very special, like meeting a girl in school or at a picnic. I missed growin' up together and planning for a future. Meetin' a woman like your mother when I was younger might have changed the direction of my life. I'm awful glad I met her when I did, Matt. I'm happy with my life right where I'm at, but I sure wasted a whole lot of time gettin' here."

The brim of the young man's hat hid his eyes. He lowered his head before he spoke. "I guess I felt like I was— like I should, ya know? Besides, well, I kinda wanted to know, you know— how it felt." Matt's voice trailed off until it was barely audible.

"Yeah, I know, Matt. I really do." Devlin stood up to her full height and placed her hands on each side of Matt's face. "Your day will come, Matt. Just don't be in such an all-fire hurry, okay? You'll grow up into the man your father wanted you to be if you think more with this," she poked a finger against Matt's forehead, "instead of that." She ended by pointing in the direction of the boy's belt.

Matt had a hard time keeping the grin off his face. Maybe Devlin did know how he felt after all.

"Hey, you hungry?" Devlin asked.

"I could eat."

"Good, 'cause I'm half starved and parched like the devil. Since we're all duded up, I might as well buy you dinner. You ever sleep in a hotel bed?"

"Nope."

"Then we're treatin' ourselves tonight. Come on."

"But, Dev, the Merchant's Hotel is that way," Matt finally said when he realized Devlin had pulled him toward the north side of town.

"That's where the riders go. This," Devlin took off her hat and directed Matt's eyes to the gold-painted sign that read *Drover's Cottage,* "this is where the trail bosses and the cattle buyers come."

Matt looked through the glass windows at the men in fancy suits and ladies in long dresses. "But Dev," Matt whispered. "I ain't no boss."

"No, but I am and you're my son. I don't reckon folks will complain to me, do you? Besides," Devlin opened the front door and pushed the boy inside. "I know the owner."

"I need two rooms," Devlin said to the desk clerk's back.

The man spun around with a smile on his face. "Why, yes, sir— I mean— uh, madam." He went from snobbishly confident to flustered once he turned and saw the tall woman at the desk.

"Two of your best rooms, next to each other. I want a private bath, too."

"Uh, yes, ma'am. If you'll just— make your mark here."

Devlin arched an eyebrow at the nervous fellow and signed her full name in her customary precise, angular script. He turned the ledger and read her name aloud. "Devlin Brown."

Devlin was sure she heard a few conversations stop in the lobby around her. She didn't let it bother her; she'd become used to it over the years. She pulled a few bills from her pocket and placed them on the polished hotel desk. Only a heartbeat passed before a large hand slapped over the money, trapping Devlin's hand underneath.

"Your money's no good here, Brown."

Matt took a step back and watched the stranger confronting Devlin. He was a large man, even taller than Hank. He had a bigger gut than Hank did, but this man's arms looked like tree trunks.

"Devlin Brown, you whiskey-drinkin', gunfightin' dally welter!" the man growled.

"Well, if it ain't J.B. Carpenter, you no-good, whorin', sorry excuse for a horse thief," Devlin hissed back.

"I told you I'd kill ya if I ever saw you again, Brown."

"And I recall sayin' you'd die tryin'."

The two stared one another down and with each passing tick of the large clock on the wall, the people in the hotel lobby waited to see what drama would unfold. Suddenly Devlin burst into laughter. The large man then engulfed her in a bone-crushing bear hug.

"I knew you'd crack first." The man laughed as he spoke.

"That's only 'cause the idea of you tryin' to kick my ass is so damn funny!" Devlin replied.

"How the hell are ya, Dev? Hank said in his last letter that you went to work for a woman."

"I'm real good, and trust me, Hank didn't tell ya the half of it." Devlin looked over her shoulder to see Matt with a very confused expression on his face. "It's okay, son, come 'ere. Matt, I'd like you to meet the owner of this rat trap," she said with a wink. "This is J.B. Carpenter, the worst drover that ever rode the trail, but one of the smartest businessmen you'll ever hope to meet. J.B. is Hank's little brother, and I use the word *little* kinda loosely."

Matt grinned from ear to ear once Devlin let him in on the joke. He shook hands with Hank's brother and stepped back once more.

"You're startin' out these drovers a bit young, ain't ya, Dev?"

"Matt's my son," Devlin answered without hesitation.

J.B. didn't think the boy's smile could get much larger. He'd never seen Devlin looking so relaxed. Obviously, his brother had saved the best part of her story for their family reunion that evening.

"Like I said, Dev, your money's no good around here. James, see that my friends get the best we have to offer," J.B. said to the desk clerk. "How about dinner, you two?"

"Well, if you're crazy enough to part with your money, I sure ain't fool enough to turn you down. A good meal is just what I'd like about now," Devlin replied. "How about you, Matt? Think you could eat enough to run up a big bill on this dandy?"

"Yes, ma'am," Matt replied enthusiastically.

True to his word, J.B. showed the two to the best table in the house. Devlin and Matt placed their hats on the empty chairs beside them. Matt seemed a little unsure of all the crystal and silver set on the table. Devlin had been there before, but still tended to feel overwhelmed at the amount of cutlery. She placed the cloth napkin in her lap and Matt repeated her actions.

"You still like the good stuff, Dev?" J.B. asked.

"When I can get it. I've grown kinda fond of Kentucky Bourbon of late."

"Rose," J.B. turned to a young woman with a tray in her hands, "bring my friends here a bottle of Madam Cliquot. You want that over ice, Dev?" he asked with a grin.

"You're kiddin' me, right?"

"Nope. They cut it from the Republican River in the winter and we store it in barns through the summer. It costs me six cents a pound, but on a hot day it's worth it."

"I'm game. Never had ice in the summer, though," Devlin answered.

"Now, what do ya say to a couple of steaks with all the trimmings?" J.B. asked, rubbing his hands together as if he were making a sale.

"Please, J.B., I been on the trail for two months. I'm sick to death of beef," Devlin complained.

"Okay, okay. We got a ham steak about an inch thick served with fried potatoes and greens."

Devlin smiled and looked over at Matthew. The young man nodded his head eagerly. "Sounds like a deal."

"Okay, I'll let you two eat in peace and I'll come back when you're having your coffee. Rose, treat my guests here well."

"Yes sir, Mr. Carpenter." The waitress returned with Devlin's whiskey. She filled the glass with ice from a silver bucket, which she left on the table. She then poured a generous amount of the amber liquid into the heavy crystal glass and turned to Matthew. "And for you, sir?"

Matt looked a little surprised that the waitress was talking to him, but Devlin answered for him. "He'll have milk."

"Aw, Dev. Don't I get to have no fun?"

"I'll give ya fun," she answered with a smirk. "Oh, okay, quit lookin' at me with your mother's eyes. You know the difference between a sip and a swallow?" she asked the waitress. When Rose nodded, Devlin continued. "He can have a sip."

Rose smiled and poured no more than a tablespoon of whiskey in Matt's glass. "Enjoy. If you need anything at all, just ask. I'll be back with your dinners in no time."

Devlin held her glass up toward Matt. "This is the smoothest whiskey you'll ever taste in these parts. You did a good job this summer, Matt. Here's to a quick train ride home."

They tapped their glasses together and Matt smiled at the musical ring the crystal gave off when they made contact. He drank the small amount of liquor in one swallow. It burned his throat going down and his eyes watered. He appeared to be holding his breath.

"Don't be proud, boy." Devlin pushed a glass of water in

front of Matt. "Take a drink."

Matt gulped the water until his throat felt better. When his breathing returned to normal, Devlin set her own glass down.

"So, what did ya think?"

"You're right– smooth," Matt replied hoarsely.

Devlin laughed at the young man's antics. "I hope you enjoyed it. That's the last alcohol I want to ever catch you drinking for some time yet."

"How long?" Matt questioned.

"Until you're as tall as me."

"Aw, Dev, that'll be forever!"

The rider laughed once more and remembered how Matt had grown this summer. "Not nearly as long as you think, son. Not nearly as long."

"Well, was he as green as I was on my first drive up the trail?" J.B. asked. They all sat around the table getting to know one another. Devlin was dead tired, but she enjoyed the conversation with her old friend.

"Nobody was as green as you were. Come to think of it, no one's ever been as bad a drover as you."

They laughed some more and J.B. turned to Matt. "She ain't kiddin' either. Dev ended up pullin' me outta quicksand, mud, and prickly pear bushes. Once I was ten seconds from goin' over a waterfall that would have left me in lots of little pieces at the bottom. Dev grabbed me just in time."

"Matt pulled me out this time. He roped me in just when I thought I was a goner," Devlin admitted.

"Is that so? Well, I reckon you've got the makings of a real cattleman here," J.B. said as he leaned back in his chair.

J.B. couldn't help but notice the look of pride in Devlin's gaze. "I reckon Dev and I became fast friends on the day I promised her I wouldn't ever step foot on the trail again." He laughed so hard that his belly shook.

"Did ya really tell Dev you'd kill her the next time ya saw her?" Matt asked.

"Sure did. I wanted to kill her something fierce. I was sore, hungry, tired, and miserable all the way to St. Louis. I cursed her name with every step I took. 'Course, I think it was the tin can incident that prompted Dev to tell me that if she ever saw me workin' as a drover again, she'd cut me up and feed me to the buffalo."

Devlin was now laughing as hard as J.B. was. She turned to Matt. "He was ridin' night watch over a herd of about fifteen hundred head. Somehow, the jackass let his horse step into a tin can. What was worse was that the animal got it stuck on her hoof. All hell broke loose. Between this one," she jerked her thumb in J.B.'s direction, "and his horse, it looked like they was doin' a dance hall act. The sound broke the herd and they stampeded in about five different directions. Took us three days to get 'em back together and we still never found all of 'em."

"Like I said, I was one bad drover."

"But he's one great businessman," Devlin added. "Well, I hate to stop all the reminiscing, J.B., but I'm about asleep on my feet and the sun ain't even down yet."

"It was great seeing you again, Dev. Matt, you watch out for her. I'll have someone show you to your rooms."

After their good nights, when they were alone in their adjoining rooms, Devlin heard a knock on the connecting door. "Come on in, Matt."

Devlin was already half lying on the soft bed. "Ever felt a mattress this soft in all your life?"

"It sure is something," Matt answered sleepily. "I just wanted to say thanks, Dev. For– well, I guess for everything ya done with me today and bringin' me along in the first place."

"You're welcome, Matt. You earned your way on this one. You ought to be proud of what you accomplished. I know I sure am. Your mother will be, too. Now, go on and get some sleep. No wanderin' around the town alone, that's an order."

"Yes, boss." Matt smiled at the rider, who looked like she was already fast asleep.

Chapter 16

"Sakli, it is time."

Tima's voice woke Sarah from a sound sleep. Once the young woman took a few moments to put her head in order, she realized where she was. She had stayed in the *chuka* of Hotti's family. The elderly matriarch's granddaughter had had a difficult time the previous evening with the birth of her first child. Tima and Sarah had stayed up through the night keeping an eye on the unstable newborn and his equally temperamental mother. It was nearly sunrise before Sarah finally laid her head down to rest.

Now that she had her eyes open, Sarah feared that Tima was telling her they had lost the baby. It wasn't until she took a deep breath of air that she realized what Tima's words meant. She smelled smoke. Not the sort of smoke that rose from the hickory kindling in the cooking fires, but the unmistakable odor of burning grass and wood.

Sarah jumped up from her prone position on the ground and hastily pulled on her knee-length moccasins. She ran from the *chuka* and had to pause to shield her eyes from the bright sun. Blinking her eyes in order to adjust them to the light, she took in the sight to which Tima referred. Far to the northwest, billows of black and white smoke rose up from the horizon like a great wall. It was quite a distance away, but she guessed that by midday, the wall of smoke that rose so high into the sky would hide the sun.

"The Elders are at the promontory, Sakli. Perhaps you can see more from there," Tima said.

Sarah nodded absently and accepted the reins to her pony. A young man stood patiently by, having already saddled Coal for her. "I'll be back," she called out to Tima as she jumped into the saddle.

"Do not forget what you have learned, my child," Tima whispered to herself as she watched Sarah's pony race up the hill.

Once Sarah was near the top of the hill, she dismounted and let Coal pick his own way among the sandstone boulders. When she reached the top of the rise, Kontonalah and the Elders were already deep in discussion. As she entered their midst, the men and women inclined their heads in a gesture of respect.

"Sakli, you have made your mark within the Thunderbird Clan. Your Vision has come to pass," Keeho said.

"I'm rather wishing I could have been wrong," she replied. The fire was a considerable distance to the west, but the direction of the trees bending in the breeze told everyone that their prairies would feel the ravages of fire before afternoon.

Sarah listened to the conversations around her. She sat quietly, since she didn't have much more to add. The Clan had been through prairie fires before, and they would be again. They already knew the way of survival from watching and imitating nature. Besides, the Clan village was a stone's throw away from the river. The water wasn't very high, perhaps knee deep this time of year, but it was three hundred yards from shore to shore. Even the small ants in the prairie knew how to defend themselves against such a predator as fire. Knowing they could not hope to outrun an open fire, the ants crawled upon the leaves that floated out onto the surface of the river. If all else failed, the Clan would do the same.

The others rose, but Kontonalah called out to Sarah. "Stay and sit with me for a time, Sakli." He directed her to sit beside him on a fallen log overlooking the prairie far below. "The Sacred Hoop makes itself known today."

"But in such a large way," Sarah acknowledged. "So much death."

"It is the way of things," the old man said. "We do not simply live, we are a part of all life itself. Everything has life and a place on the circle, even the grass beneath our feet. Sometimes renewal only comes after devastation."

Sarah thought about that statement and saw the truth of it in her own life. If her mother hadn't died when Sarah was a child, her father never would have brought her up in the manner he had. If her father hadn't taught her skills usually reserved for a son, she would never have found her way to the place she sat at that moment. She would never had met Devlin if it hadn't been for Peter's death, never had the freedom to be her own woman if not for her uncle Art's death. Her life had been a picture of the perfect prairie. Everything happened for a reason and all the events fit together in perfect harmony and balance, just like in nature.

"It is a renewal," Kontonalah said. "Mother Earth knows just when to revive herself. She has an amazing ability to know when to begin again. Do you know, Sakli, that some of the grasses on the prairie will not grow in our gardens? They die when tended too closely. They need devastation to begin anew. The seeds will only sprout after they have been through the heat of a fire. Many times we burn the hillside in the spring to provide new grass for our ponies."

Sarah listened intently to the old man's words. He had such a casual, yet dedicated way of accepting life and all its little calamities. She closed her eyes and let his words surround her. A gusty breeze upon her face caused her eyelids to snap open. Instantly Kontonalah was on his feet beside her.

"It's moving." He cast a worried glance south, in the direction of the town and the acres of cattle ranches.

Sarah saw the wall of smoke that had been moving from northwest to southeast collide with another wall of smoke that pushed in from the north. The gray and black clouds smashed into one another, forming a massive tower of smoke. She could even see the column of flames now.

"I have to get down there and warn them," Sarah said quickly. "They won't know it's moving toward them faster than it's moving east."

"Sakli, it is too dangerous."

"*Miko*, they are my people too. I can't turn my back on them any more than I could the Clan."

Long moments passed before Kontonalah finally nodded his head. "You must not go alone, though. I will send strong men with you to warn the people in the white man's village. You are the Clan's Mother, Sakli. I can only allow you to go so far in sacrificing yourself."

Sarah hugged the old man hard and found that she was staring into Devlin's eyes. It was apparent that the apple didn't fall far from the tree. The same ancient wisdom lurked beneath the pale colored irises. She whistled once for Coal and nearly ran down the rocky hill to meet the gelding halfway. She heard the old man shout out one last warning.

"Let Mother Earth be your teacher, Sakli."

She ran into the camp and immediately arranged to leave. She spoke first with Tima and Hannah. The older woman said nothing in front of Hannah that would frighten the child, but Sarah could read the concerned expression on the Healer's face. By the time she changed into the riding clothes she had originally worn to the village, ten young men waited for her.

"I have to make sure the people at my ranch know that the fire's turning, *Nali*, I have to go. I have to try to help them," Sarah explained from her position atop her pony.

"I know, Sakli. I understand that you have a responsibility to them also." Tima held onto Hannah as the small girl waved good-bye to her mother. "Take care and stay clear of brother Luak," Tima called out to Sarah as her party rode away from the village.

As they rode across the prairie, Sarah explained to the young men what she needed to do. She was thankful that Kontonalah had selected strong men who spoke small amounts of English. That way, they could separate and cover more ground at one time. She pulled Coal to a stop and instructed two of the men to head for the town and give the warning to Frank Grayson, her old friend who owned the general store. She split the other six into two groups and had them ride southwest of her ranch to warn the other cattlemen. That left Sarah with Hanan and Anoli.

Sarah turned away from the open prairie when Anoli noticed the wind had grown stronger. He brought her attention to the specks that had begun to float through the air like cottonwood seeds. The particles were ashes from the fire and the knowledge urged her to stay closer to the creek. As they rode along at a fast gallop, she spied a small herd of buffalo leaving the open land to wade into the same creek. Some of the large animals rolled in the muddy bank, coating their dense coats with a thick layer of mud.

When Sarah and her *Chahta* friends reached Double Deuce land, she was unhappy to see that the men hadn't completed the fire-breaks in time. The fire-breaks were deep ditches and furrows plowed into the ground in the hope that when the fire met with the open space, the flames would have nowhere to spread. The riders from her ranch met her just as she rode under the wooden gate that marked the entrance to the ranch house.

"Mrs. Tolliver." Bud, the ranch foreman, eyed the men with Sarah. "Strange time for you to come back."

"It's the fire, Bud. We're not that much ahead of it anymore," Sarah shouted back.

"The fire? But it looks like it's headed– "

"Not anymore. It's moving south faster than it's blowing east. No one can tell with that wall of smoke blocking the view."

"Good Lord! We're in a hell of a fix now. We had to give up working on the breaks around the main yard. The ground's like diggin' into solid granite. We got a nice one dug around the main house and that's all."

Suddenly, for the first time that day, Sarah thought of Devlin. She desperately wished her lover could have been there with her. The men respected her and she had a commanding presence that caused them to believe in her. Sarah tightened her jaw, and to anyone that knew her, it was apparent that she'd made a decision. She jumped off her pony and handed him off to a waiting rider. The *Chahta* men followed her closely without saying a word to anyone.

"All right," Sarah barked. "First thing you do is open up the barns and let all the horses free, then make sure there aren't any animals in the corrals."

"Let them go?" Bud asked in disbelief.

"That's what I said. I won't have any of them burn up in there. Let them run free and we can worry about getting them back later. Where's Angelia and Maria?"

"They're both here, in the house."

"Make sure everyone, including the girls, have mounts, Bud. If that fire sweeps down this way I plan on doing everything I can to fight it off, but if it gets to the point where it's a lost cause, have everyone left ride out toward the river."

"Yes, ma'am," Bud answered.

Sarah continued to bark orders at the men as she walked around the ranch. The foreman quickly developed a renewed admiration for the small blonde. She knew that the men would only follow her orders if they believed in her. She set her mind to the task of commanding their respect with her knowledge and an air of confidence.

"What about the ranch house, Mrs. Tolliver?"

Sarah looked around. The house had a fire-break around it, but that was no guarantee that the flames wouldn't leap it. Anything could happen to set the house ablaze, from burning tumbleweeds to hot embers falling from the sky.

"How about we douse it down real good with buckets of water?" Bud asked.

"Yes," Sarah answered with a slow drawl. Her mind focused on something she felt pertained in some way to their current predicament.

Let Mother Earth be your teacher, Sakli.

Sarah heard Kontonalah's farewell in her ears as if the old man were directly beside her. Once she opened her mind, the answer came to her easily. An image of the buffalo at the edge of the river filled her mind's eye. They had been rolling around in the mud, coating their bodies with the thick mixture.

"Mud," Sarah said.

"Ma'am?" Bud asked as the men looked at one another, then back at Sarah.

"Use mud to cover the house. Throw on a bucket of water, then a bucket of dirt, just like a mud dauber's nest. It won't stop real flames, but it'll keep falling embers from catching."

"Yeah," Bud answered. "Yeah!" He quickly realized Sarah's idea might work. He turned and shouted orders to the rest of the riders. The men didn't look particularly convinced that the plan would succeed, but Sarah's confidence was contagious. They set to work immediately.

"The other ranchers," Sarah began. "What do you know about them, Bud? Will they need our– " She stopped in mid-sentence. She had completely forgotten about Cordelia Henley. "Bud, the widow Henley. Do you know if she's there alone?"

"Damn! Sorry 'bout my language, ma'am, but I bet she is. You know she don't like the riders hanging out at her place. Besides, most all her riders are on the drive. Mrs. Tolliver," Bud cleared his throat and looked rather uncomfortable, "I don't think there's anything we can do for her at this point. I mean, if the fire's as close as you say, then it'll be at the widow's place before it ever gets this far." Bud coughed and blinked his eyes as the air around them grew thicker.

Sarah turned on one heel and whistled sharply for Coal. The pony, still saddled and ready, raced over to where she stood. Bud anticipated her actions and grabbed the reins before she could mount the animal.

"Mrs. Tolliver, don't be foolish. You can't ride right into the face of that thing," Bud said.

"We can't spare any of the riders if we're going to save this ranch, Bud, and I won't leave Cordy out there alone," Sarah shouted back, taking the reins from the man's hand.

"At least take a couple of the men with you."

"I've got my own," Sarah called out as she pulled herself onto Coal's back. Hanan and Anoli mirrored Sarah's actions, and the three raced out onto the prairie.

They rode directly toward the black wall of smoke. They all wore large bandanas tied across their faces. Even with the cloth barrier, Sarah's throat burned and her tongue felt coated with the acrid taste of smoke. She couldn't see more than what she guessed to be a half-mile in front of her, but finding Cordelia's ranch house wasn't hard. They followed the dried-out creek bed that ran right behind the old woman's house.

"Do you hear that?" Sarah pulled Coal to a stop.

"Storm?" Anoli mentioned hopefully.

Sarah listened to a sound that she was convinced she had heard before. It did indeed sound like the beginnings of a summer storm. The noise reminded her of the rumbling thunder that seemed to roll down from the wooded hills. Instead of fading away, however, it grew in intensity. She remembered where she'd recently heard the familiar sound only moments before a massive line of stampeding buffalo became visible through the smoke.

"Ride!" Sarah screamed, as she spurred her horse into a gallop. The herd looked like the animals in her Vision. They were incredibly large beasts in a herd at least five hundred yards across. Looking over her right shoulder, she couldn't see an end to the immense herd; they just kept coming as if materializing from the smoke. She slapped Coal's flank sharply with the reins. She had made the decision to ride across the front of the herd and now that they were halfway there, they couldn't turn back without being crushed by the oncoming animals. She hoped that she'd made the right choice, but if she had waited for the herd to pass it would have taken hours, and by then it might be too late for Cordelia.

They raced across the prairie, Sarah flanked by Hanan and Anoli. The *Chahta* men were sore-pressed to keep up with her, but one look to their right and they rode with the same urgency.

Sarah had to turn further south than she wanted in order to keep ahead of the now swiftly moving fire. They had to make a wide detour once they reached Cordelia's land.

Sarah cried out as soon as they reached the yard in front of the main house. The beautiful two-story structure was already aflame. A huge oak tree had fallen onto the far end of the house, and the flames now consumed it.

"Check back there!" Sarah pointed toward the open door of the barn as she jumped from Coal's back. Hanan dismounted and ran toward the barn.

Sarah ran inside the back door of the house, dodging falling pieces of wood and flame. She might have been terrified if she had stopped to let herself think about what she was doing. "Look down here, I'll go upstairs," she ordered Anoli.

Sarah took the stairs two at a time and simply threw open doors, all the while calling out the widow's name. The top floor was free from fire, but the smoke was beginning to collect there.

"Here!" Cordelia Henley's voice rang out from a bedroom at the end of the long hall.

Sarah found the old woman on the floor, looking as though she had fallen and was unable to rise on her own. "Who in the hell are you?" the old woman rasped. She coughed and Sarah pulled the bandana from around her face. "Good Lord, Sarah Tolliver! Get yourself outta here, child, before this place cooks us good."

"Come on, Cordy, I'm not leaving without you." Sarah bent down and helped the old woman to her feet. She took Cordelia's arm and put it around her neck, slipping her own arm around the old woman's waist.

They were only a few steps out of the bedroom door when Cordelia stumbled forward slightly. Somehow, her fingers caught in the rawhide strip that tied Sarah's Medicine bag around her neck. "Wait! Your amulet, it fell on the floor."

"It's okay, I can come back for it once we get you out of here," Sarah panted. At first, she had thought the old woman weighed next to nothing, but with every step they took, she thought different. Luckily, Anoli met them at the top of the stairs and easily lifted Cordelia into his arms. "Get her out of here, I have to go back for something," Sarah directed her *Chahta* helper.

Sarah ran back and picked up her Medicine bag, tying it securely around her neck as she rushed back to the stairs. The flames licked at the bottom of the stairs and smoke now filled the entire ground level of the house. With one foot still on the landing, she stepped onto the top stair with the other. A low moaning sound filled the air and when she pulled her foot back, the young woman watched in horror as the entire staircase crumbled into the fire.

Flames shot up at Sarah and she jumped back onto the landing. The fire had burned the old wooden staircase from the underside. "Hellfire!" she cursed.

Sarah ran to the opposite end of the hall to get as far away from the flames as possible, but the smoke was quickly rising into the second floor rooms, which made breathing painful. She took a deep breath and held it for as long as she could while she searched for a way out. One of the bedroom windows on the north side of the house led out onto the back porch roof. She lifted the window open and saw the flames already eating up the sides of the house. There was nowhere else to go but up.

Getting out through the window was the easy part. Sarah grabbed at the eave above her and nearly fell to the ground when a wooden shingle came off in her hand. She stopped for only a moment, her cheek pressed against the side of the house, and took a few deep breaths. She waited for her heart to ease its way out of her throat, and then the heat from the fire compelled her to continue. Using the latticework along the side of the house, she shimmied up to the roof. She wished that she had Devlin's strength in order to scramble up the vertical surface, but the fragility of the old wood made the task slow going anyway.

It took all the strength she had to finally pull herself atop the roof. She lay on her back, trying to catch her breath, and waited for the shaking in her arms to subside. Shouts from Hanan and Anoli roused her. She stood on already shaky legs, but almost immediately sank back down. A wave of nausea overwhelmed her as she gazed at the shimmering ground below. The one weakness she had attempted to hide from others all her life came back at her with a dreadful force. An intense wave of vertigo washed over Sarah, effectively paralyzing her.

Sarah clung to the eave of the attic window, caught in the grip of her own human frailty. Her fingers cramped because she was clenching the wooden shingles so tightly with only the tips of her fingers. She could hear herself breathing in loud, audible pants. She felt the heat of the fire as the flames inside the house reached the second floor. She opened her eyes to see Hanan and

Anoli calling out to her. Hanan tossed buckets of water at the flames, while Anoli beat at the fire with what looked like a wet burlap sack. Both men continued to shout up at Sarah in Choctaw and in English, but she showed no signs of hearing them.

Sarah kept trying to push her fear away, to tell her mind that the paralyzing terror was no more real than a hallucination. Each time she attempted to rise, however, the nausea and lightheadedness would pound her back to her prone position.

"Please," Sarah prayed, "please, Mothers, help me. Please send someone to help me." She felt the tears falling from her eyes, but she couldn't tell if it was due to emotion or the smoke that rose up all around her. "I can't do this alone," she whispered to the air.

Something told Sarah to open her eyes again. She would say later that everything appeared to happen so slowly. The movement on the ground below her took place as though she were viewing it in a dream. She watched as her *Chahta* friends fought the blaze below. Suddenly, like a Phoenix rising from the ashes, a figure burst through the thick haze of smoke. Leaping over a line of flames and through the wall of smoke that now surrounded the house was Devlin astride Alto.

Sarah blinked and released one hand to wipe at her eyes. It was amazing to watch– Devlin all dressed in black, a stark contrast to Alto's cream-colored body. Devlin and the animal looked as one as they leapt into Sarah's field of vision. The rider's hair whipped around her face, her cheeks smeared with dirt and soot. She was the most incredible vision Sarah had ever seen, and the young woman didn't trust what she had just seen until she heard that voice.

"Sarah," Devlin called out, and it made Sarah cry that much harder. "Sarah!" Devlin stood behind Hanan and Anoli, searching in vain for a way to reach her lover, who refused to move. Devlin knew that Sarah didn't like heights. The small blonde kept a death grip on the ladder when she climbed into the hayloft, but Devlin had never seen her in this shape before.

"Dev," Sarah called out, but the smoke had made her throat raw so that it came out as more of a whisper. She swallowed and tried to clear her throat. "Dev!" she cried out at last.

"I'm here, *Sa*! Sarah, you have to jump," Devlin yelled.

Sarah shook her head and closed her eyes again. Devlin looked for a ladder, anything that she could use to get to her lover. She gave directions to Hanan and Anoli to keep at the flames in the area below where Sarah was trapped.

"Sarah. Dammit, Sarah, look at me," Devlin shouted as strongly as she could. Sarah trained her mind to Devlin's voice and slowly opened her eyes again.

"Sarah, you have to jump. I'll catch you, but you have to, and you have to do it now."

"I can't," Sarah cried. "I can't make my legs work."

"Yes, you can. You have to, *Sa*, you just have to." Devlin paused to see if she was getting through to the terrified woman. Through the smoke, she thought she perceived a small bit of reason in the frightened green eyes. "All you have to do is push yourself off and jump. I'll catch you, *Sa*, I promise."

Sarah turned her head to look into Devlin's face. For the first time, she saw just how close the flames were to her. She also saw the fear in Devlin's expression. "I'm scared, Dev."

The rider's expression softened. "I know you are, *Sa*, but I know you can do this."

Sarah coughed as the breeze shifted yet again and blew additional smoke into her face. She held onto the eave with fingers that had lost all sensation because of their tight grip upon the wood. Her knees felt wobbly and weak as she rose to a standing position. She still faced the attic window, unable to muster the courage to turn away.

"Dammit, Sarah! You are going to die up there and then I'm going to die trying to get to you. Is that what you want?" Devlin shouted. Sarah shook her head in a furious motion.

"Then you have to jump. You don't have to look down. Just close your eyes, turn around, and jump. I'll catch you. Sarah, remember who you are! Do the *Alikchi* let fear control them?"

The remark had the same result as a slap to Sarah's face. She was letting fear control her. After all she had been through, the Visions she had experienced, now she was letting the *Keyuachi* win. They were getting the best of her at last, and one thing Sarah detested was allowing her own lack of self-esteem to beat her.

"I am *Alikchi*," she whispered, echoing the mantra until she actually felt some degree of will return to her body. She carefully turned, facing away from the house, and looked at the ground, the flames nearly lapping at the toes of her boots. A familiar nausea made her stomach lurch.

Devlin saw the transformation take place within Sarah as her words had the desired effect. At the last moment, she saw

Sarah teeter slightly and shut her eyes tight. "Don't look down. Sarah, just keep your eyes closed and trust me. If you jump, I'll be here to catch you. Now, *Sa*, you have to jump now!"

Sarah's timing was perfect. As she pushed off the building with one foot to clear the flames, the wall crumbled in. She opened her eyes when her body made soft contact with Devlin's arms. The rider half caught her, but used her own body to block the rest of the young woman's fall. They both hit the ground and Devlin rolled them away from the house as it crashed down in pieces.

Devlin had her arms wrapped tightly around Sarah, but their reunion was short-lived. Hanan ran forward with their mounts and Anoli quickly helped them to their feet, indicating that he had left Cordelia in a wagon by the river. They realized there would be no way to get back to the Double Deuce. The smoke hampered them almost as much as the actual fire. They couldn't see to navigate through the thick haze, and it was still possible buffalo might stampede them.

Once at the river, they found Cordelia in fine shape, considering recent events. The first thing Devlin did was to jump off Alto and pull Sarah down from Coal's back. She took the young woman in her arms, completely oblivious to the looks exchanged by the others in their party. They kissed one another and the rider wiped the tears from Sarah's dirt streaked face. Sarah wrapped her arms around Devlin's waist and squeezed so hard the rider thought her ribs would break. She wasn't about to complain, however.

Devlin pulled away from the embrace slightly and looked into Sarah's face, placing a gentle kiss upon her forehead. "Hi, I'm back," she said.

Sarah laughed through her tears and held onto the taller woman. Suddenly, she looked up in fear. "Matt?"

"It's okay, he's with Hannah in the village," Devlin quickly replied.

Sarah breathed a heavy sigh and reached up to kiss Devlin again. "I missed you so much."

"Me too. Let's not do this again real soon. Okay?"

"Okay," Sarah replied.

The two women sat on the wet sand at the bank of the river and continued to hold onto each other. Devlin explained that she and Matt had taken the train most of the way home. The train stopped when the engineers saw the smoke on the prairie. Devlin and Matthew unloaded their mounts from the train car and rode to the Clan village.

"Matt's not too happy, though. He spent the summer with men treating him as an equal. All I could focus on was getting to you, so I ordered him to stay there and I took off. When I reached the Double Deuce, Bud told me I couldn't have been more than ten minutes behind you. Sorry, *Sa*, I would have been there sooner, but I ran into a few buffalo. The way they were moving, I figured it best to stay outta their way."

Sarah leaned into Devlin and squeezed her hand. "I prayed for help and just like a miracle you were there."

"Don't think I've ever been the answer to anyone's prayers before," she replied with a grin.

"That's not true." Sarah sat back and looked into the blue eyes she had come to love so well. "I thought you were the very first time I ever saw you."

The look of love and adoration in Sarah's eyes stole Devlin's breath, as well as her speech. She didn't have a response for such a profound declaration. Her ears tingled with warmth when she looked up and realized they weren't alone. She cleared her throat and looked at her boots.

Sarah then remembered the people around them and smiled in embarrassment at Cordelia. "I'm so sorry about your home, Cordy."

"Sorry?" Cordelia looked at the young woman in disbelief. "That was *you* draggin' my old carcass outta that burnin' box of kindlin', wasn't it? You get nothin' but my wholehearted thanks, little lady."

"But it was your home. All your memories were there."

Cordelia placed a gnarled, weathered hand atop Sarah's. "Sarah Tolliver, that house had physical memories in it, to be sure, but havin' things around you don't keep the memories alive. A house is just a place ta rest yer body. It can be a hole in the ground or a big ol' mansion. A home– now, that's what you keep inside of yerself. Everything that means anything to me, I keep in here." Cordelia placed the palm of her hand over her heart. "You two just remember that," she winked at Devlin, "and everything else will seem small in comparison."

The wind shifted once more and began to carry the smoke away. The fire eventually ran its course, encountering riverbeds and fire-breaks that it couldn't cross, and the flames finally found nothing left to feed on. The more the wind blew, the more the blue sky became visible through the grayish haze. The afternoon sun began its descent into the western horizon and once the smoke had cleared enough for the bright light to slice across the river, it felt like a rebirth of sorts.

Sarah, in her weariness, thought of Kontonalah's words. He had told her that Mother Earth had an uncanny ability to know when to begin again. He had also told her of all the good that would eventually come to the land because of the prairie fire. The irony was that humans were the only ones to pay from the devastation, but Sarah was reminded that it might be because most humans didn't know their place in the circle. The land had existed in its perfect harmony before man ever knew what time was. Everything that had life, even the rocks and trees, understood where they belonged within the Sacred Hoop. *Does that mean we don't belong here?* The *Chahta* people had shown her the answer to that question.

Devlin had once said to Sarah that there was room enough for all. Most of the white men were merely ignorant, unschooled in the ways of Mother Earth. Many, however, were simply arrogant. They had come to this country, to this land, intent on conquest. Instead of adapting to the earth around them, they forced nature to conform to their way of life, to their will. The young Medicine Woman wondered when Mother Earth would tell man, enough. Alternately, she questioned whether man would ever realize that he had squandered the Mother's gifts and that those gifts would never come again.

The wind continued to gain strength, but the chill autumn air turned humid and close. The blue sky turned a deeper hue. Thunderheads developed in the northern sky. By the time the small party had mounted their animals and made it into town, the heavens let loose with the year's long-awaited downpour. Thunder grumbled like a testy bull and the rain finally fell as though the clouds had been saving the precipitation for just such a day. The ground smoldered and hissed as the rain soaked in, preventing further fires from breaking out.

Sarah and Devlin settled Cordelia into a room at the hotel, then decided to spend the night themselves. Frank and Maria Grayson, who owned the general store, had known Sarah and her uncle for years. The couple supplied the group with dry clothes and other necessary items.

Hanan and Anoli met up with the others that had followed Sarah from the Chahta village. They all insisted on returning to the Clan village, even though Devlin encouraged them to stay in town until morning. The men respectfully refused and she didn't push the issue. She understood that her Clan brothers probably felt uncomfortable among the townspeople. The fact that the men were returning to the village eased Sarah's mind for a different reason. She and Devlin sent a message back to Tima and the children informing them that they were safe and would be back the following day.

Sarah and Devlin stood under the roof covering the wooden sidewalk that ran from the hotel to the general store. Devlin thanked her friends for their help, and Sarah provided each of the men with jackets and wide-brimmed hats to protect them from the rain. Devlin didn't have the heart to tell her that the men were used to the elements and would probably feel strange using them.

The men were definitely nonplussed at receiving the gifts. It was well known that gift giving was something the Thunderbird Clan simply did not do. Sarah was their Medicine Woman and along with that honor came certain privileges. One of those privileges was the ability to give gifts. It would be considered a sign of disrespect for the men to refuse a gift from the Medicine Woman of their Clan.

Sarah gave the gifts because the gentle mother in her disliked seeing the young men head back home in the middle of a storm. Another reason was that the young men had displayed a strength of character that impressed her. Hanan and Anoli especially had stayed with Sarah and never gave up trying to reach her, despite the risk to their own lives.

Sarah said a personal good-bye to each of the men. "You have my thanks and my respect. Hanan and Anoli, I owe you a debt."

The men's eyes widened at Sarah's remarks. To admit owing a debt to another Clan member was a serious obligation. Sarah knew that those words, especially when voiced by a Medicine Woman, were an unbreakable oath. They formed an odd bond of friendship between receiver and debtor.

"I might have gone to the Sacred Place today if it hadn't been for the two of you. I wasn't very strong," she admitted. "The *Keyuachi* paid me a visit on that roof today."

"You see the *Keyuachi*?" Anoli asked in amazement.

"They are as real to me as you standing there. They've tried to trick me quite often lately." She grinned. "But when I remember who I am, and that I have the strength of my *Chahta* ancestors in me, then the *Keyuachi* can't defeat me."

Anoli bowed his head slightly and held Sarah's hand in both of his own. "I will remember your words, Mother."

Devlin was as impressed by the small blonde's statement as the young men were. Sarah and Devlin watched as the group rode out into the rain. They waited there until they could no longer make out the shapes of their young friends.

The rider looked down at Sarah and saw that the younger woman had changed immensely over the summer. Devlin hid her wry smile when she wondered if Sarah had really changed at all. Hadn't the young widow always been a complete enigma to her? Since the day that they first met, Devlin had suspected that Sarah could be as strong as circumstances dictated. At the same time, the young woman had a fragility about her that drew out every protective instinct Devlin had. Soft and hard, wise yet innocent. A crash of thunder punctuated Devlin's epiphany. She suddenly realized that Sarah Tolliver had been *Chahta* in her heart long before Devlin came into her life.

Sarah and Devlin lay nestled together on the soft feather mattress. They exchanged bits and pieces of what happened over the summer. They agreed that there would be plenty of time later to examine the details. For now, they were content to lie together and listen to the rain as it fell in a steady rhythm against the roof.

"I don't think I'll ever get the smell of smoke out of my hair," Sarah said.

Devlin reached down to kiss the top of the golden head. "Mmm, smells good to me," she replied as she breathed in the scent of Sarah's freshly washed hair.

"It's funny, isn't it?" Sarah asked, changing the subject. "If the rain had gotten here just a few hours earlier, the fire might never have happened."

"True," Devlin agreed. "But if you look at what might have been, then I think we have to look at the fact that the fire was probably caused by lightning up in the hills in the first place."

"You've become quite a philosopher, for a cattlewoman."

"I might say that's the pot calling the kettle black," Devlin replied with a laugh.

Sarah reached up from her position within the rider's arms

to affectionately nibble on the soft skin of her neck. One kiss turned into more until Devlin worked herself free of Sarah's grasp. She sat up and looked at Sarah as though she had never seen her.

"*Sa*, you know the walls are like paper in this place." Sarah nodded and moved closer, continuing her assault on the tall woman's neck. The rider tried to fight against the waves of pleasure that came from the intimate contact. She quickly realized it was a losing battle.

"Oh, it's all right to make love to me with your mother a few feet away, but it's not okay when I want to make love to you when we're alone in a room," Sarah drawled sweetly.

"Well, yeah, but– oh," Devlin moaned softly as Sarah's hands wandered across her body.

"I want you, Devlin." Sarah whispered the same demand that Devlin had teased her with at one time.

"Oh, *Sa*, you don't even know what you're doing to me," Devlin muttered in what sounded like utter defeat.

Sarah saw her chance as she steeled her nerves for the next move. She put her hand under Devlin's chin and tilted it upward. Her eyes locked on the blue of the rider's. She faced Devlin and straddled her thigh. Her arms circled Devlin's neck and she pulled herself toward her lover.

It was at that point that Devlin realized the oversized shirt Sarah wore to sleep in was so long it hid the fact that she wore no underclothes. Sarah's wetness coated Devlin's thigh as she slid closer to the rider. Devlin shivered.

Sarah moved her lips to Devlin's ear. "Oh, but I do, *tashka*," she whispered as her tongue ran the length of Devlin's ear. She used her teeth to gently nip at the rider's earlobe.

"Good Lord," Devlin moaned.

"I want to hear how much you want me, *tashka*."

"Please, Sarah..."

"Yes, my love," Sarah whispered into the rider's ear.

"Please, *Sa*, don't stop."

Devlin wrapped strong arms around Sarah's waist and pulled the young woman against her. With their bodies pressed tightly together, she imparted the depth of her love with one kiss. Their lips pressed together, soft flesh meeting equally soft flesh, until passion swept both women along on an immense wave. Devlin's tongue slipped past lips parted quickly for her, feeling Sarah's intense heat rising as quickly as her own. She lost herself in the kisses that, for the past months, she had only dreamed of.

Sarah had her fingers buried in Devlin's dark locks. She pulled her lover even closer with a strength and a passion she never even knew she possessed. Her hips began a slow grinding motion against the rider's thigh and she moaned at the pleasing friction against her center. Devlin's hands slid down the smaller woman's back and grasped her hips, encouraging the rocking movement.

Sarah pulled away from the kiss and leaned her forehead against the rider's chin. Both women took in a large breath of air. Sarah wondered if Devlin could feel her heartbeat pounding against her chest. She swore she could hear it echoing against the walls around them. She had never experienced a need this intense, this raw, before. All she could focus on was the overwhelming desire to take Devlin, to show the rider all the passion of which she was indeed capable.

Devlin pulled back to gaze into emerald eyes. She recognized the need there, just as her own eyes must have reflected that same passionate glaze. She saw something else there, too. Sarah had a feral look in her smoldering gaze that Devlin recognized from her own past. She had worn that expression during past sexual escapades. The look was all intensity, heat, and desire.

"Off," Sarah ordered, pulling on the soft shirt that Devlin wore.

The rider could feel her body respond immediately to the command as a raging river flowed from her aroused sex. Her body hummed like an over-taut bowstring as she unbuttoned the garment. Sarah pushed the shirt from the rider's shoulders and gazed at her lover's body with hungry eyes. Whether Devlin was willing to admit it or not, Sarah's aggressive actions excited her.

Sarah tossed off her own garment and pushed Devlin back onto the bed. Both women groaned at the long-denied feeling of skin against skin. Sarah desperately explored every inch of the rider's body. Her hand found Devlin's breast and kneaded the full flesh. Her fingers pulled gently on the rider's nipple, eliciting a mild groan from Devlin. Capturing Devlin's mouth in a passionate kiss, the small blonde thrust her tongue past her lips.

Devlin had to pull her mouth away from the kiss, but Sarah never stopped her assault on her breast. Sarah's devouring eyes watched as Devlin wet her lips and then parted them. She panted as she pulled much-needed air into her lungs.

Sarah bent to the warrior's neck and sucked at the soft flesh there. She bit the supple flesh of Devlin's throat and sucked harder. Devlin's fingers entwined themselves into Sarah's hair and drew the small blonde closer.

"Yes, *Sa*...harder," Devlin groaned.

The rider's fervent request was enough to convince Sarah that her lover desired the same thing as she. She lost awareness of the outside world. At that moment, there was only Devlin and her own need to totally consume her *tashka*, her warrior.

Sarah's thigh moved in between Devlin's legs and pressed against her mound. "Oh, yes," Sarah moaned against the rider's shoulder as she felt Devlin's wetness. Her lips slid down the rider's neck and across her shoulder. Each gentle bite and subsequent caress of her tongue drew gasps of pleasure from the writhing figure under her.

"Please, *Sa*," Devlin moaned. They seemed to be the only words of which she was capable. She arched her back, silently begging Sarah to her breast.

Sarah's mouth enclosed Devlin's aching nipple in its wet warmth. Her tongue teased the hard flesh, flicking across it lightly, then sucking and grazing it through her teeth. Devlin felt the wet pulling of her nipple straight through to her center. Her hips thrust against Sarah's thigh. Once again, Sarah reached up and captured her lips in a kiss filled with seductive fire.

Devlin could barely breathe, let alone speak. She should have known that Sarah could be such a lover. Sarah always expressed herself passionately, but that was nothing compared to the enthusiasm she put into her lovemaking.

Sarah continued to kiss Devlin. She slowly dragged the palm of her hand down across the rider's stomach and along the top of a muscled thigh. She ran her fingers back up along the inside of the same leg and rested her hand lightly against the damp curls, feeling the heat radiating from Devlin's center. The rider raised her hips toward the blonde's hand and Sarah slid her fingers across the slick folds in teasing strokes.

Devlin's breath caught in her throat when in one fluid motion, Sarah slid two of her fingers deep inside her. Devlin splayed her knees and pushed herself up to meet the gliding motion of Sarah's hand.

"Like that?" Sarah whispered with a knowing smile.

"Yes, like that...right there...oh, yes!" Devlin then felt her voice go out the window after her dignity as she shamelessly begged Sarah not to stop.

Sarah followed the rhythm Devlin's hips set, not even trying to suppress a groan when the rider lifted her thigh up and pressed it firmly upward between Sarah's legs. She ground her hips against the rider's leg. Devlin's hips thrust harder against Sarah's hand and her whole body started to tremble uncontrollably. Her eyes rolled back in her head just before her eyelids snapped shut.

"Devlin, look at me," Sarah managed to gasp, her own body begging for release.

Devlin opened her eyes. She could feel the tremors run through her body.

"I love you, Devlin," Sarah whispered.

The effect was immediate as Devlin pulled Sarah into a kiss filled with all the intense emotions she had ever felt since laying her eyes on the woman now making love to her. The fire in the rider's belly soon transferred itself into Sarah's through that one kiss. A growl of pure pleasure rumbled deep from the rider's chest. She could feel herself about to leap from the precipice, liquid fire rushing from her sex, washing over Sarah's hand.

"Sarah," Devlin moaned. It was the only sound she made to indicate her impending release.

"I'll love you forever, *tashka*."

Devlin's head slammed back into the bed at the sound of Sarah's promise. Her body convulsed and shook as wave after wave of sweetly intense pleasure swept through her. The growl that had started as a low rumble emerged from Devlin's throat as nothing short of a roar. The sound was enough for Sarah; at her lover's cry, she joined the rider in release. She felt as if flames had consumed her body, a fire just as intense as any prairie fire. When she felt as though the heat would overwhelm her, she simply melted.

Sarah collapsed against the rider's body and they melded together. Neither woman attempted to move as the small blonde lay atop Devlin. The rider's arms enfolded the spent woman and they both tried in vain to bring their breathing under control.

Eventually, Sarah lifted her head and leaned up on one elbow. Looking down into her lover's face, she grinned. "Hi, I'm glad you're back."

Chapter 17

"Oh, Dev," Sarah said tearfully as she placed her head against the rider's shoulder. Devlin wrapped one arm around the smaller woman as they looked at what was left of Art Winston's ranch house.

They stood before the burned-out shell of the main house. Many of the buildings had escaped the flames, but the fire had reduced the house and the barn to nothing more than ashes.

"I'm awful sorry, Mrs. Tolliver, Dev. We stayed until there wasn't a chance left. I feel like I let ya down," Bud said.

"We know you did your best," Devlin answered.

"Well, the wind turned the thing before it got to anything else south of here. The houses by the creek, the bunkhouse, and even the old barn we used to use for storage are just fine."

"How about the men, Bud?" Sarah asked. "Do you all have supplies or need anything?"

"No, ma'am. Thanks, but we're riders. We're kinda used to gettin' by with just the clothes on our back. We wouldn't know what to do if it was any different. I'll be sure and let you know if that changes, though. With no cattle to winter here, you probably won't need us till spring."

"I know most of you usually go down to Texas or Mexico for winter work, Bud. You tell all the men that if they're willing to take the winter off, they can rest here during the cold months.

I owe it to them. Besides, this rider here," Sarah slipped an arm around Devlin's waist, "she's made me a wealthy woman. You just tell the men to take it easy for a spell."

"We surely do thank you, ma'am. I promise you, we won't take advantage of your generous nature. Well, I best be goin'."

The foreman left Devlin and Sarah standing there. Even though the rider hadn't lived in the ranch house very long, she felt the loss of the place. "We can rebuild, *Sa*," she said.

"I know," Sarah nodded her head. "It won't ever be the same though, will it?"

"Probably not."

"I guess Cordy hit it pretty square on the head. This is all temporary." Sarah motioned to the house's remains with her free hand. "If you keep your memories tucked safely in your heart, you can't ever lose them."

"Come on, *sachu-kash*. Let's go see the kids."

They left the ranch to return to the Clan village. Sarah barely recognized her son. He was actually taller than she was, having grown three inches that summer. His long hair made him look like many of the riders on her ranch, and she noticed that he carried himself differently. She was surprised that Matt had learned a great deal of the Clan's language while he was away. It helped him to fit into the village immediately. What surprised her the most was hearing her son call Devlin *ishki toba*. His relationship with Devlin had certainly grown stronger and Sarah looked forward to her lover's detailed account of the trail drive. Eventually, even Hannah began using the *Chahta* word for "second mother."

Hard work and a great many decisions filled the weeks ahead. When the final tally sheets for the cattle drive came in, Sarah Tolliver became known as the richest woman west of the Mississippi. The ranchers who had joined in with Sarah and Devlin were so thankful to the couple that they simply showed up with the supplies one day and put up a new barn at the Double Deuce. They said that by summertime, the house would be done as well.

For Sarah, the best thing to come of the incident was that the cattlemen didn't seem in much of a hurry to put their fences back up. They went back to the old ways of running their ranches. The nesters, on the other hand, were trying to change all that. Sarah and Devlin would have quite a job when it came to dealing with people who were determined to farm land that was meant for buffalo and cattle.

The winter passed as Sarah, Devlin, and the children all learned to exist within the Clan village. Sarah never brought up the idea of marriage, preferring the rider to take the initiative. It had been quite some time since Devlin had seen an example of the engagement protocol. She went to her mother and her uncle for advice. Of course, she appeared much more enthusiastic when the event seemed much further away.

"This is very uncomfortable, *Nali*." Devlin fidgeted as Tima adjusted the special outfit she had made for her daughter. The leather was a soft buckskin, bleached as white as the snow. The garment was traditional dress for a warrior to wear when asking for a marriage bond. Once again, Devlin pulled on the choker around her neck.

"Redhawk, please be still. How will you feel if this isn't ready for today?" Tima chided.

"I don't see why I have to dress up like this anyway. I agreed to ask Sarah to marry me in the *Chahta* way, but I never said I would get all fancy."

"This is the *Chahta* way. This is what a woman will recall when she is old. I still remember the day that Tekola sat down at my father's *iksita*. I will never forget how handsome he looked in his white leathers."

"Okay, I understand that." Devlin softened. "But it's not like Sarah's going to refuse me." She chuckled, but the expression on her mother's face abruptly stopped her laughter. "What's that look supposed to mean?"

Tima still looked at her daughter with the raised eyebrow that Devlin had learned to imitate. "It means that perhaps you should not be too overconfident."

Suddenly Devlin lost all sense of reason. She had always found it hard to be rational when it came to the way she felt about Sarah. Now she felt butterflies flitting around in her stomach. What did her mother know? "What have you heard, *Nali*? Is someone else interested in Sarah?"

Tima snorted in such a way as to indicate that it was an idiotic question. "She is *Alikchi*. Of course many desire her. She is beautiful and talented. It would mean great status for the family of her spouse. Did you think you would be the only one she would consider now that she is *Chahta*?" It broke Tima's heart to tease her daughter in such a way, but sometimes the rider's confidence grew too big. Devlin's beloved Sarah might take that confidence to mean that she was being taken for granted.

If Devlin had taken the time to really think about her relationship with Sarah, she would have realized that for either of them, no other in the world existed. "Should I go early?" She now stood completely still, allowing Tima to finish the last-minute sewing.

"I think yes. It will show your enthusiasm to receive your answer. Do you have a gift for her father?"

"Yes," Devlin answered. It was a strange thing to get used to. Her mother spoke as if Sarah were an Indian girl who had lived in this village all her life.

"Very good." Tima patted Devlin's shoulder to say that she was finished. "Beautiful, very beautiful," Tima said when she looked at Devlin. The rider had her hair pulled back into one long braid down her back and tiny wisps of hair had pulled free to gently frame her face. "Okshakla would be very proud of you today."

Tima's sudden remark surprised the rider. They rarely spoke of Devlin's mother. It was an odd feeling to still love the mother who gave birth to her, but then again to feel just as strongly for the woman standing before her. "I wouldn't be standing here, with Sarah's love in my heart, if it hadn't been for you, Mother."

Tears formed in Tima's eyes and she placed a kiss on the rider's cheek. "Go now and don't forget your manners." She abruptly waved her daughter out the door of the *chuka*. She stood inside her lodge for long moments, however, remembering the tender way in which the rider had called her "Mother."

Devlin pretended not to hear the catcalls and whoops that came from the other warriors as she walked through the village in her engagement finery. If the last thing Tima had said to her had been something other than telling her to remember her manners, Devlin would have walked over and punched one or two of them in the nose. Of course, just the thought of that caused her to feel better. She promised herself that perhaps later she would go back and pound her friends. That idea made her feel much better.

"*Halito*," Devlin called out to Keeho as she approached the Medicine Man's *chuka*.

"*Halito, binili*," Keeho greeted the rider, asking her to sit at his fire.

Devlin made herself comfortable across from the old man. The pleasant spring weather meant that it was time for people to start taking their meals by the outside fires. They exchanged small talk until Sarah appeared with their dinner. They ate the meal that she had prepared and Devlin commented appropriately on how lucky Keeho was to have a daughter who could cook so well.

"It is true," the old man agreed. He smiled to himself and wondered how long it would be before Sarah broke her silence. He knew how difficult some of the *Chahta* ways were for her.

"The Spirits smiled on you when they gave you a daughter," Devlin continued with the speech she had memorized. "Surely it will be a blessing to you when your daughter marries and her spouse can provide for your *iksita*."

Keeho smiled at the respect the young warrior paid to his hearth. He nodded his head and said the words that were expected of him. "Yes, I am truly fortunate to have a daughter. Hashtahli has also given me a daughter who is talented and beautiful."

Devlin grew silent. Tima had prepared her for this, but she had said that Keeho probably wouldn't bring up this trick. It was a father's way of driving up the price on his daughter. Although no goods changed hands under *Chahta* law, fathers often wanted to hear how dedicated a suitor really was. A warrior with a silver tongue usually went home engaged.

"Yes, uh– " Devlin stammered. "I have traveled much and I have seen no greater beauty. But were your daughter of plain face, she would be no less of a prize to the warrior lucky enough to capture her eye. Her heart is pure and that makes her the most beautiful woman on earth." *Bingo*, Devlin thought, as she saw the pleased look on Keeho's face.

"Perhaps even her *banaha* will improve, given time." Keeho smiled. The Medicine Man didn't want his daughter's pride to swell too much.

Devlin chuckled as she chewed the slightly dry corn bread. "Well, perhaps perfection will take just a little longer for her to attain than we thought."

Sarah arched an eyebrow in the rider's direction and Devlin immediately realized that she obviously had issues about being teased over her cooking abilities. In all fairness, the young woman was an exceptional cook, but the *Chahta* recipes were new to her.

After they finished their meal, Devlin carefully opened the hide parcel beside her. She laid the package open before Keeho. Inside was a pipe with a cedar stem and a clay bowl. "This wood spoke to me," Devlin began. "I shaped the stem and formed the clay only to realize that I already had a very special pipe. I am unwilling to put it away. Perhaps a new pipe is something you would find useful?"

"But I could not accept a gift." Keeho stated the obvious.

"Of course not. Perhaps you have something that you could give in the pipe's place."

Keeho nodded thoughtfully. "Perhaps I do. I will try your pipe for a time and if it pleases me, then I will give you something of mine in return."

"This is a most valuable pipe," Devlin used the words that Tima had taught her. The Healer had told her that this was the way Tekola became engaged. "I would not make a trade for just anything. I have spent many hours in the crafting and this pipe has come to mean a great deal to me."

Keeho nodded again. "I agree. I can see that it is a most valuable possession. I will be sure to give you something that I hold in the highest regard in its place."

Devlin took a deep breath and reached into the pouch at her waist for a few kernels of dried corn. Her palms were sweaty and she couldn't remember ever being this nervous. *Hellfire! All this to get hitched. I'd be calmer if it were a gunfight.*

The rider casually tossed one of the dried pieces of corn on the ground in front of Sarah. She waited for Sarah's response. Traditionally, if a *Chahta* woman approved of the match, she picked up the corn, went about her chores, and the suitor left with a smile. If the young woman ran off, it was obvious that the suitor had to look elsewhere. Devlin waited. She continued to wait, as Sarah appeared not to notice the corn.

How in the hell can she not see it? It's right in front of her. Devlin tried once more. Again, Sarah looked everywhere but in front of her. On the third try, Devlin flicked the piece of corn directly at Sarah. It hit her on the hand and fell to the ground at her feet. Sarah flinched, but continued to ignore the corn.

"Pick it up," Devlin muttered out of the side of her mouth. Sarah rolled her eyes and looked up at the sky. Finally, Devlin understood. The small blonde was paying her back for her comment about Sarah's cooking. "Very funny," Devlin muttered.

Keeho didn't understand English, but he could see that the two women were acting foolishly. He had seen many matches end in argument because of adults who acted like children. "Ah, there is young Anoli. Perhaps he will visit my hearth tonight also. Do you like him, Sakli?"

Both women snapped their heads up at the Medicine Man's remark. He wanted to laugh at their expressions. Sarah reached out and grabbed the closest piece of corn. For good measure, she picked up each piece that Devlin had tossed her way. The rider sighed in relief and the women grinned at one another.

"It is decided. I like your pipe very much, Redhawk. On the next pass of the moon, I will give you something that I hold dear. Go now."

Just like that, it was over. Keeho waved Devlin away before she could say one word to Sarah. The blonde and her children would live at Keeho's *chuka* until the marriage ceremony. The two women would have plenty of time during the day to see one another, but their nights would be spent apart until they were married.

At first, Sarah worried how Keeho would be around the children. She needn't have worried. Hannah, who normally acted standoffish around men, loved the old man, and he treated her as special as any granddaughter. Matt was impressed when Keeho showed him how to make arrows with barely a hint of a curved line.

Devlin left Keeho's *iksita* feeling rather proud of herself. She would have to figure out a way to pay Sarah back for nearly stopping her heart. She would make it very fun and loving, but definitely payback. As she pondered it, she remembered her brother warriors' taunts and whistles when she had passed them earlier. She grinned a thoroughly wicked grin and headed off in the direction of where they had been.

For the most part, Sarah, Devlin, and the children lived in the Clan village after Hannah and Matthew agreed to try it. By the time that winter was over, it was as if they had always been a family there. Sarah still had quite a bit of learning to do, and some days she surprised herself by what she knew. The Clan Mothers had been right. When she needed the knowledge, it was there.

Devlin finally seemed at peace. She was living a lifelong dream. It was simple, but all she had ever wanted was to be a part of this community. She had always felt different, not merely because she was a warrior in a woman's body but because of everything that meant. She had always felt out of place in the white man's world, but had never felt truly at home with her mother's Clan. She had never thought that a family– children and a wife– would be available to her. Now all that had changed. All of their lives were changing and, as always, she worried.

"I've been looking for you, *Miko*," Sarah teased Devlin as she slipped her arms around her lover's waist.

Devlin automatically wrapped her arms around the smaller woman and bent to kiss the side of her neck. "I see you've been talking to Grandfather."

"He told me that he asked you to become a member of the council and to take his place as the family's spokesperson." Kontonalah had actually gone into detail with Sarah, discussing the Clan's system of government. Even though each family had a *Miko*, or spokesperson, sometimes families would all band together. They usually did this not for political gain or power, but because they all thought the same on important issues. In this way, they would only have to have one *Miko*. Devlin's grandfather had been *Miko* for a number of families for many years. He grew weary of the responsibility, but he had no sons. He admitted that his grandsons were not his first choice to train as successor. Now he had begun to put pressure on Devlin to stay with her people and fulfill her duty as a warrior.

"He said that your place is just as much with the Clan as mine is. He told me that my status rises above even the most battle-savvy warriors because I'm married to a powerful Medicine Woman."

Sarah grinned. "Well, Medicine Woman is true. I can't say as powerful is anything close to the truth."

The young woman chuckled and Devlin smiled. She was always pleased when Sarah was happy, and whether the blonde knew it or not, she looked like the happiest woman alive lately.

"Would it be so bad?" Sarah asked.

"It will mean truly being *Chahta, sachu-kash*. We can't live down there in that world," Devlin indicated the ranch with a nod of her head, "and then return to the Clan village when it pleases us. We would have to choose."

"I know, *tashka*, but we have time to decide, right?"

Devlin nodded her head. She was fearful about forcing Sarah to choose one world over another, but that's exactly what they had to do.

Sarah thought about Devlin's family and *Oka kapassa*'s fears about Sarah and Devlin marrying. The older woman worried that someday Sarah would pull Devlin away from her people, her world.

I am Chahta...I have always been Chahta.

Those words popped into Sarah's mind at the strangest times. She had told Keeho that the words came to her on more than one occasion. The Medicine Man merely smiled and told her that the answer would come to her once she was ready for it. She smiled to herself. Those were always the kinds of responses she received from her Clan father.

Sarah kissed Devlin's chin, which was all she could reach at the moment. "I understand the importance of our decision, Dev. Perhaps more than you realize. I've made commitments and I don't take those promises lightly. I would never have entered training if I thought for one moment that the Clan wouldn't be a part of our daily lives. I do think becoming *Chahta* has taught me one important thing."

"What?"

"You worry too much." Sarah laughed as Devlin immediately found the most ticklish spot on her body. "We're living here now. Hank is doing fine with the ranch and we trust him. Why don't we just trust that the Spirits will show us the direction they want our lives to take?"

"But we have to think of the children, too. Matt wants to be a rancher, then there's Hannah." Devlin paused to look at Sarah and gently brushed the backs of her fingers against her cheek. "I just want our children to be as happy here as we are, *Sa*."

Sarah listened in amazement as Devlin sounded exactly as she herself used to, worrying about things that might never happen. Sarah smiled up at Devlin and indicated that she should turn around. Behind them was their village and its people, doing what they did every day to live out their lives.

A group of young men battled fiercely against one another in *toli*, a sort of stickball game where each contestant had two sticks with what appeared to be baskets at the end. The idea was to carry the ball to the opponent's goal, but anyone with the ball in his possession became fair game. Only the sturdiest young men played because the sport could be quite rough. Kontonalah and the other Elders would often tell the young men of the days when the game was used to solve disputes between other tribes. They would explain to the youngsters that in those days there were few wars, but many great games of *toli*.

Devlin smiled when she saw a tall, lanky boy in the middle

of the fray. Matt had continued to grow his hair long, and he used a beaded band that his sister made to keep the hair from his eyes. His bare chest was painted in the same bright colors as the other *Chahta* boys. He received the ball and fought to keep the other team from taking it, a huge grin fixed on his face all the while.

Kontonalah and a few other *Mikos* acted as mediators. Many of the women had moved their chores near the playing field so they could complete their work, yet still place wagers on their sons or favorite players. Everyone watched as the young men ran up and down the *hitoka*, or ball field, laughing and playing.

Hannah was a short distance away. She giggled and jumped up and down as she alternated between cheering for her brother and playing with her friends in a circle under Tima and Oka kapassa's watchful eyes. Hannah looked as every other Clan girl did in her deerskin dress and moccasins. In one hand, she still clung to Dolly. The toy looked as though it was past the point of repair, but the youngster refused to part with it.

Devlin couldn't help but hold Sarah closer. They watched the happy faces of their children, family, and friends.

"I was afraid," Devlin admitted in a low voice. "Afraid that they would miss their home."

"*Tashka*," Sarah smiled lovingly up at her mate. "I think this is home."

Glossary
(unless otherwise noted, all terms are Choctaw)

aba anumpuli-a missionary
Achafa Chito-Great One (used by ancient Choctaw when speaking of their God)
Achukma hoke-It is good
akana-my friend
Akanohmi moma-To all my relations (said upon entering the Prayer/Sweat Lodge)
alakofichi-To heal, save; to rescue from (verb); a deliverer (noun)
Alikchi-a Medicine Man
ampo-a dish or bowl
Ant chukoa-Come in
bahtushi-a small bag or pouch
banaha-Choctaw bread or dumplings made from cornmeal and water, then boiled
beeve-a mature steer ; the word is used to refer to any animal in a herd (English)
Binili-Sit down.
blattin' cart-an extra wagon to transport calves born during a cattle drive (English)
Chahta-Choctaw
Chahta isht ia-Choctaw blood
Chahta Okla-Choctaw tribe
Chalakki-Cherokee
Chiksa-Chickasaw
chopi-a dung chip, usually buffalo
chuchupate-osha root
chuck wagon-a provisions wagon, usually driven by the cook
chuka-a house or dwelling
chukash-a person's spirit or center of being
cooney-storage space created by slinging a cowhide under a chuck wagon (English)

fahpo-Magic
folota-a round; a period of time
hakchuma ashuka-a pipe
halito-hello
Hashtahli-the sun god
hashtula-winter
Hasimbish humma-a red-tailed hawk (Devlin's Clan name)
hatak isht atia-human beings
hitoka-playing field for toli
Hushi Ninak Aya-the moon, wife of Hashtahli (the sun god); literally, "the sun that travels at night"
ikhananchi-a teacher
ikhish bahta-a Medicine bag
ikhish bahtushi-a Medicine pouch
ikhish chuka-a Medicine Lodge
ikhish itampo-a Medicine bowl
iksa-Clan
iksa achafa-One clan; the same clan
iksa inla-another clan; a different clan
iksita-a hearth
inola-good luck
ipokni-grandmother
ippok tek-granddaughter
ishki-a mother
ishki toba-a stepmother or second mother
isht ahalaia-to take a personal interest in, be responsible
itauaya-marriage
itauayachi-a marriage ceremony
keyu-no, not
Keyuachi-the enemies of Hashtahli who attempt to sway those looking for answers via a Quest, coming most often in the form of "doubts"
kiva-a Pueblo Indian ceremonial structure, usually round and partly underground (Hopi)

Long Journey, The; "The Trail of Tears"-A number of Native tribes were forced by the American government to not only give up their lands, but to make the inhumane journey without the promised wagons, food, and supplies, to Oklahoma, then known as the Indian Territory.
Luak-fire (friend of Hashtahli, the sun god)
Magic-the controlling of events, effects, or forces of nature (English); many Shamans spell the word "magick," to distinguish it from present-day sleight-of-hand entertainment
Miko-a Clan spokesman
moshi-an uncle
na hollo ohoyo-a white woman
nakni or **hatak nakni**-a man
Nali-smiling one (Tima's nickname)
Nanih Waiya-The sacred mound in Mississippi that is the legendary birthplace of the Choctaw Indian nation. There is some debate as to whether the mound was in Mississippi at the time; the mound itself was built between 1500-2000 years ago, likely by the Choctaw themselves. Construction is thought to have taken two to three generations to complete and the mound served as the base for a temple.
nighthawk-the member of a cattle drive who herds the remuda all night and drives the other riders' sleeping gear to the next night's camp; usually a young man or teenager (English)
nita nipi itaba nusi-bear meat with acorns; a favorite dish of the Ancient Choctaw
ohoyo yukpali-a woman pleaser; lesbian
Okla-people
omi-yes
remuda-a loose herd of horses (Spanish)
sa-my; mine
sachu-kash-my heart (term of endearment)
saibaiyi-a nephew
Sakli-a salmon, trout, or fish (Sarah's Clan name)
Sí-yes (Spanish)

tapadero-a leather stirrup covering (Spanish)
Tasa-a shortened version of "tashka," or "warrior" (Tima's nickname for Devlin)
tashka-a warrior (Sarah's nickname for Devlin)
tekchi-wife
tekhanto-a mud dauber; wasp-like insect
toli-a game played with sticks and balls
topa-a bed; a place where sleeping furs are spread
ushta-the number four, sacred in the Choctaw religion
vaquero-a rider (Spanish)
wrangler-the member of a cattle drive who trails the remuda during the day and does chores for the cook, such as loading and unloading the chuck wagon, washing dishes, gathering firewood, and keeping the water barrel filled (English)
yakoke-thank you
yatahe-welcome (Southwestern Indian dialect; used by Apaches, Comanches, Shoshone, Potowatamie)

Also from
Yellow Rose Books
be sure to read

Tumbleweed Fever
by LJ Maas

In the Oklahoma Territory of the old west Devlin Brown is trying to redeem herself for her past as an outlaw, now working as a rider on a cattle ranch.

Sarah Tolliver is a widow with two children and a successful ranch, but no way to protect it from the ruthless men who would rather see her fail. When the two come together sparks fly, as a former outlaw loses her heart to a beautiful yet headstrong young woman.

Available at booksellers everywhere.
ISBN: 1-930928-05-X

Other spellbinding stories by LJ Maas
available from
Yellow Rose Books

None So Blind

It's been almost 15 years since Chicago writer, Torrey Gray has set eyes on the woman she fell in love with so long ago. Taylor Kent has become one of the most celebrated artists in the country, and has spent the last 15 years trying to, unsuccessfully, forget the young woman that walked out of her life, stealing Taylor's heart in the process. Best friends forever, neither woman was ever able to find the courage to speak about the growing passion they felt for one another.

Now an unusual, but desperate request will throw the old friends together again, but this time, will either of them be able to voice their unspoken desires, or has time become their enemy?

Available at booksellers everywhere.
ISBN 1-930928-13-0

Meridio's Daughter

Tessa (Nikki) Nikolaidis is cold and ruthless, the perfect person to be Karê, the right-hand, to Greek magnate Andreas Meridio. Cassandra (Casey) Meridio has come home after a six-year absence to find that her father's new Karê is a very desirable, but highly dangerous woman.

Set in modern day Greece on the beautiful island of Mýkonos, this novel weaves a tale of emotional intrigue as two women from different worlds struggle with forbidden desires. As the two come closer to the point of no return, Casey begins to wonder if she can really trust the beautiful Karê. Does Nikki's dark past, hide secrets that will eventually bring down the brutal Meridio Empire, or are her actions simply those of a vindictive woman? Will she stop at nothing for vengeance...even seduction?

Available at booksellers everywhere.
ISBN 1-930928-53-X

Other titles to look for in the
coming months from
Yellow Rose Books

Strength of the Heart
By Carrie Carr

Red Sky At Morning
By Melissa Good

Faith
By Anj

Thicker Than Water
By Melissa Good

Honor Bound
By Radclyffe

Something To Be Thankful For
By Carrie Carr

Tomorrow's Promise
By Radclyffe

LJ Maas is the author of *Tumbleweed Fever, None So Blind, Meridio's Daughter*, and *Prairie Fire*, published by Renaissance Alliance Publishing, Inc. (http://www.rap-books.biz).

Originally from Chicago, LJ now resides in Oklahoma with her partner of almost 6 years. They have an eight-year-old daughter (a blonde, lab/retriever mix who simply doesn't believe she's a dog). Along with writing full time, she teaches computer graphics and a variety of fiction writing classes at a local college. Her online works can be located at: http://www.art-with-attitude.com/artist/Alt_FanFic.html.

Printed in the United States
6446